THE TRAITOR

Silent Phoenix MC Series: Book Four

SHANNON MYERS

Cover Model: Sonny Henty

Photographer: Wander Aguiar

First Printing: 2017

Paperback ISBN- 978-0-9994716-3-0

❀ Created with Vellum

ALSO BY SHANNON MYERS

(Charm & Neve's Story)
Through The Woods

(Killian and Ari's Story)
Through The Water

Fictioned Series
(Hayden & Jake's Story)
Protagonized

To the Mikes and Laurens of the world—those who refuse to give up even when the deck is stacked against them.

Lift your head.
It ain't over yet.

TERMINOLOGY

1%er (One-Percenter)- *If 99% of motorcycle riders are law-abiding members of society, the rest is the 1%. Advertised through a patch or tattoo, usually on a diamond shaped back field.*

13 - *Patch worn by a biker, usually a 1%er. May stand for the letter "M" (13th letter of alphabet), and indicate the wearer smokes pot, or uses "crank" (methamphetamine). Can also mean "The Mother Club", or original chapter of a motorcycle club.*

1916- *The nineteenth letter of the alphabet (S) and the sixteenth (P). Stands for Silent Phoenix.*

3-Piece Patch- *Configuration of back patches, consisting of: a top rocker (club's name), a center patch (club's emblem), and a bottom rocker (geographical territory).*

69 - *Patch indicating someone who has performed cunnilingus with witnesses present.*

Air Condition- *Riddle with bullets*

ATF- *Bureau of Alcohol, Tobacco, Firearms and Explosives.*

Broad- *A female whose sole purpose is being used as a sexual object; similar to a one-night stand.*

Cage- *Non-biker's car/truck.*

Church- *Club meeting.*

Club Whore- *Also known as a Mama. Sexual equivalent of a public well. Anyone can dip into her, at any time, as often as he wants. These are woman who belong to the club at large. They belong to every member and are expected to consent to the sexual desires of anyone at anytime. They perform menial tasks around the clubhouse, however do not attend club meetings.*

Colors- *Patches, logo, or uniform associated with a motorcycle club.*

Fly Colors - *To ride on a motorcycle wearing club's kutte.*

Gathering: *A scheduled social event or meeting. This is not Church.*

Grocery-getter- *A biker's car/truck.*

Hang Around- *a person that hangs around a motorcycle club and may be interested in joining.*

Jacket- *Arrest record*

Kill-Light- *A flashlight used as a weapon.*

Kutte- *A jacket which has had the sleeves cut off. All club patches are sown onto kuttes, which are worn as the outer-most layer of clothing. Most, if not all, outlaw clubs have kuttes as their basic uniform.*

Mother- *Founding/original chapter of the club.*

Nomad- 1) "Nomad" on a bottom rocker patch means that motorcycle club member travels between geographical chapters. Kind of like working in a secretarial pool, a Nomad goes where he's needed. 2) "Nomad" on a top rocker patch or car plaque means "Nomad" is the name of that club.

Ol' Lady- *Wife or long-time girlfriend of club member. She is considered property of the member and is off-limits to other club members.*

Property Of- *displayed on a shirt, patch or tattoo to show who the woman "belongs to." Example: Monica wore a "Property of Torch" vest in Renegade. That meant that she associated herself with Torch and would do anything he needed/wanted.*

STRUCTURE WITHIN CLUB

National President- *Many times the founder of the club. He will usually be located at or near the national headquarters. He will be surrounded by bodyguards and organizational enforcers.*

Territorial or Regional Representatives- *In some cases called the National Vice President in charge of a specific region or state.*

National Secretary / Treasurer- *He is responsible for the club's money and collecting dues from local chapters. He also records any by-law changes and records any minutes.*

National Enforcer- *This person answers directly to the National President. He acts as a body guard and gives out punishment for club violations. He has also been known to locate former members and retrieve colors or remove the club's tattoo from them.*

Chapter President- *This person has either claimed the position or has been voted in. He has final authority over all chapter business and members.*

Chapter Vice President- *This person is second in command. He presides over club affairs in the absence of the president. Normally, he is hand picked by the Chapter President.*

Chapter Secretary / Treasurer- *This is usually the member with the best writing skills and probably the most education. He will maintain the chapter roster and maintain a crude accounting system. He is also responsible for collecting dues, keeping minutes and paying for any bills the chapter accumulates.*

Chapter Sergeant (SGT) at Arms- *This person is in charge of maintaining order at club meetings. Because of the violent nature of outlaw gangs this person is normally the strongest member physically and is loyal to the Chapter President. He may administer beatings to fellow members for violations of club rules. He is the club enforcer.*

Road Captain- *This person fulfills the role of a logistician and security chief for club sponsored runs or outings. The Road Captain maps out routes to be taken during runs, arranges the refueling, food and maintenance stops. He will carry the club's money and use it for bail if necessary.*

Members- *The rank and file, fully accepted and dues paying members of the gang. They are the individuals who carry out the President's orders and have sworn to live by the club's by-laws.*

Prospect- *These are the club's hopefuls who spend from one month to one year in a probationary status. They must prove during that time if they are worthy of becoming members. Some clubs have the prospect commit a felony with fellow members observing in an effort to weed out the weak and stop infiltration by law enforcement. Must be nominated by a regular member and receive a unanimous vote for acceptance. They are known to carry weapons for other club members and stand guard at club functions. The prospect wears no colors and has no voting rights.*

Associates or Honorary Members- *An individual who has proven his* *value or usefulness to the gang. These individuals may be professional people who have in some manner helped the club. Some of the more noted are attorneys, bail bondsmen, and auto wrecking yard owners. These people are allowed to party with the gang, either in town or on their runs; however, they do not have a voting status or wear colors.*

AUTHOR'S NOTE

Please be aware that The Traitor is not recommended for readers under the age of eighteen, as it contains strong language, sexual situations, drug use, and graphic violence.

If you, or someone you care about has been a victim of sexual assault, RAINN is available to provide confidential support.

RAINN Hotline: 1 (800) 656-4673

TRAITOR

/ˈtrādər/

noun

noun: **traitor**; plural noun: **traitors**

1. a person who betrays a friend, country, principle, etc.

CHAPTER ONE

Lauren: July 2015 (Age: 28)

I parked behind Torch's motorcycle, staring wearily at the house. Work was kicking my ass. My heart wasn't in it anymore and it showed.

As much as I'd wanted to keep what happened to my car from Josué and Isaac, I really needed something to drive while I fought it out with my insurance company.

While I agreed my car being bombed was an act of terrorism, I disagreed with it being considered an act of war—something the insurance company explicitly did not cover. Until we could settle, I was without a vehicle and had been forced to call and listen to Josué lose his mind, switching rapidly from Spanish to English and back again.

Isaac had gotten on the phone and calmly offered me the use of one of his vehicles before handing the phone back to a worried Josué. "*Mija*, they won't be happy until you're dead. Please come home. Your heart belongs here with us."

My heart actually belonged in a farmhouse just outside of town, but I'd kept that to myself.

What good would it have done?

I'd made my decision when I left Mike sleeping in bed... again. Only, this time around, he hadn't come after me. Sex was supposed to have given me closure—a way of releasing my frustrations on his body before moving on with my life.

Instead, he had become an even more prominent fixture in my mind.

Maybe because I was now nine days late.

I swiped the stray tears from my face and tried working up the courage to go inside the house. Torch might have been home, but he wasn't really there.

Most evenings, I stayed in my room while he drank himself into a stupor. On others, I'd come in to find empty beer cans and liquor bottles cluttering the counters, Torch nowhere in sight. Wherever he was, I knew damn well it wasn't an AA meeting.

A week ago, I'd gotten up for some water. He'd mistaken me for Monica and cried for hours. Now, I tried not to leave my room until I knew for sure he was asleep.

With a deep sigh, I grabbed my purse and keys off the seat and headed inside. I followed the scent of food to the kitchen, my stomach already rumbling.

Torch was busy chopping onions and talking to a woman who had her back to me.

"Hello," I ventured, shocked to see Torch up and moving around, much less entertaining someone.

"Lauren, *mijita*," she said, clapping her hands. "Come and let me hold you."

"*Abuelita?* What are you doing here?" My voice was muffled as she had my face crushed against her ample bosom.

She released me to gesture around the kitchen proudly. "I am here to take care of you and Dave. Josué tells me about your car and you know what? I say to myself, '*Gloria, you must go to Texas.*' So, I get on the airplane. I can sleep when I am dead."

I nodded along before asking, "Who is Dave?"

Torch put the knife down and waved a hand. "Me."

Leave it to *Abuelita* to get a biker to give up his real name.

She jerked her thumb toward him. "This one? Oh, boy. He wants to lie around all day, but I say no. We must carry on."

He held up the cutting board and showed her the onions. "Like this?"

Abuelita patted him like a small child. "*Sí,* very good, Dave. Next, we are going to get you showered up so I can trim this mess on your head. You look homeless." She eyed me next. "Lauren, what has happened to your hair?"

I patted my head self-consciously. "Nothing. It's just in a messy bun."

She shook her head. "Messy—why do all the kids want to look messy? You have been at work, not the bed all day."

Torch shot me a sympathetic look. He'd probably been on the receiving end of a lecture since she arrived. "*Abuelita,* why don't you and Torch finish up here while I change out of my work clothes?"

"His name is Dave," she called down the hall after me. "He is not a torch."

I closed my bedroom door and leaned my head against the wood, tempted to call Josué to inform him that his mother was going to drive me *loco.* I shed my blouse and tossed it onto a bed that was no longer unmade. *Abuelita* had been busy.

My slacks soon joined the blouse, and I pondered what to wear. Normally, I'd throw on some cotton shorts and a tank top, but with *Abuelita* here, casual was out.

After perusing my closet, I finally settled on a black sundress with cherries on it. Simple, yet guaranteed to meet the dinner dress code. I laid it on the bed on my way into the small en suite bathroom, where I fussed with my hair.

It was when I sat down to pee that I saw it.

Blood.

I'd gotten my period.

My face crumpled with despair. I didn't know why I was reacting like this. I should have been relieved—a baby was a complication I didn't need at this point in my life.

But I'd had a little over a week to grow used to the idea, only to have it ripped from me like everything else.

My tears became full-on sobbing. I buried my face in my hands, trying to stifle the sounds. I'd known we couldn't make it work, but a baby would have been the part of him I could hold on to. A piece untainted by the world.

There was a knock at the bedroom door. "Lauren? Are you okay?"

I took a deep breath. "I'm fine, *Abuelita*. Just give me a minute."

Ignoring me, she entered the bedroom. The bathroom door opened next, and she slipped inside to find me sitting on the toilet, sobbing hysterically.

"*Mijita*, what has happened?"

It took a couple of tries, but I finally choked out, "I got my period."

I expected questions or worse, reprimands. Instead, she found a washcloth and ran it under the faucet until the water grew warm. Then she came over and wiped it over my face.

"When I was young, I think I will have a big family. Your *Abuelo*— God rest his soul—and I marry and I think this is my chance. It was not so simple, though. Each month was another reminder my body was... *defectuoso*." She paused and looked away.

"He broke my heart," I admitted, swallowing another sob. "But when I found out I was late, I thought maybe there were worse things than carrying his baby."

She patted my knee. "You will carry a child, LoLo. I tried for years and one day, the Lord saw fit to give me my Josué."

My eyes were swollen and my nose was running like a faucet, but *Abuelita* stayed by my side, wiping away the tears and snot.

"I don't want to just carry a child, I want to carry his child. How messed up is that? He refused to help me get Monica out of jail. Then, I told him when I planned to go into the station and my car got blown up. In what world do we ever work?"

She cupped my chin in her hand. "Do not be so quick to close his chapter, *mijita*. I got my miracle. Things can work out—*sí Dios nos da licencia.*"

I didn't know what the last part meant, but nodded anyway. "It hurts—I've had this crushing weight on my chest since January. And I don't know how much longer I can take it."

She squeezed the washcloth out and ran it under warm water again.

"*No hay mal que dure cien años, ni cuerpo que lo soporte.* Do you know what that means?"

I shook my head.

"It means nothing bad lasts forever, and even if it did, you could not withstand it. That makes you feel better, right?"

It didn't in the slightest, but I was certain she'd made tamales and *sofrito,* and I didn't want to miss out, so I nodded as if it did.

She ran the warm cloth over my face again. "That's a good girl. I am going to help Dave with dinner while you get freshened up. I brought my hot water bottle—you can use it for the cramping."

I sniffled again. "Thank you, *Abuelita.*"

She pressed a kiss to the top of my head. "Maybe fix your hair a little before you come out, too." She squeezed my cheek. "We've got to fatten you up, LoLo. You are nothing but skin and bones. You do not want to lose *las montañas.*"

And now we were back to normal.

CHAPTER TWO

Lauren: July 2015 (Age: 28)

I was going to get fired. It was really just a matter of when. I'd lost an invoice, and another vender hadn't been paid on time. It might have been manageable had Dr. Mulloy not called an order in herself today. When they explained there was a hold on our account because of nonpayment, she'd stormed into my office, guns blazing.

"What the hell is wrong with you?" she'd hissed. "Do you realize how this makes me look? Like I'm not seeing enough patients to cover the bills. Lauren, this is unacceptable. I don't care how late you have to stay, but you will stay and make sure every single account is up to date."

It was now almost nine, and I was just pulling into the driveway. Torch's bike was missing, but at least I could visit with *Abuelita* for a few minutes before collapsing from exhaustion. She'd been with us for two weeks, but hadn't mentioned any specifics for going back to Denver. Torch and I weren't complaining. The house was clean and there was always something to eat. With the third bedroom, I doubted either of us would have cared if she moved in permanently.

I let myself in, tossing my keys and purse on the small hall table. A table that hadn't come from Torch. There were hints of my mother all over the house. I found her presence comforting.

"*Abuelita?*" I called out, walking through the dark house.

When I flipped on the light to find a man sitting on the couch, I screamed.

"She's not here right now," said the large blond biker.

I took one look at the leather vest and reached for my Glock.

He placed his hand on the gun in his lap. "Wouldn't do that, Lauren. I'm a lot faster than I look and I didn't come here to put a bullet in your head. If I had, I would've dropped you in the hall as you put your keys down."

I let my shirt fall back over the holster, hands shaking violently. "W-why are you here? Where's my grandmother?"

He took his hand off the gun. "Torch took her to the movies. Needed a chance to talk to you. Alone."

I tried to imagine my grandmother on the back of a motorcycle, but failed. The man was menacing, yet strangely familiar.

"What could we possibly have to talk about?" I asked, crossing my arms over my chest to hide the shaking.

He grinned. "I like you—most people would be cowerin' right now. I wanna talk about why the fuck your car burned to the ground in a gym parkin' lot. Who knew you were tryin' to get your mother's case reopened?"

I fell into a nearby chair, shocked. It shouldn't have come as a surprise the bikers were watching my every move. But it did. "I—I told Mike, my ex. He's a cop, but—"

"I know who Mike is," he interjected. "No one else knew?"

I shook my head. The man continued staring, as if waiting for me to crack and admit I'd given the story to *CNN* as well.

"I swear to you. No one else knows."

"That means I've got a fuckin' rat in my clubhouse then. No wonder he didn't trust them." He stroked his beard, staring right through me.

I realized who he was when I looked into his eyes.

"You brought my car back, didn't you? You're Jared—no—Josh. Don't tell me, it's Jeremiah."

Why couldn't I remember?

The biker watched patiently before offering, "Do you want to keep guessin', or should I just tell you?"

I sighed and gestured for him to go on. "Just tell me. I'm too tired to think."

He laughed deeply. "It's Jamie. And, yes. I brought your car that night."

"So close," I lamented.

"You didn't tell anyone other than Mikey," Jamie reiterated as he paced the room. "And I know he's not a rat, so that leaves one of the club members."

I watched him walk from one side of the room to the other, wondering if Mikey and Mike were the same person.

"How am I supposed to help you with this?"

He stopped. "Did Monica leave you anything the night she died? I know she told you she'd overheard some shit. Might mean nothing to you, but it could to me."

"Back here." Without another thought, I grabbed his arm and led him down the hall to my bedroom. He didn't resist when I walked into the closet and slid a section of hangers back.

Jamie's brow raised as he took in my wall of clues and he let out a low whistle. "Wow. You're quite the detective. Walk me through this." He pulled a small notebook from his back pocket along with a pen, waiting for me to give him something.

I took a deep breath. "Okay, I found these bits of paper, but I haven't been able to make sense of them." I pulled one scrap free and held it up for him to see. "Like this—Brianne. October 2. I searched the archives for any public record relating to a Brianne and the date October 2. Nothing came up, though."

He nodded, and I moved down to the coaster. I removed the tack and handed it to him, pointing out the name at the bottom. "This meant nothing to me until Chon Ramos tried to kill me. I'm assuming they're the same person."

Jamie turned it over in his hands. "Leather & Lace."

I nodded. "Yeah. That's what led me to Torch. I don't know what *SOD* and *roll over* mean—do you?"

He clicked the pen on and off in frustration, his jaw tightening. "SOD is the Sons of Death MC. Roll over means someone turned on the club. Fuck!"

He roared the words, and I shrank back, instantly realizing I'd just trapped myself inside a small closet with a biker who probably killed girls like me for breakfast—*wait, that wasn't how the saying went.*

Ate girls like me for breakfast?

It wasn't much better, although Jamie was pretty handsome for an older man. I doubt I would complain much if he wanted to eat me.

When he paused to pinch the bridge of his nose, I gasped.

He gave me an odd look. "Are you okay?"

I nodded shakily. "I—I thought I saw a mouse."

He laughed lightly and went back to studying the wall, while I focused on his profile, the pieces falling into place.

The pen clicking.

The blue eyes.

Fuck, even his profile was a dead ringer.

The resemblance was uncanny. Jamie knew Mike wasn't the rat because a father would never suspect his son.

And Mike was most definitely Jamie's son.

It was why Carnage had apologized profusely when Torch told him I belonged to Mike. I knew next to nothing about bikers and their gangs or clubs, but I was pretty sure you couldn't mess with the head honcho's family.

Oh god.

Mike was in deep with outlaw bikers, but if he was the son of the leader, wouldn't that mean he would have done everything in his power to keep Monica safe?

What if I'd made a horrible mistake?

CHAPTER THREE

Mike: August 2015 (Age: 32)

"Never send in a beer to do the job of a tequila shot," I said proudly.

The bartender raised her eyebrows and slid the shot across the bar to me. "Whatever you say, man."

I downed it and immediately requested another.

Who gave a fuck how I got to my destination?

Lauren wouldn't answer my calls, but her *abuela* was much more understanding and had ushered me inside for a snack when I showed up at the front door.

After hearing my plight, the woman naturally invited me over for dinner. Unfortunately, my nerves had gotten the best of me, so I'd made a pit stop at a nearby bar just to take the edge off. I hadn't seen my girl in a month and needed to be my best if I wanted to win her over.

Twenty minutes later, I stumbled outside, wincing at the sunlight. There was a chance I'd overdone it.

"Fuck," I grumbled as I climbed into my truck.

I kept my speed ten miles under and leaned over the steering wheel, as if doing so would help me see the road better. The one person I was looking forward to seeing was Lauren.

Eight weeks.

My dick had promptly stopped working again once she was gone. The only way I could get hard was by imagining her face. At night, I'd lay in bed, stroking myself and wishing it was her hand instead of my own.

My pants grew tighter just from the thoughts of seeing her again and I fumbled with them one-handed until they were unzipped. My cock tented my boxer briefs, but it was a hell of a lot better than strangling it with the zipper on my pants.

The reds and blues that lit up my rearview mirror would not likely share my point of view. I pulled over with a heavy sigh.

Fuck.

"*Sayonara*, Detective Sullivan. Nice knowing ya." I placed both hands on the steering wheel.

The officer sauntered up—a rookie, or blue flamer, as I liked to call them. There wasn't a snowball's chance in hell I was getting out of this one. I'd be in cuffs within five seconds of him talking to me.

"Good evening, sir. Do you know why I stopped you tonight?"

With zero fucks left to give, I gave him a cocky grin. "You realized women weren't into you, so you thought you'd try to grab me. Sorry to disappoint, but I'm not into chubby dudes. Lose some weight and we'll talk."

The officer frowned. "License and registration. I stopped you because you were weaving all over the road." He glanced down at my unzipped jeans and limp cock before replying, "Guess that explains that."

I handed over my driver's license, insurance, and badge. His eyes widened. "Sullivan?"

"In the flesh," I dryly responded.

"Kyle. Kyle Barton. Fuck, you're a legend around the station. I waved to you once as you walked to your truck, but I don't think you saw me." While he rambled, I zipped my pants up and tuck in my shirt.

"Look, Kyle. I hate to cut this short, but I've got a dinner to get to and I'm already twenty minutes late. Can we keep this little 'mishap' to ourselves?"

He hesitated for a second, but then nodded. "Just this once. Try to keep yourself—uh, decent."

"You got it, man," I agreed, slapping him on the shoulder. "Have a good night."

I made it to Torch's house in record time, having sobered up during the impromptu traffic stop. I checked my reflection in the visor mirror and gargled some mouthwash from the console before getting out.

Fresh as a fucking daisy.

Torch answered the door with an amused grin. "This oughta be good."

"What the fuck does that mean?"

He gave me another shit-eating grin. "Does she know you're stopping by?"

I rolled my eyes. "Of course she does—she invited me. Why?"

He jerked his thumb toward the kitchen. "Why don't you go see for yourself?"

I shoulder checked him on my way in, coming to a sudden stop just outside the kitchen. Lauren's *abuela* had apparently been inviting all the strays to dinner. Jimmy sat next to Lauren, arm draped casually over the back of her chair.

"What the fuck is this?" I bellowed and forks clattered down to plates.

Lauren gave a small sigh and dropped her head into her hands. "Mike, why are you here?"

Gloria pushed her chair back and stood up, leaning over the table toward me. The only thing she was missing was the wooden spoon. "Language. You do not walk into someone's home and start cursing like *un pirata*. Manners."

"Uh, *Abuelita?* I think you mean *un marinero*—he's cursing like a *sailor*... not a pirate," Jimmy offered helpfully before going back to his enchiladas.

Fuck this guy.

"Oh, look everyone! Jimmy speaks Spanish. Isn't that just the most delightful thing ever?" I clapped slowly, taking immense pleasure in his sudden scowl.

Lauren stood, dropping her napkin to the floor. "Excuse us for just a minute."

Her fingers dug into my arm as she dragged me down the hallway and into her bedroom. "Why, Mike? Why are you here?"

"You won't take my calls." Saying it aloud made me sound like a petulant child. I should've just thrown myself down on her bedroom floor; it would have gotten my point across a lot faster.

She crossed her arms over her chest—which was unfair, because after the night I'd had, I deserved to see a nice pair of tits. It would have cheered me up immensely.

"Are you drunk?"

I crossed my arms over my own chest and faced her. "Are you fucking *Slim Jim* out there?"

Lauren let out a sarcastic laugh. "You're unbelievable, you know that? Not that it's any business of yours, but no, I am not fucking Jimmy. I feel like we've been over this before, Mike."

I glanced around her bedroom. I hadn't really known much about Torch's place when I suggested Lauren stay with him. He was just the only biker I trusted to be left alone with her. His house was actually more modern than I'd imagined—she even had her own en suite bathroom. I stared at the sink, imagining her bent over it.

"Can I fuck you in the bathroom right now?" I asked.

Her eyes widened with shock, and she cracked her palm against the side of my face. "What the hell is wrong with you?"

I winced and rubbed my stinging cheek. "What's wrong with me? My dick's been hard for eight weeks! Eight fucking weeks, Lauren. And suddenly he's a goddamn pussy critic. Nobody else's pussy will do. It has to be yours. So, excuse me, but I think he deserves a little somethin' somethin'."

Lauren closed her eyes, inhaling and exhaling slowly. She was probably imagining how good it would be. I realized I was sorely mistaken when her hand connected with my other cheek.

"Leave," she demanded.

"But, I just got here. Gloria invited me to dinner and fine—I'm sorry, but I wasn't expecting Jimmy the Giraffe to be here, too."

She shook her head. "I can't do this. Seeing you just makes everything harder—"

"That's what she said," I interjected, but Lauren's face remained solemn. "C'mon, Red. We're good together. Why can't you see that?"

"Because we were never together, Mike! You were always working on a case and when we saw each other, it was late at night. Let's be honest and call a spade a spade. What we had was long-term sex. You never opened up to me about your life or family—I left you in January feeling like I never even really knew you at all."

What could I say?

I hadn't given her much—I couldn't. David didn't even know the half of it. I'd thought giving her my body was enough. Shit, I'd tried the same thing when she'd shown up at my house.

"What do you want to know, darlin'?"

Her mouth opened in surprise. "Really? You'll just give up your secrets now when it doesn't matter?"

I shook my head. "I'll give up my secrets when it matters most. I want you with me and if you need to know more about my life, I'll tell you anything you want."

She blurted out, "I want to know about your dad."

Well, that escalated quickly.

I chewed on the corner of my lip.

How much could I say without sending her fleeing for her life from the room?

"My father... okay. My old man is a psychopath with a predisposition to violence and drugs. Those traits led to him joining a biker club where he is just thriving."

Her eyes held pain as she watched me talk. "Did he hurt you?"

I laughed bitterly. "*Did he hurt me?* Does a bear shit in the woods, baby?"

Lauren bit her own lip worriedly. "Would he—would he hurt women? Like women who didn't know him?"

Where the hell was this coming from?

"Yeah. He's not known for his gentleness. Looks like a fucking homeless bum, though, so most women and children steer clear of him."

Her face paled right before her eyes rolled back into her head and she slumped forward into my arms.

"Red?" I patted her cheek, but got no response, so I lowered her onto her back on the carpet. I'd expected a reaction, just not one this dramatic. I lifted her legs up onto the side of the bed, trying to get the blood back to her head. Her shirt was looking a little too restrictive for my taste, so I took the liberty of unbuttoning it.

Within a couple of seconds, her eyelids fluttered open, and she gave a weak groan. "Mike? Why am I on the floor?" She struggled to sit up, but I held her down.

"You just fainted. Apparently, you don't want to get to know me better." Lauren winced and I could see her heart pounding steadily against her chest. She was terrified.

"Baby, take a deep breath. There is no way you're going to meet my old man. I won't allow it."

She nodded slowly. "And why is my shirt unbuttoned?"

I tried to keep the need out of my voice as I answered, "It was too tight."

Instead of being upset, she looked amused. "Well, thank the lord that you were here to keep my clothing from killing me when I passed out."

"You joke, but it's a real issue. I was just following protocol."

There was a soft knock at the door before Gloria called out, "Lauren? Is everything okay?"

Lauren closed her eyes. "Well—"

The door opened before she could finish her statement as Gloria rushed in and knelt beside her. "What has happened?"

"She fainted, Gloria. She just needs to stay like this for about ten more minutes Then we can get her up and moving."

Her eyes widened, and she covered her mouth. "Does this mean that a few weeks ago was a fluke? Are you—*estás embarazada*?"

Lauren shook her head vigorously, narrowing her eyes at her grandmother. "*Abuelita*, could you please get me a glass of water and never speak of that again?"

Was she what?

Why didn't I speak Spanish?

Realization hit a second later.

This time, it was my face that paled.

Gloria nodded. "I'll get a shot of tequila, too. It will help."

I resisted telling Gloria I was going to need an entire bottle before helping her to her feet and ushering her from the room. Once she was gone, I sank down to the mattress near Lauren's feet. "What happened a few weeks ago? Are you pregnant?"

Lauren closed her eyes and shook her head. "I was nine days late, but got my period, so we don't even have to have this discussion."

I pinched the bridge of my nose and leaned down, feeling incredibly disappointed. Over what, I didn't quite know. It wasn't like I'd had something and lost it. She'd never even been pregnant.

When I brought my head up, she was watching me curiously. "Are you okay?"

I nodded and then shook my head. "I'm disappointed—does that make any fucking sense to you?"

Her lower lip began trembling, and she nodded. "Complete sense. What are we doing, Mike?"

I briefly wondered if Gloria had gone in search of a blue agave plant because that tequila shot was taking a long fucking time.

I ran my thumb along my jawline. "I don't know, darlin', but I need you. Wrong. Right. Whatever. I just need you."

I didn't give a shit if Jimmy was listening in. It had to be said. Maybe Lauren needed to hear me say it. I'd climb up on the fucking roof and shout it for the entire neighborhood if it meant we could be together again.

"I can't keep doing this back and forth. We're fighting... we're not. It's too much." Her hand came to rest against her forehead.

"So, stop fighting me. Let's get together and make it work this time around. You want to know what my life was like? I'll tell you. We'll work together to find out who killed Monica—like a team."

It wasn't the greatest of offers.

Listen to my shitty childhood. In return, I'll drag you into a biker war.

Jesus, where were my brilliant speeches when I needed them?

Gloria finally returned from the distillery with three shots and a bottled water. "Take this." she handed one to each of us before taking the third. "To health," she stated before downing hers.

"To health," we repeated.

"It was not so easy to get this. Dave, he's a drinker. I had to have Jimmy drive me over to the liquor store to pick some up," Gloria admitted in a conspiratorial tone before realizing Lauren and I still had some things to discuss. She slipped back out and closed the door behind her.

Lauren turned her emerald eyes on me and sighed. "Can I get up now?"

I pulled her legs off the bed and helped her into a sitting position. When she remained conscious, I brought her back up to her feet. She closed her eyes briefly before righting herself. "I'm okay."

I pulled her into my chest. "I'm not."

She looked up at me. "I didn't mean it like that. Obviously, I'm not fine with the way things are between us. I just need some time to think about it."

I pressed my lips to her forehead. "Take all the time you need."

It was done. I could only sit back and hope the pros outweighed the cons for us.

CHAPTER FOUR

Mike: August 2015 (Age: 32)

"How many of your prospects have gotten picked up in the last few weeks?"

Grey mulled it over before responding. "Six. Can't get any charges that'll stick, though."

I kicked my feet up on my coffee table, leaning back into the couch. "I think it might be time to leave runs to the Ol' Ladies and hang arounds. Until I know who's working against us from the inside, it's not safe."

"Yeah, you're probably right," he agreed, scratching at his jaw. "Can't stand to lose my prospects if there's a bust. Jarvis looked into Lauren's new man—he's a Fed."

I shook my head, not surprised in the least. The guy had given himself away at the gym.

Not that I wasn't grateful as fuck he'd kept her safe.

I was.

No civilian could have pulled off what he did and come out of it without a single scratch, though.

"Let me guess... FBI?"

"Nope. CIA operative of some sort. Jarvis hacked as far as he could, but this guy's security clearance is pretty high. Nearly everything we could find was heavily redacted. Had a fiancée, but she died in a terrorist bombing."

I took a long pull from my beer bottle. "That's heavy shit. Think he's investigating the club?"

He shook his head. "I think he's runnin' from something. I mean, why else settle in Lubbock when you've got the ability to live anywhere?"

He had a point. If you weren't a college student, there wasn't a hell of a lot else to do to stay entertained.

"Been to *Leather & Lace* lately?" Grey asked nonchalantly, as if he and I frequently hit up biker bars together.

"Haven't seen the inside of that place in years. Are there still patch whores waiting outside the men's room?"

Grey chuckled. "That ain't changed. Like to stop by once it closes here in a few—see if anyone knows shit. You in?"

"Okay," I hedged. "What are you thinking they know?"

His jaw gave a soft pop as he ground down on his back teeth. "Someone's using a bar I fuckin' own to pass information along to the Sons. Explain to me how that happens."

I didn't know how any of it was happening. All I knew was a small-scale war had grown to wildfire proportions. And right now, it was impossible to guess which way the wind was going to shift.

We finished our beers in silence before heading out. Grey insisted on taking his bike. "Ain't wearin' my colors in a cage."

I'd forgotten that bit of protocol. SPMC rules stated no club member desecrate their colors by wearing them inside a cage—or what non-bikers referred to as a vehicle.

Despite my warning, he insisted his men still wear their colors when riding. Once they arrived somewhere, they were under strict orders to shed the kuttes and not draw attention to themselves.

We pulled up outside *Leather & Lace* just as the sun lightened the sky. There were still a few bikes parked alongside of the bar, the die-hards who just didn't know when to quit.

I could make out the bikers—the ones who decided they weren't going down until the sun came up—through the permanent haze of smoke. Grey moved on toward the back, but I stopped at the bar, distracted by the multitude of colored wings on one of the biker's kuttes.

I touched the patches. "Jesus Christ, man. The hell did you do to earn all these? Fuck every club whore in the state?"

Colored wings were trophies indicating a member had engaged in sex acts while being watched by other members of the club. I couldn't give two fucks about earning my wings, but I'd be willing to do some freaky shit for tequila and blow.

The biker removed my hand from his kutte with a snarl. "Touch my patch again and I'll ram this bottle down your fuckin' throat and watch you choke on it!"

Grey hauled him off the bar stool by the back of his kutte. "So goddamned wasted you thought you'd talk to Detective Sullivan like that? Get the fuck out of here!"

The biker scrambled up from the floor, apologizing profusely. "Sorry, Pres. It was a mistake—"

Grey leveled a glare at him. "Get. Out. I'll deal with you back at the clubhouse. And you better pray Comedian don't find out about this."

His last line almost had me chuckling. Comedian wouldn't do jack shit if he knew one of his brothers was threatening me. Fuck, he'd probably buy them a drink for it.

The biker was escorted out by his buddy, looking less confident than he had only moments before. Grey walked around the room, stooping to check under tables and chairs.

"What the hell are you doing?"

He popped out from under a booth. "Lookin' for bugs, Mikey."

I walked over to where he was crouched down. "Is there a rat in your club or not? When we went over the plans involving Lauren, we were down in the canyon. Either the Sons managed to infiltrate every single one of your hangouts or you've got someone with big ears and an even bigger mouth."

He scratched at his jaw. I'd watched him do it more and more lately. This was getting under his skin. He paused and looked back toward the bar. "Brianne... October second. Holy shit."

"What? What does that mean?"

He shook his head as if in a daze. "Right in front of my fuckin' nose the entire time. Didn't put two and two together. Ian—it's the same night Ian was killed. Someone here handed him over to the Sons."

I struggled to keep up, wracking my brain for the name Ian. "Ian? Who the fuck is Ian?"

Grey slammed a hand down on the table in front of him. "Ian was the prospect the Sons gutted October second. Saw the name and the date, but it didn't mean shit. I can't believe I didn't catch on."

"Where are you getting this information?" I asked, knowing it sure as hell wasn't me.

He dismissed the question with a wave. "Not important. What is important is I now know who Brianne is—and more specifically, where Brianne is."

"Everybody out!" Grey bellowed, storming back toward the bar.

Bikers marched out like ants, leaving us alone with the bartender. The guy looked rough as hell, worse than all the bikers he served combined. A long scar ran down one side of his face, one he'd tried covering it up with a scraggly beard.

Instead, he was a few missing teeth and a banjo away from a job as an extra on the set of *Deliverance*.

"Get Brianne," Grey ordered. The man hesitated, and within seconds, Grey had his gun pressed to the man's temple. "Now."

He nodded shakily and reached for his cell phone. Grey turned back to me. "Call the boys. Get 'em down here for this."

Once I was done playing event planner for the club, I was going to have to drag my ass to my day job. It was shaping up to be a banner morning.

Carnage, Little Ricky, Torch, and Comedian arrived at the bar soon after. All were in varying stages of drunkenness, except for Torch, but that was only because Gloria hid the alcohol from him.

"What do we got, Junior?" my old man asked.

I jerked my thumb toward the door. "Brianne rolled over. That's all I know."

I didn't know who the woman was, but if Grey thought she had something to do with his club members getting killed, it wasn't going to matter one fucking bit by the end of today.

She'd be long gone by then.

Our boots crunched over the gravel as we made our way back inside. A female, who I could only presume was Brianne, sat bound in a chair in the center of the room.

She'd miraculously appeared in the time it had taken me to step outside and call for backup, leading me to assume she'd been hiding somewhere in the bar the entire time.

Brianne was a tweaker—just one look at her and it was inherently obvious. A canvas of open sores and scratch marks riddled her face and her once bleached blonde hair was ringed with jet black roots, making her look like a skunk. What she lacked in looks, she made up for in weight. Brianne had clearly not let her drug use affect her eating habits.

Her eyes darted to the various faces surrounding her while nervously chattering to Grey. The bartender sat behind the bar, arms crossed over his chest and a deep scowl on his face. Obviously, he'd realized his fuck buddy was in a shitload of trouble.

With the way she kept looking past Grey, it was apparent Brianne was hoping one of us would step in to save her.

"Stop lookin' at them," he snapped, jerking her chin. "Ain't a single one gonna help you. Now, tell me who you been talkin' to."

She silently pleaded with Carnage before answering, "Don't know what you're talking about—"

The bartender slammed a glass down on the counter with a thud. "Dammit, Brianne—don't fuck with these guys."

"Listen to your boy, girly. He's tryin' to keep you breathing," my father encouraged.

"Fuck you!" She spit in Grey's face, before throwing her head back in a laugh, revealing a mouthful of rotting black stumps. "I owe you nothing."

Grey closed his eyes, wiping the saliva from his cheek. "Shouldn't have done that. It's gonna fuckin' cost ya."

He gestured to Carnage. Without a word, the burly biker drove a fist into her stomach. She gasped in pain and tried curling her body inward, but the cuffs restricted the movement.

"That's a warnin'," Grey stated flatly. "Now, tell me who you've talked to."

She shook her head. "He said I could never tell. I'm his good girl."

"Jesus Christ! We're not gonna get a fuckin' thing from her at this rate!" my father roared, before kneeling in front of her chair, stroking her thighs with his palms. "Brianne, baby, tell Comedian what he needs to hear."

She bit down on her cracked lip in consideration before shaking her head tearfully. "No."

He smiled and patted her on the back. "It's alright. I understand. I do."

The tension fled her body, and she nodded, unaware of his fist until it slammed into her cheek. I felt sick to my stomach. The only thing keeping me in this hellhole was the need to find out if she'd been responsible for what happened to Lauren.

Brianne howled in pain, her face swelling. My old man knew just where to strike and had probably shattered a few bones.

"Just tell us what we need to know, and this'll all be over," Grey commanded.

The bartender had disappeared to the back at some point, probably unable to witness his girlfriend being beaten. Just to be safe, I pointed it out to Little Ricky, and he drew his gun before going to check.

The last thing we needed was for this guy to call it in.

Grey continued to urge her to reconsider. Every time she refused, she earned herself a fist.

I was ready to call it a bust when she blurted out, "I followed the redhead."

My head whipped around at the same time as Torch's.

"He said to follow her. So, I did. She went to the gym and then home with someone else. I had to wait around until she went back to her car and make sure she was alone, but I messed up—"

"You goddamn bitch," I roared, storming over to where she sat. As my fists rained hell down on her face, I only saw red.

"We need more out of her, Mikey. Gonna need ya to hold back," Grey said, pulling me back. He continued talking softly until my vision cleared and I could take in the damage I'd inflicted. Brianne's face was unrecognizable. Her lips looked as if she'd been stung by a thousand bees, eyes nothing more than slits.

I'd battered her—granted, she'd almost gotten Lauren killed, but I'd raised a hand in anger against a woman.

The transformation was complete—I'd become Comedian.

I leaned against a table, trying to hear over the sound of the blood rushing in my ears.

"Jesus," she whimpered through her tears.

"He can't save you now," Comedian answered with a grin.

"Time to give us your contact," Grey urged.

She spat a mouthful of blood onto the bar floor. "Don't know. I never met him—he'd message me through the computer, leaving me drugs when I followed through. We're in love," she said, almost wistfully.

She'd turned on the club for cyber-sex and drugs. The tweaker had lost her goddamned mind.

Carnage spoke up. "The shit with Ian and Monica? You behind that?"

She struggled to find him through her swollen eyes before nodding. "All I had to do was tell him where they were or where they were going. Didn't do nothing else to them. Just watched them. You have to bel—"

"Enjoy hell, cunt," Torch growled, firing a round through her forehead. Before storming out of the bar, he stopped to spit on her corpse.

A meth-head had ended Monica's life and almost Lauren's as well.

Little Ricky reappeared with the bartender in tow. "This one was running like a scared bitch."

I pulled my gun and fired a clean shot through his left eye from across the room. Little Ricky didn't realize I'd done it until the bartender's body slumped down to the floor.

"Jesus, Mikey. What the fuck?" he protested, looking for the other club members to intervene.

"We don't leave any witnesses," I explained amid complete silence, before heading for the front door.

"I taught him that," Comedian bragged.

I looked over my shoulder and called out, "I've got to get to my actual job, so I'll leave clean up to you fuckers."

The bright morning sunlight beat down on my face. I'd just earned my skull and crossbones patch. I'd killed for a club I hadn't even patched into.

Had that ever mattered to them?

CHAPTER FIVE

Mike: August 2015 (Age: 32)

I walked through the front door of my house nine hours later, delirious from lack of sleep and the reality of what I'd done. I'd taken a life in cold blood and instead of remorse or guilt, I felt numb.

Brianne and her guy deserved everything they'd gotten. Their actions had destroyed multiple families. Now, I just had to hope the department never got wind of my involvement.

I stripped out of my clothes as I climbed the stairs, praying sleep would bring some clarity and shake off the penetrating numbness. I'd just reached the second floor landing when someone knocked, sending me back downstairs to retrieve my gun from the holster near my jeans.

I wasn't sure who I was expecting, but it sure as hell wasn't her.

Lauren took in the gun and my state of undress with raised brows. "Did I catch you at a bad time?"

"Not at all. What can I do for you, darlin'?"

Please let it involve sleep...

"I came to tell you my answer is yes," she said with a grin, the corners of her eyes crinkling.

I scratched at my head. "Yes to what?"

There was a brief spark of recognition, but the fog of exhaustion made it impossible to follow. I'd unbox it once I'd slept. Lots of delicious, life-giving sleep.

Lauren bit down on her lip. "Us—I guess if that's even still a thing. I told you I needed to think about it and it's only been a week, but maybe—"

"Shut the fuck up. You had me at us." I stopped her rambling with my mouth. It was a stupid line, but I was running on fumes. I'd have to save the impressive speech for another time.

My hands slid up the sides of her neck and rested against her hairline, anchoring her lips to mine. I enjoyed having control over her movements. Judging by her soft moans, she didn't mind it one bit.

Turned out I didn't sleep after all. I just needed her. The numbness was gone, replaced with relief. She was my home. As I held her in my arms, I didn't feel guilt over what I'd done. In fact, I could have killed a hundred people for her and felt nothing but satisfaction.

This was what David had experienced after killing Landon. Lauren was my family, and I would do anything to keep her safe.

Her hand came up to cup my chin, fingernails scraping against my stubble. She was mine again and this time—I wasn't going to let anything come between us.

CHAPTER SIX

Lauren: October 2015 (Age: 28)

"Don't drop it down like that. You're flinching." Jimmy held my Glock in his hand. "Let's try group shooting again. We need to improve your accuracy."

After witnessing Jimmy's skills first hand, I'd asked him to train me. I carried a gun every day, but my first instinct wasn't to reach for it during signs of trouble. My instinct was to run away.

We'd been training together since July and it was clear there was still a lot of work to be done. I seemed to always anticipate the shot, which left me tense, completely missing my mark every time.

Initially, I considered asking Mike, but was quickly reminded that the man had absolutely no free time. By week two, I wondered what had possessed me to agree to another chance.

I never saw him.

Maybe it was enough for him to know I was there, but I yearned for more. He only seemed to put in the effort when our relationship was on the line. Otherwise, it was business as usual. Relationships needed to come with mandatory performance appraisals. Without them, we were just collecting pink slips before the termination.

"Lauren? Are you listening?" Jimmy patted my arm, breaking me away from my thoughts.

I nodded. "Sorry, just got a lot on my mind. I'm ready."

"Distracted shooting is—"

"Deadly shooting," I finished for him. "I know, but I'm focused and ready now."

I once asked Jimmy where he learned to shoot. He vaguely hinted at a government job before changing the subject. The man might have kept his past under lock and key, but he was willing to train me on my lunch breaks, so I didn't complain. How could I when I had a few secrets of my own?

Mike knew I still went to the range. He was just under the assumption I was there alone. It was an assumption I never bothered to correct. He hadn't exactly reacted well the night Jimmy came to dinner —a dinner I'd planned as a way of thanking him for saving my life.

It didn't matter. He would never be Mike's favorite person. Telling him about my midday meetups would only cause trouble.

"Okay, holster your gun and let's get moving. You're still too slow on the draw. I'll time you for this so that we can get a baseline." Jimmy got out his stopwatch, and I worked to clear my mind.

I hadn't told Mike the real reason behind my need to be a sharpshooter.

Jamie.

He hadn't offered anything about his family or past since that night in my bedroom, and I didn't have the courage to ask. I wasn't sure I would have been able to remain conscious.

The scary thing was that I prided myself on being an excellent judge of character and never once had I gotten the impression Jamie was going to hurt me—even when he pulled his gun. I'd only seen a father who cared about his son and was committed to finding out who took my mother from me.

It was why I needed Jimmy's help.

I couldn't even trust myself anymore.

CHAPTER SEVEN

Lauren: October 2015 (Age: 28)

"You're late... again," Sandra noted as I set my purse down on my desk. "I tried calling you, but you left your phone here."

I hadn't been taking my phone in case Mike got the urge to track it. That way, he would think I was just working through lunch. The last thing I needed was him showing up and seeing me with Jimmy.

"I'm so sorry," I said with an apologetic smile. "I had an appointment that ran over—"

"Every day for the past month? I swear, Lauren, your ability to handle your role here has decreased drastically since January." She began ticking items off on her fingers. "Late payments, missing orders, payroll errors, and the inability to get to work on time. What has gotten into you? I'm supposed to trust you with my practice, but you're running it into the damn ground!" Her voice remained quiet, even as she hissed the words at me.

I cringed. I had been slacking off, and I needed to get my shit together before I ended up unemployed. "Look, Dr. Mulloy, things have been difficult for me..." My voice wavered and she immediately closed the door behind her.

"What's wrong?"

Maybe it was because the concern in her eyes seemed genuine, or maybe I was just sick of keeping it all to myself. Either way, I let the words come tumbling out of my mouth.

"My mother died in January, and then the stuff with Mike—it's just been really hard trying to manage it all." I brushed away a stray tear.

She squeezed my hand. "I know exactly how you feel. I lost my mother last year and am still working through the pain of her death."

I frowned. "Last year? When? I didn't even know."

She took her free hand and patted my arm. "Honey, that's because I never let it affect my work life. I have a practice to run. So, I attended her funeral on a Sunday and flew back late that night to be in clinic Monday morning. We all make sacrifices."

I hated her a little more at that moment.

Minimizing my grief just because she coped differently. It was as if she thought she was better than me because of it. I'd bet anything they hadn't found her mom with a needle in her arm on a dirty street, either.

I shoved down my feelings of indignation and instead responded with, "Well, except for one Tuesday in May and the Friday I requested off, I've shown up every day. I'm handling it the best I can."

She nodded, as if she were placating a child. "Of course you are, honey. It would just be really helpful if you could handle it and keep the office running smoothly at the same time. Now, what's the problem with your ex? I thought you'd moved on from him."

"I don't know that there's such a thing as moving on. He's it for me." It felt good, saying it aloud, despite the distance I'd felt between us lately.

Sandra pursed her lips. "Look, I don't know how to say this. I just think you should move on, because he is so not worth it."

I protested, "That's not really something that I need advice on—"

"I fucked him, Lauren," she said with a sigh.

The room suddenly felt smaller than it actually was. "Excuse me?" I squeaked out.

Hadn't I known the man was a whore? I'd known and blatantly ignored it.

When had they been together?

Was it after he brought me breakfast? Was that why he never showed up at the office again?

Oh my god, this room was sweltering.

I began unfastening the top buttons on my blouse and fanned my face.

She nodded. "Yeah, he and I were together in Galveston... the night you were feeling sick. He saw me in the bar and one thing led to another."

Goddammit!

The one thing I'd held on to for all these years—the one thing that had been pure.

I'd measured every man up against the man he was on the beach— and he'd gone from what we shared to her bed?

I pulled the trashcan out from under my desk and leaned over it.

"See? Now, don't you feel better getting that out of the way? Okay, for the afternoon—the new patient at three goes to my church, so obviously we need to discount their visit. And, I'm going to need more time for that permanent filling at three-thirty, so move what you need to move to accommodate that. Did you order those new burs I showed you?"

I nodded, even though I hadn't. She told me to stay in the room that night—told me I'd hate myself for having a one-night stand. And then the bitch had gone downstairs and fucked my Jack.

Mine.

He would have come looking for me had she not shown up. Every-thing could have been different had she not played me to get laid. My stomach twisted and a bead of sweat formed along my hairline. He had been inside my boss.

Sandra stood up and patted my arm. "Okay. You get composed. I'm gonna get in my op."

I nodded again and sat staring dumbly at my computer screen. I'd reached a crossroads. If I stayed, then I was spineless. And if I left? Well, I was unemployed. I had to decide which was worse.

I continued staring at my computer as the screen saver switched from mountains back to beaches. Then I pushed away from my desk and grabbed my purse and my cell phone.

Someone called my name, but I refused to stop. I kept on until I was standing just outside one of the op rooms.

"Sandra?" I called into the room and she turned away from the patient and toward me.

"Yes?" She smiled.

I glared at her. "I'm leaving."

The smile faded slightly. "Another appointment?"

I shook my head. "No. Like for good. I quit."

She laughed while Dara watched me uncertainly. The patient was on enough nitrous that I doubted he even knew I was standing there. "C'mon, Lauren. Enough joking—we'll talk in a minute, okay?"

"No!" I growled. "You fucked up my world. So, now I'm fucking up yours. Find a new office manager!"

Her mouth fell open, and Dara worked to cover the patient's ears. To drive my point home, I flipped her off. Her eyes were as wide as saucers and she began sputtering excuses as I hit the back door. The gray sky fit my mood perfectly.

I got into my car and screamed until my throat burned.

Unemployed.

I needed to drive until my head was clear again. When I left the parking lot, I had no destination in mind. Maybe I'd go to Austin and see my dads—Isaac might know of some work in the area. Nothing was keeping me in here anymore.

It was refreshing, really—not being tied down.

A cry ripped from my chest, immediately followed by laughter. I was fine.

Better to know before I did something crazy, like give him a second chance, right?

Everything we'd shared had been a lie. Mike hadn't fallen in love with me that night on the beach. He'd fallen in Sandra's vagina.

One hour turned into three, but my mind was still as dark as the sky outside. I took a detour outside of Winters that led me down a dirt road and away from the highway. I'd panicked for a moment before remembering I truly had nowhere else to be.

For the time being, I was just existing.

The sky grumbled and fat raindrops pelted the windshield,

obscuring the road and forcing me to turn on the wipers. The dry earth couldn't handle the deluge and the dirt road became a mud pit within minutes. I sped up, somehow convinced I could outrun the storm and make it back to the highway.

That thought ended as a giant rooster flew up from the road right in front of my car. I didn't think. I just reacted and jerked the wheel to the right. The tires left the road and dropped into a bar ditch, leaving my car high-centered. I lost all traction and muddy brown water began flowing into the passenger side of the vehicle.

"Oh, fuck! Help!" I yelled to the dashboard as the car lurched hard to the right before coming to a complete standstill.

A quick glance confirmed my worst fears. I had officially stranded myself in the middle of nowhere, not a gas station or house for miles. I freed my phone from the pocket of my purse to find I had no cell service, either.

Hadn't there been a signal just a few minutes ago?

"Okay. Don't panic," I told myself as I panicked.

I couldn't stay inside the car and hope that help showed up. In the last hour and a half, I hadn't passed a single vehicle. I'd be out here for days and by the time someone came upon my car, there'd be nothing but a waterlogged zombie where I now sat.

I shuddered at the thought and peered up at the sky. The storm didn't show any signs of breaking, either. If I didn't start walking now, I'd be spending the night in it.

That was almost scarier than turning into a zombie.

I threw open the driver's side door, using my foot to prop it open as I grabbed my purse from the passenger seat. Mud on the side of the car smeared across the back of my skirt and calves as I climbed out.

My heels instantly sank into the muck and I let out a cry of surprise at the cold before bending down to save them from drowning. They were my best pair—I'd gotten them on clearance at Dillard's and was not about to give them up to the storm from Hades.

I tossed them onto the driver's seat, praying they'd be there when I made it back.

If I made it back.

Lightning lit up the sky, chased by a booming clap of thunder. I shivered again and walked around the front of the car to survey the damage. The damn rooster was embedded in the grill of Isaac's BMW 5 Series. I didn't even want to think about how badly that conversation was going to go—most children at least had the decency to wreck their parents' cars when they were teenagers.

About a mile in, I began ugly crying. The urge to call my mother was overwhelmingly strong. It damn near took me to my knees. I was soaked to the bone and at one of the lowest points I'd ever been in my life.

Was it too much to ask for me to just have some semblance of normalcy?

"Shit!" I howled when my big toe caught a stray rock, before launching it at the sky.

"Red, where in the hell do you think you're going?"

At the sound of his voice, I turned, convinced I was going to find some spirit impersonating him. That was going to be how I died out here. Not from exposure, but from fright.

Mike had the driver's side door open on his pickup truck and was standing up on the chrome cab step, concern etched on his face.

"I don't even know anymore," I admitted.

He slammed the door and came over to me; the rain soaking his hair and suit. I tried to ignore the way the material clung to his skin as he pulled me into his arms and asked, "What happened?"

"I quit my job after I found out you fucked my boss. So, now I'm unemployed and running away to see my dads," I finished with an unhinged laugh.

"I can explain," he began, his body already going stiff.

"Of course you can," I said with another maniacal chuckle. "You can always explain away the wake of damage you leave in your path, can't you, Mike? I can't do this with you anymore—just when I think I'm coming up for air, you're shoving me back under!"

He ran his hands through his wet hair. "Don't do this, Lauren. Don't run away because it's not perfect—"

"Not perfect?" I screamed. "Not perfect is you forgetting our anniversary. Not perfect is having to cancel dinner plans. It's not you fucking a woman I despise because I didn't show up to meet you. I thought that night meant something!"

Mike threw his hands up in the air. "It meant something, goddammit! I fucked up—I know that. What she and I had was just sex, but you stayed with me for years. Shouldn't that count for something? I never once cheated on you!"

I smacked his wet arm, stinging my hand. "You son of a bitch! It should count for something? How could you go to her after what we had?"

My screaming dissolved into sobbing again. This was about so much more than Sandra. I knew I couldn't voice my real question —*how could you leave my mother to die after everything we had?*

Had it only ever been a big thing to me?

He gave me a warning look before growling, "Don't you hit me again."

I slammed the palms of my hands into his chest, sending him stumbling back. "Why? Are you gonna hit me like your daddy hit you?"

I immediately regretted the words and tried reaching for him, but he jerked away from my grip.

"Mike," I started, but he shook his head. "Mike, please. I'm sorry!"

His jaw clenched, and I could see his pulse jumping in his neck. He opened his mouth and then closed it again before shaking his head angrily. "I witnessed my first murder on my eleventh birthday. My father killed a woman right in front of me—didn't understand why I wasn't in awe of him."

I started to apologize again, but he stopped me. "I'm not finished. When I was eighteen, I got jumped. My old man was so afraid of me turning into a pussy, he forced me to learn how to fight like he did. I hit the kid, and he fell back, cracked his head on a curb. Killed him with one stupid, unlucky punch. I called my mom and do you know who she sent to bail me out?"

I nodded. It all made sense.

"She called my father. He and the club took care of it. Now, I'm nothing more than a crooked cop on the MC payroll because of a mistake I made at eighteen!"

I covered my mouth to stifle my sobs. He'd sold himself to his father's biker gang before he'd even had a chance to go straight.

Mike continued, "I've done a lot of fucked up things in my life and you're right, I may be no better than he is. I've covered up a lot of shit for the wrong people, but what I have with you is real, and I have never once faked my feelings. I am so far from perfect and I feel like I ruin you just by looking, but I am not letting you run away from this." He dropped to his knees in the mud. "Forgive me. Forgive me, Lauren. Please. Forgive all the fucking stupid things I've done to hurt you."

He kept repeating the words until something inside of me broke. The armor surrounding my heart gave way, leaving me exposed.

Raw.

Two broken souls—who'd had their childhood stolen from them and been forced to resort to other means to survive.

Were we really all that different?

CHAPTER EIGHT

Lauren: October 2015 (Age: 28)

The rain battered our bodies, yet cleansed our souls. He knelt in the mud in front of me and, for the first time; I saw him—truly saw him.

The man behind the badge.

The scared boy behind the cocky man-whore.

And I knew that there would never be anyone else that made me feel like he did—whose scars mirrored mine so perfectly.

No one had ever seen the real Mike Sullivan. Until now. And I could keep running away every time we had a problem or I could stand by my man, at the gates of Hell, ready to fight anything that came our way.

As a team.

I'd hesitated in forgiving Monica, but if I had it to do over again, I would have willingly handed it over immediately if it meant more time with her.

His face ran with a mixture of tears and rain. Decision made, I reached out and wiped them away. My voice faltered as I gave him what he needed most. "I forgive you."

He buried his face against my belly and mumbled, "I wanted to keep you out of it all. It's too fucking much to burden someone with."

My hands slipped down to his jaw, tipping his face up toward mine. "I swore to love you in the gray areas. Tex. It doesn't get any grayer than this."

He was back on his feet in an instant, scooping me up and carrying me back to his truck.

"I had to get you out of that rain. You'll get sick," he said, carefully setting me down on the leather backseat before climbing in after me.

"And where'd you get this sound medical advice?" I asked with a smile.

He rubbed away the moisture on his splotchy face and grinned. "Abuelita—the woman's better than any doctor. My shoulder was giving me trouble last week, and she rubbed Vicks all over it. Worked like a charm."

That sounded like my grandmother.

Mike leaned forward and cupped my neck in his hand. "I almost had a fucking stroke when I saw you leaving Lubbock. I thought—" He grew quiet, and I realized what he thought. That I'd been taken.

Like Elizabeth. Katya. My mother.

At that moment, I was so damn grateful that he'd insisted I download the stupid tracking app. Without it, I would have been well on my way to becoming a zombie.

He leaned in until our noses were touching, breathing me in. "I don't know what I'd do without you, Red."

All of my anger evaporated. A tear fell onto my cheek as I nodded. "Me too. Thought I was going to die after hitting that rooster. He just came up out of nowhere."

Mike's mouth twisted into a smirk. "Rooster? Darlin', that was no rooster. Was it flying around?"

I nodded. "And then it came right for me."

He chuckled. "Baby, if it's the same thing that's hanging out in the front of your car, that's a turkey buzzard. Roosters can't fly."

"Oh," I replied. "Right."

His eyes dropped to my mouth. "Can I?"

When I nodded, his hand tightened around the back of my neck, pulling me in closer. His mouth pressed against mine, tentatively at first, before becoming more urgent.

It reminded me of showing up at his house after my car was bombed. We'd ripped each other wide open, needing to let the pain bleed out. This time, though, we were rebuilding everything we'd lost since January.

Mike kissed me so hard my head fell back, hitting the window with a soft thud. His stubble scraped against my skin, but instead of fighting it, I welcomed the pain.

Where I was still shivering from the rain, Mike's body radiated heat, and I tried to burrow into him. He was like my personal heating pad. My top lip fit perfectly against his bottom one and, as impossible as it sounded, it reminded me of something I'd never experienced before.

Home.

His kiss reiterated everything he'd said out in the rain and I wanted to make it work. To make us work. No matter the cost.

He pulled back to admit, "I'm an addict, baby. After everything that happened with us, I fell apart. Hard liquor. Coke. I was hell-bent on self-destructing. The thing is, I got clean, walked away from all of my vices. Except one. *You.* You're an addiction I'll never be able to kick, and darlin', no matter how many times I think I've sobered up, I will relapse again and again until I take my last breath."

I sucked in a soft breath and cupped his cheek in my hand, my eyes misting over. "I only ever wanted you, Mike. Not some version of you that was acceptable to society, but you. All the messy and broken parts."

His mouth flattened into a thin line, tears running down his face. "I want to take care of you, baby." At the look on my face, he amended, "Fuck, I know you can take care of yourself, but you shouldn't have to —not anymore. That's my job."

I had taken care of myself for longer than I could remember. To rely on anyone else was just begging for trouble. Was I capable of putting my wellbeing in someone else's hands? I knew then that I at least wanted to try.

"Okay," I whispered, feeling the last wall come down. I was vulnerable and still bore the wounds of my past, but I felt it. He was piecing me back together with his love. I only hoped I could do the same for him.

I wrapped my hand around the back of his neck, guiding him back down to my lips. With his forehead resting against mine, his hands found my hair. Mike wound the strands around his fingers, yet his mouth never left mine.

His tongue pressed lightly against my top lip, and I grinned before opening up to him. The hands that had found my hair so fascinating were now furiously undoing the buttons on my blouse and pulling it off of my shoulders. Our kiss had gone from lazily snacking to ravenous in a matter of seconds.

I worked to loosen his tie while simultaneously removing his light gray suit jacket. "Even if it is covered in mud, you in a suit is so incredibly hot," I murmured against his cheek.

His tongue darted out and licked along my jawline before he growled, "Yeah? Let's see how hot it gets you, baby."

My bra joined my blouse on the floorboard and then Mike's hands were on my skirt, unbuttoning and unzipping until I was wearing nothing but my panties. He pulled them to the side before easily pushing two fingers inside of me.

"That's my girl," he praised, moving them in and out. My walls worked to grip his fingers tightly, yet he still pulled away before pushing them back in even deeper, forcing me to accommodate him.

His lips moved impatiently against mine as if we'd been apart for years, while his fingers worked me up into a frenzy. With a pant, he broke away and his head dropped to my chest. His lips hovered over my left nipple, each warm exhale sending shivers throughout my body.

My eyes closed involuntarily as he sucked it into his mouth, his teeth closing lightly around me. When he curled his fingers inside of me, my back arched, but I remained pinned in place with his teeth. His hand moved again, and I saw stars. I bit down on my lip, but before I could get there, he pulled his hand free. Cold metal closed around my wrist with a click and my eyes flew open in surprise.

"Mike? Did you just handcuff me?"

There was a wicked glint in his eyes as he answered, "Just in case you get cold feet and decide to run on me again."

I didn't protest. It just made me wetter, especially when he looped the cuffs through the handle at the top of the window and placed them on my other wrist.

"That's a damn good look on you, darlin'." Even I could appreciate the sight of me with my chest thrust out, nipples hardened into stiff peaks.

"Please," I whispered.

The grin returned. "Please what, baby?"

I pushed my thighs together, trying to ease the ache. I was about to have a serious case of lady blue balls if he didn't do something soon. "Please," I tried again. "I need you inside of me."

Mike removed his shoulder holster and began unbuttoning his shirt almost casually. By the time he got down past his navel and the light blond hairs began peeking through, I was straining against the cuffs, craving the feel of his skin beneath my hand. Happy trail indeed. He slipped it off, and I admired the canvas of ink and muscle that greeted me. A sight I would never grow tired of.

He undid his belt slowly, and I groaned my disapproval. His eyes softened as he looked over at me, and I relented. The way he stared— like I was a small child who'd just performed my heart out in the school play. I never wanted to be cute or adorable. I'd insisted on being taken seriously. Until him.

"Patience, Red. Good things are worth the wait."

It couldn't have been more perfect if I'd planned it—the rain beating steadily against the glass and him sliding those slate gray slacks down his muscular thighs.

His erection jutted up toward his stomach, demanding my full attention. The cuffs rattled against the plastic handle as I instinctively moved to reach for him. I didn't have to wait long before he was kicking his boxer briefs into the floorboard and rubbing the tip of his cock up and down my slit.

A shudder wracked my body and my mouth dropped open in both orgasm and shock.

How?

I looked up at him in awe, and he reached down to run his middle finger through my wetness before spreading it down his shaft. "That was fucking hot, baby. Daytime sex is mandatory now."

I gave him a drowsy nod. I'd have agreed to anything at this point. The tinted windows had fogged up, giving the illusion we were in our own private cocoon. Safe from the world and all of its problems.

Mike cupped my ass in his hands, shifting me until the head of his dick was notched at my opening. "I wanna fuck you bare—need to feel you around me."

It wasn't a question, but a demand. I nodded again, knowing there were reasons it wasn't a good idea. At the moment, none of them seemed to stand up to his logic.

He needed to feel me.

Nothing else mattered.

He kept stroking the base as he worked his way in, and I let out a mewling whimper. He was holding back, trying to ease my body into it.

"Just fuck me, baby," I begged through clenched teeth.

That was all the invitation he needed. He surged inside of me, filling me to the point I thought I might black out. Mike growled when I released a hoarse cry and began making longer strokes. The cuffs clinked together loudly as my walls squeezed around him, my breath growing shallow.

"Mike... Mike... I'm—" My words cut off, as did my breathing. Our bodies were slick with sweat and the inside of the truck felt like a sauna, but we never slowed down. His skin slapped loudly against mine, pushing me to the brink and then over, again and again.

Just when I thought I had nothing left, his mouth sought mine. Plundering. Taking. I willingly handed everything I had to give over to him before locking my legs behind his back, drawing him deeper.

I thought he'd hit every pleasure point until his hands moved between our bodies, squeezing my breasts. His thrusts became erratic, and he moved his hands up behind my shoulders, forcing my body further down on his, before coming inside of me with a loud growl.

"Fuck!"

It was enough to send me over the edge with him. Mike clung to my body, our chests heaving as we floated back down to earth.

"I fucking love you, baby," he breathed.

Before I could answer, there was a gentle rap at the window behind us. I yelped in surprise and tried to cover myself, but the handcuffs refused to budge.

Mike wiped some of the steam off of the glass and looked out before muttering, "Fuck. Here." He tossed me his suit jacket and it hit my chest before falling to my lap.

"Um, Tex?" I questioned.

He pulled his boxers back up distractedly. "Yeah, Red. Just throw that on and button it."

I cleared my throat. "Mike? I, uh, can't really move here."

His eyes widened when it registered. "Shit! The key is around here somewhere. Okay, uh—look up." I did, and he held the jacket up under my chin before directing me to look down again.

The only thing keeping me covered was the power of my neck to chest action right now. Mike hurriedly buttoned up his shirt and rolled down the window, still in his boxers.

"Hello," he called cheerfully to a man in an oil covered t-shirt and farm supply hat.

The man narrowed his eyes as he took in the handcuffs. "I stopped by to see if you needed help getting the car out. That storm came up while I was out on my tractor." His eyes cut over to me again.

"Good afternoon." I smiled widely, trying to look like I wanted to be in cuffs.

He reached for a cell phone and backed away. "I'm just going to make a quick call."

I expected Mike to identify himself, but he didn't. "Mike?"

He pinched the bridge of his nose. "Red, we're gonna have some explaining to do when the Winters Police Department shows up here in a minute."

"Then pull out your badge," I hissed.

Mike gave me a wry smile. "Darlin', I've been accused of whipping out my badge any old time I need to get myself off the hook. I say we just wait it out and maybe the boys headed our way will have an extra set of keys for those cuffs."

I shook my head. "No! You get me out of these cuffs right now,

Michael Sullivan. I'm not even playing with you! So help me god, if you wait for the police to get here, I will lose my shit."

He frowned. "But using my badge is taking advantage, isn't it? I don't want to do the wrong thing."

I went to kick him, but he was faster. He easily wrapped my foot up in his hand with a chuckle. "Watch it there, Red. I saw your gorgeous pussy when you did that. You don't want me getting hard again right now, do you?"

"Mike!" I snarled. "Get me out of these goddamn cuffs and tell that poor man not to call us in!"

"Please?"

"Please," I growled.

He gave me a dopey smile and pulled his pants back on before jumping out and going after my would-be rescuer. Poor guy probably thought I was being trafficked.

The man reluctantly made his way back over to the truck a few minutes later, Mike's arm casually slung around his shoulder. "—Yeah, you can do anything you need to do to get a confession out of a prisoner. Even mouthy little gingers like this one."

The man shook his head in surprise. "I never imagined they gave you free rein like that."

"They don't," I responded dryly.

Mike shook his head and rolled his eyes at his new friend. "I wouldn't listen to anything Grand Theft Auto over here has to tell you. She's gonna be going away for quite some time with the charges I've got against her."

"Well, let's get that car pulled out so you can tow it and her back to Lubbock. Unless..." He trailed off, staring at me in a way that made me shudder. The only things missing were the cartoon eyes bugging out of his head and a tongue rolled out like a red carpet.

Mike immediately stiffened, his hand digging into the man's shoulder. I could tell it was causing him pain when his head dipped lower and lower toward the affected side.

"You know, Farmer Brown, I think we're good with just the tow. Touch her and that's assault. You don't have a badge." Mike's voice had a joking tone, but his eyes looked murderous.

"You got it, man." He winced. "I'll—ow—I'll just grab the tractor now."

He stumbled off. Mike spun his key ring until he found the one he needed. "Let's get you out of those cuffs and fully dressed, darlin'. Before I have to kill someone."

I relaxed my head and let the jacket fall. "Thank the lord. I thought I was going to be stuck like this forever."

Mike unlocked my wrists and gently pulled my arms into his, getting the blood flowing again. "Goddamn, Red. If I thought we had more time, I'd ask for round two."

I slugged him weakly in the bicep and smirked. "Just get me out of here, Tex. Before that farmer tries to jump my bones."

His booming laughter filled the cab of the truck as he helped me back into my underwear. "No duh—I'll get you back to your crib before he decides that you're all that and a bag of chips. Can't have Old MacDonald gettin' jiggy wit' it."

The man had just managed to work a lot of nineties references into one sentence. If I had more feeling in my arms, I would have hit him again.

"You know, Red? You're pretty phat. P.H.A.T."

I sighed. It was going to be a long three-hour ride home.

CHAPTER NINE

Mike: October 2015 (Age: 32)

I woke up in a sweat with a gorgeous redhead sprawled across my body, feeling like I'd won the lottery. Lauren mumbled something in her sleep before her breaths evened out again. After the night we'd had, she needed the rest.

Then again, so did I. She would never know what seeing her location move out of town had done to me. I had raced out of my office, convinced the Sons had gotten to her. I lost service outside of Winters and had been flying blind when I drove up on her minor mishap.

Sandra? My shitty childhood? None of it had been part of the plan, but that downpour had done more than soak my clothes. It left me with a sense of heaviness in my chest at the lies I'd been feeding her from day one. So, maybe I'd been lying by omission, but it hadn't lessened the hurt I caused.

I traced the freckles on her shoulder, thanking whoever controlled destiny that she was mine. Everything I'd kept hidden for years was now out in the open, and for the first time, I felt I could breathe easily.

After the war between the clubs was over, I was going to get that ring from the gun safe and knock the dust off before asking her to marry me. Shit, maybe I'd give it to her after Katya's case wrapped up. We could take off, maybe find some all-inclusive resort down in Mexico to hole up in for a week or two. Lauren had been forced to grow up at an early age, just like me. It was time for the two of us to make new memories and plans for a future that didn't involve Silent Phoenix MC.

If that made me a pussy, so be it. I'd wear the title like a badge of honor.

Platinum Pussy, at your service.

My phone lit up with a blocked number. I carefully reached for it, trying to ensure Lauren remained asleep. It was just after six, so whoever was on the other end of the line better have had something important to tell me.

"Hello?" I whispered.

"Junior, need you to come outside. We got a problem."

Next to hearing my father's voice on the other end of the line, my least favorite thing was quickly becoming the phrase, We have a problem.

They always had fucking problems.

Maybe Lauren and I could get hired on at the all-inclusive resort and just stay permanently.

She stirred briefly when I got up, before rolling back over with a soft sigh. What hadn't been used up in the backseat of my truck was spent when we got back to my place. She was probably going to sleep most of the day away. I only wished I could join her.

I pulled on a pair of sweats and met my old man out on the porch.

"Ain't talkin' to you inside when your bitch is over," Comedian said as I shut the front door behind me.

"Morning to you too, Dad. It's always a pleasure to see your—"

He cuffed me upside the head. "Don't fuck with me right now, Junior. You left the club in an uncomfortable position, so I'd show a little more respect if I were in your shoes."

Having left my patience upstairs in bed, I growled, "What is it this time? Did I not get my cookies to the club bake-off in time? Did Grey need his ass wiped, and I wasn't nearby? What? What did I not do to make your fucking club happy now?"

My father's jaw popped out as he forced through clenched teeth, "Your model rolled over, son. It's all over the fucking news." Seeing my expression, he laughed and tapped his nose. "I think that trail is going to lead right back to you. And, if it leads back to you, then it's gonna lead back to the club. And that just won't do."

Katya?

She'd seemed better the last time we spoke and had made amends with her neighbor. Fuck, she'd made it sound like they were more than friends—had even gotten defensive when I told her to be careful.

Then, he'd called me up out of the blue a few days ago, wanting to help in her case. Had the timing been more than mere coincidence?

Comedian held up his phone and my face went numb. This wasn't just a few secrets. What TMZ had was a goddamn exposé.

And perhaps the most disturbing claim Katya has made is that Landon Scott has been dead the entire time. Police have spent countless hours searching for her kidnapper. According to Detective Shane Strohn with the Arapahoe County SD, "We've reached out to the Lubbock Police Department and informed them the search into Scott's disappearance could be a homicide investigation." Police said they're not considering Katya a suspect at this time, but are interested in questioning her further.

If they'd reached out to the police department, I hadn't heard a word of it.

Probably because I was suspect number one.

My word had become the official narrative of what happened the night we rescued the girls. I never considered the possibility they would question it. Working for the club had given me a god complex, and I was sure as shit going to be paying for it now.

I scrolled through my contacts and angrily stabbed her name when I got to it. It rang several times before clicking over to an automated voicemail. I hung up without leaving a message before turning back to Comedian.

"What do we do?"

He let out a rough bark of laughter. "What do we do? We ain't doing shit here, son. You're gonna get your ass up to Colorado and neutralize the goddamned threat."

He wanted me to kill her?

The thought left me feeling sick.

Killing a club slut had been one thing. Brianne dug her grave proudly, but Katya—Katya had been abused and raped. If she talked to anyone, it was a therapist. God knew she'd seen her fair share of them. This was what this was—some psychologist wanted a payday and broke confidentiality.

I'd gladly fly up there and end one of their lives. Not hers, though. I was no better than Landon if I hurt her. Scratch that, all I'd need was a name change and I could've filled in for Comedian.

"Just make it look like a suicide," he instructed, clapping me on the shoulder. "Glad we had this talk, Junior. You been making me real proud lately—showin' initiative and taking care of club business like a man."

I wasn't feeling like much of a man at the moment—just a spineless drone. He hopped back onto his bike and took off down the driveway as the first rays of dawn lightened the sky. I sank down onto the porch swing with my head in my hands.

I had to call her first—I owed her that, at least. I'd keep calling until she answered before making any sort of decision. If she sounded unhinged, then I'd go up there and put her down. Christ—I was even starting to think like him.

She didn't answer the first five calls. I redialed like I was trying to be the one hundredth caller on a radio show, losing count after forty. But she still wasn't picking up.

Maybe she'd taken care of it herself.

If Katya had fallen back into one of her spells, it wasn't far-fetched to believe her capable of hurting herself.

I needed to get into the office—find out more about her neighbor. What was his name? Trevor? Travis. Travis Logan.

I crept back inside and up the stairs, finding Lauren in the same position I'd left her thirty minutes ago. My heart clenched in my chest.

She was my world.

I leaned down and kissed her hair before grabbing a large duffel bag from the top shelf in my closet. I snagged my gun case and a small metal box of ammo, knowing I'd have to declare them at the counter. But I wasn't worried about that. As far as they knew, I was assisting with the Christine Stevens' investigation.

CHAPTER TEN

Mike: October 2015 (Age: 32)

Katya had admitted to talking to just one person. The neighbor, Travis Logan. Since then I'd combed the system, trying to make the connection between him and the notes. It didn't fit. Like forcing a round peg into a square hole. They'd been seeing each other—if he was my guy, I'd have expected him to make his move months ago.

While at the station, I'd gotten word Sergeant Rendell wanted to see me. I knew what it was about. If Katya's story had changed, then mine had, too. I promised to get with him after lunch before skipping out and heading for the airport.

If I wanted to keep everything I'd worked for—including Lauren— I was going to have to accept the club's terms. I'd called Grey on the way, hoping he'd talk me out of it, but he'd quietly agreed that Katya disappearing would take the heat off of everyone.

I replayed what I was going to have to do for most of the flight. I'd left my girl in bed asleep to commit a murder. Another one. Just when I thought I'd cleared my conscience, another sin reared its ugly head. As the wheels touched down on the tarmac, I decided to not only take out Katya, but the neighbor as well.

Just to be safe.

A lead ball of dread rested in my stomach. There was no coming back from this. Killing in self-defense or for Lauren, I could justify either and sleep like a fucking baby at night. Killing just to cover my own ass didn't settle well with me, though.

My cell phone rang while I was waiting for my luggage. Lauren had called twice already, but I couldn't talk to her until it was over. This time, a blocked number flashed across the screen and I answered with a tired, "What?"

"Mike, it's Jeremy—uh, Jarvis. Listen, I looked into the computer records you had on the Egorichev case. You're not gonna like this."

I'd already known it was the neighbor, but decided not to spoil the momentum he had going. "What'd you find?"

"It's not the neighbor—uh, Travis Logan. I looked into him too, though. Marine veteran... wounded in combat. Other than that, guy's clean."

I snatched my duffel bag off the conveyer belt and headed for the rental car counter. "If it isn't him, then who the fuck am I looking for?"

Finding a stalker for a supermodel was like searching for a needle in a goddamned haystack. If Jeremy had just called to tell me who it wasn't, then I knew we were going to be hard-pressed to solve this.

"Lee Watkins. Guy was a journalist for Huffington Post around the same time Egorichev was rescued. Fabricated a story and lost his job. So there's motive. I traced the IP addresses back to Cedar Ridge. Mike, he's in the same town as her right now. Every message traces back to wherever she's been. He's our guy."

I froze, rental car keys in my hand. "You're saying this guy's location shows him in the same town as Katya and you didn't think to fucking lead with that information? I don't need to know who isn't responsible!"

I took the winding curves toward Cedar Ridge, accelerator smashed against the floorboard. She hadn't answered a single call since I left the airport, but I kept trying to get through, anyway.

"Katya, where are you?" I demanded when she finally picked up.

"I'm at home—why?"

"I need you to get into your car and drive back into town. It's not safe for you. We found evidence. Facebook released records—you were right all along. Get to a police station or somewhere safe. Okay?" So I'd lied about Facebook releasing the records, but couldn't tell her the club had hacked the system.

"Mike?" she questioned before my phone gave three short beeps and disconnected.

No service.

I punched the steering wheel in frustration and forced the SUV to move faster. He was within blocks of her. If I didn't get there soon, she was going to die.

Katya's cabin was dark when I pulled into the gravel driveway. Her Jeep sat in the driveway, proof she hadn't made it out of the house. The question was, who was inside with her? I killed the headlights and coasted to a stop behind her vehicle. My cell phone vibrated from the passenger seat and Lauren's smiling face greeted me.

"Can't talk right now, baby. Kind of in the middle of something," I muttered to myself, declining the call. I should have told her what was going on, but I hadn't wanted to make her a part of it. I needed to make sure nothing pointed back toward her.

I retrieved my gun from the duffel bag and loaded it with a heavy sigh. I didn't notice the neighbor's truck until I got out. His house was just as dark as Katya's, though.

The sound of music reached my ears as I got closer to the back porch —Sinatra. I kept a wary eye on his windows, anticipating an ambush at any second. My instinct was to rush in, guns blazing, but I fought it. Until I knew for sure Lee hadn't brought accomplices, I was going to have to wait it out. Other than the faint strains of music, things were calm. The sky spat snow and I burrowed further into my jacket, waiting for a sign.

Katya screamed, but before I could move, a figure approached from the lake. Without knowing if it was a threat or an ally, I hung back, gun at my side.

When I saw the dog, it clicked. It was her neighbor, Travis. He and the dog jogged past before I could call out a warning. If Travis went in there, he was going to get killed. If he got himself killed, it saved me the trouble.

Goddammit. I never wanted this life.

He knocked on the front door, and I took a chance, peering in the back window. Lee held a gun on Katya and gestured toward the door. She was cradling her wrist, but nodded at his words.

Think, Mike. Think.

Lee was alone. I could take him. I needed a plan, though—some way to end the whole fucking thing without Travis or Katya getting hurt. Katya sent Travis away, closing the front door with a silent sob. She was going to sacrifice herself to keep him safe. Hadn't Lauren done the same thing the night she found out I killed Landon?

By staying with my sorry ass, Lauren had given up on a normal life with a man who would have shown her every day how important she was to him.

I spent every ounce of my free time with her, but was it enough?

Screw it. I didn't have time to consider all the reasons I didn't deserve Lauren. I slipped on my gloves, knowing I had to focus on my mission. Just as I began inching the window open, Travis and his dog silently entered the house.

Shit.

Get the fuck out of here, man.

Lee immediately turned the gun on him, and I cursed again. Now, I had to find a way to get them both out alive. Jeremy had mentioned something about Travis being in the military, but I failed to see how it was going to help since he'd walked in unarmed.

Katya went back over to Lee, letting him hold a gun to her head like an obedient animal. If I got the window open enough, I could take out Lee from here, but I'd likely hit Travis too.

The second Lee turned his attention to Katya, Travis barreled into him. It was the only opportunity I'd get. I ran for the back door, the unmistakable blast of a gun shattering the illusion of calm.

I kicked in the door to find Lee lying motionless on the floor.

"Is he dead?"

Travis shook his head, panting, "He had a gun... put him in a chokehold."

Unconscious.

Good. This plan actually had a chance of working out. I holstered my gun and retrieved Lee's from the floor, before kneeling beside him.

I placed the weapon in his limp hands and brought the barrel up under his chin.

"Detective?" Travis questioned.

Combat veteran.

Combat veteran.

I came to my senses long enough to bark out, "Travis, look away."

With my index finger over Lee's, I pulled the trigger, blowing his lower jaw off.

He was dead—it was over.

Travis stared at me in openmouthed horror, his chest rising and falling rapidly.

Almost over.

I raised the gun again, hearing my father screaming in my head.

Kill him! Don't leave another fuckin' witness to take us all down!

Katya was on the phone in the other room, worry evident in her voice. I had to kill him and then her for it to truly be over. I would never have to worry about anyone else looking into the Landon Scott disappearance.

Travis eyed me warily, winded from his fight with Lee. His eyes narrowed in a glare as if saying, *get it over with.*

Kill him, my father urged, and my index finger moved off the guard and toward the trigger.

When I grow up, I'm gonna be one of the good guys.

Suddenly, I was eleven years old again.

I hope you are, kiddo. Hope to hell you can do it. Grey's voice broke through the haze, puncturing my resolve.

I shook my head and slowly lowered the gun. I wouldn't take an innocent person's life just to keep my shit under wraps.

Plan B it was.

I pulled the plastic bag from the inside pocket of my jacket. Landon's wallet. I slid it into the pocket of Lee's pants and stood, somewhat satisfied with the change of course.

Travis sank down the wall until he was sitting with his back against it, watching my every move. Katya came down the hallway, phone pressed to her ear. Her focus was entirely on Travis as she patted his arms and chest. "I'm here. I'm here. Did he shoot you?"

Travis didn't take his eyes off mine as he answered, "He's gone—you're safe."

He was watching to see if I reached for the gun again. Hell, he'd probably channel his inner Marine strength to snap my ass in two before I even got close to Katya. She deserved a man like him. I hoped he woke up every day and realized what a lucky son of a bitch he was to have a woman like her.

She'd been willing to die for him.

I nodded my head at his statement, and he marginally relaxed his shoulders.

Katya finally noticed me, along with what remained of Lee. "Jesus Christ."

I muted her phone. The cops were on their way, leaving me little time for explanations. "I need Landon's ring."

Her eyes studied mine briefly, as if reading my thoughts. It lasted maybe a second before she went to her bedroom, returning with the ring in her hand.

Travis watched the exchange with wide eyes. She'd have to explain our history to him, because I was out of time. I wiped the ring clean before slipping it onto Lee's finger. It was maybe half a size bigger than what he would have worn normally. Not enough to draw suspicion.

"I was never here," I warned both of them, slipping out through the back door and into the rental. I drove around the lake to avoid the red and blue strobes coming up the hill, processing what needed to be done next.

Ten minutes and I'd return to give my statement to the media before catching the last flight back to Texas.

I could only pray Lauren would be waiting for me.

CHAPTER ELEVEN

Lauren: October 2015 (Age: 28)

"*M*ijita, it's the little mice. Your favorite." *Abuelita* patted my foot through the blanket and pointed at the screen before telling Torch, "LoLo loved this movie so much when she was a little girl."

I frowned and stared at the television screen. It was *Cinderella* and for the life of me, I couldn't recall why we were watching it. "Um, *Abuelita?* You met me when I was seventeen."

Torch took another handful of popcorn from the bowl, watching our exchange with an amused expression.

She huffed, "You let me have this, LoLo. You are my only granddaughter. If I want to imagine you loved *Cinderella* as a *niña*, humor me. I am nothing but an old woman now."

Torch began chuckling, but stopped when she turned her glare on him. "Her guilt trips are some of the best I've seen."

I should have been at Mike's—arguing over which movie to watch or getting tangled up in his bedsheets. Instead, I'd woken up alone and more than a little confused. He was gone.

No note or text letting me know where he'd gone or even if he was okay.

Morning turned to afternoon, but my calls and texts went unanswered. It was as if the man had fallen off the face of the earth.

I had given him my trust—just willingly handed it over, only to be ghosted within the first twenty-four hours. When it felt as though the cavern in my stomach was going to swallow me whole, I got behind the wheel of my busted-up BMW and drove back to Torch's.

If he wanted me, he knew where to find me. I snuggled into the couch, burying myself under one of *Abuelita's* blankets—a woven throw depicting the image of Our Lady of Guadalupe.

"Can we watch something else?" I pleaded from my polyester fortress. "Like a grown-up show?"

Torch flipped over to one of the local channels where a baseball game was being aired. *Abuelita* immediately began questioning everything about the sport, forcing him to explain.

"A strike is an action, Dave," she argued. "If he gets the strike, it should mean he hits the ball far away."

I dozed off to the sound of his laughter. My dreams were disjointed—filled with farmers, handcuffs, and roosters playing baseball. I woke with a jerk when my phone vibrated against my thigh. My heart sank to find it was just a news alert until I caught the name mentioned near the bottom.

"Torch, find me a news channel!" *Abuelita* lowered her crocheting with narrowed eyes and I quickly amended, "Please."

"Terrifying news coming out of Colorado tonight. Just one day after police identified the body found in Cherry Creek as that of model, Christine Stevens, another model was held at gunpoint in her own home.

"Katya Egorichev is safe after alleged stalker, Lee Watkins, broke into her home. She escaped with a broken wrist and concussion and is recovering at an undisclosed location tonight."

After covering the details of Katya's kidnapping and subsequent stalking, they went live to Colorado and twisted the knife a little deeper. My lungs constricted when Mike's face filled the screen, making it hard to take a full breath.

Why are you there?

Why didn't you tell me?

Torch reached over and squeezed my thigh. "It's okay, kid."

I nodded and fought the trembling in my chin.

Abuelita looked up in awe. "LoLo, that looks like your man. Sí?"

I pointed to the caption at the bottom of the screen with a forced smile. "See that, *Abuelita*? Detective Michael Sullivan, Lubbock PD. It looks like him, because it is him."

She nodded and went back to crocheting. I stared desperately at the screen, needing answers. He hadn't faked things with me. He said that. So, why was he in Colorado, refusing to take my calls?

"I can confirm the decedent was in possession of some jewelry belonging to Christine Miller, along with a wallet and college ring belonging to Landon Scott," Mike reported. When he looked directly into the camera, my blood ran cold.

He'd killed again.

His eyes looked the same as they had the night I confronted him about Landon.

"I'm pretty tired," I mumbled to no one in particular. "Think I'm gonna head to bed now."

I stripped out of my jeans and found a pair of sweats, suddenly chilled to the bone. Then I buried myself under the comforter and considered what it meant that he hadn't told me anything before drifting into a restless sleep.

Sometime after midnight, a warm body slid into bed behind me. I recognized the smell of him immediately, and my chest tightened. He tucked me against his chest and laced his fingers through mine.

"I'm sorry," he whispered against the shell of my ear.

"How did you get in?"

He shifted closer and yawned. "Gloria. Apparently, the woman never sleeps. I took the last flight out of Denver—I had to see you."

I turned my head to look up at him. "Did—did that man kill the other girl?"

He nodded and ran his thumb across my knuckles. "Yeah, he was also the one sending Katya letters. I guess he wanted her to think Landon was back, not realizing it would've been impossible."

I squeezed his fingers. "Then you did the right thing."

He sighed, his breath warm against my cheek. "Red, as far as the world is concerned, he was dead when I got there."

I rolled until I was facing him. "I saw your eyes, Michael Sullivan. You can lie to them, but not to me."

He froze. "How can you even look at me?"

"You did what had to be done," I said with a frown. "I'm not gonna lie and say I didn't have second thoughts when I couldn't reach you, but you kept Katya safe, Mike. That's all that matters."

He shook his head, flexing his jaw muscle. "I ignored your calls, so you didn't go down with me. And I didn't go up there to kill Lee."

"What? Who did you plan to kill?" I felt like I knew the answer, but it didn't make sense.

His heart beat against my shoulder. He was bracing himself for me to run. "When I woke up yesterday morning, all I could think about was how perfect it was between us. Then I got word that *TMZ* was running a story on Katya, where she admitted Landon had been dead all along—"

"So, you thought killing her would fix that?" I hissed, my voice growing louder. If I didn't lower it, *Abuelita* was likely to burst in, demanding details.

He sat up and moved away from me. "The department had launched an investigation. Suddenly, no one believed I didn't know what happened to Landon that night. Everything I'd worked for was going up in flames. I thought if she was gone, then maybe it would balance everything out."

I closed my eyes. It didn't fit—Mike wasn't a cold-blooded killer. It wasn't him. Then again, I thought his father seemed like someone with a lot of heart. Maybe the Sullivan men were just exceptionally skilled at hiding their true selves.

Mike continued, "Even after figuring out Lee was responsible, I planned on neutralizing the threat."

"Neutralizing the threat? Does saying it like that make you sleep better at night?" I thought of Katya and all she'd endured. Knowing the man I loved had come close to ending her life left me feeling sick.

His hands moved to rest on top of his head. "No! Jesus, Lauren! I— I couldn't do it. Do you want to know why?"

I nodded, even though I wasn't sure that I did.

"Growing up, I swore I was going to be one of the good guys. Tonight, I realized I was nothing like the man I wanted to be. Katya's boyfriend risked his life to keep her safe and then there was me—so scared of the truth coming out that I'd been ready to end an innocent person's life. A fucking coward with a gun."

I wrapped my arms around his neck and pulled him to my chest. "Mike, you're not a coward. You're a good man."

He shook his head, and I wasn't sure whether he was disagreeing or burrowing into the space between my breasts. "I'm not," he said in a muffled voice. "Not yet. But I want to be that for you and, more importantly, for myself."

I rubbed his back. "Why didn't you answer my calls? I would've helped you."

Mike moved back and looked up at me. "Why didn't I answer your calls? Because, Red, I didn't want you going down with me if it all fell apart. I've dragged you into enough of my shit."

I couldn't help myself. I laughed. "Dragged me into it? I'm pretty sure I found most of it on my own. Apparently, asking the biker stalking me at work who the fuck he thinks he is was a bad idea—as was barging into a biker bar and demanding to speak to people."

This time, it was Mike who pulled me into his arms. "A biker was watching you at work? When? Who was he?"

I inhaled deeply. He smelled like aftershave and firewood. It was nice. Judging by the way his hands dug into my skin, he was worked up and needed me to calm him before he snapped.

"I don't know who he was. He had the leather vest like the guys, but they said he wasn't with them. Maybe he's with the other biker gang. I don't know—it doesn't even matter, to be honest. You're not responsible for my choices, Tex. Trying to keep me out of it further proves what I've always known was true—you are a good man, Mike. Even if you can't see it yourself."

He gripped my hip tightly in his hand. "Move in with me."

"What?" I whispered back, certain I'd misheard.

His throat bobbed in a swallow. "Move in with me."

He'd given me his secrets, the parts of him no one else had. Now, he was offering the one thing I'd yearned for—a safe place to call my own. His arms to fall into every night.

He was my home.

I bit down on the corner of my lip, even as it turned up into a small smile. "Okay."

CHAPTER TWELVE

Mike: May 2016 (Age: 33)

"What do you mean, you're getting married? You're already married."

David took a swig of beer from his pint glass and grinned over the top of it at me. "Thank you for stating that, Captain Obvious. We're renewing our vows—with everything that happened, I thought it'd be good for us. An outward display of an inward change."

I winced. "Jesus, you sound like an inspirational greeting card right now. Is this what marriage and having a kid do to you? If so, do not sign me up for that shit."

Actually, I wanted the stability of having a wife and kids—didn't mean I wouldn't give him hell when he brought it up, though.

He flipped me off with a smirk. "Say what you want, asshole. Beth was kind enough to agree to you being the best man again, despite the speech you gave at the last one."

I clapped my hands together. "Does this mean another bachelor party? More strippers?"

"Jesus, Mike. You never change. You're in your thirties now. Don't you want to do more than just fuck around?"

The anger behind his words made me pause. I'd been screwing around with him under the assumption he knew I was dating Lauren and hadn't bothered telling him myself, figuring Elizabeth had beaten me to the punch already.

"So, Lauren—"

"She'll be there, okay?" David interjected with a sigh. "From what Beth said, she's hot and heavy with some guy at the gym. Bring a date if it'll make you feel better about things, but for the love of all that is good and holy, do not fuck this day up for us."

The blood left my face, and I sat in stunned silence. Lauren had been living with me for seven months. Seven months of being in the same bed every night. I didn't know where Elizabeth had gotten her information, but it was wrong.

I held up a finger. "Excuse me for a second."

The phone rang three times before Elizabeth answered with a cheery, "Hello!"

"I was just informed that you're to be wed... again. My congratulations."

"Well, thank you—" she began with a giggle.

"Where did you get your information on Lauren's dating life?"

Her laughter ceased immediately. "Mike, I know it's hard to hear, but—"

"Just answer the question," I ground out through clenched teeth. David's head shot up and he gave me a warning look, mouthing, *Don't speak to her like that again.*

"Mike, I've been working out with her. Jimmy's a good guy and he seems to really care about her. Let her go—she deserves to be happy."

Jimmy?

Fucking Jimmy was still in the picture?

My head pounded, and my vision blurred from the surge of adrenaline. I hung up on Elizabeth and tried to stand. Instead, my legs were like Jell-O and I fell, striking the table on my way down.

David was on his feet and over to me within seconds. "Fuck, Mike. Are you okay? Did you have too much?"

I shook him off.

She was cheating?

Of all the things I could have imagined her doing, cheating wasn't one of them. Was this payback for the Sandra incident? Or her mom?

Had she taken me back just to see if she could rip my fucking heart out all over again?

"I have to go," I said, more to myself than David.

He tried to talk me out of it. "C'mon, you're obviously in no condition to leave. Stay—maybe we can find someone here for you."

I grabbed the front of his shirt and snarled, "I don't fucking want anyone else. Okay?"

I was going to find out where Jimmy lived and pay him a little visit. I stormed out of the bar and into my truck, not giving a fuck if he was eight feet high or not.

The son of a bitch had messed with the wrong man.

———

I slammed the door of my pickup truck and hobbled up the front porch steps. There wasn't a single part of my body that didn't ache.

"Christ, I'm not fucking your girl. We're just friends."

Turned out, Jimmy hadn't wanted to fight me, at least not until I threw my fist into his jaw. Instead of falling down like I'd hoped, he'd thrown several hits of his own—all while calmly explaining again that he and Lauren were nothing more than friends.

Apparently, she'd been working out and shooting with the man every day, but had kept it from me. I let the screen door slam shut behind me and stood in the doorway to the living room, where she sat facing the television.

"You're home early from boy's night. I thought you'd be gone for hours," she said, pausing her show to look back at me. Her face paled. "What the hell happened? Are you okay? Was it the other gang?"

I shrugged off her attempts to help and stormed into the kitchen to grab an ice pack. "Jimmy says hello."

And there it was. She blinked rapidly and shook her head. Some detective I was. How had I missed the deception in her eyes before? "Oh my god, your eye is swelling. Jimmy did this to you? Why?"

I pressed the ice pack to my face and leaned against the cabinets. "Why don't you tell me, darlin'. I was just informed I'm not the one taking you to their wedding re-do or whatever the fuck they're calling it. Apparently, you and Jimmy are pretty hot and heavy."

Lauren ran a hand over her face and sighed. "Shit. Look, Mike, I haven't really told anyone we're back together yet—didn't want to get their hopes up, you know?"

The entire fucking house of cards was coming down in front of me. I pinched the bridge of my nose and took a deep breath, struggling to keep my voice calm. "No, I don't know. You've been it for me from day one and I'm sure as fuck not keeping it a secret."

"I just wanted to wait until we were in a more concrete spot! I'm not hiding it!"

My fist came down against the counter with a loud thud and she jumped in fright. "Goddammit, Red! Look around you—we fucking live together. It doesn't get much more concrete than that. Why are you hiding this?"

"It's not like that. There just hasn't been a good opportunity to tell her."

"You're telling me in all the months you've lived here, Elizabeth has never once asked to stop by your place—never offered to pick you up? Jimmy has known about us from the beginning, yet you kept the fact that you're seeing him daily from me. Where do the lies end with you?"

She glared at me. "We're together until we're not together. We're fighting, but then we're not fighting. There is so much shit that goes along with us. You'll forgive me if I'm not big on sharing that with everyone I know."

I wanted to grab her by her shoulders and shake her until her teeth cracked together. Maybe knock some goddamn sense into her until she realized what she was doing to me.

"When was the last time we fought? If you're referring to the time you drove to fucking Winters because you found out I fucked your boss when we weren't even together yet, then sure, we fight all the time! Do you even think before you speak?"

Except for the nights I had to help the club, we were like a normal couple.

I thought.

Little did I know she was off pumping iron and shooting targets with Paul Bunyan.

"Do I think? Do you? You come in here, beaten to shit, because you heard I was cheating. Do you come home and ask me? No, you go to Jimmy's first, because that's obviously the more rational choice. This —this right here is why I've kept my mouth shut!" She roared.

I shook my head, but kept my voice steady. "You're still looking for a reason to leave, baby. You blamed me for what happened to your mom, then the Sandra thing, and now? Fuck me, I don't even know why you're walking away anymore. I'm willing to fight for you, but I can't put in all the effort—"

"All the effort? You're never here! You're at the station or you're at the club! When do I get to be first, Mike?"

Should have just gone with shaking her.

"You wanna be first, darlin'? Okay, as soon as I'm done hustling to keep us on top, I'll make sure you feel important. I swear to Christ, you don't work—you're too busy playing single girl with Jimmy while I bust my ass!"

Her face darkened to a dangerous shade of red. "You said you wanted to take care of me! You told me to rely on you!"

I grabbed an ice pack and headed for the front door. "Yeah, well, I'm not sure why I ever agreed to that. I've gotta get out of here and clear my head."

Lauren reached for my arm. "Don't leave mad—we can talk this out! You're right, I fucked up. I kept us a secret, but it wasn't out of some ploy to get Jimmy, I swear. Honestly, I don't know how to do this! I don't know how to trust this is all going to work out, no matter how much I want it to." Her eyes filled, and I had to look away. Her anger I could take, but her pain would break any resolve I had.

"I can't look at you right now," I said softly, closing the door behind me.

I just needed to drive until my head was clear, until I knew what to do. If this was all a part of David's prediction that I'd find a woman who'd turn my life upside down, then I was going to have to send him a fucking fruit basket to thank him.

I wanted a drink.

I wanted to use.

God, love was a fucking gem.

After driving aimlessly for about fifteen minutes, I realized something. Lauren had never been shown how to trust. Never had anyone show her how to love. When I told her I'd take care of her, hadn't that come with it?

Sure, she had Josué and Gloria, but they'd come around when she was damn near grown. Her behavior was learned; ingrained into her at an early age.

As her man, it was my job to provide a place where she felt safe. Even on nights like tonight when I wanted to strangle the life out of her.

I'd had women... a lot of them. No one had ever gotten under my skin the way she did. She was feisty as fuck and not afraid to stand up to me. That meant something. I just had to get her to let her guard down and trust me.

I'd given her a house, but maybe there was something I was missing.

Had I ever truly given her a home?

I turned the truck around. She and I weren't going to bed until this was worked out. We had come too far to throw it all away now.

Just needed to stop for coffee first.

CHAPTER THIRTEEN

Lauren: May 2016 (Age: 29)

U ntil Mike slammed the door, I'd thought things were going well.
Sure, *Abuelita* had been pushing for a wedding, but I'd brushed
her off, not wanting to put any pressure on him. My grandmother
claimed she was a romantic, but secretly, I think she just wanted an
opportunity to plan a wedding for her only granddaughter. She had never
forgiven Josué for eloping in Boston without the entire family present.

When Mike proposed, I wanted it to be one hundred percent his
decision.

If Mike proposed...

God, I was so stupid. I should have been honest with Elizabeth,
especially when Jimmy suspected she had the wrong idea about us.
Instead, I'd screwed up the best relationship of my life and proven I
didn't know how to act like a normal human.

The man had given me his home and the ability to do what I
wanted during the day. How had I repaid him? By making him think I
was cheating. If I was in his shoes, I would have reacted poorly, too.
The only difference being I'd need bail money after.

What was wrong with me?

Without a full-time job, my life had become a constant reminder of my failures. I was no closer to finding my mother's killer, had no lucrative way of supporting myself, and was pushing away the man of my dreams to sneak around with a former secret agent, trying to become what? Black Widow? It was depressing.

When Mike came home, I'd tell him I needed to find a job, something to take my mind off my mother's case. The gun range was probably the only place I felt like I had some sense of control. Maybe they were looking for somebody.

I stared at my mother's urn, wishing for the umpteenth time that she could give me some advice. When I moved in, I hadn't known where to place her. Putting her in a closet or drawer felt wrong, like I wasn't honoring her memory. Then again, I hadn't wanted to rub it in Mike's face either.

Luckily, he'd made the decision for me and I'd come home to find her urn on a bookshelf in the living room. My chest tightened at the thought of losing him and I grabbed my keys, prepared to scour the countryside until I found him.

My phone buzzed, and I scrambled for it, praying it was him.

Restricted: Ask him about the text he received the night your mom was killed. Mike's a good soldier, always following the orders of his club Pres.

I swallowed past the sudden lump in my throat, trying to make sense of the words. He'd gone home after his shift. That was the extent of his involvement. A knot of dread formed in my stomach.

Right?

Me: Who is this?

Had he been under orders to keep her in jail? Was that the reason he'd refused to help me? I sank down onto the carpet, willing the person to respond. They were insinuating it had never been other bikers but Monica's own club who had killed her.

It had to be a mistake. The clubs had rules and codes, even the illegal ones. Torch said that. They didn't just go around killing Ol'

Ladies. Unless they became a threat to the club. Monica had overheard something—had even insisted I not drag Torch into it.

Why else would she have done that unless a fellow gang member was behind it all?

I forced myself up the stairs and into the bedroom on shaky legs. After dragging my suitcase down from the top shelf of the closet, I tossed it on the bed.

No. I couldn't run. I needed answers—needed to look into Mike's eyes and have him tell me it was all some sort of mistake.

I jumped as the door slammed downstairs.

"Lauren?" he called out.

Tears pricked the back of my eyes. "Up here."

He must have taken the stairs two at a time, reaching the bedroom in a matter of seconds. He held a cup of coffee. "I got this. Look, I don't want to fight, but if fighting is what's gonna make this work, then I'll stay up all night with you."

His eyes dropped to the bed and the empty suitcase before looking back at me questioningly. "Are you leaving me? Because of the Jimmy thing?"

I shook my head. "No—yes. I don't—did you get a text the night my mother died?"

The spark that had been in his eyes moments earlier faded almost instantly. "What are you talking about?"

My eyes burned, and the urge to cry was overwhelmingly strong. I held it together and repeated, "The night my mother died, did you or did you not receive a text ordering you to keep her there?"

His Adam's apple bobbed up and down and he set the coffee on the nightstand. "I—where is this coming from?"

I handed him my cell phone, and his face took on a greenish hue. That was when I knew it was true and, incidentally, the moment I realized there were worse things than death. For the last sixteen months, I'd carried the belief that, had Mike known what was to come, he would have stayed on shift and kept my mother safe.

He'd told me as much.

He stared at the phone screen, eyes moving as read the words again. As if doing so would change what had happened. "Lauren, I can explain—"

"I think it's pretty self-explanatory. You were following orders— kind of like the Katya thing, right?" The words were out of my mouth before I had time to consider them, but my intuition told me I was right.

"The Katya thing was different..." He glanced around the room helplessly.

I saw the battle being waged in his mind the night he came home from Colorado. He'd claimed killing her would have kept his secrets safe, but I'd been certain there was something else there.

He struggled to be the man he wanted to be and the man the club wanted him to be. Had it just been that, I might've been able to over-look it. Unfortunately, he'd chosen the club that night and I lost someone I was just getting to know again.

Unlike the morning after she died, there was no screaming. I wouldn't hit him. The fight had gone out of me when I received that text.

"You knew they were going to kill her all along—" I clapped a hand over my mouth as it hit me. "That's why your father came by that night. He wanted me to tell him what I knew, and I fell for it!"

Mike's eyes widened. "My father? He was here? When?"

I shook my head. "Does it even matter? It was when I still lived with Torch. He came over and wanted to talk about her case; said he thought there was a rat in his clubhouse—"

He waved both hands out in front of him. "Slow down—you're saying my old man showed up at your place and wanted to talk about the case?"

I rolled my eyes and zipped up the suitcase, ignoring the fact that it was still empty. "Yes. And it all makes sense now. You're both in it together. Does Torch know what you did? And then blaming it on another biker club? It's just sick. Were the biker in the parking lot and the ransacked apartment just ploys to get me to come running to you for help?"

I mashed the button down until the handle on the suitcase extended before hauling it off the bed and toward the stairs.

Mike reached for my arm, stopping me in the hall. "I don't know who sent you that text, but it sure as hell didn't come from someone in the club. We don't kill our own."

"Your own? God, you even talk like one of them. Do you have a leather vest hidden around here too?" His grip tightened, and I looked up at him warily. "Let me go, Mike. Please."

He released my arm and threw up his hands in frustration. "You can't run away every time something goes wrong, Lauren. I can't be the only one who fights for us."

I swallowed past the lump in my throat as the first tear jumped the gun and ran from my eye. "I wanted to stay and work things out," I croaked. "But this text—Mike, you can't come back from that. You can't talk your way out of it. And the sad thing is I convinced myself you were telling the truth. I didn't hold her death against you because you swore to me you had nothing to do with it."

I left him standing on the landing as I dragged the empty suitcase down the stairs, letting it jar my body as it hit each step. I wasn't leaving behind a house this time, but a life. My feet faltered, begging me to turn around and run back to him. And as I rounded the corner into the kitchen, I almost did.

There was the large dining room table David had made as a house-warming gift for Mike—a table I envisioned sitting at, surrounded by little faces that were a perfect mix of the two of us.

My brain urged me toward the door, even as my heart begged to stop. I stepped out onto the porch, refusing to look at the swing where we sat and talked in the evenings. A swing I imagined us sitting on when we were gray and old.

I glanced into the rearview mirror as I reached the end of the dirt driveway and, just like the whisper of a breath against a flame, watched my dreams as they were extinguished into darkness.

CHAPTER FOURTEEN

Mike: May 2016 (Age: 33)

"Get the fuck out of my way," I growled, shouldering past a couple of prospects on guard duty at the front of the clubhouse.

They immediately reached for their weapons.

"Do it, and I'll fucking end both of you. I need Comedian right the fuck now!"

The two hesitated with their hands on their hips until the younger one chose to speak. "Uh, he ain't here. Club business. If you want to stop by later—"

I grabbed the patch-free kutte and yanked him toward me, keeping my voice low. "I don't want to stop by later. Tell me where he is and don't give me that club business bullshit!"

The door swung open, and I instinctively reached for my throwaway.

"Mike? What the hell's going on?" Torch looked me over carefully before calling the prospects off and ushering me inside.

"Shouldn't have kids on watch duty. Not with everything that's going on."

He patted my back and led me toward the common room. "Sure,

Mikey. I'll have Pres get right on that. But first, tell me why the fuck you're here."

I almost sat down on the leather couch until I remembered where I was and what usually went down on it before deciding to keep standing. "I'm looking for my old man. Did you know he paid Lauren a visit when she still lived with you?"

A look of horror on his face passed over his face. "He showed up there? Why?"

"That's what I'm trying to figure out. You didn't know?"

The biker suddenly looked as if he wanted to be somewhere else, not having this conversation. "Well, I mean, Grey stopped by, but I don't remember Comedian ever showing his face. Believe me, I would've kept Lauren safe."

I laughed. "That's a good one, Torchy. Kind of like how you kept her safe from my father? I want to know why he showed up there and who the fuck is texting her about Monica. God, I need blow!"

He closed his eyes before shaking his head. "No. I'll help you find Comedian, but you gotta do it clean and sober, kid. Can't be around that shit."

"I don't have time for this. We're in the middle of a fucking outlaw's paradise! Where are the sluts and the drugs? Goddammit!" I left Torch in my wake and stormed through the clubhouse, opening door after door, in need of a fix.

I got to the door marked President and threw it open into Grey's chest. He stopped the motion with his arm before taking in my appearance. "Jesus, son, you look like shit. The fuck happened to you?"

I searched his office. "I need blow. And answers. Mainly the blow, though."

He led me over to the couch in the corner. When I hesitated, he let out a booming laugh. "Sit down, Mikey. Ain't no one here dumb enough to fuck on my couch. Now, tell me what the hell is going on with you."

I sank down onto the black leather. "Lauren left. Probably forever this time. She got a text from a restricted number telling her to ask me about the night Monica died and the text I received from you. Said I was nothing more than a good soldier who followed orders."

Grey's face remained the same, but he began cracking his knuckles, a sure sign that he wasn't thrilled with the development. "So, whoever sent the original text likely sent this one. But why? Why now?"

I shrugged. "Beats me, old man. Listen, I hate to cut this short, but I need some blow and to find my piece of shit father. Can you help or not?"

"Comedian's on a run, what do you need?" Grey calmly ignored my request for cocaine, moving onto the next topic.

"Lauren said the text made sense because my old man showed up at Torch's, wanting to talk to her and see what she knew. She thinks he and I conspired to kill her mom and cover it up. So, what I need is to find him and ask him who the fuck he thinks he is."

His face paled, the first genuine reaction I'd gotten out of him since I walked in. "Mikey, listen—"

There was a sharp knock at the door.

"Come in," Grey barked.

Crossbones peeked in. "Pres, we got an emergency. Storage facility over on University is going up in flames."

I jumped up. "Flames, as in fire? Or is this club speak for some shit I don't know about?"

Crossbones rolled his eyes. "Nope. Literally means that it's on fuckin' fire."

Grey led me to the door. "Gonna need your help on this one, Mikey."

It wasn't until I began following the line of motorcycles out of the clubhouse that I realized I'd been duped. Grey needed my help about like he needed another MC moving into his territory. He just wanted to distract me from using.

You OD once and suddenly everybody loses their shit the next time you need a fix.

———

"I've got it!" Jeremy shouted, startling me awake. After watching the fire department put out what was left of the storage buildings and speaking with arson investigators, all I'd wanted was to go home and get lost in the bottle.

Unfortunately, Grey had other plans and sent Jeremy home with me to see what we could find on Monica's autopsy report. I'd come really close to hitting him in the face for it, too.

Just because the almighty Grey decreed it didn't mean I had to listen. So, while Jeremy had worked tirelessly on his computer, I'd gotten drunk on the couch and passed out.

It was a win-win for both of us, really.

"What the fuck do you have?" I asked, rubbing the sleep from eyes.

He spun the laptop around.

"Her autopsy report? Great, but we've already seen it. Overdose."

He shook his head and began scrolling down. "You've seen the doctored one, but never the original. Read it and weep, motherfucker!"

My eyes scanned the length of the report. "Holy shit—they found nothing in her system?"

"Nope. They found patterned abrasions along the base of her skull, consistent with a crowbar—inflicted antemortem. The M.E. noted—" Jeremy scrolled down the screen. "Here. The drugs were injected post-mortem, as they were not absorbed into her bloodstream. Tox screen came back clean."

We sat in silence, staring at the report. I'd assumed a forced over-dose, never imagining they had beaten her to death.

"Explains the defensive wounds on her hands," Jeremy added somberly.

I nodded. "Now, we need to pay a visit to the M.E. Find out why his name is on both reports—see what they're holding over him."

Having overdosed myself, I'd been convinced Monica hadn't experi-enced any pain. But the report threw that theory right out the window. She'd fought, all while knowing she was going to die. Her attacker's face was the last thing she'd seen—maybe he'd even been a friend at some point, somebody she'd trusted.

"I-uh-I traced the texts off Lauren's cell, too—while you were sleeping."

I looked at him and shook my head. "And? What did you find?"

He swallowed nervously. "You're not mad at me for hacking her phone?"

"Jeremy, I couldn't give two fucks at this point. If it helps us find her mother's killer, then hack away."

He clicked the mouse, and another screen popped up. "So, I ran this with the text you received the night Monica was killed. Here's where it gets interesting—they sent both messages using an app that scrambles the number every time you use it, similar to what we do with you. After some digging, though, I found both messages trace back to one phone—a phone belonging to Monica McGuire."

I cracked my neck. "Jesus—they used her phone while she was still sitting in jail?"

Jeremy nodded. "I'd assumed it would've come from two different phones, but it's the same damn one. That's not all—I found the mole."

I looked at him in shock. "How? We've been trying to identify this bastard since last January and you found him just like that?"

Jeremy shrugged. "Guy fucked up. I started tracing the message sent to Lauren tonight, and that led me back to the original message sent to you last year. Once I had the phone in question, I knew where to look."

I gave him an incredulous look. "You knew where to look?"

He grinned and clicked the mouse again, pulling up the surveillance cameras inside the station.

"Holy fucking shit," I breathed.

"I knew when and where to look once I traced the phone. Monica was sitting in jail when the first message was sent and I played off a hunch that the phone had been with her when she was arrested. See anybody that looks familiar?"

I stared at the black and white images, watching my colleagues come and go. None of it seemed noteworthy, and I was ready to tell Jeremy we had shit when I saw him.

Detective Aiden Rangel.

He'd been the first one on scene after Lauren's car was blown up. God, he'd even asked for Jimmy's information and knew he was a Fed before we did. I hadn't considered him a suspect at the time—hadn't considered anything but getting Lauren somewhere safe. I pointed him out to Jeremy. "That's him. Let's go. Call it in to Grey."

He nodded, and I jogged up the stairs, emptying my gun safe into a bag. We were taking out a cop—a dirty cop, but a cop nonetheless. I wanted to be prepared for anything.

When I got back downstairs, Jeremy was loading his gun. "Talked to Grey. He's sending Torch, Carnage, and Crossbones. The others will meet us back at the clubhouse. We torture him and it could bring this whole thing down on their fucking heads, Mike. War might be over by sunrise."

I smiled. This was it—we knew at least one man responsible for Monica's death. By taking him out, we were destroying any chance of them getting away scot free on this. Taking away their police protection was cutting off the head and this time, instead of three more growing back, they were going to bleed out thanks to the intel I was going to get from this guy.

"Has a wife. No kids," Jeremy noted, still tapping away on his laptop. After discovering Aiden wasn't at the station, he'd found his home address and punched it into the GPS.

Good.

I wasn't messing with kids, but I bet anything Aiden would give up the Sons if he thought it'd save his wife. We parked down the street from his house, waiting for the others. Everything in me was raring for a fight, but I forced myself to wait until I heard the low rumble of bikes.

Torch, Carnage, and Crossbones met us, the latter two demanding we treat it like a stealth mission. The two had served in the Army together; most likely doing recon missions and shit. There would be no blazing guns or Wild West shootouts.

In and out, without waking the neighbors.

Carnage noted a light on upstairs before bringing his finger back to his mouth. Crossbones picked the lock and silently pushed the door open. We moved through the downstairs, guns drawn. The house was deathly silent, leaving me optimistic we could get Aiden and his wife out without having to make use of our weapons.

Torch moved up the stairs, followed by Carnage and Crossbones.

Jeremy and I brought up the rear. My body tensed with anticipation of what was to come. I'd done SWAT early on, and the feeling was the same. Ambushing someone came with too many fucking variables.

The bedroom door was closed at the end of the hall. Without a word, everyone began moving along the walls, just in case Aiden got the urge to shoot through the door. Jeremy and I may have had tactical gear on, but the same couldn't be said for the other three.

We reached the door and with a nod, Torch opened it silently before we stormed in. The copper scent of blood hit my nostrils immediately and my heart sank.

Carnage must have realized it at the same time I did because he threw the master bathroom door open without even trying to mask our presence. It was the one room of the house that had a light on. And it confirmed my suspicions.

Aiden lay in the empty tub, a gun resting near his hand. His eyes were open, but unseeing. The back of his head was splattered across the wall and along the rim of the tub behind him.

"She's gone," Jeremy whispered from the bedroom, and I cursed. No matter what it looked like, they'd gotten to him first. Sirens wailed in the distance and Crossbones rolled his eyes.

"They knew we were coming. It's a fuckin' setup."

We raced out of the house and down to our vehicles as the wailing grew louder. It was obvious someone inside the club had tipped them off.

But who?

We'd gone in with gloves, so fingerprints weren't an issue. But as we drove away, I couldn't help but think that we'd just lost our one opportunity to end things before they got worse.

CHAPTER FIFTEEN

Lauren: June 2016 (Age: 29)

"Are you sure you're going to be okay?" Elizabeth asked as I fastened the small pearl buttons on the back of her baby blue gown.

I brushed off her question. "Why wouldn't I be fine? My best friend is getting married... again."

She caught my eye in the full-length mirror. "Lauren, you didn't make rehearsal last night. I know you're trying to avoid seeing him again, but it's inevitable. I just wish you and Jimmy had worked out—it would have made today easier."

I closed my eyes and admitted, "Elizabeth, Jimmy and I would never have worked out. We went out twice, but it was never serious. I should've corrected you, but I thought with everything you had going on, it was better if you assumed I was happy."

And I was actually living with Mike during a sizeable chunk of that time period, but there's no reason to tell you any of that now.

She frowned, but nodded. "Can we agree to be honest from here on out? Good or bad—you're my best friend and I want to know what's going on with you."

I nodded and lowered my gaze to the carpet. My emotions were all over the place. Walking down the aisle may as well have been a death-row march.

Elizabeth's mother, Susan, arrived with a bundle of fresh flowers. "Okay, I think I've got enough here to make a crown."

I swiped lip gloss across Elizabeth's bottom lip, stepping back to admire my work. It was nice to know I performed well under intense pressure. Despite lightheadedness and an overwhelming urge to vomit, I was a regular Bobbi Brown.

David's mom, Louisa, poked her head into the dressing area. "Oh my goodness, Elizabeth, you look absolutely breathtaking!"

The woman had been a gem since day one and I seriously questioned how she'd remained friends with Betsy "The Ice Queen" Sullivan for so many years. Elizabeth had warned me she was in attendance. As long as I stayed away from hot wax and kept my dress on, I thought I actually stood a good chance at dodging her completely.

Her son was another matter entirely.

I wanted to run until I was safely back home. My heel tapped out an anxious rhythm against the Saltillo tile and I wondered if it was too early to start drinking.

Louisa checked her watch. "You're up, kid. You nervous?"

She wasn't asking me, but I answered anyway. "I'm a little nervous, to be honest. Lou—you got anything in that purse of yours to take the edge off?"

Elizabeth's mother passed me a flask from her handbag with a big grin. "What? So, I drink. How else do you think I've gotten through all these years of quilting club at the church?"

"It's going to be okay," Elizabeth said, taking my hand firmly in hers.

I nodded. *Sure it was*—just as soon as the alcohol kicked in. It wouldn't be a permanent solution, but it would get me through today. And that was enough for now.

After helping Elizabeth into her heels, we began the trek out to a small orchard connected to the event center, passing a small chalk-board sign that read: *I Do: Take Two*. She'd made it herself, along with most of the other decorations.

The coordinator met us with a manic grin and began going over the timeline of events. She reminded me of a terrier, and her nervous energy only reinforced my anxiety, sending dread coursing through my body.

"Five minutes," she trilled into her headset.

I was going to puke. I turned around and met Susan's stare. She shook her head slightly and slipped me the flask, ordering, "Drink."

I complied, even though I didn't know what I was drinking. It burned the entire way down. That was all that I could make out. I hoped it meant I'd be oblivious within minutes.

Susan patted my arm. "You still love him. Judging by the way he keeps scanning the crowd every few seconds, he's in love with you, too."

Louisa caught the last bit of the conversation. "Who, Mike? I've known that boy since he was thirteen, and I can tell you he is a wreck right now."

I wanted to catch a glimpse of him, just to see for myself. But I had to remember why I was here. For Elizabeth. Both moms pulled me into a hug before going to get Kaden from David.

Elizabeth was deep in conversation with the wedding planner about job openings, slightly lessening my guilt over stealing her spotlight. Had she invited people from work? Was Sandra here? Unlike me, Elizabeth was still on good terms with people from the office.

I poked my head around a large topiary, trying to spot my former boss's blonde hair in the crowd. I hadn't told Elizabeth about the situation and suddenly wished like hell I had.

Oh god, what if she was here?

Mike was single now; there was nothing stopping him from hooking up with her again. What if they fell in love and got married? Now, I was absolutely sure I was going to hurl. Susan and Louisa may have had faith he was still in love with me, but the man thought with his dick most of the time, so I was a little more reluctant to accept their words. The music kicked on and the wedding terrier grabbed me, stuffed a bouquet into my hands, and sent me down the aisle.

My eyes found him immediately. Mike looked sexy as hell in dark denim jeans and a cobalt blue button down that matched my strapless tea length dress perfectly. It didn't matter how many times I'd rehearsed this moment in the past month, nothing could have prepared me for seeing him in the flesh. His mouth fell open, those blue eyes moving over my body as if there was no one else around.

I would only ever belong to him.

It was the truth. He'd sparked a fire in me—one that would never burn out. He could torch everything, and my heart would still turn over in my chest when I saw him. It didn't matter the destruction. I would never love anyone the way I loved him. And that scared the shit out of me.

Right on cue, Elizabeth appeared with her father by her side and within seconds, various guests began leaving their seats to join our procession. I skipped back to join her, and we linked arms, just like we'd practiced. She'd wanted to surprise David with a flash mob performance. I wanted to say the surprise worked, but I couldn't take my eyes off of Mike long enough to notice. I was a moth, and he was the flame, blinding me with his light.

I took some solace in the pain reflected on his face, knowing he felt just as wretched as I did. Then he winked at me, mouth curving up in that familiar cocky grin. I knew what the slight ache between my legs meant—my lady-bits had betrayed me yet again.

I'd tried satisfying the itch, spending almost every evening in bed with a vibrator. But the desire had only grown to wildfire proportions —unmanageable and untamed.

The bastard had hard-wired my vagina to need him.

Once the officiant began speaking, I saw the problem with David and Elizabeth's planning. Mike and I were the only members of the wedding party, and as he refused to take his eyes off me even once, every word felt like it was being directed at us.

David gripped Elizabeth's hands in his, reciting the vows he'd written and memorized. "Six years ago, I pledged many things to you, including my faithfulness. I broke that vow and almost lost you forever because of it. The past two years have been some of the most trying in our marriage. I never imagined I would face losing you, or the over-whelming despair I would feel at the prospect. Thanks to our enduring love, we made it out of the fire unscathed, and I am a lucky man that I get to continue doing life with you.

"Others come and go, Beth, but you are the constant in this life. I will love you until there isn't a breath left in my body. Once again, I promise to love you, honor you, and keep you, for better or worse, in sickness and in health, for as long as we both shall live."

Mike nodded along with David's vows and I had to look away, choosing instead to focus on Kaden, who was happily shoving handfuls of grass into his mouth at Louisa's feet. She caught me staring and gave a puzzled look until I discreetly pointed down. Her eyes went wide as she dug it out and settled him back on her lap.

I made it through Elizabeth's vows by staring through Mike and toward the outer edges of the orchard, the tears in my eyes distorting everything. The late afternoon sun broke through the cover of the trees enough for me to know I'd be leaving with a sunburn.

Everyone clapped when David leaned in and kissed Elizabeth, and I released the breath I'd been holding. I made it through the ceremony. Now, to get through pictures and the reception.

I was going to need to find the bar as soon as possible.

———

"*Malibu* and pineapple—that's got to be the cutest thing ever. You have a theme drink!" My words ran together, but that was to be expected with as many beverages as I'd consumed.

Elizabeth nodded, a bemused expression on her face. "Yeah, you've told me that three times now. Are you having a good time?"

I looked around at the wildflowers in mason jars and the fairy lights twinkling from the eaves of the old barn and bobbed my head. "I am— it's perfect."

It was.

Sandra and Betsy were nowhere to be found, and I'd avoided Mike by faking the need to go to the ladies' room anytime he was near. Except for pictures. The photographer had insisted on getting a shot of just the two of us, and his arm was around my waist before I could protest.

"Smile for the camera, baby."

Elizabeth looked around proudly. "It's a lot different from the wedding in Galveston, but I think it's fitting for us."

"Sandra isn't here, is she?"

She shook her head and leaned in. "No, Mike requested she not be invited. Would you know anything about that?"

I slurped the few remaining drops of pineapple goodness into my mouth and shrugged. "Doesn't make a damn bit of sense. I'm thirsty, so I'm just gonna grab another from my friend at the bar."

Elizabeth appeared to be fighting a grin. "Okay, Lauren. Knock yourself out. Oh, there's Katya. I want to meet her guy."

I turned and watched the supermodel walk in on the arm of a very attractive man. She turned and said something to him and he broke into a wide grin, displaying blindingly white teeth and the most perfect dimples I'd ever seen in my life.

I felt a small pang of jealousy that had nothing to do with them. I just missed the familiarity that came with being with someone for a while.

"Thought if I camped out here long enough, I'd catch you." Mike looked up from his pint of beer.

I'd been so focused on Katya and her lover that I'd unwittingly walked into the very man I was trying to avoid.

I leaned across him and signaled for the bartender. "Um, hello. I'll take another *Malibu Barbie*—I mean, pineapple. *Malibu* and pineapple. Please."

Mike chuckled, and I frowned at him. "What's so funny?"

"You, darlin'. Sure you need another one?"

I crossed my arms over my chest. "I'm a big girl. I'll decide when I've had enough." My ankle rolled at that exact moment and I stumbled on my heels.

He just raised an eyebrow and took another drink. "Yep, looks like you've got it all under control."

"Why'd you tell Elizabeth not to invite Sandra?" I hadn't meant to ask, but the rum had loosened my tongue.

If my question surprised him, he hid it well. "I knew today would be hard enough for you; didn't think you should have to deal with her shit, too. I didn't want it to even cross your mind that I could want anyone else here but you."

I stood, dumbfounded, until the bartender slid my drink over. Then I pulled the little red straws out and sucked it down straight from the glass.

Mike continued, "You know, Red, I'd like to think that if I got the opportunity to marry you even once, I'd die a happy man."

I inhaled the liquid and began coughing. My body buzzed, and it had nothing to do with the rum. I could have sworn he just referenced marrying me. "You can't say things like that to me, Mike."

He nodded and stood. "You're right. Dance with me."

I sputtered, "What? No!"

Several guests turned to look over at us, and Mike grinned. "C'mon, you don't want me to cause a scene. Do you?"

I sighed and put the glass back down on the bar. "Fine. One dance. And then we'll leave each other alone for the rest of the night."

He agreed and went over to the deejay booth. I stood at the edge of the dance floor, watching the couples slow dancing to country music. Katya giggled as her guy spun and dipped her, not at all in time to the music. David had one arm around Elizabeth and Kaden asleep on his shoulder as they moved in circles around the room.

One dance.

Then we'd go our separate ways.

Mike came back over. "We'll wait for the next one. One complete song, or it doesn't count."

We stood in silence until the song ended, and then he gently took my arm and led me out to the center of the room. I closed my eyes as the first few bars began to play. It was our song—the first thing we ever danced to.

It transported me back to Galveston. He wrapped his arm around my waist, pulling me into him.

"Do you feel like coming a little closer and strippin' it down?" he whispered in my ear. My hand had to be a sweaty mess in the palm of his.

"Mike," I protested. "Why are you doing this to me? After everything, why can't you just let me go?"

He continued singing softly before fixing me with another one of his trademark grins. "A man protects his home. Well, darlin', you've always been mine. Twenty years from now, I'll still want only you. So, if you wake up one morning and find you've changed your mind, come find me. I'll be waiting. There's still a lot of shit that needs to be said, and you can be damn sure I'm gonna clear my name. But right now, I just want to hold you in my arms and pretend we're Jack and Charlotte —the two least screwed up people I know."

Mike voiced everything I felt. Despite all of it, he was my home. For better or worse. I didn't want to fight with him tonight. He waited for me to say something.

Instead, I used my hand on his neck to guide his mouth down over mine. It was soft and slow, my lips barely brushing against his. His hand tightened against my hip and I moaned softly. This was wrong. I was going to hate myself when I sobered up.

I didn't care.

One song faded into the next, but we remained in the same spot on the dance floor, wrapped up in each other, oblivious to everything around us.

Mike broke our kiss. "I've missed you."

I blinked rapidly to dispel the gathering tears and pressed my lips to his chin. "I've missed you too, Tex. God, I've missed you."

"Come back to my room?" He bit his lip, giving me puppy dog eyes.

I nodded. He was the only choice.

We said hurried goodbyes before bolting back toward the inn, giggling like children as we ran. Mike lost his patience and scooped me up in his arms with a roar. It took the two of us twenty minutes to get up the stairs to his room. I kept getting lost in his kiss. The minute his mouth met mine, all I could think about was keeping it there.

The room spun slowly as Mike closed and latched the door behind him. I felt so good. My hands came up and cradled my breasts—it wasn't my hands that I wanted, though.

"Damn, baby. I could watch you touch yourself like this all night."

I dropped my eyes back down to him with a small smile. "Oh, yeah?" I unzipped my dress and let it hit the carpet. My skin tingled in anticipation of what was to come.

One last dance.

One last time.

CHAPTER SIXTEEN

Mike: June 2016 (Age: 33)

"Um, perhaps I should come back another time?"

"Oh no, Reverend. What was it you said yesterday? *Time is promised to no man?* I think that's how it went. Anyway, I've got the bride and the ring. I'd say we're good to go."

So, I did a thing.

The minister looked beyond me and into the room where Lauren was still sleeping. "She has to be conscious and agree to the marriage. Until that happens, I'll be in my room." I grabbed him by the back of his shirt as he tried to walk off.

"Now, hold on. I'm not making you do this for free—I've got five hundred dollars in my wallet if you perform the ceremony. What do you say—"

He wrenched himself from my grasp. "I am a man of the cloth, sir. I do not accept bribes—"

I kept my voice low to avoid waking Lauren. "*Man of the cloth?* What the fuck does that even mean? Everybody accepts bribes—it's how the world works!"

He shook his head and headed for the stairs.

"Do I need to use the handcuffs on you, too?" I hissed after him before stomping back into the room and slamming the door.

Shit.

I was going to have to find a new officiant.

Lauren groaned and shifted around in the bed. She'd fallen asleep in my shirt, but hadn't bothered with the buttons. My dick got hard just looking at her.

"All of me is dying," she whimpered. The handcuffs clinked against the headboard and her eyes popped open. "What the fuck?"

I waved from the end of the bed, her chest turning scarlet. "Michael Sullivan, did you handcuff me to the bed?"

"Yes, but only because you keep running away from me. I told you I was going to clear my name. It shouldn't be a surprise that I'm using the cuffs to keep you compliant during questioning."

The redness swept up her neck. "Mike," she bit out. "You cannot handcuff people to get what you want. Jesus, fuck, what is on my stomach?"

I picked up the velvet box. "It's your engagement ring. You'll get that in a minute. But first, I wan—"

"You can't do this shit, Mike! You can't put a ring on my finger and make it all go away! What happened last night was just a onetime thing!"

I ran a hand across my face. "Well, you're not getting the ring with that attitude. Look, I know you think I had something to do with what happened to Monica—Jesus, I feel like I've started almost every sentence over the last year and a half with that line—but I swear to you I didn't. Someone is setting me and the club up."

Lauren rattled the cuffs in frustration. "You keep saying that, but the evidence points to you and your father. What am I supposed to believe?"

"Me!" I roared. "For fuck's sake, I want you to believe me. The club had just declared war on the Sons of Death and one of Grey's prospects was murdered. This kid couldn't have been over the age of eighteen. We knew they were targeting prospects and family members.

"I fucked up—I got that text and thought it was from Grey. I fell right into a trap and the whole time I thought I was keeping her safe. Do you understand what it's like to live with that guilt? I've questioned

Grey on damn near everything—that night was the first time I just followed orders."

I sank down on the edge of the bed in defeat. This had been a mistake—all of it. The ring. Taking her back to my room. She'd never see me as anything other than the man who killed her mom.

She watched me quietly, no longer struggling against the cuffs. I was going to have to let her go—both physically and emotionally.

I sniffed and ran the back of my hand across my eyes. "I shouldn't have brought you here. Being with you over the last two years has been a shit show—"

She sucked in a breath. "But—"

"Just let me finish. But, they've been the best two years of my entire life. Someday, you're going to meet someone who makes you happy like I never could. And you'll deserve every bit of it. We couldn't get it right in this lifetime, but in the next one? Darlin', you're all mine."

I didn't look at her face. It would've only made things worse. Instead, I kept my focus on the floral wallpaper before standing up to retrieve the keys from my pocket.

"Mike?"

I glanced down to see tears streaking her gorgeous freckled face. "Yeah?"

She bit her lip. "Who is Grey?"

I poured my soul out and that was where she stopped listening?

I exhaled. "The President of Silent Phoenix. C'mon, Red. You know who he is."

She frowned, and her eyebrows moved together. "But I thought your dad ran it. That's the impression that I got, anyway."

Thinking about my father being in a room alone with her made me sick to my stomach all over again. "Michael Sullivan, Sr.? Jesus. He can barely manage himself, much less an entire club."

Instead of being relieved, Lauren looked even more confused. "His name is Michael Sullivan, Sr.? Why does he go by Jamie then?"

Now, it was my turn to be confused as fuck. "Jamie is Grey," I said slowly, hoping she'd figure it out and move on to another part of my speech—one that actually concerned us preferably.

She nodded. "Your father. Grey is your father."

"No... Grey is the club Pres. Comedian is my father."

Lauren sighed. "The giant with blond hair and blue eyes is—"

"Grey," I finished helpfully.

Her eyes were as wide as saucers as she exclaimed, "Oh my god, you don't know! Mike, Grey is your father!"

God, how many times had I wished for that exact thing?

"No, Red. As much as I wish that had been the case, my old man is Michael Sullivan, Sr. The nastiest motherfucker around."

"I don't understand. You look just like him. Even your mannerisms are the same. He was clicking the pen just like you do when you're thinking. It made sense. You protect the club because your dad runs it. Are you sure you're not related to him distantly?"

I shook my head. At least now I knew where her confusion stemmed from. She'd never been alone with Comedian. She'd been with Grey. That was why Torch had seemed confused and why Grey's face had paled—*oh, fuck.*

I swayed on my feet as I moved for the door.

"Mike?" Lauren called. "Mike, please don't leave me in these!"

I couldn't catch my breath as I marched down the hall to my mother's room. My fist connected with the wood loudly three times before she answered.

"Mike, what are you doing here?"

I slammed the door shut behind me and gestured to the bed. "Sit. I've got some questions and I'm going to need you to be completely fucking honest with me."

She immediately began trembling. "I don't know what you mean."

The jumping pulse in her neck said she knew exactly why I was here, though. "I wanna know about my dad, Betsy."

She swallowed with an audible gulp, just like a cartoon. "What is there to know about your dad? He's rough around the edges, but he loves you—"

"My real dad," I added.

My mother dissolved into tears. "Why are you asking me this? Your dad is Michael Sullivan. You know this."

But I didn't.

Once Lauren said it, everything clicked. Michael Sullivan hadn't shown up to my Little League games, but Jamie Quinn never missed one. My so-called dad never gave two shits about me, but a biker Pres seemed to always go out of his way to keep me out of trouble.

"Grey's my father." I said it as a statement. My mother refused to look at me, but nodded slightly.

"Does he know?"

She nodded again. "You can't say anything, Mike. If your father—if Michael were to find out, we'd all be dead." Her hand came up to cover her mouth as she wept. I could have comforted her, but she'd kept the truth from me for over three decades to save her own ass.

I could've had a different childhood entirely had I known. Instead, I'd spent the last ten years convinced I was turning into Comedian. I'd been certain his DNA was stronger than anything I'd gotten from my mother, and I was nothing more than a ticking time bomb.

I left her sobbing on the bed and walked downstairs. I continued walking until I was outside, needing some fresh air and a life exchange.

CHAPTER SEVENTEEN

Mike: June 2016 (Age: 33)

"Mind if I join you?" David gestured toward the long wooden bench I was sitting on.

I nodded and continued staring blankly down the aisle. We'd stood here just yesterday; back when I was naïve enough to think I could convince Lauren to stay. Back when I thought I knew who my father was.

"I thought you and your bride would've been sleeping in since your mom has Kaden."

David chuckled. "That was the plan, but Lauren was screaming the entire fucking inn down. I thought she was in trouble."

I jumped up. "Fuck, Lauren. I've still got the keys!"

He laughed again. "Relax. Beth had a bobby pin. I picked the lock. Next time though, make sure your girl's decent before you restrain her, especially if you plan on bolting. That is more of her than I ever needed to see."

Jesus, she was going to kill me.

"How'd you know how to do that?" I was surprised, more than anything. David didn't seem the type.

"Have you really forgotten all the shit we got into growing up?

Knowing our way out of cuffs kept us on the right side of the law. Don't you remember?"

I nodded. "For all the good it did. I can't even remember the last time I was really on the right side of the law. Probably before I turned eighteen."

David leaned over and rested his forearms on his knees. "You've made a lot of sacrifices, brother. Not all of them have been selfish. You covered for me the morning after my wedding and again with the Landon thing. You saved my wife's life. The good in you outweighs the bad, no matter what you think. And I haven't said it enough, but thank you."

I clapped my hand on his shoulder roughly and nodded. "Thanks, man." It was as deep as either of us was ever going to venture without growing a vagina.

"So, the handcuffs?"

I sighed. "What would you say if I told you that Lauren and I have been on and off since last June? Or that we'd been living together until last month?"

His face screwed up in confusion. "Are you serious?"

I nodded and told him everything from the last six years—how I sold my soul to the devil the morning after meeting an angel. How I got her mom killed and ultimately lost her. It seemed like I talked for hours, finally feeling my chest lighten by the time I reached the end.

"Wow." David kept shaking his head. "Jesus."

I leaned forward until my arms were on my legs, matching his stance. "Tell me about it. I was actually dumb enough to believe I could keep her cuffed to the bed until she started listening to reason."

"Well, I would say you're tied for the stupidity award with that and thinking now was a good time to propose," David said with a grim smile.

The breeze whistled as it moved through the orchard, cooling our skin, yet not clearing my head one damn bit. "So, I just let her go?"

David bent down and picked a blade of grass, splitting it between his fingers, completely lost in thought. "I can't answer that for you. If you and the club had nothing to do with what happened to her mom, then eventually, she's going to see the truth. What about the shit with your dad?"

I pinched the bridge of my nose and sighed. "My whole life, I wanted nothing more than to be Jamie Quinn's kid. Now that I know I am, it fucking complicates everything. So, I'm not the son of a sociopath. I'm the son of a man who was too much of a pussy to acknowledge me. It's not much better."

"The one thing I can't figure out is how Lauren knew." He began twisting the grass around his finger like a ring, the carpenter in him building something out of nothing. If I tried, I'd just end up with grass stains on my hands.

"She said it was his mannerisms." We slipped back into silence and I wondered if there was anyone else on the planet who knew me as well as she did—if there was anyone who would ever know.

"Well, I think you know what to do," he said as he dropped the grass and stood up.

"I do?"

David nodded. "Yeah, you're good at thinking on your feet—always have been. Nothing is impossible to overcome. I'm living proof of that. Give her some space, but don't stop chasing her—even after you've caught her. Don't make the same mistakes I did."

I laughed. "David, I don't think anybody's stupid enough to make the same mistakes as you. Like how hard is it to not put your dick in her best friend?"

He cuffed me upside the head. "How hard is it to not keep kidnapping women and proposing to them?"

"Touché, asshole."

I stood and stretched before following him back toward the inn. I was going to give her the space she needed while working to find the actual killer.

We parted in the upstairs hallway as Elizabeth came around the corner. She gave him a small smile and nodded before looping her arm through his, letting him lead her back toward their room. He winked at her in return, and I found I hadn't understood a bit of their exchange.

"What's with all the secret codes?"

"See you later, Mike," she called cheerfully over her shoulder to me.

I stood in the same spot. "That doesn't answer my question. Are y'all really just leaving like that?"

David looked back at me. "I'm kid-free for the next two hours, so unless you have some life-threatening emergency, go the fuck back to your room."

I flipped him off and rounded the corner toward the room. Lauren would be long gone by now, but I planned on spending the next few hours before check-out working on the case and trying not to think about all the ways I'd let her down.

Maybe it'd keep my mind off of Grey too.

I slid the key card in and waited until it flashed green before swinging the door wide open. Lauren stared out the window, back in her dress from the wedding.

"Hey," I breathed. "I wasn't sure you'd still be here."

She turned around. "Yeah. I dropped a bombshell on you and didn't want to leave until I knew you were okay. I would've come after you, but you handcuffed me to the bed."

I winced. "I'm sorry. I saw that going differently in my mind. You didn't have to wait around though, Red. I'm gonna be just fine."

She eyed me skeptically. "You sure about that? It's a lot to take in."

I shook my head. "Nope. I'm great."

"Okay."

I wasn't ready to watch her walk out of that door, though. Not yet. "I found the original autopsy report, Lauren. You deserve to know that the needle found in her arm was a cover-up. Monica, even in the end, stayed clean."

Her eyes filled, and she mashed her lips together with a brisk nod.

I continued. "We found the mole, too. Unfortunately, the Sons got to him before we could." I ran my hands through my hair. "I don't even know why I'm telling you all this—guess I just want you to know that even though it didn't work out between us, I'll never stop working on her case."

"Okay," Lauren answered weakly, snagging her purse from the small table by the bed. She held out the ring box.

I took it and placed it in my pocket, avoiding her stare.

"How long have you been carrying that around?" She asked with mild curiosity.

I met her eyes. "If you're asking when I knew I wanted to marry you, that would have been two years ago. And I bought the ring right before your mom died."

Her eyes filled, and she blinked rapidly. "Well, that's a long time to hold on to something. It was good to see you, Mike. I'm just going to—"

She walked over to the door without finishing her sentence and I didn't think. "I've carried you with me since May 2010."

Her hand hovered above the doorknob, but she turned around. "Ask me," she whispered.

I shook my head. "Ask you what?"

She pointed at the box. "Ask me again, Tex. And do it right this time."

I didn't know what had changed in the last five seconds. Frankly, I didn't care. "But I haven't even scratched the surface on helping you find the truth about your mom."

Lauren smiled, several tears spilling over onto her cheeks. "Torch has been telling me for the last month that the club wasn't responsible —that you weren't responsible. The stubborn redhead in me didn't want to accept it. I got some damn good advice and a healthy reality check this morning. You didn't do it, I believe you. You're right, Mike. Chaos together is a hell of a lot better than a lifetime apart."

I dropped to my knee. "Marry me, Lauren Santiago-McGuire. Let me be your home like you've been mine—"

"I still want to work-out with Jimmy—oh, and shoot guns. But, go ahead."

She smiled down at me, but I frowned. "You're not putting stipulations and conditions on my proposal, are you, darlin'?"

Lauren chewed at the corner of her mouth. "I'm more making a request or two."

I didn't want to agree to her terms, but her eyes narrowed, and I realized I never had a choice in the matter. "Fine," I grumbled. "I'll allow it. Anything else you need to put on the table, or am I allowed to finish my fucking proposal now?"

She smirked. "You're ruining it with your language."

"You're ruining it with your amendments." I mimicked her voice as I popped the ring box open, only to find it empty. The blood left my face as I mentally retraced my steps. "I swear there was a ring in here," I said, more to myself than her.

Lauren nodded and held up her left hand. There it was, sparkly as fuck, sitting on her ring finger. "I tried it on and found I didn't want to take it off."

"Just like that, huh? And you were just going to waltz out of here with it on?"

Her cheeks reddened. "Well, not exactly. I was going to give you another chance to ask me and then I was going to waltz out of here with it on—"

"You got it stuck on your finger, didn't you?"

She nodded. "Little bit, yeah."

I pulled her into my arms. "God, I've missed you. So, what do you say? Marry me?"

Wild strands of red hair tickled my face as she reached up and pulled my mouth down toward hers. "Absolutely yes."

CHAPTER EIGHTEEN

Lauren: July 2016 (Age: 29)

"Hold still. Winged tip eyeliner requires absolute focus. One wrong swipe and you'll look like a nightmare." The tip of Elizabeth's tongue peeked out from the corner of her mouth as she popped the lid on the eyeliner and leaned in.

Now and then, a girl just needed a bitch slap across the face from her best friend. A proverbial bitch slap—not actual.

It had been just over a month since the morning David stormed into Mike's room, ready to defend my honor. Six weeks since he found me handcuffed to a bed in nothing more than his best friend's shirt.

He and Elizabeth were like some *MacGyver* dream team, freeing me with little more than a bobby pin and some elbow grease. Once David went off, presumably to find Mike, Elizabeth had ordered me to tell her the truth.

And I had, culminating in the bombshell confession that had sent Mike running from the room. She had cried when I did, but otherwise, sat in silence as I dragged every secret out into the light.

I admitted to pinning the blame for my mother's murder on him, and for the first time, saw the walls I'd put up under the guise of safety. Torch had already told me of what Mike had done—how he'd taken on a corrupt medical examiner and dirty detective. For me. For my mother.

A mother I loved, but one who had never shown me how to trust—how to let myself be cared for. So I'd spent most of my life always waiting for the other shoe to drop. Those idiosyncrasies wouldn't disappear overnight, but the revelation was enough for me to consider Mike's proclamation—consider that maybe I truly deserved someone who would make me happy.

There was only one person on earth who gave me a sense of calm and stability. After promising Elizabeth I'd take our conversation to heart, I opened the velvet box and slipped the sparkling band onto my finger. Where I'd expected something foreign, it felt right. Like it had always been meant for me.

"What are you thinking about? The wedding night?" Elizabeth teased as she put the final touches on my eyes, pulling me from my thoughts.

The woman staring back at me in the mirror was almost unrecognizable. My hair was swept to the side, loose curls trailing over my right shoulder. My eyelids were a champagne gold and I must have been a statue, because my eyeliner was perfection.

"I look so pretty," I breathed in wonder.

"Every woman should feel like that on her wedding day. Are you nervous?"

She swept bronzer over my cheeks and I waited until she finished before admitting, "I'm not. Just so ready—I've wanted to marry him since I met him in Galveston."

It was true.

No matter how much had happened, he was my person. Now, six weeks later, at the exact same location, I was going to become his wife. I'd thought it was a long-shot, but fate must have been smiling down from above, because they had a cancellation for a Friday evening wedding.

Elizabeth had put her event planning talents to work and, even with an unruly one-year-old to look after, managed to throw together the entire thing in a matter of weeks.

With Abuelita's help, of course.

"Let me get a look at my LoLo," Josué called, as he and my grandmother stepped into the room. She made it three feet before stopping to rummage around in her purse for tissues.

"You are stunning, *mijita*. You will knock his *pantalones* off."

Josué looked down at her in horror. "*Mamá*, you mean socks. She will knock his socks off."

Abuelita just grinned wickedly before giving me a wink. "I know exactly what I meant."

Elizabeth mashed her lips together, trying not to crack up as she lined mine. I finally held a hand up to stop her before losing it. Eventually, we composed ourselves long enough to finish makeup. Elizabeth and *Abuelita* helped me into my gown before stepping back to embrace each other.

"I was right. The man is going to lose his pants when he sees her." *Abuelita* elbowed Elizabeth with a snort.

I'd found a white sleeveless gown with a deep v neckline—it stopped just under my breasts and while I'd worried that it was too sexy for a wedding, Elizabeth assured me that with a little double-sided tape, I'd look like a celebrity on the red carpet. I still had my doubts and was convinced I was going to have a wardrobe malfunction at the worst possible moment.

She adjusted the train, and I realized she was right. I felt like royalty as I swished my skirt from side to side. As I stared at my reflection, I suddenly missed my mom so much my chest ached. I swayed slightly and Elizabeth was by my side within seconds to steady me.

"You okay?"

My eyes clouded with tears, and I shook my head. "I just—I wish she was here to see this. You know?"

Abuelita reached into her purse and pulled out a thin silver chain with a locket at the end. "Dave and I, we made this for you. The locket belonged to my *Mamá*, but the chain is new."

I took the necklace from her hand and opened it with a gasp. Inside was a picture of my mother. She had her hands up by her face, laughing at whoever was behind the lens. Someone had taken it not long before she died. "But, how? I don't have any pictures of her."

Elizabeth fanned both of our faces as *Abuelita* explained. "Dave found this on his phone. He thought it might be a nice way for you to have your mother with you on the biggest day of your life."

I choked back a sob, determined not to ruin all of Elizabeth's hard work. "Thank you, *Abuelita*."

Elizabeth clapped her hands together. "Okay, everyone. It's time."

My belly fluttered, but I quashed down my fears and headed toward my future. My skirt swished loudly as we walked through the inn, and I resisted the urge to twirl around in circles until it billowed out around me. I was almost thirty; way too old to be dancing around in a wedding dress.

The photographer met us outside. Elizabeth leaned in to whisper something in her ear before they both snickered.

"Okay, Lauren. Let's have you spin in a circle, arms overhead. I'm going to snap some candid shots."

My face lit up. "Seriously?"

I did as she asked, letting my eyes drift closed as the sun beat down on my face. When I opened them, Elizabeth handed me an envelope.

"For you."

I tore it open to see a note from Mike.

Today, I have loved you for 2,225 days, and I will love you for a million more.

My eyes blurred with unshed tears and I began fanning my eyes yet again. I would not be one of those brides who ugly cried down the aisle. I was going to be radiant.

Flawless.

Torch walked up to give me a hug, and I threw my arms around his neck, pressing a soft kiss to his cheek. "Thank you for what you did— my mom. It means so much—"

He shook his head and embraced me. "I didn't do nothin'."

I pulled back to look at him. "You did everything."

His eyes went cloudy, and he blinked rapidly before excusing himself to go find a seat. Most girls only had one father figure in their lives. I was lucky enough to have three.

Elizabeth handed me my bouquet just as the song began. "Okay. Do you remember your cue?"

I nodded shakily as Josué and Isaac walked up. "Yep." My voice had taken on a high-pitched squeak, indicating tears were on the way.

Flawless.

Radiant.

I could do this.

Mike summed up his feelings in a note—I chose our wedding song to convey mine. I just hadn't expected to choke up upon hearing it. My dads offered me their arms and led me down the aisle, while Rascal Flatts crooned about finding love in the middle of broken roads.

It was perfect for us... *and I was now sobbing openly.*

Mike was grinning, his bottom lip tucked between his teeth. He mouthed: I love you, and I hiccuped as another sob broke free. Somehow, this made his smile even bigger.

C'mon, Lauren. Hold it together.

Josué squeezed my arm tighter in what I thought was an attempt to quiet me down, but when I looked to my left, I realized he was crying almost as hard as I was. Isaac was the only one out of the three of us who was keeping it together; and his eyes had suddenly become suspiciously shiny.

Mike's hand was reaching for me before we even made it to the end of the aisle and I didn't hear anything the officiant said. I was lost in my groom's eyes; everything else had just become white noise.

He winked at me as he began his vows. Vows that were not at all what we'd rehearsed. "Six years ago, I was just a guy who was drifting along and then I met you. You changed my entire life, Red. It took a lot of work to get to Plan C, but fate didn't let me down."

I quirked my brow, but he continued. "I know what you're thinking —Mike, if this is Plan C, what were Plans A and B? Well, baby, Plan B was marrying you while I had you handcuffed to the bed in my hotel room last month and Plan A—"

His voice cracked, and he clenched his jaw for a few seconds to get his emotions under control. "Plan A was marrying you six years ago on that beach in Galveston, because that was the night I found my purpose. I didn't realize it, but I'd been waiting for a Charlotte my entire life. So, Lauren Santiago-McGuire, I stand before you as a man with absolutely no reservations, choosing to spend the rest of my life with a woman I have the utmost respect and love for. I want to grow old with you on our front porch swing."

I stood in stunned silence.

How the hell was I supposed to compete with that?

I pushed through my vows with an unsteady voice and more tears, while Mike gripped my hands tightly in his and raised his eyebrows dramatically every so often to make me smile. We exchanged rings, but my mind was still wrapped up in his words. Only when the officiant pronounced us man and wife and Mike's lips met mine was the spell broken.

———

"Does this song make you want to cry?" Mike teased as we walked out to the dance floor amid clapping. "It is our first dance as husband and wife."

I swatted his arm. "Don't make fun of me. I was supposed to be stunning."

"Oh, darlin', you stunned me. I didn't know it was possible for someone to cry so much just from walking down the aisle. I thought Josué and Isaac were going to have to get you a paper bag to breathe into." His arm locked possessively around my waist, pulling me into his firm body, reminding me it had been days since we'd been this close.

I rested my chin on his chest and looked up at him with a sly grin as he led us around the dance floor. "And what about you? Either your eyes got a little misty or you choked up reading the vows you wrote— which, I thought, we'd agreed we weren't doing."

He shook his head. "Must've been allergies, and as I recall, we never had a formal discussion on the vows."

"You were totally crying, Mike. Admit it. Also, we had an agreement—just the traditional vows, since we were short on time."

His lips curled up into a smile. "Okay, you might've seen a few tears. I still held it together better than you." He spun me around in a small circle before completely losing his train of thought. "Damn, Red. That dress—fuck. I can see your tits. Do we have to stay for our entire reception?"

I let out a shaky exhale before nodding. "Sorry, Tex. It's the rules, and our wedding planner would kick my ass if we left now."

He looked over at the bathrooms and waggled his eyebrows suggestively. "We could—"

I groaned. "Subject change—when did you decide to write your own vows and when did you even find the time?"

Mike bit down on his lower lip. "Look at you, baby. You're worth more than the same shit everybody spouts off at weddings. You deserved something better. And can we take a moment to appreciate me not saying fuck once during it?"

I cringed. "Yeah, you're a real humanitarian, Mike. I kinda feel like a jerk for not writing something for you now. Can we redo it?"

He laughed softly. "I don't give a fuck about that—you said, 'I do,' and that was good enough for me. A wise ass once told me to never stop pursuing you, even if I caught you."

I giggled. "*Wise ass*? Don't you mean wise man?"

Mike shook his head. "Nah, I meant wise ass. It was David. I never want to make you feel you're not the most important person to me. Because I tried living without you and I failed. There's no one who knows me like you do and somehow, you look past all the bullshit and still want me. You are the most important thing in my life."

I rested my cheek against his chest, breathing him in. "You're my person, Mike. My best friend."

The hand that was draped across my shoulders came to rest against the nape of my neck, squeezing lightly.

With a little luck and a lot of thigh clenching on my part, we made it through the reception, surrounded by the people who loved us. I thought perhaps I was missing some bride gene, because I'd spent most my wedding and reception eager to get my new husband into bed.

David gave a toast that somehow didn't involve threesomes with sorority girls, much to Mike's chagrin, while Elizabeth talked about how I'd helped her through one of the lowest points of her life.

I cried. Again.

Abuelita spent her time out on the dance floor with Dave, teaching him how to dance, while Isaac and Josué danced circles around them.

"Showoff—I taught him everything he knows," she'd claimed.

Grey had even made a last-minute appearance, dressed in a suit, no less. He'd insisted on a dance with me, which I'd nervously accepted. I'd been certain that he was going to bring up me telling Mike the truth, but he didn't. He asked me about random things—like my favorite type of flower and whether I'd gotten enough to eat—before telling me I made a beautiful bride. It had been like looking at an older version of Mike.

Well, I was looking, and I was liking.

As our dance ended, people said their goodbyes. But Grey sought me out again. This time, to ask me to watch out for Mike and keep him safe. It was the easiest promise I'd ever made. Betsy had been a little standoffish at first, but even she couldn't deny how happy her son was and had come up near the end of the reception to embrace me. Everything was perfect—there were no biker club issues or police emergencies. It was a day that was truly ours.

We made it back to the room, and I kicked off my heels almost immediately, stretching my toes on the carpet. "I should've listened to Elizabeth when she insisted on flip-flops."

Mike scooped me up and carried me over to the bed. "Lay back."

I reclined on my elbows. "You planning on handcuffing me to something, Sullivan?"

His lips quirked up. "Well, that all depends on your behavior, darlin'. If you resist, I just might have to break them out for old time's sake."

I suddenly had a powerful urge to misbehave.

He grabbed a tiny bottle of lotion from the bathroom and poured some out in his hands before grabbing my left foot and massaging it in.

I moaned loudly, and he chuckled. "I'm just getting started, Red. Calm your tits." His thumbs kneaded the arches of my feet, immediately undoing the damage I'd caused by wearing heels all day. I was mesmerized, watching his hands move from one foot to the other, his black titanium wedding band catching the light from overhead.

A foot massage wasn't meant to be erotic, was it?

Mike's hands moved up to grip my calves and my teeth sank down onto my lower lip, silently urging them higher.

"Are you sore here?" He asked.

I nodded and he moved up to my knees. "And here?"

"So sore," I whispered.

His fingers gripped the inside of my thighs. "What about here?"

My mouth suddenly dry, I nodded dumbly.

Mike grinned and ran his thumbs along the outer edges of my panties. "What about here, Red?"

"Aching." The word tumbled from my lips just as his mouth brushed up against the white lace.

"You're fucking soaked, Darlin'." He yanked my panties down before moving his head back between my legs. My hands dug into the comforter, needing something to grab onto—anything to steady myself against the onslaught of his tongue.

Mike pushed my body to the brink, using his mouth and hand. My climax hit me like a freight train and I clapped a hand over my mouth, screaming into it.

"Be as loud as you want, baby." Mike stripped down to nothing within seconds, flipping me onto my stomach so he could unbutton my dress.

I shook my head. "I—I—I can't. David might hear."

"Jesus. Point taken." Mike slipped the sleeves of my dress down my shoulders while I lay limply across the mattress, doing absolutely nothing to help him.

My body still shuddered from post-orgasm aftershocks as he lifted my hips, pulling layers of lace and tulle down my legs, before pushing against my entrance.

My body stretched around him and I marveled at how the sex only got better. His lips pressed against my neck as he pulled my back into his chest, fully sinking into me.

"I love you, baby," he murmured against my earlobe before taking it between his teeth.

"I love you too."

He growled and thrust harder into me. The aftershocks grew into another full-fledged orgasm and this time, when it hit, I didn't cover my mouth.

Hopefully, David knew not to come running this time.

Mike pulled out and gently moved me onto my back again. "I need to see your gorgeous face." His hands brushed the stray hairs off of my forehead before his mouth claimed mine with a brutal intensity, bruising my lips against his as he sank back into me.

I was never coming down from this high.

He looked into my eyes with such love. Knowing he was the only man who would ever see me like this pushed me into yet another free-fall. The room fractured around me, yet his face remained crystal clear.

Grey should have made me promise something that would've actually required a sacrifice on my part. Taking care of Mike came as easily as breathing to me.

We moved around on the bed, constantly changing positions, but never once looking away from each other. His hands tightened around my face as his body went stiff with his release—filling me entirely—and marking me as his forever.

The road that had led to this moment was paved with tragedy, but I would never regret choosing him. We'd gone through life alone, but now we were a team. Given what we'd already overcome, there was nothing that would stand in our way.

CHAPTER NINETEEN

Dakota: September 2016 (Age: 22)

I studied the piece of paper in my hands, trying to make out the numbers with the help of a nearby streetlight. Carol Danvers, my little red Cavalier, was a hand-me-down and had lost her interior lights long before she was passed down to me.

With a frown, I looked out at the darkened house again. A house Jackson Blake, my ex-fiancé, had told me to meet him at.

I didn't recognize it.

Then again, I supposed his stupidly rich father could have bought it for him after he ended our engagement and relationship of two years. Maybe the house was a congratulatory gift for ditching the mouthy blonde.

We had never seen eye to eye, which was why I was keen to get this over with. Jackson had called just as I was closing my store for the night, demanding the engagement ring back.

Seemed Mr. Blake had caught wind of the ring still being in my possession and was threatening to call the police if it wasn't in his son's hands within the hour.

As I had few options, and didn't even know anyone who practiced law, I'd dragged my exhausted butt to an unfamiliar but well-established neighborhood.

I'd planned to return it, eventually. It was of little sentimental value to me now that I had Zane.

My Big Guy.

A six foot six, golden-haired god of thunder whose muscles had little baby muscles. Dating a man who worked at a gym definitely came with some perks. If his co-worker, Kyle, wasn't an absolute trash bag of a person, I might have considered swinging by to surprise him afterward.

Unfortunately, the guy was a slimy little greaseball I wouldn't set up with my worst enemy.

I slid out of my car and slammed the door with my hip, trying to recall if Zane had said he was going to call when he got out of his late-night gym meeting or stop by.

Either way, my plan was to be in and out long before then. He'd never even have to know I hadn't followed his stern warning to go straight home after work.

I approached the front door before remembering Jackson's instructions to go through the side door of the garage. I felt like I should have been dressed in all black, rolling across the neighbors' lawns like a ninja with all of his weird directions.

The side door gave a quiet groan as I pushed it open and slipped inside. The sound of raised voices carried from down a hallway and I froze, wondering if Jackson's dad had stopped by—or worse, if he'd already called the police.

I considered tossing the ring onto the kitchen counter and running like hell for my car, but talked myself down. If the police were here, they would have swarmed when I pulled up out front.

This was fine.

I was fine.

Once the ring was in his hands, I could go back to my regular life. Some day, I'd probably even look back on this moment and laugh. With that, I squared my shoulders and knocked on a closed door at the end of the hall.

"Kyle?" I asked when the door swung open beneath my hand, revealing Zane's co-worker along with four men I didn't recognize. "What are you doing here? Where's Jackson?"

A man sitting on the opposite side of the table smiled widely at me, a gold tooth peeking out from under his lip. "Kyle, is it? You two know each other?"

I nodded dumbly and Kyle's face paled.

"Well, in that case..." The man stood and fired three bullets into Kyle's chest from a gun I hadn't seen him grab.

My hands moved over my head instinctively, and I dropped to my knees with a scream, ears still ringing from the blast.

"Please!" I pleaded when the man turned the gun on me, knowing it wouldn't be enough to save me from the same fate as Kyle. "Please!"

Oh, god of thunder, please let me make it out of this alive.

Glass shattered from somewhere else inside the house, and the others rushed out of the room, leaving me alone with him. Tremors wracked my body as he studied my face, probably looking for a good place to stick a bullet. Whatever he found gave him pause, and he lowered the gun with wide eyes.

"This never happened," he growled before brushing past me and toward the sound of gunfire.

I sobbed an exhale and crawled on my belly to where Kyle lay, unmoving. I had never been a fan of his—didn't mean I wanted to watch him die, though.

"Kyle?" I whispered, getting no response.

Please don't be dead, Doucheface.

"Kyle? Answer me," I begged, staying low to the ground. I'd read enough comics to know if I stood I'd be shot to death immediately.

Then Zane would totally know I hadn't gone straight home like he'd asked.

When I reached his body, I felt his throat, finding a pulse. Not that it meant much. He'd taken three bullets to the chest—who could survive that?

"I'm here," I whimpered, placing a hand on his shoulder. "I'm gonna get you some help."

The next logical step was retrieving my phone from my purse, but my head felt as if I'd taken cold medicine—my reflexes sluggish.

"It's just shock," I told myself, trying to remain calm even as tears flooded my eyes. "Why didn't I just stay home? Zane's going to be so mad."

Now I was talking to myself. Definitely a sign of shock.

I swiped at the tears and found my purse lying on its side just feet away. A sudden blast sent me back onto the carpet with a yelp, knocking the air from my lungs.

The ringing in my ears became a definitive roar, but I forced myself back up, needing to reach my phone.

"Police! Freeze!" The voice was little more than a whisper, as if they were a million miles away.

I jerked my head up to where a man in a helmet and bulletproof vest loomed in the doorway, looking as if he belonged on a battlefield and not inside an office that was growing smaller by the second.

My butt hit the carpet, and I scooted back, trying to get to my feet.

"Stay down! Hands in the air!"

I choked back a rising sob, my lower lip quivering in terror. "This is a m-m-mistake! I didn't do this. I don't know... I don't know... please!"

"Turn around!" he roared, raising his weapon. "On your knees—put your hands on your head! I will not say it again!"

I dropped to my knees, no longer trying to hold back the tears. "Please! I can explain... I just... I can explain!"

The police officer shouted over my voice. "Put your hands on the back of your head!"

My hands immediately went up. "Please..."

He roughly grabbed one of my wrists and cuffed it before reaching for the other. "You have the right to remain silent. Anything you say can and will be used against you in a court of law. You have the right to an attorney. If you cannot afford an attorney, one will be provided for you. Do you understand the rights I have just read to you?"

"Please..." I began shaking again, arms bound behind my back.

"Radio it in," he called to someone outside the room as he hauled me to my feet. "Code eight—Barton's down."

"But, Kyle! My purse—I need to call for help. I need to call for help!" I tried to break his grasp, but he only held on tighter, leading me through a war zone of glass and drywall. We passed cops standing in what used to be a dining room before heading to where more stood outside, surrounded by flashing red and blue lights.

Another cop stepped in and grabbed the front of my work t-shirt, shoving me toward an unmarked car. My heart pounded violently in my chest.

"Get off of me!" I shouted, squirming away from his bruising grip. "Get your hands off me! This is a mistake!"

He wasn't as patient as his friend and shoved my head against the side of the car. "Stop! It's over!"

"Don't fucking touch her like that!" a deep voice growled from behind us.

Zane?

I struggled to turn my head. "Zane?"

The cop released me with a sound of disgust.

"Zane!" I yelled, my voice hoarse from crying. "Tell them I didn't do anything!"

He didn't say anything, though. He didn't have to—it was written all over his face. *Why are you here?*

I shook my head. *I don't know.*

They were going to let me go. They had to—I'd done nothing illegal. Just the wrong place, at the wrong time.

"Zane—I'm sorry," I blubbered. "I'm so sorry!"

Why are you here? You're supposed to be at work.

Having lost interest in humoring Zane, the cop latched onto my arms again, pushing my face against the side of the car again. "You get an ID?" he yelled to someone behind us, but with the way he had me pinned, I couldn't see a thing.

"Got it," the voice confirmed. "She's been Mirandized."

It was all a big mistake.

"Here we go." The cop turned me to face him. "Dakota Quinn, you are under arrest. Do you understand your rights as they've been read to you?"

Under arrest?

"I didn't—what? This is a mistake." Any bravery I may have felt fled, and I began weeping again. "Zane? Tell them... tell them I didn't do anything!"

The cop holding me opened the car door and pushed me in while I was still pleading. Zane stood with his head down near another group of cops, refusing to acknowledge me.

Look at me... please.

"Zane?"

He glanced back briefly and then turned away.

CHAPTER TWENTY

Kate: September 2016 (Age: 26)

There was only one person in the entire world who could drive me out of a man's bed in the middle of the night.

Dakota.

Not that I had much experience with other people's beds, per se, but I assumed running out of someone's house after mind-blowing sex was frowned upon by most people.

Then again, most people didn't have a sister like mine. The same sister who knew every single relationship within the *Marvel* universe had been arrested for drug possession after being found in a home with five pounds of cocaine.

She claimed to have been set up by her asshole ex-fiancé, but it didn't change the fact that I was going to have come up with the money to get her out.

Money I didn't have.

Which left me with only one option. With trembling fingers, I scrolled through the contacts list on my phone until I found her name. There was only one person I knew who could come up with the money they were requesting.

My mother. *Celia Quinn.*

———————

Dakota stared listlessly through the passenger window as we drove home, nodding in response to questions but otherwise refusing to make eye contact with me.

It had taken one phone call and a promise I had no intention of keeping to get the money needed to bail my sister out of jail.

She hadn't said much of anything since I picked her up, which was completely out of character. While free, the charges against her weren't going anywhere. To make matters worse, there was apparently a good chance she would be hit with federal charges as well.

I'd been lost in my own thoughts most of the drive, wondering if I was going to have to triple my case load to pay for a good lawyer. There was decent income in counseling, but was it enough to keep my sister out of prison?

I wouldn't ask my mother for help—not again.

"Kate, I'm sorry," Dakota said to the window, almost too quietly to hear. "For telling you to stay away from Nate and, well, all of it, really. I clearly have no room to talk, and you can do whatever you want with your life."

Nate.

She didn't see the flash of pain in my eyes at the mention of his name.

He had been calling non-stop since the night I took off without so much as a goodbye, begging to know if I was alright—wanting to know if we could talk. I hadn't been able to bring myself to answer, not after overhearing him on the phone with his ex-wife.

What could I say? Hey, sorry I haven't been in touch, but my sister's in the clink and I know you're still in love with your ex?

I swallowed my grief, pushing it down for later, when I was alone and could rip the scabs off and let myself bleed.

"Dakota—stop," I said, using the no-nonsense tone I'd perfected by the age of seven. "You were just looking out for me. It's what we do. I haven't given it another thought and neither should you."

We pulled up in front of the house to find Dakota's next-door neighbor waiting on the porch.

"They let you out?"

"For now," Dakota said with a sigh. "Look, Ramon. I'm exhausted."

He patted her arm as if she were a small child. "Girl, it's Ricky, remember? Little Ricky? How could you forget about ya boy, Little Ricky? My ma was a big fan of I Love Lucy and named me after Lucy's kid? Damn, they beat you, didn't they? Man, fuck the police!"

I stared at him, trying to keep it together.

Who the heck was this guy?

Dakota was dead on her feet and needed to be inside resting while I figured this whole mess out. I stepped in between them and guided her up the sidewalk. "Alright, Little Ricky—I'm gonna get Dakota inside to rest now, okay?"

He nodded toward the house. "Good luck with that shit—they tore everything up. You know pigs never clean up after themselves."

"They what?" I asked, feeling the blood drain from my cheeks. "They searched the house?"

Dakota's own face paled, and she reached for me. "Kate, keys!"

I found the spare in my pocket and handed it over, but we were too late. The house was utterly destroyed and everywhere we turned, more chaos greeted us.

"Oh god... no!" she wailed from the kitchen, sending me running after her.

The sight was one that would haunt me until the day I died. Dakota's comics littered the floor—some she'd collected but most had belonged to our father, passed down after his death. Every single one now lay gutted on the floor. Altogether, they had to be worth over fifty thousand dollars, but she and I knew they were worth so much more.

They were the last pieces of our father.

"Oh Dakota," I breathed, watching helplessly as she began trying to piece them back together. "Oh, honey."

"FUCK!" she screamed in anguish, tears falling in a steady stream down her face.

I tried reaching for her, only to be shoved away.

"Don't touch me! Oh my god—who would do this? Why would someone do this to me, Katy?"

My heart shattered at the brokenness in her voice. It didn't matter how hard I tried to make a good life for us; we would never get there. Everything good had always been just out of our reach.

"I don't know, kid. I'm so sorry."

She scrambled to her feet and bolted outside. I followed, holding her hair back when she sank to her knees and began vomiting into the flower bed.

"You couldn't have put in a good word for us, so we didn't have to fight for every single thing?" I hissed at the sky, to a father who either didn't know or care about the constant struggle his daughters had been in since his death.

Little Ricky sauntered back up the walkway. I wasn't entirely sure he'd ever really left.

"Damn girl, who do I need to kill?" he asked as he surveyed the damage.

"I want whoever is responsible for this taken out," Dakota answered, staring through him.

"Dakota!" I yelped. "I don't think retaliation is the best idea for you right now—"

"You got it, Cap," Little Ricky interjected with a manic grin. I assumed the nickname was due to Dakota's love of Captain America but wasn't entirely sure how her neighbor would know that.

She glared at both of us. "Don't call me that anymore. Cap's dead. I'm gonna need someone to run to find me a t-shirt with a skull on it."

He nodded eagerly and took off, the wheels on his SUV squealing as he backed out of the driveway. Meanwhile, I was still wracking my brain for the link between the skull t-shirt and her sudden desire to take out her enemies like a 1920s gangster.

"I'll have to increase my workouts, but first, cupcakes. I am in mourning after all," she murmured to herself, continuing to stare across the street. I wasn't entirely sure she was talking to anyone in particular.

I knelt beside her, aching to help take the pain away. "Want me to go buy you some cupcakes?"

She nodded, her lips pressed into a thin line.

I tried again. "Okay, but can we talk about what happened? I'm still wondering how you ended up in jail."

A part of me was also curious why a man I saw myself falling in love with had taken a call from his ex after having sex with me. Not just any sex, either—but toe-curling, make you forget your name sex. Unfortunately, I could only deal with one problem at a time, so Nate and amazing sex were going to have to wait.

"After," she mumbled, looking up as if seeing me for the first time. "After you buy the cupcakes, I'll tell you everything. Then we'll plot."

It was then I realized which Marvel hero she was channeling. "You're really going to become Punisher, aren't you? That's your grand plan? Well, I'll give you credit for originality. He's definitely a hero you've never chosen before."

She patted my leg. "Kate? Sweetie—I'm gonna need a fucking cupcake, sooner rather than later."

I propped my hands on my hips, completely frustrated with the alien posing as my sister. "Jail changed you, didn't it?"

CHAPTER TWENTY-ONE

Dakota: September 2016 (Age: 22)

M y entire life—the only possessions that meant anything to me lay in tatters across the kitchen linoleum. Marked by unclean hands and boot prints. The savages had smudged and bent the pages, ripping them from their bindings. Some were even missing covers.

Not a single one was salvageable.

All because I was lured into a house where an active drug bust was taking place. I stupidly thought the officers would believe my story and let me go. Apparently, one guy arrested with me gave false testimony. He claimed I had evidence in my possession, but said evidence was never found.

Instead, they booked me.

Possession with intent to distribute.

Until this point, my only experience with booking had been of the comic variety.

Now, I was painfully aware of what that entailed. A cop took my fingerprints and mug shot, not caring that I looked like a drowned raccoon. But the icing on top of the cupcake had to be the strip search, though—to ensure I wasn't trying to smuggle weapons or drugs in. I jokingly asked the female officer to buy me dinner first before bursting into tears.

Jail was nothing like they portrayed in movies. I expected I'd get my one phone call and someone would bail me out immediately. When I asked, I was told I'd have to go before a judge for a bail hearing.

Two days—two days spent inside a jail cell. I'd missed work shifts, and besides Kate, no one knew where I was. With nothing else to do, I sat with my thoughts and the unanswered questions that had been nagging me since the night of my arrest.

Why were Zane and Kyle at a drug house?

It made no sense. He told me he had a meeting at the gym. Was he using drugs? If so, I had missed all the signs.

As I sat on the front porch step of a house police had destroyed, I couldn't help but come back to the biggest question of all. Why in the hell had Jackson set me up?

Maybe it was time to put my old heroes out to pasture in favor of one whose vision better aligned with mine. Captain America stood for all that was good and right. Meanwhile, I'd just been busted for drugs and had murder on my mind.

Frank Castle.

I'm going to become *Punisher* and bring hell to everyone who was involved in framing me, starting with Jackson Blake.

CHAPTER TWENTY-TWO

Celia: September 2016 (Age: 44)

"What do you mean you didn't tell her, Kate? You promised me you'd tell her right after you bailed her out."

"Look around you," she hissed back at me. "She came home to this. At what point should I have dropped that bomb on her? She's in bad shape."

I took in the ransacked living room, my heart thudding dully in my chest. The cops had done a thorough job of searching the house; even going as far as taking a knife to the throw pillows on the couch in their search for contraband.

My daughter was in trouble.

I'd played by the rules my parents set and kept my distance, knowing there was no way to ensure the girls' safety from behind bars. I should've realized when my letters and calls went unanswered that it was no longer about doing what was best for my kids.

They were hellbent on punishing me.

Somehow, I'd stayed off my parent's radar while doing everything I could to be near my daughters. I thought they'd go off to college and live a normal life where their biggest concern was whether they'd remembered everything on their grocery list.

Once the men who hurt me were all gone, I'd planned on reaching out to them.

I'd become Jamie; living in my head, convinced that someday we'd be a family again.

Someday had come in the form of bail money.

Instead of going home after her shift at the mall, Dakota, who'd never cared about anything but her superhero comics, managed to evade the biker sent to watch over her. She'd landed herself in the middle of a drug bust and had promptly been arrested. To make matters worse, she'd caught the attention of an undercover cop.

Zane Masterson.

Fate hadn't been kind to me, but I'd always hoped things would be better for them.

Life didn't work like that, though.

I ran a hand over my face, suddenly craving a cigarette after going years without one. "I know things are a mess right now, but Dakota deserves to know the truth about where the money came from."

You both deserve the truth.

Kate tucked her lip between her teeth, studying me through narrowed eyes. "Why don't we start with how you had my cell phone number? You didn't get it from Nan. I know that for a fact."

"College directory," the lie rolled off my tongue.

If it hadn't been for Jeremy's hacking skills, I wouldn't have been able to reach out to her over the past year. Granted, our conversations had been brief and filled with awkward pleasantries, until tonight.

When Kate found out Dakota had been arrested, she could have called anyone, but chose me. It left me feeling hopeful that I could somehow undo the mess my mother had caused when she took them.

"And why is it so important for her to know the truth? You left us. You can't just change your mind and expect everything to go back to normal."

Bile rose in my throat, and I swallowed. "I know what you must think of me. I really should've been here—"

"Mama?" Dakota stood frozen in the hallway.

"Hey, baby girl," I rasped, tears pricking the back of my eyelids. "Come here."

As she walked toward the couch, a line of sweat trailed down over my spine, leaving me feeling faint.

"Why are you here? Why now, after all these years?" she demanded, eyes darting from me over to Kate. "You bailed me out, didn't you?"

I sucked in a strangled breath and nodded. "I did. I couldn't let my baby sit behind bars."

Dakota shook her head. "But you can sure leave your baby and run off to a casino for ten years. Like, I'm grateful you got me out, but it doesn't make up for everything you've missed."

Kate intervened. "Dakota, please hear her out. I didn't know who else to turn to when I found out you were in jail. If it weren't for her, you'd still be there."

I patted the couch next to me, praying she didn't see the way my hands had begun to shake. "Come here. It's time you know the truth."

Kate shook her head. "Mama, not now. She's had too much for one day."

I could've taken her advice, but I refused to wait any longer. If what I suspected was true, then someone had set my daughter up.

Dakota dropped onto the couch, suddenly interested. "No, I haven't, especially if you're about to come clean over where you've been for the last decade."

I could do it.

They deserved to know.

"When you and Kate were little, you remember how we struggled a lot financially?" They both nodded, and I continued. "Well, I found a way to make money. Gambling. But I got in a little over my head."

Celia, sweetheart, where's your old man?

I looked up at the ceiling, fighting to stay in the present. My skin crawled with the memory of their hands on my body, but I pushed through it. "Sorry, it's still hard to talk about. The men I got mixed up with threatened to hurt not just me, but both of you girls, too. I was so young and scared. I went to a man that I knew could take care of the threats, but that came with a price. His world was even darker than I could've imagined, and by choosing him, I opened us up to even more danger."

I was raped and beaten.

I'd been confident that if I ever got the opportunity to sit down with my daughters, I'd tell them the truth about how they ended up with my parents.

Instead, I was repeating the same worn-out lies.

Dakota rubbed at the sides of her head with a frown. "Mama, what you're saying sounds a lot like a movie. And not necessarily a good one."

"I know how it sounds. When you were a little girl, you asked me if I was in love with the man that would stop by from time to time. I didn't know how to answer in a way that would make sense to you, but you're an adult now. Dakota, I do. I love him, but his world is so different from ours. When I chose to be with him, I faced an even more difficult one—walking away from both of you. I'm so sorry. Please know that I never wanted to make that decision, but I couldn't provide for both of you and keep you safe." A sob broke free from my chest, and I covered my face, trying to compose myself.

She took you from me.

Why couldn't I just say it?

Reaching for Dakota, I took the coward's way out, knowing they'd never believe the truth. "I decided to have you live with my parents and sent money there every month. I told your Nan to make sure you both had everything you needed."

Kate jumped up off the couch with a yelp. "Everything we needed? First of all, we needed a mother! Second, we never saw a dime of that money! I've tried to help Dakota out as much as I can, but doing so has put me in a tight spot. You're telling me we were supposed to be receiving money every month from you? Yet, you never followed up with that?"

The pain in my throat intensified. "You never got it? There was enough to cover clothing, a car when you got older, and even college."

Kate kicked the edge of the coffee table before exploding. "You're telling me I've been taking on double the patient load to pay off my student loan debt and car while Nan drives around in a shiny Cadillac? You're telling me she and Pops stole the money?"

I should have been honest.

It was bad enough she'd ripped them away and made them believe I was off gambling, but the entire time I'd been laboring under the delusion that my mother was using the money we sent her every month to give them everything they needed.

Before I could say a word, she marched over to the front door and screamed across the street. "Little Ricky—we're gonna need another skull t-shirt. Size small!"

"You got it, boss!" he yelled back.

Initially, I'd been skeptical when Jamie told me he'd recruited Molly's idiot son to keep watch over Dakota, but it was a job he'd taken very seriously.

"Rick's always been a good kid," I mused with a small smile, wondering how much I could give away.

They both turned to me in shock before Dakota found her words. "You know him? How?"

"Well, he works for me... technically."

She nodded slowly, waiting for me to elaborate. When I stayed silent, she sighed, "And what is it you do exactly, Mama, that you can afford to pay for cars and college?"

I met Kate at the front door and led her back to the couch. "You're gonna want to sit down for this, Katydid. How familiar are you both with the Silent Phoenix Motorcycle Club?"

They both shook their heads, and I laughed while trying to decide how to best explain the club. "Well, they don't exactly advertise themselves. They're more of a one-percenter MC. Um, this is harder than I thought it would be. They're one of the most powerful clubs in this region, and have made quite a few enemies over the years doing what they do..."

Enemies that were now coming after them.

"What is it they 'do' exactly?" Kate quietly asked, the color draining from her face.

I picked at the cotton guts protruding from one of Dakota's mangled pillows, pushing the batting back in. "There's, uh, there's drug and weapons trafficking... for starters."

Kate's eyebrows raised, but she quickly channeled her expression into one of indifference before asking, "And what is your role in this —business?"

It was probably the same expression she used when counseling unstable clients.

Deciding there was no salvaging it, I plucked a wad of cotton from the pillow and began shredding it in my lap to keep my fingers busy. "I'm—I'm married to the Pres, okay?"

Kate's mouth hung open, and I knew I'd pushed my luck. Instead of alleviating her worries, I'd made things worse.

"Mama, why did you come here?" Dakota's voice wobbled as she slumped back against the couch cushions.

"I came here to help you. I know what you're facing in charges, and we have the means to make it go away." I reached for her hand, only for her to jerk it from my grasp.

"Why is this 'club' so willing to help me? They don't know anything about me."

My mouth flooded with saliva. "Because you're important to me."

Because you're important to your father.

Dakota stood up and walked over to the door. "Well, it's been lovely, but I'm gonna have to ask you to leave now. Like right now, now."

"Don't push me away, Dakota. Let me help you," I begged.

"I've managed just fine on my own for the last decade. I can handle it. Plus, I'd rather use a more legal means to deal with my problems. Go." She pointed toward the door.

I pushed down my grief, knowing I needed to warn her about the badge that she'd been spending time with. Somebody within the department was working with our enemies, I was sure of it.

With traitors around every corner, leaving them ignorant was no longer an option. "Kota-Bear, a word of advice? If you want this to be over quickly, quit talking to cops. It's only making it worse."

As I climbed into my car, it struck me how much damage had been done. I'd never understood my mother's obsession with taking my children; never imagined the lengths she'd go to get them.

Now, my daughters regarded me with little more than contempt, and I realized what she'd wanted all along—me, left completely alone in this world as punishment for choosing Jamie.

Never mind that she'd stolen the money. My daughters were now solely focused on what my affiliation to Silent Phoenix would mean for them.

The time I'd lost with them was gone forever, and just like that, the tiny flame of hope in my chest flickered out.

CHAPTER TWENTY-THREE

Celia: September 2016 (Age: 44)

"Celia, you believe this shit? They sent the badges in to tear up Cap's superhero magazines. Man, fuck that. I say we pump 'em all full of lead—"

There was so much to unpack that it was hard to even know where to start. In the six years Rick had been with us, I'd found it was better to intervene quickly when he went off on one of his tangents. Otherwise, things got completely out of hand. "You want to go after the cops... and shoot them? I can't see how that could backfire."

"It only backfires if the gun's pointed the wrong way... kinda like that time you shot me." He grinned and waved his fingers in the air like he was Yosemite Sam.

"Rick," I said slowly. "I didn't shoot you... I stabbed you. There's a difference, you know."

He dropped onto the porch swing beside me with a laugh. "It's Little Ricky, Celia. We been over this. And yeah, see, I tell people you shot me because it seems more badass. But we got bigger fish to throw in the bush right now. Cap is in serious shit."

I sighed. "Quit calling her Cap. Her name is Dakota. What I'm still stuck trying to figure out is how she ended up at that house, in the middle of a drug bust, while you were supposed to be watching her. Jeremy watches Kate, and she stays safe—"

"Yeah, Jarvis keeps her safe, alright." He waggled his eyebrows up and down before lighting up a joint.

"What does that mean?"

He inhaled and shook his head. "*Nada*, and just so you know, I didn't even come up with that nickname. That was the cop. I think Cap is short for *Caparina*, which is like a butterfly or some shit—"

"Rick," I interjected, knowing full well the nickname had everything to do with Dakota's penchant for *Captain America* t-shirts and nothing even remotely related to winged insects.

"I mean, what girl wants to be compared to an insect? Nah, if Dakota was my lady, I'd call her mi cielo, because why she give two shits about bein' a bug when she could be the entire sky?"

Angel, who'd been sitting quietly in the shadows, stood up and slowly walked over to lean against the railing in front of the swing. "Goblin," he said, using the road name that Rick hated so much. "She ain't ever gonna be your lady, but I ain't opposed to takin' out some badges for what they did to her comics."

The headache I'd been fighting for most of the day intensified, leaving me restless and ready to snap. I'd tried doing the math in my head but had given up once the figures reached a hundred thousand. She'd kept the money for herself, and had Dakota not been arrested, I never would've known they were struggling.

Some mother I was.

"Celia?" Angel waved a hand in front of my face.

I forced myself back to the present. "I'm sorry?"

"Asked how you knew she'd been arrested."

"Oh, Kate called... like a last resort type of thing." I clenched my hands into fists as my tears threatened to spill over again.

The sound of a bike cut through the dark and Rick jumped up. "Angel? Wasn't there that thing in the kitchen you wanted to show me?"

"Yep. It's a neat little gadget for bread." He hurriedly followed him toward the door.

"That's called a toaster," I snapped as the screen door slammed shut behind them.

As if sensing the storm that was brewing, the cicadas fell silent. I was off the porch and waiting on the front lawn by the time he pulled up. The full moon acted like a spotlight, illuminating everything around us.

"Hey, darlin'."

I stabbed a finger into his chest. "Don't you 'hey, darlin'' me, Jamie Quinn. Do you know how our daughter ended up in that house? Jeremy and I looked into it. Two words—Jackson Blake. Her ex-fiancé. Care to explain to me why a family that's partnered with your club set our daughter up?"

He ran his tongue over his teeth with a grin. "Jesus, you're cute when you're pissed."

"Jamie," I warned.

"Fuck, Celia. Yeah, the Blake family has been tryin' to change the terms of our partnership for quite some time, but I thought they knew better than to involve my kids. I've got Mikey lookin' into this and if— why you cryin'?"

I sucked in a ragged breath and angrily swiped at the tears before fanning my face with trembling hands. "I'm fine, it's just—" A sob tore from my throat, releasing a river down my cheeks.

Jamie's eyes widened, and he cupped my chin in his hands, brushing my tears away with his thumbs. "What's goin' on, princess?"

"I—I can't do this anymore! I can't sit back and watch as everything falls apart around us. We swore to keep them safe, and we're failing!" My lungs heaved, and I pulled myself from his arms before stalking toward the orchard.

"Celia." He caught my elbow and spun me around to face him. "Tell me what happened."

He was going to kill them.

"My parents took the money. All of it. Girls never saw a dime. Don't you see?" My voice raised. "Everything we did was for nothing! She took my babies from me and made them struggle while she lived like royalty!"

The muscles in his jaw popped out as he ground his teeth together.

"She did what? Thought those girls were as stubborn as their mama, refusin' to spend the money on themselves..."

He calmly walked over and drove his fist into a tree with a roar. "Goddammit! I don't care if she has an entire army camped out in her front yard. I'm sendin' her to the Reaper, Celia! Don't you try to change my mind!"

I shook my head as I sank down to my knees in the soft dirt. As much as I wanted to dredge up an emotion, I couldn't. After ten years, I finally cared for my parents as much as they had for me.

"When does it end, Jamie? The Sons of Death MC is growing stronger every day. We've been chasing Cobra for sixteen years, somebody named Saint for six, and now we have to worry about the people who see our girls as collateral?"

As if another rival MC wasn't bad enough, it was also becoming apparent that someone in his own clubhouse was working against him.

I didn't even know what we were fighting for anymore.

For years, I'd held myself together with the idea that someday Jamie and I would have a relationship with our daughters, but we would never be a family.

At least, not in the way I'd imagined.

Because my girls would never know this life.

"I've got every chapter workin' together—" His eyebrows pulled together as he looked at the tree and then back down at me. "Oh, my god."

"What?"

Jamie ran a hand over his face. "Hawk told you Death was comin' for you, right? The entire fuckin' time I thought he meant the Reaper, but what if he was talkin' about the Sons?"

A ball of lead settled in my belly, and I was glad that I was already sitting as I was suddenly lightheaded. "That doesn't make any sense. Why would they want me?"

"Maybe we ain't heard from the Serpents because they've been working with the Sons. Fuck, I don't know, but I ain't takin' any chances. From now on, you don't go anywhere without Carnage. I've got Jarvis and Goblin on the girls."

Instead of calming me, Jamie's words only made my tears fall faster.

He didn't know, but I'd been reading up on the Sons of Death. They were never mentioned by name, but there were countless news stories detailing their crimes. They'd started out taking down crime families but had more recently shifted their focus onto other MCs.

It didn't matter how much security was in place. In the last year, the Sons had executed the Outlaws Pres as he sat at a red light in broad daylight, along with the head of the Russo crime family while he ate dinner with his kids.

Jus in bello had never applied to the one-percenters, but there had always been an unspoken agreement that families were off-limits.

Until me.

I'd come a long way in sixteen years, but the idea that we'd forever be running from something pierced my armor, leaving me vulnerable.

I pushed past the tunnel vision and planted my hands in the dirt before getting my feet back under me.

"Celia?" Jamie called after me as I turned back toward the house. The pounding in my ears made it sound as if he was miles away.

I squeezed the pads of my fingers into my palms until the knuckles cracked, but still my skin vibrated with a need to hurt someone.

"Celia! Fuckin' talk to me!"

My throat was dry, and my body had trembled, but I refused to give up what little power I had left. I refused to sit and do nothing.

Jamie caught my wrist and dragged me backward, the muscles in his neck straining as he fought me for control. His rough breathing was the only sound between us, and I swallowed hard, letting him pull me deeper into the orchard.

I wanted to rake my nails down the sides of his face for letting our enemies stack up against us.

I wanted him to yank up the skirt of my dress and bury himself inside of me until none of it mattered.

"I don't want to be afraid," I whispered the words, as if doing so might make them less real.

Jamie inhaled deeply, and I studied his face, searching his blue eyes for signs of disappointment. "You're scared?"

I nodded, biting down on my lower lip and he shifted his weight, guiding my body back up against a tree. I rested my forehead against his chest and breathed in the comforting scents of leather and cigarette smoke.

His chin rested on top of my head. "I love you, Celia. Ain't one motherfucker gonna lay a hand on you or my kids... not as long as I'm still kickin'."

Something strange happened at that moment. I exhaled a shaky breath as the tension left my shoulders because, for the first time in a long time, I believed him.

I freely handed over my trust, knowing that he'd keep his word, or die trying.

He released my wrist and brought his arms around my body, and I tilted my head back to look up at him. "I love you—" His head moved down, and my lips parted instinctively, knowing exactly what it was he wanted.

His mouth collided roughly with mine while the hands that had been around my waist moved down to the back of my thighs, gripping the hem of my dress and dragging it up over my hips. He paused, letting his fingers trail over the completed phoenix tattooed on my hip, reminding me of who I was.

I pulled away when he paused and found him watching me with heavy-lidded eyes. Clenching my thighs together, I scraped my nails across his beard while tracing his lips with the pad of my thumb, sending a shudder throughout his body. "What do you need, Jamie?" I asked, even though I already knew.

"Need to fuck you. Hard," he growled around my hand, forcing my nipples into hardened points that ached to be touched.

My core clenched, and I wondered if he knew how wet I already was for him.

He reached up and tucked a strand of hair behind my ear with a slow grin. "You gonna give me an answer, princess?"

"Did you ask me something?"

His eyes darkened with lust, even as he lowered his hands. "I wanna feel you clench around my cock. Wanna watch your tits bounce with every motherfuckin' thrust before I suck them one at a time in between my teeth, bitin' down until you moan. But you know I ain't touchin' you until you say it."

My mouth fell open, not in shock, because what he was asking was nothing new. It was pure desire; a fervor that coursed through my veins every time he asked for my consent.

As if he knew that even after all these years, I still needed it.

"I'm in control."

He blew out a long breath. "That's right."

His fingers moved quickly over the buttons on my dress, pushing it from my shoulders as my nails raked along his scalp. I tightened my hold on his long hair, fighting to keep myself from dissolving into a puddle at his feet.

Our breaths turned ragged as we shed the clothing in our way, finding that there was no need for words after almost three decades. We easily navigated the slope of the other's skin, taking none of it for granted.

Jamie jerked the cups of my bra down until my breasts spilled over into his hands before grinning up at me wickedly. The edge of his thumbnail lightly scraped across the sensitive flesh, and my hips rolled forward, seeking release.

Keeping his eyes firmly fixed on my face, he pulled one of my nipples into his mouth while dragging a finger down past my belly, teasing me over the lace of my panties. I arched my back as he ignited multiple points of pleasure, no longer sure what it was I was offering him.

"Please," I whispered.

Jamie groaned, and his tongue darted out to lick around both nipples once more before he rocked back onto his heels. "What do you need, princess?"

"I need you to touch me."

Jerking my panties to the side, he ran his middle finger over my folds before pushing it up inside of my body with a low growl. "So fuckin' wet for me."

I was painfully aroused, and any chances I had of coming down from my high disappeared when he pulled his finger out and popped it into his mouth, tasting me.

His shaft jutted up against his abdomen, and I reached between us, covering it with my palm. I used slow, deliberate strokes, knowing it would push him to the edge. He gripped my wrist again, breaking the contact between us before lifting me up in his arms and impaling me on his shaft.

The tree bark scraped against my back, but there was no time for soft and sweet. We were in the middle of a war, with enemies on all sides.

We succumbed to our base instincts, knowing that every second we had might very well be our last. Our bodies came together in a frantic rhythm that the saints themselves couldn't have stopped.

His body conveyed the things he couldn't say, driving out my rage and fear; silently reminding me we'd face the threats together. There was nothing gentle about the way he moved inside of me, but with every thrust, I knew I was safe.

I was home.

The pressure built until I was convulsing around him in pulsing waves, my body holding him in a death grip. He didn't slow down, but began moving faster and faster until the world spun out of focus.

At that moment, we were invincible.

Life may have dealt us blow after blow, but we'd gotten up and kept fighting. We'd survived on our own, but together, we were unbeatable.

"Fuck," he ground out as his thrusts became erratic and shallow. Sensing he was close, I used his shoulders to lift my body up, and he spilled his seed between us with a labored groan.

His arms tightened under my thighs as his forehead dropped to rest against mine. "Fuck, how does it get better every time?"

I'd just opened my mouth to reply when a twig snapped, and we both jerked our heads toward the sound.

Rick stepped out into the clearing with raised palms. "It's just me. It looks weird, right? Okay, I'm just gonna cut to the chase. I came out here because I can't find any more cereal."

"You're telling me you just came out here for food?" I asked, laughing when I realized that while Jamie had covered my body with his, his jeans were somewhere around his ankles, leaving his ass on full display for our intruder.

"Yeah." He nodded thoughtfully before adding, "But I stayed for the fucking. Never thought I'd wanna see two old people boning, but that was hot as fuck."

"Goblin," Jamie growled. "Get the fuck out of here before I beat your ass into the ground."

"You got it, Pres. I'mma just be in the kitchen with Angel, waiting for the cereal. Take your time, though. No rush. I found a frozen pizza in the back of the freezer, and it's heatin' up right now. You know, boss, you earned your colored wings... for your kutte. I'll totally vouch for you if anyone gives you shit—tell them loud and proud that you fucked your Ol' Lady good... right out in the open—"

"Jesus Christ!" Jamie and I exclaimed at the same time.

He gently set me down before yanking his jeans up with a snarl. "You better start runnin' now, boy."

CHAPTER TWENTY-FOUR

Dakota: September 2016 (Age: 22)

The sound of the doorbell interrupted my crying fest. Of all the people I could have run into tonight, it had to be Jackson.

"You know the connections my family has. Zane Masterson is an undercover cop and you've been the target of his investigation for the past few months."

I needed it to be a lie—my entire revenge plot centered on Jackson being the reason I'd ended up in handcuffs that night. Not Zane. Not a man I'd pictured a life with.

But it was true. Every kiss, every touch—they were meant to gain my trust, to entice me into letting my guard down. He had never cared for me—he'd wanted evidence that would lock me up. I was just another case.

The doorbell rang again and I hastily pushed my glasses up to my forehead to wipe my eyes before answering it.

"Hey, Cap." Zane held a coffee in one hand and flowers in the other, an expectant smile on his lips.

Seeing him up close did nothing to ease the ache in my heart and my eyes filled again.

Stop it right now, Dakota Mae—you are angry, not sad. You are not some sniveling little teenager with a broken heart. Make him witness your pain, and then when he lets his guard down, rip him apart.

I closed my eyes and took a deep breath, fueled by my little pep talk.

Zane moved closer. "Have you been crying?"

I jerked my chin and turned to go back inside, leaving the door open for him to follow.

Channel the tears into something you can use.

He took in the destruction, eyes widening in shock. "What the hell happened here?"

Like he didn't know. As if he wasn't the ringleader of the entire operation.

"After I was arrested, the police ransacked—I mean, searched—my house. Guess someone gave them intel I was hiding a large stash of drugs here." I walked toward the kitchen. "But this—this might be the icing on the cake."

I gestured toward the china cabinet he'd helped me work on for days. Back when I was stupid enough to believe he loved comics as much as I did. It was all part of the cover.

"Oh, babe." Zane placed the coffee and flowers on the counter before sinking to his knees, gathering the destroyed comics in his arms. "Can they be salvaged?"

Anyone who knew anything about comics would have known they were worth nothing now.

"I don't think so," I said coldly, resisting the urge to brush his long hair out of his eyes.

Anger, Dakota. Hold on to that emotion.

If Kate were here, she would have argued that anger was a blanket emotion—a defense mechanism covering up how I really felt.

He got back to his feet, towering over me once again. "Can I hold you?"

I allowed him to embrace me and tried not to notice how good he smelled and felt beneath my cheek while getting my scrambled thoughts in order.

"I need to tell you something, Dakota," he admitted, his chest vibrating against the side of my head with each word spoken. "I think I'm falling in love with you."

He loved me?

It was just another ploy to get information. Unfortunately for him, I had ways of getting information too.

"Really?" I asked, running a hand down his chest, feeling his heart beat faster. "Are you familiar with the Enchantress from the Thor comics? The way she feels about him?"

"Yeah," he breathed, his voice gravelly. "Absolutely."

"I think—" I paused and toyed with his belt buckle, earning a low groan of approval. "I think that's the best way to describe how I feel about you right now."

"Should we move this to the bedroom?" he whispered against my hair, but I shook my head.

"No. I think we can do it right there." I moved my hand to cup his balls, tightening my grip.

"E-easy there, Cap."

I smiled at the strain in his voice. "What's the matter, Big Guy. Can't handle it?"

"Not sure if I told you, but I'm not really into BDSM," he wheezed, trying to move away when I squeezed harder.

I loosened my grip slightly and tilted my face up to meet his, whispering, "See, this is how we get closer. You tell me you're not into BDSM, and I tell you that I know you're an undercover cop. See, we're really bonding now."

Zane's jaw tightened. "I was going to tell you—"

I squeezed viciously. "When, Zane? When you had me arrested again? Look around you—does it fucking look like I'm hiding drugs?" His blue eyes went wide. "Oh, I forgot what hearing me curse does to you. Are you turned on, Big Guy?"

My face was the picture of innocence while I kept his balls in a death grip.

"Jesus Christ, Dakota! You have every right to want revenge on anyone involved in this—but I didn't do this to your house. I didn't have you arrested! I told you to stay home that night!"

I moved to crush his balls but he caught my wrist, gripping until I had no choice but to release him.

"It's not revenge—it's punishment," I snapped. "And I was going to stay home, but Jackson's father was ready to press charges against me over the engagement ring unless I returned it. So, I went." My voice cracked and I fought to anchor myself to the anger.

Zane backed me up against the wall and leaned down. "Do you know what it did to me seeing you in handcuffs? I thought—I thought I was a fool—"

I made the mistake of looking up, and he released my wrist before bringing his mouth down over mine. I bit down on his lower lip, drawing blood. If anything, it fueled the fire between us. His beard scraped against my skin, but I welcomed the assault, tightening my fists in his t-shirt.

"Feel what you do to me?" He growled into my hair, his hands moving down to my butt, pressing me against his hard length.

Like a rubber band, I snapped back to the reality of the situation. He was the reason my life was in shambles.

"Let me go," I hissed, jerking out of his grip. "I was nothing more than a job to you, and it's over now. So let me go."

Zane swiped a spot of blood from his lip. "It was never a fucking job—what we have between us. You know that."

I brushed the hair back off of my face. "I thought I did. I let you into my life—I slept with you, for crying out loud! Oh my god, I can't believe I did that!"

"You think I'd do that as a job?" he bit out in frustration.

"What—you want me to believe undercover cops have never used sex as a means to get information?" I asked with a bitter laugh. "Because the search I just did online would beg to differ."

He ran his hands over his face. "Yeah, it's been done before. It wasn't like that with us, though. Trust me."

"*Trust you?* Are you kidding me? Look around you, Zane! I'm going to be facing federal charges if the others even get dropped. My comics —something I collected for sixteen years, are gone because of you! You were investigating me the entire time and now you want me to *trust you?*" I was powerless to stop the sob as it worked its way free.

"Dakota, wait," he pleaded, holding his hands up.

I stepped over broken glass and comics and gestured toward the front door. "Get out."

He reached for my arm, but I jerked back. "Last chance. Stay away from me. If I run into you again, I won't be as forgiving. In the beginning, I thought you asked me out as a joke. I never imagined you did it as a job."

Zane shook his head. "You were so much more to me, please know that. I'm sorry and I won't rest until your name is cleared. Let me do that for you. Please."

"If it weren't for you, there'd be no reason to clear my name!"

He tried to say something else, but I slammed the front door in his face before screaming in frustration.

"Whoa, Cap—you sure got some pipes on you!"

I spun around to find Little Ricky leaning against the back door, dopey grin plastered across his face.

"What are you doing here?"

He shrugged "I heard yelling. Thought you were starting the punishment phase without me. Plus, your ma would have my balls if I didn't check in on you."

I sank down onto a chair at the kitchen table with a sigh. "For a second there, I forgot you worked for my mother, The Criminal. You can show yourself out."

"Nah, Cap. I'm in it to win it now. You're gonna need a right-hand man to pull this shit off. That's where I come in. Nope, I'mma be stuck on you like glue from now on." He smiled contentedly and took the seat opposite mine.

Of course he was.

My own personal thug.

"I'm just not comfortable being involved in any more than I already am."

His smile faded. "You think you know so much because you were in jail for forty-eight hours. But my entire life has gone about like the last two days for you. Growing up, it was just me and my ma. Well, Bear was there too, but he don't count."

I didn't know who Bear was and didn't have the mental capacity for an explanation, so I nodded, encouraging him to continue.

"When I was sixteen, I fell in with some bad people. Don't get me wrong, the money was great, but it was a bad situation. Until I found the club, I was always one step away from doin' time. You see your ma as a criminal, but she saved my life. Took in a kid with no prospects and taught him a motherfuckin' trade!" He ran a hand roughly over his face, trying to hide his tears.

It was impossible to stay mad at him. How could I fault him for things I obviously knew nothing about?

"You becoming a drug dealer made your life better than before?" His childhood must have been pretty shitty, if he considered a biker club to be a lucrative career option.

"I know what you're thinking, but I came from nothing. They gave me a chance to join a family. At the same time, I got the knowledge and freedom to run a business. So yeah, my life is a helluva lot better."

"How old are you?" I asked, genuinely curious.

"Why, *Caparina?*" he asked with a knowing smirk. "Looking to get over Thor already?"

"No, I think I'm done with relationships. I asked because you can't be older than eighteen, yet you talk about life as if you've been around for a while."

"I'm twenty-five." My mouth dropped open and he grinned. "It's all in the baby face. I'm ageless."

I wouldn't ever admit it, but I kind of liked having him around. It was like hanging out with an older brother—a brother who just so happened to deal drugs on the side for a motorcycle club. But a brother, nonetheless.

"Alright, you're in. Be ready at five-thirty tomorrow morning. We're going to start training. I can't have you looking so scrawny. Plus, I don't have a car so I'm going to need a ride."

"You got it, Cap. Tomorrow morning."

I fought to hide my smile.

It was time to punish some people.

CHAPTER TWENTY-FIVE

Kate: October 2016 (Age: 26)

"Remind me to never again get involved with someone I met at a gym," I snapped into the phone while gnawing on a hangnail.

"Ooookay," Dakota drawled. "Seeing how Nate is technically the only person you've ever picked up at a gym and, like, the only relationship you've been in, not counting Ben—"

"Ben is completely irrelevant to this conversation," I interjected, about as eager to discuss my ex-boyfriend as I had been to discover him in bed with the head of the finance department hours before he'd planned to propose to me. One year later and it was still a sore subject.

"Right, so why are you and Nate calling it off this time?" Dakota asked, a note of boredom creeping into her tone. Given that I'd supported her through a break-up, helped her move, and then bailed her out of jail—all within a two-month span—she owed me one.

Or a thousand.

"For starters, we have nothing in common." Well, almost nothing. We seemed to share an interest in having sex with the other.

On my desk at work.

At my apartment.

In the hot tub at his place.

For obvious reasons, I would be admitting none of that to my sister.

I cleared my throat and my thoughts before moving onto the next point. "Not that it would even matter after last night. I mean, I felt like he'd been off lately, but thought maybe he was just busy with work or something. I should have listened to my gut, though. Do you know what I found in his bathroom cabinet?"

"Um, towels?" Dakota guessed, not even bothering to mask the sound of her yawn.

"Yes," I admitted, taking a second to unclench my jaw and breathe. "But next to the towels was a bottle of perfume and a pretty pink toothbrush. How do you explain that?"

"Maybe the perfume belongs to his sister or mom, and they accidentally left it after coming for a visit? And a lot of men like the color pink, so the toothbrush can hardly be considered evidence of any sort."

A male voice piped up in the background, and Dakota began explaining my predicament with the same level of enthusiasm one might have when discussing a root canal.

"Here, talk to Little Ricky. He's a man and knows how they think."

"But I don't—"

"Hail Mary, full of grace. How's it hangin'?"

I didn't want to discuss my love life with my Dakota's neighbor and new best friend. A man who had shared the history behind his name within seconds of meeting me, but was suspiciously vague when I asked what he did for a living. I wanted my sister to give me the same attention I'd given her for the past twenty-two years.

"Rick," I forced out through gritted teeth. "It's Kate. As I've told you at least a hundred times by now. May I speak with Dakota again, please?"

He laughed easily. "Nah, *Caparina's* gettin' ready for the gym. I hear there's trouble in paradise. Tell ya boy all about it."

I couldn't fathom why Little Ricky refused to call either of us by our real names. Dakota never bothered to correct him, though it was obvious she didn't know what *Caparina* meant. Meanwhile, I had wasted more time than I cared to admit trying to determine if his nickname for me was a football or Catholicism reference.

Against my better judgment, I laid out the case against Nate, starting with the nagging feeling that I was missing something to the discovery of *female shit* in his bathroom, as Little Ricky had so eloquently put it.

"And you're sure they weren't there before?" He asked after a brief pause. "You said he was married before. Maybe his ex moved out and left some of her shit behind."

I considered it before remembering the most damning piece of evidence. "I also found a pair of panties wedged in between the couch cushions."

He let out a low whistle. "*Caparina*, get your *culo* back in here. Hail Mary's got actual problems this time—"

"What do you mean, *actual problems*? I'm not calling for fake problems."

He laughed as if he thought I was joking. "Okay, Hail Mary. Whatever you say. Personally, I feel you need to take a chill pill most of the time."

"Don't tell her that," Dakota said, taking the phone. "Kate, what do you have for me? Do I need to add him to the list? Come on, a girl needs a name."

I massaged my temple with my free hand. I should have just called Nicole, my co-worker and best friend, like I'd originally planned. "No. He doesn't need to be on your list and will you stop with the Game of Thrones talk?"

"Let me know if you change your mind. Ooh, real quick, have you seen our grandmother lately?"

Little Ricky began cackling.

"Um, no. Seeing her isn't really high on my list of priorities right now, kid. I'm still trying to come to terms with the fact she was stealing from us the entire damn time we lived with her."

"Thought so. Just one small favor? If you see her, ask her if she's feeling royal lately—maybe work in something about me, if needed. What do you think, Little Ricky? Implicate ourselves or work like the group Anonymous? You know, '*we are legion*.' I think that might be more terrifying for her. Scratch that, Kate. Just ask her how she likes the dye job."

I groaned. "What did you do to her hair? I thought we were going to discuss things before you began punishing people. I seriously just called for some advice."

"Uh, we discussed it," Dakota said, with a click of her tongue. "You didn't make the meeting. As for the advice? I'd say your chances of having an honest, long-term relationship with the man are about as good as my chances of getting back together with the undercover cop sent to ruin my life. What do you think, LR?"

"Oh, Hail Mary. You're completely fucked on this one."

I hung up with a growl and paced my apartment. Once, over one too many drinks, Nicole had speculated that my father's death was the reason behind my sky-high standards in relationships.

As much as I'd wanted to deny it, her assessment rang true. I left people before they could leave me, because I never wanted to feel pain like I had when they told us my father had died—didn't want to relive watching my mother drive away after leaving us on our grandparents' front porch.

The guilt over knowing my grandparents stole the money must have gotten to her, because I'd woken up to twenty-five thousand dollars in my bank account this morning.

I'd planned to report it as an error but was now considering doing something completely irresponsible, like using it.

I needed a vacation—to get out of town and clear my head and my heart.

Maybe somewhere fun—like Vegas. Apparently, what happened there stayed there, which would be a delightful change of pace from the problems that seemed to keep piling up on my doorstep.

Maybe this was just another example of me running from my problems, but I'd save the psychoanalyzing for later.

I deserved a break.

CHAPTER TWENTY-SIX

Dakota: October 2016 (Age: 22)

I hid a yawn and hoisted my bag over my shoulder before heading out to the dark parking lot. I'd been hitting the gym twice a day, once before work and again after. And while I'd never understand how men bulked up so quickly, Little Ricky actually looked like he could withstand a fight now.

Since my arrest, the cops had cleared out, leaving actual trainers in their place. I was more than a little surprised to discover that, besides Zane, Kyle was an undercover cop as well—although it explained his poor training skills.

His inability to take a bullet, or three, while wearing Kevlar was another matter entirely.

The district attorney had dismissed the charges against me, citing recent evidence. My lawyer had nodded smugly as though he had something to do with it, but I knew who was behind it.

My mama.

Hadn't she admitted as much when she showed up at my house? The people she worked with must have been pretty powerful to make charges like mine disappear almost overnight.

Two days in jail and a subsequent court appearance had cured me of any desire to join their criminal underworld. Still, I could admit it came with some perks.

In addition to a brand new Chevy Tahoe sitting out front, my entire house had been cleaned from top to bottom, and the broken furniture replaced. The little corner china cabinet sat empty, a reminder of what trusting the wrong person had cost me.

Mostly, my life had returned to the boring normalcy I'd grown accustomed to. I didn't think of Zane and the way the sunlight would highlight every strand of blond on his head. I didn't cry myself to sleep most nights, wishing his arms were around me—missing the feel of his mouth on mine.

Nope.

That would have been crazy. Who missed the person responsible for launching a criminal investigation against them?

Not this girl.

"Dakota!"

My shoulders sagged at the sound of Jackson's voice.

I'd been avoiding him since the night he told me who Zane really was. When I finally got around to replacing my cell phone, I found about a hundred texts and voicemails from him.

Clearly, he thought, with Zane out of the picture, I'd go crawling back to him. Truthfully, I had no plans to date anyone ever again and hoped he'd eventually take the hint.

"Hey," I said, reluctantly walking over to where his SUV sat idling. "I was just heading home."

"It's about Zane—do you have a minute?" Concern etched Jackson's face, and I hated how my body immediately went taut just hearing his name.

"Is he okay?" I asked, trying to keep the worry out of my voice. I wasn't supposed to care anymore.

He shook his head grimly. "You'd better get in. Something's happened."

No!

He couldn't be hurt. His name was last on my list of people to punish. If anything happened to the man, it would be at my hands—and mouth.

I climbed into the front seat of his SUV and slammed the door, pushing the sexy thoughts aside. *For now.* I'd come back to them later once I was alone, and knew what was going on with Zane.

"What happened, Jackson?" I asked, turning to see the gun resting in his lap.

He gestured toward the backseat with a smile. "You remember my employee, Bill, don't you? He's got a gun aimed at the back of your seat in case you decide to run."

My heart hammered in my chest, but I tried to remain completely still in case Bill had an itchy trigger finger. "I'm not running—where's Zane?"

Please let him be okay.

He cocked his head and snarled, "I couldn't give two fucks about where Zane is! I told you that to get you in the car, idiot."

I breathed a small sigh of relief. He was safe.

He pulled out of the parking lot, continuing an epic monologue he no doubt worked on for hours. "I love that you were so quick to move on after we broke up, but you're still pining after a man who wanted to see you rot in prison. You've probably convinced yourself he cared about you too, haven't you? He didn't. You were a job. Pretty similar to our story, now that I think about it."

"You cared about me," I argued. "Don't change the facts now."

He laughed easily. "Oh, poor Dakota Quinn. Nobody loves her. You were a job for me too—although I guess I wasn't as convincing as Thor in gaining your affection. It was supposed to be a simple enough job. I'd marry you and unite the two families while still getting what I wanted on the side. Win, win, yeah? Well, it was until he fucked us over on his end of the deal, forcing me to call off the wedding. Blake's don't negotiate, after all. It's ridiculous how everyone's so scared of this guy, talking about how ruthless he—"

"Who are you talking about?" I interrupted, completely lost.

He glanced toward the backseat. "You hearing this, Bill? She wants to know who I'm talking about. This is too good. Your father, Dakota. You just accepted a vehicle from the man. Don't act like you didn't know."

My eyes widened, and I stumbled over my words. "What—my father's dead, Jackson. You know this. My mama gave me the vehicle."

My mama, who was married to the Pres of Silent Phoenix. The blood drained from my face. It was impossible. He'd died when I was two.

"I think she's connecting the dots now, Bill. Smoke's coming out of her ears! Your mama's nothing more than an Ol' Lady. Grey's the brains behind the operation—a fucking genius, really—but he pissed off the wrong family this time. Suddenly, Daddy got a conscience and didn't know if I'd make a good husband. Like it fucking mattered. Why do you think Zane was so interested in you? He found out who your daddy was."

My brain fought against despair, trying to come up with a way out. I began noting every sign and landmark we passed. "So, why am I here? How is you hurting me going to make my father want to work with you? Your family owns a furniture business—what do they want with a biker club?"

"You're so pretty... and stupid," Jackson noted with a cruel smirk. "I'm not gonna hurt you. I'm taking you as collateral. Grey will have no choice but to work with us when he finds out we've got his baby girl. If he still refuses, we'll put a few bullets in Kate to make the decision easier on him."

"You won't lay a hand on my sister!" I swore.

"Of course I won't. I pay people for that. To answer your original question, the furniture business alone wouldn't benefit much from Grey's club. But if someone were transporting drugs inside said furniture—that might change things a bit, yeah?"

I swallowed the lump in my throat, unsure which was worse—dating an undercover cop without knowing, or agreeing to marry a man who ran a high-powered drug ring.

Neither spoke highly of my choices in men.

"He'll never agree to help you."

Jackson laughed. "Of course he will. If not, I promised Bill here a taste of you, and he's not known for his gentleness. I doubt Grey wants to see his baby assaulted."

We pulled into a gravel lot toward a large metal building sitting inconspicuously off in the distance.

"Here we are. Home sweet home."

Bill opened the door and jerked me out, keeping my arms pinned behind my back as we walked.

"I can't believe you didn't know your old man was still alive and well," Jackson continued, gesturing with the gun as one would their hands while talking.

I was so focused on watching the weapon that I missed a large rock in my path. It caught the toe of my sneaker and I stumbled forward. With Bill holding my arms, I had no way of breaking my fall. My glasses collided with the bridge of my nose when I hit the ground and I cried out, feeling the break.

"Jesus Christ, Dakota!" Jackson shouted, flipping me onto my back. Blood ran down my throat, and I turned my head to the side, trying not to gag. A beam of light shot out from the cell phone in his hand, blinding me almost instantly. "Your face—fuck! Grey's gonna think I did this! Clean her up when we get inside."

Bill yanked me to my feet, and I struggled to right myself, feeling as if my head was going to explode at any moment. My right eye was swelling, but I could still make out enough to see we'd reached the building.

I lost my balance when Bill shoved me through the doorway, but Jackson grabbed my waist, keeping me from face-planting on the concrete floor.

"Easy, asshole! God, Dakota, have you lost weight? Maybe I'll keep you for myself. Just like old times."

I ground my teeth together as his hands roamed over my stomach, fighting the rising fear that I would not make it out alive. Worse was the knowledge that Jackson wasn't likely to give me a quick death, either.

With a deep breath, I centered myself, keeping my voice steady as I replied, "Maybe you should."

If he tried anything, I'd end him.

CHAPTER TWENTY-SEVEN

Dakota: October 2016 (Age: 22)

"Hold still." Bill's breath reeked of garlic, and I had to turn my head away. He was supposed to be cleaning the blood from my face, but his hands kept dropping to my breasts, bringing a hideous smile to his face every time. I swallowed back the rising bile. If I incapacitated him, there'd only be Jackson left to deal with.

I just needed a weapon.

"Jackson wanted you to come to him," he said, while making another pass over my chest. "You didn't ask him for help. That made him mad." It was the most I'd ever heard Bill speak. Judging by the slow speech and delayed reactions, his IQ was definitely on the lower end of the scale. If I wanted to stay alive, I'd have to use it to my advantage.

He continued, "Jackson had a backup plan. You fell right into that one. Know what it was?"

I nodded. "The ring. He wanted me to return it and, in the process, dragged me into a drug investigation."

"That's right," he said, patting my head.

"Damn! Bill, I left my phone in the car!" Jackson shouted from outside the bathroom. "Keep an eye on her while I rub back to grab it!"

"Bill," I purred as the large outside door slid shut. "Why do you let Jackson take all the credit when it's obvious you're the brains behind the operation?"

It was so over-the-top, only an idiot would think it was genuine. What Bill didn't know was that, in addition to working out twice a day, Little Ricky had taught me a few self-defense techniques he'd picked up after years of doing jiu-jitsu.

His face reddened, and he looked down. "You really think so, Dakota? I've always had a soft spot for you. Could treat you real good, too."

"Yeah?" I ran a hand through his hair, grease instantly coating my palm. I hid a grimace and brought it down to his chest, wiping the grease on his shirt.

Plan B. I thrust out my chest, immediately drawing his attention to it.

Never underestimate the power of The Mighty THOR t-shirt.

"You know, there's something I've been wanting to do to you since I first saw you."

"What?" he asks, panting through his mouth. Mama always said to never trust a mouth breather.

I inclined my head toward the door. "We've gotta be quick, but I need you."

He caught my meaning and unbuckled his pants, letting them drop to the floor with his gun still in the pocket. His hand lingered over the waistband of his white cotton briefs, but I stopped him with a shake of my head.

"Let me."

He dropped his arms down by his side, completely unprotected. I thrust my foot out and connected with his balls, expecting him to drop instantly. He didn't. I barely had time for more than a startled yelp when he dragged me off the counter and tossed me to the floor.

"I was gonna make it real sweet for you," he growled, tugging his underwear down before dropping all of his weight onto me. "But now I'm gonna make you cry."

Little Ricky's training came back to me and I relaxed, letting my body do what it had done hundreds of times before in the four weeks.

Remember this, Cap. You think you're in a position of weakness, but you have power.

I closed guard around his back with my legs, bumping my hips forward and shoving his shoulder to the side. The movement pushed his weight back and allowed me to sit up and come at him from the side. I slipped my arm around his neck in a guillotine choke and fell back to the concrete, crossing one ankle over the other and extending my legs until his body went limp.

Hold tight, and he'll be out in six seconds.

I held on for fifteen, just to be sure.

"Bill?" Jackson called, jiggling the door handle. "You know our agreement. No touching the merchandise."

I retrieved the gun from Bill's pants and tucked it into my yoga pants, adjusting my shirt to cover it before opening the door.

"What the fuck happened here?" He took in the discarded jeans and half-naked idiot passed out on the floor.

"I told him not to touch me," I said coldly. "He didn't listen, even when I told him you wouldn't like it."

He sighed and rubbed his forehead. "Damn right I wouldn't want him touching you. Jesus, why is it so hard to find decent employees? Let's go. Looks like we're gonna have to blame your face on Bill— maybe turn him over to your dad? I don't know. What a fucking mess." He twisted around and latched onto my arm in a bruising grip. "If I find out you're lying, what happened to your comics will look like child's play—got it?"

My blood turned to ice. "My comics?"

"I might've had my men tell the cops the buyer list was hidden in one of your comics. Maybe you should have been a little nicer to me when I tried to take you back, yeah?"

I was going to break every bone in his body, one at a time.

He led me through the large warehouse. I ached to reach for the gun, but knew I'd have to bide my time and wait for him to let his guard down. Then I'd slowly and painfully take him out.

The sound of glass shattering echoed throughout the metal building. Jackson grabbed me roughly, hissing, "Did you call someone?"

I jerked away. "How would I do that? You have my phone."

"Stay right here," he demanded. "So help me—if you run, I will shoot you. My dad is going to be so pissed at the way this is going."

The second he disappeared from view, I began searching the dark building for a place to hide. My foot connected with a pipe sticking up out of the floor, and I fell to my knees with a strangled gasp. Before I could get back on my feet, a hand came down over my mouth. When I tried to scream, the hand clamped down even harder, squeezing my jaw.

"Shh... it's me, babe. It's me."

"Zane?" I asked, my voice muffled against his palm. He released me just as light flooded the large room, fluorescent bulbs humming as they warmed up. Seemed Jackson had found the switch, taking away any chance of an ambush.

"What are you doing here?" I hissed at the giant crouched behind me.

He glared at me. "Saving your ass, Cap. What the hell does it look like I'm doing?"

I kept my eyes on the hall, making sure Jackson wasn't lingering nearby. "I have it under control and don't need saving—especially by you."

"Babe, I don't doubt that for a second. But this isn't a comic book. You're inexperienced and you could get hurt."

"You're inexperienced," I retorted.

Zane pinched the bridge of his nose with a sigh. "Real mature, Dakota. I'm just trying to get us out of this in one piece. Little help, please?" I turned to face him and his gaze instantly darkened. "What the hell did he do to you?"

I brought my fingers up, palpating the swollen areas. "Well, I'm like ninety-nine percent certain my nose is broken."

His jaw tightened. "Which is why you need my help."

I nodded, suddenly tired of arguing. "Fine—what's the plan, Big Guy?"

He crept toward the sliding door. "How many are there?"

I held up a finger. "Just one. I took care of the other guy."

There was a loud groan from the bathroom. Zane raised an eyebrow. "Just one?"

"Well, only one who's armed," I said, lifting the edge of my t-shirt.

He nodded, impressed. "Okay, here's what we're gonna do—"

"Well, well, well. What do we have here?" Jackson's booming voice filled the room. "Thor here to save his woman—lame!"

Zane drew his gun. "Let her go, Jackson."

"No, I don't think I will," he responded with a chuckle. "I've worked too hard to get this deal with her father. You remember her dad, don't you, Zane? After all, he was the only reason you were even interested in little Dakota here."

"That's a lie!"

I reached under my shirt for the gun, my eyes darting between the two warily. Their pissing contest was wasting precious time—time that could have been spent taking Jackson out.

One second, the door was closed. The next, it was open. Men swarmed in like bees and Jackson lifted his gun, aiming it at Zane's head.

I freed the gun from my waistband and launched myself at him with a roar. We fell to the floor in a tangle of limbs and a gun went off, but I couldn't tell if it was his or mine. Strong arms latched onto me from behind, but I kept fighting.

"Let go of me! He's going to hurt Zane. Let me go!" I kicked wildly, hitting my captor right in the groin. He released me, doubling over with a loud exhale.

Zane groaned, and I forgot about the men surrounding me and ran to where he lay near the door. "Oh my god, Zane! Are you okay?"

"Do I look like I'm fucking okay?" he snarled. "You fucking shot me!"

"N-n-no, Jackson shot you! Remember?"

"Nope," he bit out through clenched teeth. "You did."

He was losing an alarming amount of blood, and it was making him delirious. An older man with long blond hair squatted beside me, reaching for Zane.

I placed my hand on his arm, noting the black leather vest with a growing sense of dread. "Please don't hurt him!"

"Ain't gonna hurt him, baby girl," he responded gently. "Just checkin' the damage."

He pressed near Zane's shoulder, causing him to jerk upright with a growl. The biker stripped off his vest and shirt, passing the latter off to me. "Hold it right here. We need to keep pressure on the wound. You hit anywhere else?"

Zane shook his head, sweat beading along his hairline. A wave of dizziness washed over me as I pressed against the wound, feeling the blood pumping its way out. I needed a distraction—anything to keep from passing out. I focused on the biker, studying the colorful tattoos covering his body. There was a large one in the center of his chest, but I couldn't see it without craning my neck.

He noticed and turned back to me with a small frown. "You okay, baby girl? Lookin' a little pale."

When he faced me completely, I realized the tattoo taking up most of his chest was that of Mjölnir, Thor's hammer.

"Grey, you want me to call it in to Sullivan?" another biker asked.

The man, Grey, nodded.

"Daddy?"

He nodded again, reaching for me. I reached for his hand, only to find it covered in Zane's blood.

Then, everything went dark.

CHAPTER TWENTY-EIGHT

Grey: October 2016 (Age: 52)

"Your girl's got a strong kick," Bear groaned. "My fuckin' balls are still lodged somewhere in my throat. The fuck you grinnin' about? You think this is funny?"

"I think it's funny as fuck that a woman half your size took you down. Might have to change your name to Cub, 'cause you're losin' your touch." I couldn't fight the smile that was plastered on my face, and it had shit all to do with Dakota's well-placed kick.

She knew I was alive.

Granted, I'd been busy trying to keep her cop boyfriend from bleeding out and had only managed to get one word out of her before she saw the blood and blacked out on me, but I'd live on that word for the rest of my life.

Daddy.

Celia had been right to question the Blake family's motives. Proving that some men never learned, they'd gone after my daughter. Blake's idiot son had been stupid enough to kidnap my daughter, taking her to a facility I owned. He and his father would pay for that. But first, I had to deal with one of my own.

"Goblin," I called out.

He came running. "Yeah, Pres?"

I sat on the edge of the desk in the back office of our warehouse, scratching at my jaw. "Thought you said she ended things with the cop."

His brown eyes widened, and he stuttered, "S-she did! I swear it. I was on her like peanut butter on a sidewalk, boss. Ain't no one could've done a better job than me."

I shook my head with a frown. The kid was shit with analogies. "See, that don't add up for me because the cop's fuckin' ass over teakettle for her and plans on poppin' the question."

A line of sweat ran from Goblin's hairline down the side of his face. "That don't make no sense! We broke up with him because we don't need no man... even one that looks like Thor. We go to the gym twice a day, and she only cries in the shower. We made motherfuckin' progress, Pres!"

My lips twitched, but I fought it, wanting to see how far the kid would go to get himself out of trouble. I lasted all of three seconds before I was doubled over, wheezing with laughter. "Goddamn, son. I'm just fuckin' with you. I'll talk to Mikey, make sure this guy, Zane, knows how to keep his fuckin' mouth shut."

I couldn't have stayed mad at Goblin if I tried. He'd kept my daughter safe and shown her how to defend herself using the kung fu shit that he and Celia were so fond of.

Considering she'd just shot her soon-to-be fiancé, I might've spent a little more time showing her how to use a gun, but it was a start.

He laughed nervously. "Oh, yeah. See, I knew you were just fuckin' around, boss. That's how we do, right? You got me, and now I gotta come up with somethin' to get you back—"

"Goblin?"

"Yeah, boss?"

"Get the fuck out."

"You got it," he chuckled. "I'll just be out here, beatin' the shit outta the Blake kid if you need me."

Bear watched me from the couch with an amused smirk. "Jesus Christ. Kid runs his mouth more than me. So, how's it feel to be back from the dead?"

I stood up. "It feels fuckin' amazing. Walk with me. I lost my shirt, tryin' to keep the cop alive. I feel fuckin' naked without at least my kutte. You feel me?"

We passed Goblin, happily pistol-whipping our prisoner, and moved outside. "We any closer to findin' our rat?"

Bear shook his head. "Jarvis is lookin' into it, but between our guy and whoever they got inside the department, they've covered their tracks. It's like a fuckin' game of cat and mouse, only I can't figure out what the goddamn prize is."

I sighed. "I'm startin' to feel like this Saint guy ain't real. Only person who copped to knowin' jack shit about him was Hawk, but I ain't seen a goddamn thing that proves he's out there."

"Serpents were spotted outside of Houston. Got some of our Nomads trackin' to see where they lead."

I ignored the pang in my chest as I thought of Slim. Three years later, and it still didn't feel real. Every day, I expected him to walk through the door of the clubhouse, bragging about how he'd pulled off the world's most epic prank.

"Cobra with them?" I asked, pushing my grief back down.

"Haven't gotten confirmation on that, but as soon as they know, we'll know." Bear kicked at stray pieces of gravel with his boot, sending them rolling across the parking lot.

In two years, the Sons had wiped out the Outlaws and recruited most of the local gangbangers to their cause, but no one seemed to know exactly what that cause was. Torch's Ol' Lady had turned up dead after overhearing something she shouldn't have, but the notes she'd left behind had led nowhere.

As much as I wanted there to be a connection between Cobra and the Sons, the evidence wasn't there. Despite what Hawk had wanted us to believe, no puppet master was pulling at strings to get to my wife.

I'd been looking for hidden meanings and chasing after loose ends when it could've been nothing more than a turf war. Most ended as soon as they began, but the Sons had been smart and infiltrated my clubhouse.

"Sullivan's here." Bear pointed at the truck pulling in. "Bet you never thought you'd live to see the day that he was the one with his head on straight," he chuckled.

"What do you mean?" I asked carefully as I retrieved my kutte from where I'd left it, hanging on the chain-link fence. I tucked it under my arm and meandered back toward the warehouse. Comedian had snagged Blake Sr. and with the way Goblin was working Junior over, nobody was going anywhere.

Plenty of time for me to find out what exactly Bear knew, and how.

He looked around before leaning in. "I mean, out of the three of your kids, he's the only one who has his shit together."

Dread wrapped its icy fingers around me, and I swallowed. "You know about that?"

Bear nodded. "Pres, I got two eyes and been ridin' with you for years. You and I both know the conversation that's gonna have to happen. You know how hard it was for me to tell Ricky I wasn't his old man? To see the hurt in his eyes?"

"You two are good now, though. Right?"

"I don't know. We're brothers in the same club—whether he'll ever see me as his dad again? Who the fuck can say? You know, me and Molly had a one-night stand not long before she ended up with the gangbanger. When I found out she was knocked up, I had this stupid thought that maybe the kid was mine."

He paused, chewing on the inside of his cheek. "Only I used a rubber, and that prick didn't. Some of the other guys gave me shit, sayin' that she was gonna try to get me on the hook for child support, but I was so fuckin' gone for her by then, it didn't matter."

"Did she?" I'd been so preoccupied with taking out Los Dictadores back then I'd missed out on the drama taking place within my own club.

Bear shook his head with a grin, lost in his memories. "Nah, she straight up told me the baby wasn't mine, tried to push me away. I showed up to every goddamn doctor's appointment and was the first one to hold him when he was born—fuck, what am I tryin' to say? Just don't wait too long. Hell, maybe if I'd been honest from the beginning, things would've turned out differently."

I clapped him on the shoulder with a jerk of my head before walking back inside. There was nothing I could say to make things better. Bear and I were in the same boat—both stuck and wishing our boys could see who we really were.

CHAPTER TWENTY-NINE

Dakota: October 2016 (Age: 22)

"There you are, sunshine," a woman chirped, giving me a warm smile.

I struggled to sit up, taking in the blue curtain surrounding me. "Where am I?"

"You poor thing," she tsked. "You're in the emergency room—you and your husband are lucky people."

My what?

"Targeted because he's a cop, and them going after you too—just makes me sick—"

"Get your fucking hands off of me! Where is she? Let me see her!"

I winced. "Is that—"

She nodded. "Been yelling for you ever since they brought him in. Never mind, he has a gunshot wound to the shoulder. We've even given him a sedative, but it's taken just about everyone on staff to hold him down while we get ready to transport him upstairs for surgery."

I didn't know why the nurse thought Zane and I were married, but wasn't about to correct her. If my fake marriage meant I wouldn't be arrested for discharging a weapon into a police officer, then I'd agree to whatever they wanted me to at this point. Upon remembering I was the reason he was in the hospital, I sucked in a ragged breath, unable to stop the sob from escaping my throat.

"Hey now," the nurse said, gently patting my hand. "He's going to be just fine—"

"Mr. Masterson, do you know what type of gun was used?" someone on the other side of the curtain asked.

"A 9mm," he groaned.

"Are you sure about that?"

"I'm a fucking cop! Of course, I fucking know what type of fucking gun was used! Touch my shoulder one more time and you're gonna be dealing with a head injury, pal!"

The nurse strapped a blood pressure cuff on my arm while Zane shouted as if the medical staff were trying to kill him. I couldn't help it and began laughing through the tears.

"He's not normally like this..."

The nurse cackled. "Honey, no one acts right when they've been shot. Now, as far as your injuries—your nose was broken, but we were able to set it when you arrived."

"I figured."

She paused to enter my blood pressure reading into the computer and tapped the screen. "Looks like we've got your lab work back as well, Mrs. Masterson. Can you tell me the date of your last menstrual cycle?"

I rattled off the date, and her grin widened. "Well, that puts you about six weeks along, which matches up with your hCG levels. Congratulations!"

"Wait—what does that mean?" I asked, my voice rising in panic.

She gestured at the screen. "You're pregnant, hon."

My hand came up over my mouth and I fell back against the pillow in stunned silence.

Pregnant?

I couldn't be pregnant!

I was only twenty-two and in the middle of a pretty extensive punishment plot. Besides, Zane and I were only together one night— well, and the following morning.

"Is that her?" Zane yelled from the other side of the curtain. How he heard either of us with the noise he was creating was beyond me.

"Were you not late?" she asks with a frown.

I gave her a shaky nod. "I'd been working out so much, though, I thought it had just thrown everything off."

"Dakota! What'd I say about the shoulder, buddy? Babe, answer me, please," he pleaded in a strangled tone, as if he was locked in a death battle.

The nurse gestured toward the curtain separating our rooms and I nodded again, pressing a hand to my mouth to silence my sobs.

She hadn't been lying. Every available nurse was trying to restrain him.

He turned, his massive body going lax once he saw me. "Are you okay, baby?"

I could only shake my head in response. Nothing about any of this was okay.

"Your wife is fine, Mr. Masterson. Just a little overwhelmed at the moment," my nurse said, smiling brightly.

My what? He mouthed, eyes searching my face. "Don't cry, baby. I'm right here."

I nodded, hastily swiping the never-ending tears from my eyes.

"Do you see this woman?" he asked a man in scrubs. "I'm in love with her."

The man nodded absently, much like an adult would for a child, while another nurse injected something into his IV.

"Marry me."

My heart slammed against my ribs and as much as I wanted to jump up and down with joy, I was aware of the questioning looks being passed among the nurses. "We're already married."

He bobbed his head up and down. Whatever they gave him was beginning to take effect. "Right. So, marry me again. I don't remember the first time. I love you—you love me. It's a done deal."

I willed my bottom lip to stop trembling. "You sure about that, Big Guy?"

I just shot you.

He licked his lips as if he'd never used his tongue before. "S'always been you, baby. Since the moment you wanted to work your quad-ry-ceps. I said to myself, 'Self, you marry that girl.' Well, maybe I said it the first time I saw your tits... I don't remember. What d'ya say?"

A nurse raised his eyebrows at me, and my face heated.

"I say yes," I whispered, watching as his eyes drifted to a close. A smile played on his lips and I wondered if he would even remember asking once he woke up.

"We'll have someone let you know when he's out of surgery—take you up to his room," someone said as they wheeled his bed out.

"Okay," I said before turning back to my nurse. She waved a hand over her eyes. "Whew! I've got something in my eyes. Let's get you discharged so you can get upstairs to your man."

I reached down to place a hand on my abdomen, letting another round of tears wash over my face.

I was carrying a superhero's baby.

And I had never been so scared in my entire life.

CHAPTER THIRTY

Dakota: October 2016 (Age: 22)

"Mind if I catch a ride down with you?"

I sniffled and shook my head. "What are you doing here, Mama?"

She waited until we stepped inside the elevator before answering. "Your father told me what happened. I wanted to be here for you."

"Where is my dad? Already gone back underground?" I asked with a bitter laugh.

She watched the floor numbers light up as the elevator descended. "Dakota, it's not that simple. By sticking around, he puts you in danger."

"Where's Jackson? Did they arrest him?" I hoped so. If anyone needed to rot in a prison cell for the rest of their life, it was him.

Her mouth curved up in a smile. "Let's just say that Jackson and his father have been handled. He'll never bother you again."

I pursed my lips. "Tell my father Jackson is mine to deal with. I want to be the one to inflict pain on him."

"Baby girl, your daddy said you passed out from seeing Zane's blood. I don't think you'd do any better with Jackson."

I exhaled loudly. "That was a fluke thing."

She bit her lip. "Somehow, I don't think so."

"If I can't do it, can I at least watch?"

"Absolutely not. God, I don't think anyone needs to see that."

Damn. I thought she'd agree.

I was curious to know what was going to happen to him and simultaneously terrified the answer would change how I viewed my parents. I didn't want to think of my dad as anyone other than the man who saved mine and Zane's lives.

"I saw his tattoo."

The elevator doors opened, and we walked out, side by side. "Mjölnir, you mean? Well, you definitely came by your love of comics naturally."

I smiled with pride. Daddy's girl. "Would—" I paused to clear my throat. "Would there ever be a time I could sit down—maybe get to know him?"

She nodded, her eyes filling with tears. "We'd have to look at how to make it work, but I know he'd love nothing more. We just want to keep you and Kate safe, baby girl."

My steps faltered when we reached the parking lot, and I shook my head. "I walked all the way out here and my car's still at the gym. I don't even know where my bag is with my keys."

Mama laughed. "Your daddy got your stuff from Jackson's car. It's in mine now. If you like, I can take you to get your car tomorrow."

I nodded, needing to get some things off my chest first. "How'd you do it? How did you fall in love with someone so dangerous and then have kids with him? You had to know that every time he kissed you goodbye, it could have been the last."

"Is this about your daddy, or Zane?"

Both.

I didn't meet her eyes. "My dad."

She studied me with a frown. "What are you not telling me, Dakota Mae? Did something happen with you and the cop?"

I swallowed hard and stared at the pavement, eyes brimming with unshed tears. "He—it's complicated. I mean, he was investigating me for a good chunk of our relationship, so..." My voice trailed off. I didn't know what else to say. A relationship based on lies had no little to no chance of working out.

Mama placed a hand on my shoulder. "You can tell me—if there's something going on, let me help. As far as your dad and I go—we were young and I got pregnant with Kate while we were dating. Pops and Nan felt like I could've done so much better—married someone who was wealthy. But I knew no one would ever love me like he does. I thought he could run his club, and we'd still get the white picket fence life. It wasn't reality, though." She fell silent, lost in her memories.

"I'm pregnant, Mama," I confessed. "And I love him, but I just don't know what to do."

"Oh, Dakota," she breathed, pulling me to her chest.

And then I let her hold me while I fell apart.

CHAPTER THIRTY-ONE

Mike: October 2016 (Age: 33)

I shoved my way into the metal building, taking in the chaos. "Jesus fuck, what the hell happened here?"

Goblin held a gun on a douchebag in a suit—there was no other way to describe the guy. He looked like a spoiled little rich boy who'd been handed everything on a fucking silver platter.

I'd been curled up with my girl, watching the History Channel when Carnage called. This prick would pay for interrupting my night. Lauren hadn't even gotten a proper honeymoon as the Sons had attacked Leather & Lace the same night we got married.

The morning after my wedding had been spent helping with cleanup. Minus a club whore and a prospect, there had been no other deaths, but the timing was suspect. Grey had been at my wedding. Someone knew that and chose to strike while he was thirty miles away.

As I got closer, I realized who the douchebag was.

Fucking Jackson Blake.

"What's the matter? Daddy not here to bail you out?"

He spat out a mouthful of blood and laughed. "Fuck you, Sullivan. You can take me down to the station, but you won't get shit on me."

Goblin laughed along with him before bringing the pistol down sharply against the back of his skull. "Shut the fuck up. You talk too much. Thanks for getting down here, Mikey. We got all sorts of fucked up shit for you to deal with tonight."

I saw the puddle of blood and looked back to Goblin. "What the fuck?"

He shook his head. "Shit went south. Dakota shot the cop—"

I held up my hand. "Dakota was here? Start at the fucking beginning, Little Ricky."

His face lit up. "You called me Little Ricky—not Goblin or kid. Sweet."

I gestured with my hand to hurry him along. "Sometime tonight would be good."

He nodded. "Right. Well, Dakota was engaged to this pendejo. Then she was fucking around with Thor until she found out he was a cop. Oh, Grey's back. He'll tell you everything."

I looked over as Grey walked in, missing his shirt and kutte. "You wanna tell me why I'm down here?"

"Yeah. One second," he said with a heavy sigh before turning back to Little Ricky. "Goblin, you and Crossbones get this piece of shit out of my sight and back to the clubhouse. Wouldn't want Jackson's old man getting lonely."

The prick's face paled. "I'm not being arrested? Where's my dad?"

I actually found myself breaking into a wide grin. "I don't really work like that anymore. Found a better way to deal with guys like you, and it saves the taxpayers money, too."

He began begging for his life as the men dragged him outside. Grey ordered a prospect to clean up the blood and led me back toward an office at the end of a hallway.

"Let's talk in here." I sat down, and he rubbed his eyes wearily. "He fuckin' took Dakota, Mikey."

Growing up, I'd been closest to Katy. Other than a brief encounter at the gym and some covert monitoring, I knew next to nothing about my youngest half-sister. We shared the same hair and eyes, but that was where the similarities ended, as far as I could tell.

Grey continued. "Agreed to their marriage months ago—thought it was a win-win for everyone. The Blake's transported for us for years. Seein' Lauren on your wedding day, though, I had second thoughts.

Dakota deserves the same happiness, and Jackson would've made her miserable.

"I backed out of the merger and he called off the wedding. I thought that was the end until he took her tonight. Guess he thought he'd use her as leverage to get what he wanted from the club."

I blinked slowly, trying to absorb the information he was hurling at me, while also calculating how little sleep I was going to be getting tonight. "And the blood?"

Grey's mouth fell flat. "Dakota's got a broken nose and Zane took a bullet to the shoulder, tryin' to protect her."

I grimaced. Zane was undercover—there was no covering up on this one. I wracked my brain. "What's the story with them?"

He smiled. "He fucking loves her—"

"Great. I can use that. Okay, what if we use the cop angle and run with it? It might be enough to keep suspicion low as long as Masterson plays along." I wasn't sure if I could pull any of it off, but it was worth a try. "What's going on with the Blakes'?"

Grey ran a finger across his throat, adding, "They're thinkin' of fleeing the country once it comes out that they've cooked their books."

Okay. This wasn't too bad. I'd handled far worse.

Jarvis burst into the office, panting, "Slight problem."

Fuck.

"I know I was supposed to keep an eye on Kate, but I got busy with club shit and she—um, well, she's in Vegas."

Jesus, keeping the Quinn girls safe was more work than dealing with the club. They were like kindergartners left in a room without a teacher while hopped up on sugar—absolute fucking holy terrors.

And we were blood relatives.

What did that say about me?

CHAPTER THIRTY-TWO

Grey: October 2016 (Age: 52)

Jarvis had the same look of panic on his face that Goblin had, but for an entirely different reason. I'd put the kid through college and gotten him a job as a realtor for the real estate company I owned. He'd repaid me last year by taking my daughter home and fucking her.

The only reason the fucking ginger was still breathing was because it had only happened the one time, and then Kate had gone out of her way to avoid him.

Didn't mean I'd planned to let it go unpunished.

Trouble was, the prick had fallen for my baby girl, and I realized him being forced to watch her day in, day out was better than any of the shit I could have doled out.

Sensing he was about to hyperventilate himself onto the floor, I casually said, "So, she's safer there than she is here. She's a grown woman, Jarvis. I think she'll be okay."

He shook his head. "Well, she's with the trauma surgeon—uh, Nate Davis. Based on their credit card trail, I think they're getting married."

I pinched the bridge of my nose at the same time Mikey did. "What do you mean, married? Celia said they weren't even serious."

My phone vibrated against my hip, and I quickly answered when I saw it was my wife. "How's our girl?"

She sniffed, and I knew she was crying. She had every right to, because it shouldn't have happened. I'd put measures in place to keep them safe, and it hadn't meant shit.

Hades and Persephone had come from separate worlds, and she'd simply divided her time between the two. His world had never bled over into hers.

Until now.

The kids we'd fought to keep safe were now in the middle of a war, being used as pawns by our enemies. I'd always thought my biggest challenge would be getting Mikey sober and clean and keeping him that way.

It turned out the secret I'd been keeping was the only thing that had saved him from becoming a target. Bear was right, though. It was only a matter of time until our enemies noticed the similarities between us and put two and two together.

Jackson had insisted he was in love with Dakota, and I'd been too blind to see the truth. If I'd missed that, then none of them were safe. Our enemies had disguised themselves as friends.

"Hey Jamie, Dakota's got a broken nose, but she's going to be okay. Zane came out of surgery with no problems. It's just—she, uh, she wants to get to know you—" Her voice cut off in a soft sob.

I ran my hand over my face, fighting back the tears with a smile. It no longer mattered who the fuck was in the room with me. My daughter knew I was still kicking and wanted a relationship. "Darlin', that's the best fuckin' news I've had all night."

Celia hiccuped loudly. "That's not why I called, though."

"Believe me when I say I'm takin' care of it, darlin'—"

"She's pregnant, Jamie." Except for her ragged breaths, the line was silent.

Pregnant.

In my mind, Dakota was still a baby, screeching that her favorite superhero was *For*, because she couldn't make the th sound. She wasn't old enough to be having babies of her own.

Fuck, she wasn't old enough to even be thinking about sex.

"She's knocked up by a badge?" I roared. Jarvis backed out of the office with his palms raised while Mikey shook his head with a wince. "I'm gonna fuckin' kill him."

I looked over at Mikey. "What are those charges you can get on someone for fuckin' your kid?" I asked. "You're a cop. You know that shit."

He frowned. "Statutory rape? Grey, I think the age of consent is seventeen, and what is Dakota? Twenty-two?"

"Thought you'd know all about the laws regarding that," Celia deadpanned through the phone. I didn't need to be reminded of how young she'd been when I popped her cherry.

"I got one elopin' in Vegas, one knocked up by a cop... the fuck is this world comin' to, Celia? I think right now, the only kid I got doin' a goddamn thing right is—" I caught myself just before saying the words, not missing the way Mikey's head shot up in expectation.

He knew.

The truth was looking me right in the eye, and I still couldn't say it. "Well, I think it's pretty fuckin' obvious that raisin' kids is like tryin' to herd feral cats."

"Did you just say that Kate is getting married in Vegas?"

"Celia, I can't hear—think—breaking up—" I pressed the end button with a sigh and leaned back.

When I worked up the courage to make eye contact with my son again, he was watching me with an unreadable expression. "You know, Grey, there isn't an easy way to say this, but..."

Here it was.

Time to set club bullshit aside and come clean.

"Between Celia and the girls..." He grinned. "You're fucked."

CHAPTER THIRTY-THREE

Kate: October 2016 (Age: 26)

I groaned into the pillow, unable to determine if the incessant buzzing that had jolted me out of a dead sleep was from my phone or aching head. The sour taste of booze lingered on my tongue, leaving me fighting a sudden wave of nausea.

Mistake. Such a mistake.

The buzzing continued, and I slowly peeled myself off the mattress.

"Never again," I swore before blindly swiping at my phone screen. "H-hello?"

"Kate?" My mother sounded strange, and for a moment, I prepared myself for a lecture on the dangers of leaving town without telling anyone. Just as quickly, the more rational part of my mind sluggishly chimed in to remind me that Celia Quinn had lost the right to condemn any of my life choices when she walked out on me at sixteen.

"Listen, Dakota's up at the hospital with Zane. He was shot earlier tonight but is going to be okay. He's out of surgery and resting in a room right now, but Dakota wanted me to let you know."

I sucked in a sharp breath and sat up before the pain in my head kicked in, forcing me back down. "Oh my god. I can meet you there. Just let me throw some clothes on—"

And get rid of the hangover from hell.

"Katydid, take your time. Do you need me to book you a return flight?"

"A return flight?" I parroted, forcing my legs over the side of the bed. "What do you mean?"

"From Vegas," she said before quickly correcting herself. "Or wherever you are."

I frowned, knowing it wasn't a random guess. "How did you know—"

"That doesn't really matter. Just get here and we'll talk, okay? I love you, baby."

She ended the call before I could say another word. I should have known I couldn't just skip town. Clearly, there were people within the club watching my every move. My shin connected with the corner of the nightstand and I bit back a curse before stalking over to the window.

The strip was lit up, a kaleidoscope of colors against the still dark sky. So much for a weekend of irresponsibility and room service. My twelve-hour reprieve from reality had ended.

I released a heavy sigh and pushed my hair off my face, catching several strands on my ring. Slowly, I brought my hand down, blinking rapidly at the rock on my finger as if it was a hallucination.

An obscenely large diamond ring on a very important finger.

I felt my body heat rise as the gem winked in the light from outside, sending sparkles across the glass. How?

"Fuck, babe," a deep voice groaned from the bed. "Never drinking again."

My legs buckled, and I dropped to my knees on the plush carpet, clutching my chest. I was confused and frightened and—*what in the actual hell had I done last night?*

"Nate?" I tried. "Is that you?"

"Who the fuck else would be in your bed?" he growled, kicking off the comforter.

I glanced down at the offending object on my finger, feeling light-headed. It meant nothing. Maybe I just liked the ring and had decided to treat myself. "We—" I swallowed. "We might have a problem."

He gave a low chuckle. "Yeah, we do. Why don't you come back to bed, Katy girl, so we can solve it?"

"I'm not talking about sex," I hissed.

"Babe, we're in a hotel in Vegas for the weekend. Let's get romantic."

I inspected my left hand again. "Oh, we got romantic alright."

"What? What are you doing over there?" Nate sat up and felt along the nightstand until he found the light switch. We both winced at the sudden brightness, and I blinked through the tears until he came into focus.

He sat on the edge of the bed, his dark hair poking out in all directions. With a yawn, he stood and stretched—either unaware or unbothered that he was completely nude. His cock jutted up against his abdomen, momentarily distracting me from the problem at hand.

On hand.

"Are you sick?" he finally asked, coming to kneel at my side. His eyes moved over my body, silently assessing the situation.

I shook my head and placed my hand on his arm, trying to steady myself. "Worse—I think."

Nate sagged against me when he saw the ring, bringing a shaky hand to his forehead. "We didn't—I mean, it could just be jewelry, right?"

I wanted to agree—to reassure him it was probably nothing. Instead, I could do nothing more than stare, glassy-eyed, at the black titanium band on his left hand. Without thinking, I backed away from him, jerkily scooting my bare ass over to the wall.

He reached for me with a frown, visibly paling when he realized what had spooked me. "Did we—fuck! Oh fuck. Did we get married, babe?"

"No," I gasped, covering my face. "No, no, no!"

But the evidence suggested otherwise.

CHAPTER THIRTY-FOUR

Mike: October 2016 (Age: 33)

"Check your inbox now and tell me how fucked I am." Jeremy sounded as if he'd been sitting in front of his computer for the last two days. Knowing him, he probably had.

I clicked on the message and a surveillance video popped up. There was Kate, completely shit-faced, clinging to the doctor as they left a chapel. He wasn't too sober either, if the swaying was any indicator.

Her dark hair was pulled up in a bun, which was typically how I saw her. She'd always been gorgeous, but in an ice queen sort of way. The woman took herself way too seriously and—she looked up at him and grinned.

I'd be damned.

She was in love with him. I'd never seen her smile once—hadn't understood why Grey's guys fell over their dicks trying to get close to her.

Without his knowledge, of course. Go after one of his girls and kiss your balls goodbye. She was pretty under normal circumstances, but the smile took it to another level entirely.

"Well, Jarvis," I deadpanned, using his road name just to piss him off. "You are completely and utterly fucked. This is worse than the time you hooked up with her."

He went silent before asking, "How the fuck did you know about that?"

I wouldn't have known anything had I not been monitoring Dakota and Kate as well. It started when I moved back to Lubbock—during a time I still believed Grey was dead. He had been such a huge part of my childhood that it felt right to check in on the girls, to make sure they were safe.

"Thought you were the only one called in to babysit? You wanna know the difference between you and me? I kept my dick in my pants while I did my job."

Granted, she was my half-sister, so the thought turned my stomach completely. Even when I hadn't known we were related, something had kept me away. Maybe it was just my fear of Grey.

With Dakota, it had been easy to see how we were related—the blonde hair and blue eyes made it obvious. I hadn't seen the resemblance with Kate, though—she seemed to favor Celia more. The only indicator that she was Grey's was her mouth. When it was set in that hard line, she looked just like her father.

"Goddammit, what am I supposed to do? He's asking for an update. Why did she run off and marry him?" Jeremy continued talking, but I zoned out the rest, lost to my own thoughts.

"Look, we've investigated Nate. He's clean and in no way affiliated with the Sons. Just give Grey the footage and face him like a man. You did the best you could—she's twenty-six, not two." There was no way that advice was going to work—Grey would place the blame solely on his shoulders.

I didn't see it as his fault. But then again, I didn't have daughters—or sons—to look after.

"Knock, knock," David called out before sauntering into my office.

"I'll call you back." I cut off the call and stood up to shake hands with him. "What brings you downtown?"

He just grinned stupidly before sinking down into a chair. "I've got some news..."

I grinned back. "I knew you were going to come out eventually, asshole. So, who's the lucky guy? And don't say it's me, because I am married now and not down for any funny business."

He shot me the bird. "After that comment, I should leave your ass hanging, but I'm feeling mighty fucking generous today. We just left the doctor's office—Beth is pregnant."

My smile wavered slightly, but he didn't appear to notice. "Congrats, man! That's great news!"

David leaned in. "You better get on it, Mike. Unless you've found that your sudden need for men has made it hard to get it up."

"Well, dickwad, we did just get married three months ago. I think we'll enjoy the honeymoon stage a little longer if that's alright with you."

I smiled and laughed, all the while resisting the urge to batter his fucking face. So, maybe we'd only been married for three months, but we hadn't used protection in a year. We'd left it up to fate.

And fate was a cunt.

Anytime I brought it up, Lauren would change the subject and find another room in the house to redecorate. If she wasn't at the gym or out on the shooting range, she was on Pinterest, finding ideas for remodeling.

Her latest project was the master bathroom. Before that, it was the master bedroom. She'd Feng shuied the shit out of it and then promptly gotten her period the next day. I'd heard her crying in the bathroom and tried the door handle, but it was locked. Later, I saw the box of tampons near the sink and, with a sinking feeling, knew for sure.

I felt so fucking helpless. She was going through this and, no matter how much I wanted to be a part of it, she was alone. I'd thought that losing her was the worst thing I'd ever been through.

I was wrong.

Watching her go through this hell, month after month, was the hardest thing I'd ever dealt with. When we were dating, I'd been oblivious to it, and maybe it hadn't been on her radar either. Since we'd been married, though, everything had come to light. It was in the way she'd look at Kaden with a huge grin on her face while her eyes told a different story.

I was seeing my wife fall apart a little more each month, and it killed me to know there was nothing I could do about it.

"Hello? Earth to Mike?" David waved a hand in front of my face.

"What? Sorry, I've just got a lot on my mind."

He frowned. "I asked if you were doing anything special for Lauren's birthday. Beth said it surprised her you hadn't planned a raging kegger with strippers."

I laughed hollowly again. "We're just keeping it low-key, per the birthday girl's request."

Today was Lauren's thirtieth birthday and instead of a huge celebration, my wife had requested we stay in and watch movies. Well, that wasn't exactly true. Initially, she'd asked if we could forget it completely, before finally agreeing to movies.

No cake.

No candles.

No singing.

No acknowledgment whatsoever that thirty years ago today, my better half had come into this world.

It wasn't exactly something I could share with him. *Hey, Lauren's severely depressed over our infertility issues, but come on by and bring your pregnant wife, just to rub more salt in the wound.*

David checked his watch before standing up. "I've got to get over to meet an inspector on one of my sites. We have a gift for Lauren. Care if we run it by later tonight?"

I shook my head quickly. "Just give it to me now and I'll take it home."

"You sure everything's okay?" David gave me another strange look.

I nodded. "I've been up most of the night and am kind of in the middle of ten different things. It's just bad timing, that's all."

He slapped me on the shoulder. "Okay. I'll just get it out of my truck and be right back."

There was no way I was letting them stop by tonight and announce their pregnancy, crushing her on her birthday. She didn't need that shit. Tonight was about letting her know how fucking important she was to me, regardless of whether we could have kids. I had her, and that had always been enough.

David brought the gift bag in, checking to make sure I was okay once more before leaving.

I sat at my desk for another four hours, staring mindlessly at the computer screen, before giving up any pretense of being productive.

I grabbed my suit jacket and headed out, needing to clear my head and find a way to fix things.

It was a little after four when I got home to find Lauren fast asleep on the couch.

I kissed her on top of the head. "Hey, Birthday Girl. It's time to wake up."

She gave me a sleepy smile and sat up. "I must've dozed off watching The Pioneer Lady."

I pointed to the television screen. "Uh, Red? It's The Pioneer Woman. And since when do you watch cooking shows?"

"I need to learn," she said with a shrug. "We can't eat out all the time."

Now, I was getting really concerned. The last thing I needed was for her to burn the fucking house down in an attempt to learn how to cook. It had taken forever to get rid of the burned spaghetti smell.

I also knew that if I told her any of that, she'd burst into tears and any chance of me getting her out of the house tonight would be gone. So, I led with, "Well, Darlin', that's why God made grills. I can keep you fed just fine with that."

"I just feel like it's time I learned."

I pulled her hand. "C'mon, Rachael Ray. Up off the couch. I've got plans for us."

Lauren immediately began shaking her head, trying to move back to the comfort of the couch. The damn thing was starting to take on the imprint of her body. "No, no. We said no plans—I said that, didn't I?"

I kept a tight grip on her hand, moving us both toward the stairs. "Alright, no need to go full-redhead on me. I just thought it'd be good for us to get out of the house for the night—switch things up."

Her eyes filled, and I silently cursed myself for trying to force her out of her comfort zone, but then she did something that shocked the hell out of me. "Okay. Do I need to dress up or am I okay like this?"

I led her up the stairs, suddenly feeling like she was made of glass. "It's pretty fucking chilly out there, so let's find you a sweater and some leggings or some shit."

I dug around in the closet and came out with some black leather leggings and a blue hoodie. Lauren sat on the edge of the bed, chewing the corner of her lip, a look of confusion on her face. "Um, Mike? What the hell are you doing?"

I held up the clothes. "What? What's wrong with this?"

She walked over and took them from my hands. "You're hopeless, you know that?" Then she stood up on her tiptoes and pressed a light kiss against my mouth. "And I love you for it. Let me find something."

I took her place on the bed and watched as she put the leggings back on a hanger and reached for a pair of jeans. Watching her get undressed was something I would never grow tired of seeing.

And it wasn't just because of her fantastic tits. She was so comfortable in her own skin—always had been around me. I was the only man who would ever see her like this. My cock grew hard, and I adjusted myself through my slacks, willing him to calm the fuck down.

"Tonight isn't about you," I warned.

Lauren turned to me. "What'd you say?"

I shrugged. "I just said tonight's all about you."

She smiled happily and slipped the hoodie over her head. I realized then that I would've moved heaven and earth to see her smile like that again.

So, I did what any red-blooded male would do if he found himself in my situation. I went into that closet and lifted my woman up into my arms, trailing rough kisses across her face and neck while she giggled and tried to move away.

"Mike—babe, stop. Your beard is scraping my face off!"

I sank my teeth into her neck, and she looked down at me breathlessly. Her lips parted slightly and then she leaned down, pressing them to mine. I was transported back to that night on the beach in Galveston. Every fucking time. The taste of her sparked such a vivid memory that it was like I was reliving it all over again.

If I would have known then that she'd be the woman I'd spend the rest of my life with... "I would have found you sooner—"

"What?"

I didn't hesitate. "If I would have known that night in Galveston what you were going to mean to me—I would've found you sooner. Fuck, I would have combed every inch of that hotel until I got to your room."

She pulled back slightly and frowned. "Even knowing—even with—"

I knew where her sentence was headed and nodded. "Absofuckinglutely."

At that, her lip began quivering, and she buried her face against my neck. "You're the best man alive, Mike Sullivan."

I wasn't.

Not by a long shot.

But with her in my arms, I knew I'd done at least one thing right.

CHAPTER THIRTY-FIVE

Celia: October 2016 (Age: 44)

"You're shakin', Celia. Here, watch this." Rick thrust his cell phone into my trembling hands. "If this don't work, we'll go out back and..." He held his thumb and index finger up to his lips like he was smoking a joint.

"I'm fine—" At the sound of giggling, I looked down at his phone just in time to see a cat launch itself off a counter and into a wall. "How is this supposed to help?"

He tapped the screen knowingly. "You watch a few minutes of this, and you're chill as fuck. Most hilarious and funny cat videos, see? Says it right there. If this doesn't work, we'll break out the weed."

My body tingled in anticipation, and I raked a hand through my hair, fighting to calm my nerves. Dakota had done surprisingly well with the revelation that her father was still alive—so well, in fact, that she'd insisted I come over to help her tell Kate.

Knowing what Jamie's death had done to her, I was dreading every second.

"Look at this one," Rick jabbed a finger into the screen again. "You think Grey would let us get a cat for the clubhouse? Man, I bet he'd be a great mascot... representin' the club and shit. We could even call him Phoenix."

I glanced up at the ceiling, silently pleading for help.

At the sound of voices in the living room, my mouth went dry, and everything in me fought to run away. Telling Kate the truth was only going to make things worse between us.

Rick took a bite of cereal from the bowl in front of him before cracking up, sending a stream of milk onto the table in front of us. I glanced at the video of a cat tangled up in blinds, wondering if being high was a requirement to finding cat videos funny.

"Holy shit, Hail Mary." He looked up with a grin. "I thought I heard you in there. How's it hanging?"

Yet another nickname that made no sense to me.

It was as if Rick was incapable of just calling them by their names.

"What are you two doing here?" Kate asked with a furrowed brow.

Patting my leg under the table, Rick answered. "Hail Mary, I'm always here. You know that. I got a little hungry, and *Caparina* gets the best cereal. What are you doing here?"

She glanced around the small kitchen as if searching for answers. "I —are you high?"

"Kate, it's not polite to ask people if they're high," I said, more out of reflex than anything else.

"Mama, I'll get to you in a minute. Little Ricky, answer the question."

He took another bite of cereal with a big grin. "Hail Mary, I was up late last night working, and I couldn't relax, so I partook of the herb. It's all-natural, with none of the harsh side effects of *Ambien*."

I shot him a warning glance as Kate sank down onto the kitchen floor, muttering to herself. "This is psychosis—disorganized thinking and hallucinations."

Rick paused the video to ask, "Is she talking to herself, Celia? Hail Mary, you're thinking of peyote—not psychosis."

"You said you were working late. What were you doing?"

I knew what she was getting at, but what had happened to the Blake family was not up for discussion. I squeezed his arm and shook my head. "Don't."

Kate continued watching Rick before leaning against the refrigerator with a groan.

"C'mon, Kate," Dakota snapped as she walked in. "Quit moping on the floor."

"Are you kidding me right now?" Kate screeched in reply. "You were so upset with me earlier, and now you're acting as though all of this is fine. You shot your boyfriend after getting kidnapped. Mama is watching cat videos with the stoner over here. I'm sorry, I'm just having a hard time keeping up with everything taking place in front of me."

Proving that weed only made him more unpredictable, Rick chose that moment to announce, "*Caparina's* emotions are gonna be all over the place—at least until the second trimester."

Kate's eyes narrowed as she looked up at Dakota.

"I was going to tell you..."

Her hand came up over her mouth in shock. "How? When?"

Dakota joined her sister on the floor. "I found out last night in the ER; and when two people really love each other—"

"Stop. I get it."

Kate's breaths became ragged, and I knew there would never be a good time to tell her the truth. Rick squeezed my shoulder as I stood up and made my way over to my girls.

"Kate, there's something I want to talk to you about—"

Jeremy and Zane walked in, leaving me with a sense of claustrophobia. Dakota's kitchen wasn't made for this many people.

"Kate told you guys she got married in Vegas, yeah?" Jeremy casually asked, stopping me in my tracks. I was convinced Jamie had to be mistaken—couldn't believe she would have done something so reckless.

I knelt beside her. "You got married, Kate?"

Do you love him?

Are you scared?

Is he worthy of someone as unique as you?

I rocked back on my heels; the questions stuck in my throat. I couldn't question Kate's decisions without revealing my own.

Misreading things entirely, Dakota ran over to hug Jeremy. "Congrats. I have a brother now."

Rick chuckled to himself before cryptically muttering, "You're so dead, Jarvis."

Jeremy looked around for help before blurting, "She didn't marry me…"

I winced when Dakota connected the dots and confronted her sister. "God of thunder, Kate. Tell me you didn't do something as stupid as marrying that asshole!"

The asshole happened to be a doctor, but I understood her frustration. From what little I'd seen, the two were oil and water, never managing more than a couple of days without blowing up at each other.

Kate pushed herself to her feet. "Well, it's time for me to go."

"No, you don't, Mary Katherine," Dakota snapped. "I need details!"

"You just called my husband an asshole, Dakota. You don't get to make demands now. Jeremy, let's go."

"If you're married to Nate, then why are you here with Jeremy?" She called after her.

I'd come to tell Kate the truth, but my head spun with more questions than answers. I'd assumed the two had put their childhood differences aside, but with the way they were in each other's faces, it was clear that I was mistaken.

Just one more thing I'd missed.

"Kate—Dad's alive," Dakota quietly admitted, pulling me back to the conversation.

Her green eyes met mine, and I nodded, blinking against the sharp sting of tears. She was no longer a woman, but a little girl, battling her anxiety in the middle of a grocery store.

I can't breathe, Mama!

"My dad died," she breathed.

I shook my head, watching her break all over again. The stolen money was the least of their worries when their entire childhood had been drenched in lies.

"Nah, Hail Mary," Rick said with a laugh. "Your padre is my boss."

"So, your husband is my dad?" she spluttered.

"Kate, I wanted to tell you—" I started.

"Wow, I'm hearing a lot of that tonight. I need to get out of here."

With that, she was gone, along with any chance of redemption. Dakota shook her head and wrapped her arms around me as the air left my lungs. Kate was still that lost little girl, grieving for her daddy. Telling her the truth hadn't changed that. If anything, it had only forced her to relive it.

Maybe my mother had been right all along.

The girls had been better off without me.

CHAPTER THIRTY-SIX

Lauren: November 2016 (Age: 30)

"You will need three eggs, half a cup of vegetable oil, and—" I wiped a smudge of yellow powder off the box. "One cup of water."

It was Mike's birthday. After the trouble he went to for mine, I wasn't going to sleep the day away.

Even if that was exactly what I wanted to do. I wasn't even sure how I was getting through each day anymore—infertility consumed my every thought. The past few months had been hell. If I left the house, I was bound to see a baby, so I'd stopped going anywhere.

Jimmy had grown tired of my excuses and shown up one afternoon. *"They're asking for you at the range. Why aren't you going in anymore? You said you loved working there, but suddenly you've fallen off the face of the earth."*

I'd tried justifying my actions, but he'd seen right through me. *"You know what I never see at the range? Babies. You know why? Because it's a fucking gun range. But fine, you want to hide out inside your house until the end of time—do it. I'll be here every afternoon. You can't phone it in and lose everything we've worked for."*

He drove out to the house every day for target practice—even had me running laps up and down the long dirt driveway.

I knew Mike wanted to talk about it—wanted us to see a specialist.

It was almost better not knowing, though. If we didn't know for sure, then I could pretend we both had issues, even if my gut screamed that it was all my fault.

Doubt had begun to creep in as far back as April, but I chalked it up to stress and poor timing. Since we'd gotten married, I'd been charting my BBT—basal body temperature—just like the pregnancy websites had instructed. And every single month, I had to suppress any hope that it had worked when my period showed up right on time.

I began lurking around the infertility message boards online, hoping to find something that would explain why my body was working against me. When I ate out, I tried to go with the healthiest option. I'd never taken synthetic hormones, smoked, or done drugs. For all intents and purposes, I should have had a whole damn litter by now.

On my birthday, Mike took me out to his land—a tradition he'd started two years ago. After building me a bonfire, he'd presented me with Italian takeout to eat under the stars. The choice of spaghetti hadn't been lost on me, nor were the remarks that it wasn't as crunchy as mine was.

Wrapped up in an oversized sleeping bag, he'd pointed up at the sky, tracing the constellations with his fingers. *"That one there is Cepheus. Now, old Cepheus was a king and he married Cassiopeia—that's like being married to Heidi Klum, in modern day hotness quotients. Well, Heidi and Cepheus, they had themselves a beautiful daughter that they unfortunately named Andromeda. Andromeda was like—Kate Upton.*

"Well, Heidi thought it'd be a great idea to tell the entire world how Kate was more beautiful than anything or anyone else. The sea nymphs got word and were like, 'Fuck that bitch.' Then Poseidon heard and basically battered the kingdom with the power of the sea until Cepheus agreed to sacrifice Kate to the sea monster, Cetus. So, he chained his daughter up to some rocks and peaced out. Luckily, Perseus dropped out of the sky and said, 'I'll kill this monster if you give me that pussy,' which, of course, Kate agreed to because Perseus looked like Channing Tatum."

I'd rested my chin on his chest, watching his face as he animatedly told the story, feeling completely at peace for the first time in months.

I loved him so much that it made my heart ache and I hoped for a million more nights just like it.

Mike dragging me out of the house on my birthday had awakened me to the possibility it could just be the two of us forever. I realized then that Jimmy was right. I could watch my life pass me by while obsessing over whether I was ovulating, or I could face the harsh truth and somehow still be a good wife to a fantastic man despite it all.

It had been a bitter pill to swallow, but I'd woken up the morning after and thrown away the ovulation predictors. Today, I'd left the house and gone to a grocery store, where I saw six babies and only teared up twice.

It was progress.

I turned the mixer on high, sending bits of yellow batter flying from the bowl, before hurriedly lowering the speed and wiping down the counter.

Okay, so I still had some areas to improve upon in the kitchen.

But still. Progress.

I got the cake into the oven to bake without another mishap and was just debating whether to watch a YouTube video on cake frosting when there was a knock at the door.

Elizabeth stood on the porch, juggling several boxes in her arms.

"Hey, stranger." I smiled and took one of them from her hands. "What do you have here?"

She grinned. "Just a few things we thought your husband might need for his birthday."

I looked down into the box in mock confusion. "But I don't see the stripper."

Elizabeth shook her head. "Seriously, Lauren? Stripper-grams are delivered separately. Mmm... are you baking?"

Did she have a bionic nose all of a sudden?

"You're good—I just put a cake in the oven."

Her smile faded, and she immediately held the back of her hand up to my forehead in mock seriousness. "Are you okay? Feeling feverish?"

I slapped her hand away. "Stop it. I can bake!"

She arched an eyebrow before heading into the kitchen. "This I've gotta see." She cracked the oven door and peeked in. "Lauren, this looks great!"

I rolled my eyes. "I'm not a child—I told you I can bake. The Pioneer Lady does it all the time on her show."

"Woman," Elizabeth corrected. "The Pioneer Woman."

"Whatever. This cake is going to be delicious."

She glanced around the kitchen. "The house looks amazing. I can't believe how much it's changed in just the last couple of months. And now you're baking too? You're a regular Suzy Homemaker."

"Don't say that. I'm just baking a cake—that's it. Sometimes, it's nice to break up the monotony of just going to the gym and the gun range. It makes me miss having a full-time job. Speaking of—why aren't you at work this fine Thursday morning?"

Once the event center saw her creative side, they'd snatched her up immediately. She was now an official wedding coordinator, which kept her pretty busy.

Elizabeth pulled a barstool out and sat down at the island. "I am— just took the morning off to run some errands and I haven't talked to you in forever. I thought it might be nice to catch up."

I hadn't meant to avoid her calls, but everything had just become a little too overwhelming to deal with. Just the thought of having to make small talk with another person exhausted me.

"I know—I'm sorry. It's just that life gets so hectic—" I stood up and walked over to the Keurig. I needed to tell her, if for no other reason than to get it off my chest. Maybe she knew of a doctor I could see. "Do you want a coffee?"

She shook her head vigorously and sighed. "No, thank you. God, I really thought it would be better the second time around with the food aversions, you know?"

I froze with my hand resting on a coffee mug as I reeled from the news. "You're—you're pregnant?"

My vision blurred as I stared into the cabinet, refusing to turn around and face her. I was a complete coward.

"Yeah. Mike didn't tell you? David said he told him on your birthday—and here I was, wondering why you hadn't said anything! Stupid pregnancy hormones making me overthink every little thing." If she suspected I was anything other than happy for her, her voice didn't give it away.

Of course, Mike hadn't told me. He knew exactly what it would have done to me. After everything we'd been through together, he was not going to be the one to inflict that wound.

I took a deep breath and forced a smile before turning back around. "I can't believe it. Kaden's going to be a big brother—do you know what you're having?"

Elizabeth's smile disappeared, and her eyes widened in alarm. "Lauren, are you crying?"

I tried to shake my head, but more tears gathered in my eyes. "I'm just—I'm just so happy for you."

The stool scraped across the floor as she climbed down and came over, pulling me into her arms without another word. "There's a reason he didn't tell you. Oh my god, I'm such a moron. I should've given him a head's up that I was going to be stopping by."

My tears dropped one by one onto her shirt. "No, seriously. I'm so happy for you both. I just got off my period so everything makes me cry—no *Hallmark* channel for me right now!" I laughed, even as my heart shattered.

She eyed me skeptically. "You're sure?"

I nodded and tore a paper towel off the roll, holding it under my eyes as a catchall. "Oh my goodness, look at the time. I forgot I'm supposed to meet with the tile guy about redoing the downstairs bathroom. I've got to go."

I walked toward the front door and held it open for her.

"Lauren—" she tried.

I waved my hand. "I'm fine. Stop asking. I just have to get over to meet with him. Call me this weekend and we'll work on stuff for a baby shower. It'll be great."

"Okay," she mumbled, still eyeing me with concern.

"Okay. Take care." I slammed the door and locked it as the timer went off in the kitchen. On legs that no longer felt like they belonged to me, I pulled the cake from the oven and set it on the counter to cool.

Then I wandered into the living room, anxiety wreaking havoc on my brain. An anguished sob burst from my chest, quickly followed by another. Until I was wailing. I'd been able to control so much—had worked so hard to not be seen as a victim, while taking active steps to move on with my life. But I couldn't control my own damn body. I pulled a blanket from the chair and curled up into the fetal position on the couch, letting my tears bathe the fabric, until exhaustion pulled me under.

CHAPTER THIRTY-SEVEN

Lauren: October 2016 (Age: 30)

"*M*ijita, open your eyes." *Abuelita's* sharp voice forced me back to consciousness.

I blearily opened one eye and then the other.

"What has happened?" she asked, peering into my face. Little Ricky popped up over her shoulder, along with a woman I didn't recognize, and I jumped back in fright.

"Jesus Christ! How did you get in here?"

Abuelita made the sign of the cross before answering. "We have come with *la curandera*." She wiped the still damp tears from my cheeks and pulled me into her bosom. "Come here, my LoLo. It's okay."

I didn't know what a *curandera* was and was still more than a little confused about how she and Little Ricky had gotten into the house. But being in her arms dredged up the events from earlier, causing me to fall apart all over again.

Her hands moved up and down my back—it felt so nice to just be held and comforted.

The strange woman muttered something in Spanish, her voice raspy with age. Little Ricky turned to her and nodded before looking back toward the front door. "Torch, we're going to need your help for this."

I broke away from *Abuelita*. "What's happening? Why are you all here?"

Little Ricky grinned. "We're here to get you knocked up. She promised me tamales if I helped. Same for Torch."

I immediately scooted away from him on the couch with a look of horror, shaking my head vehemently. "Oh, no. No, no, no!"

Abuelita interrupted my little rant. "LoLo, they are not here to make you pregnant. You need to listen to me—I know you cannot conceive. *La curandera* is here to help—I just needed the men for the *¿como se dice?* Heavy lifting. We are going to perform a fertility ritual to help open your womb."

I hadn't told her I was having problems—I hadn't even verbally told my own husband. How had she found out? Nobody else knew we hadn't used protection in over a year. Maybe she'd gone through the trash?

I massaged my temples, briefly wondering if all of this was a hallucination caused by my depression. "*Abuelita*, you cannot just show up at people's houses and demand to perform fertility rituals on them."

The *curandera* began walking around the room, picking up various knickknacks and turning them over in her hands. *Abuelita* frowned. "Lauren Gloria Santiago-McGuire-Sullivan, I am an old woman and you are my only grandchild. Is it too much to ask that I receive the blessing of a great-grandchild before I die?"

I cocked my head to the side. My middle name was not Gloria, nor would she be considered elderly by any stretch of the imagination. "You're only sixty-five, woman!"

She nodded, as Torch and Little Ricky backed slowly out of the room, clearly not willing to offer me any sort of help in the matter. "*Sí*, and your *Abuelo* wasn't even given that, so humor me?"

The strange woman clapped her hands together and began speaking in rapid Spanish. I looked to *Abuelita* to translate, but it was Little Ricky who spoke.

"The healer wants to know if you have any fertility—" His serious expression fell away and he choked with laughter. "Or phallic sculptures."

At *Abuelita's* stern expression, he transformed back into his role of innocent bystander immediately, all traces of humor gone from his face. Torch was staring out the front window earnestly, completely avoiding making eye contact with anyone in the room.

I owned a lot of phallic sculptures... how was I not pregnant?

All kidding aside, I wasn't even sure how a statue was supposed to help me get pregnant. I shook my head and *Abuelita* patted my hand.

The healer came over to me and placed her hands on my abdomen. Heat shot out from her fingertips, warming my skin better than any heating pad. She nodded at *Abuelita* and I could only catch a few words as she began chattering away again in Spanish.

Abuelita's hands came up to her face as she gasped at the healer's words.

"What? What's wrong?" I looked over at Little Ricky when she didn't answer.

He frowned. "*Mi sirenita*, the healer says that you became afflicted when you were a child. Your body has been spooked and cannot bear children."

Despite my unwillingness to buy anything the woman was selling; my lip began trembling, and I teared up again. "I'm broken?"

She looked at me and nodded as she spoke. I looked around furtively for someone to translate.

Abuelita gripped my shoulder. "You have never known stability, *mijita*. *La curandera* says the body has only known how to exist in chaos and in chaos it will remain. Your heart knows that you have made a home with your husband, but the body and mind are still dealing with the past trauma." She paused and listened for a moment before nodding. "We must align all three and only by doing so can we convince the womb that it is safe for a child."

I wanted to laugh the four of them right out the door, but somewhere deep inside of me, her words clicked. I had grown up in an unstable environment—something she'd obviously picked up on just by laying her hands on me.

I took a deep breath. "What do I have to do to fix it? I'm not having sex with Little Ricky. I just want to put that out there now."

He gave me a suggestive wink and puckered his lips. "You would be pregnant within minutes. Maybe consider that before you turn it down."

"That's enough—do you want the tamales, *o vas a seguir hablando?*" *Abuelita* placed her hand on her hip.

"*Sí*, I want the tamales."

"Okay then, we are ready to begin. I will run the bath. Dave, you need to boil water for the tea. Little Ricky, you will set up the massage table."

Abuelita launched into action, dragging me along behind her. She plugged the drain and began dumping various herbs into the water. "You just had your monthly visit, yes?"

I nodded, still more than a little nervous about what it was I was going to have to do and wondering how in the hell my grandmother knew my cycle as well as I did. "Um, what is the healer going to do? Is it invasive?"

She cupped my cheek in her weathered hand. "*Mijita*, take a deep breath. This will be like a spa day."

She stepped out while I undressed and slipped into the water. The smell of the herbs mixed with the steam enveloped my senses, leaving me with a surreal sense that this wasn't an absolute waste of my time.

I was just planning on baking a cake today. I totally had time for a fertility ritual, right?

Abuelita slipped back into the bathroom with a towel in her hands. She even went as far as insisting on drying me off like a small child before handing me a t-shirt and a pair of sweatpants and leading me out onto the landing.

The healer closed her eyes and breathed deeply. Everything about her was deeply intense. It was as if she saw past the physical and straight into my soul. Her heavily lined face split into a grin after a few moments and she nodded, stating that it was time to begin.

It was the first thing to come out of her mouth that I actually understood. She took my hand in hers and helped me up onto the massage table with a strength a woman her age shouldn't have possessed. She lifted the edge of my t-shirt until it was right under my breasts. I prayed Mike didn't decide to come home early, because this would have been impossible to explain.

I was having enough trouble understanding it myself.

Torch came up the stairs with a coffee mug in one hand and a bowl in the other. The healer took both from him and began arranging things near my feet. He did the weird staring off into the distance thing again.

"Torch."

He continued staring at the wall.

"Torch," I tried again. "Look at me."

He glanced back reluctantly.

"Um, can we keep this whole thing between ourselves? No telling Mike... or Grey... or anyone. Okay?"

He nodded and gave me a small smile. "You got it. I'll just, uh, be downstairs—"

Abuelita shook her head. "Dave, stay. We need to align her body before she can begin." She looked over the railing. "Little Ricky, come up here."

I noticed he shared the same expression as Torch when he came stomping up the steps. She must have promised them a hell of a lot more than tamales for this.

The healer gave instructions to Little Ricky, and he shook his head before muttering, "Not again."

"What?" I asked hesitantly. It was going to get weird. I knew it.

He pointed toward the stairs. "She's going to align your body. We did this before, for my *Tía* Mary. She got knocked up right after."

I looked at the stairs and back at him. "How is she going to align me?"

Abuelita chimed in. "Dave and Little Ricky will hold your legs so that *la curandera* can work easily."

I tried to sit up, but the healer pushed me back down with her superhuman strength. "So, like upside down?"

They both nodded, and I sighed before agreeing. I'd lost my damn mind. The healer handed me the coffee mug that Dave had carried upstairs, urging me to drink. It had more herbs floating around in it and tasted like flowers.

The next few hours were a blur. The healer spoke a blessing over me before rubbing my body with an egg wrapped in basil. From there,

Torch and Little Ricky held my legs so that she could pound the bottoms of my feet with a mallet. I was a bit disoriented from the rush of blood to my head by the time we got to the massage.

She spoke in a faint voice as she dug into my abdomen and I cried out. Her hands were like fire on my skin, scorching me, and I had the strangest sensation that she was pulling something from my body. I either fell asleep or passed out before it was over and awoke to *Abuelita* peering anxiously at me.

"How do you feel?"

I started to tell her that her healer had made things worse, but the pain in my abdomen was gone. My body felt strange—unfamiliar, even. I gave her a small nod, and she helped me up. Torch and Little Ricky were nowhere to be found, and the healer was packing her things as if it was just another day at the office for her.

She asked *Abuelita* a question and my grandmother began stumbling over her words as she tried to respond. "We did—I do every year for the ones we have lost. Was—how did you?"

The healer smiled so widely that her eyes crinkled before replying, "*Ella es bendecida por La Virgen.*"

Abuelita was so overcome with emotion that she could only nod before making the sign of the cross again over her chest. I waited until the woman left before asking what it was she'd said.

All I got out of her was, "*Día de los Muertos*—your *mamá*—she heard my prayers," before she said she had to go. "I frosted the cake for you. You are all set for Michael's birthday. I put his gift in the kitchen." She kissed me on the cheek and left me standing in shock in the middle of the living room, trying to regain my bearings.

For the first time in months, the fog lifted, and I felt the stirrings of desire. Depression had buried a lot of those feelings, forcing me to rely on my need to conceive in order to 'get the job done.'

I didn't know exactly what the curandera had done, but I felt weightless. Maybe it was all in my head and nothing was different—like some sort of placebo effect.

I heard the front door and jumped up just as Mike walked in. He didn't see me and I watched him as he opened the closet and hung up his coat before pulling his gun from his shoulder holster, placing it on the small table near the door.

My heart beat a little faster when he turned and saw me.

"Hey, baby. You're up." He grinned.

I nodded, my chest rising and falling rapidly. I'd never wanted him more than I did in this moment.

I crossed the room and jumped into his arms. He made a sound of surprise before his arms locked protectively around me. My hands moved from his neck and up into his hair, as if searching for something, before they settled on the sides of his face.

He was rough. The hands that cupped my body had taken lives; his eyes had seen things that could never be unseen. Yet, deep in his chest beat a heart that was good, despite the world he lived in.

Mike looked up, and I saw it—a softness he reserved only for me. A monster only I could tame. My thumb traced along his lower lip before I brought my mouth down to his. Instead of taking it for granted, I lost myself in the way his lips yielded to mine and his arms tightened their grip, drawing me in.

I'd had him so many times, but it never got old.

He nipped along my jawline, and I arched my neck, giving him better access. My hands were restless again, so I pushed the suit jacket from his shoulders, needing to feel his skin against mine. He must've had the same idea because he set me down on my feet and pulled my t-shirt off in one move. I fumbled with the buttons on his dress shirt as his hand slipped into my sweatpants.

My back hit the wall in the entryway with a thud, but he never paused. I moaned and gave up my efforts as his fingers pushed inside, stroking. His mouth moved down to latch onto my bare skin, his teeth grazing my nipple, sending me through the ceiling.

"Mike," I panted as his fingers moved faster. My mouth went slack and black spots danced before my eyes as he milked the orgasm from my body.

Cool air hit me as he pulled his hand free and yanked my sweats down before reaching for his belt buckle. I stopped him with a shaky hand. "Let me."

He exhaled slowly and nodded as I kicked my pants across the hardwood floor and dropped to my knees. Seeing him standing above me in an unbuttoned shirt and dress pants that were tented from his erection sent a surge of white hot heat coursing through my body.

I took a mental picture, wanting to keep the image of his rippled muscles and swirls of ink inside my head forever. Luckily, I got his pants down on my first try. I brought my hands up and ran them lightly down his torso, just to watch his reaction. His hips rocked forward so slightly that I didn't think he was even aware he'd done it.

I pressed my lips to his boxers, feeling the hardness of him against my mouth. He groaned, bringing his hands up to rest on the wall. "Jesus, Red. You're killing me here."

I smiled at the compliment and hooked my fingers under the waistband, inching them down slowly. His hips rolled forward again as his breath quickened. His cock glistened under the light and I stroked up and down his length before tentatively licking the moisture from the tip of him.

"Fuck," he cursed, rattling pictures as he pounded his hand against the wall.

I took him fully in my mouth and watched as every muscle in his body went taut. I'd never considered the possibility that I'd get pleasure from going down on him, but his facial expressions had me turned on more than I thought physically possible.

I relaxed and took him in fully, stroking and sucking. He dropped his gaze down to me just as I touched myself with my free hand.

"Goddamn, baby. I need to be inside of you." His arms hooked underneath mine, pulling me back up his body. His shirt fell from his shoulders as he lifted me up and pushed inside roughly.

My body began buzzing almost immediately. I clenched down around him with a small cry—wanting to savor it, to make it last, but my need for him was too strong. The heels of my feet dug into his back as I pulsed around him and his thrusting became erratic, his breath catching in his throat as he stretched my body.

"Come inside of me," I moaned, as if we hadn't been doing just that for the last year—as if it was our first time together.

The air crackled from the electricity between us—unbridled and wild. Even the sky rumbled, lightning streaking across the glass.

Mike's hands tangled in my hair, forcing my face toward his. He groaned against my lips as he found his release before his legs gave out and we sank down to the floor, breathing heavily.

"Happy Birthday," I managed to get out as I rested my head against his chest, listening to his heart as it slowed.

His chest rumbled as he chuckled. "Best. Present. Ever." He leaned up and pressed a kiss to my hair before frowning. "But Red, why do you smell like a fucking salad?"

CHAPTER THIRTY-EIGHT

Grey: December 2016 (Age: 52)

"I want to know where those photos came from. Is Kate even safe here? Fuck, maybe we have Mikey put her back in that holding facility—"

Jarvis cut me off. "Grey, I'm tracing the IP address. Trust me, we'll find these guys. Sullivan says she's safe here. If that changes, we'll move her and Dakota somewhere else."

I glanced back toward the closed bedroom door and whispered, "You think the doctor she married had somethin' to do with this?"

"I've run him through everything. Not counting his crazy ex-wife, the guy's completely clean."

"Bet that really chaps your ass, don't it, Jarvis?" I clicked my tongue against my teeth.

"I'm not following."

"Never mind. We look into the ex-wife? Maybe she had something to do with the pictures?"

The guys at *Inked* had reached out after photographs of Kate popped up in their inbox. It was bad enough knowing she'd run off to marry a man she barely knew, but seeing full-color images of the two going at it in a hotel elevator was enough to send me to an early grave.

Me, and anybody else who saw them.

"Uh, the ex-wife checks out too. Well, other than the whole trying to get Kate sent to prison thing."

I ground my teeth together. "And you can bet your ass as soon as I take care of this, I'll be handlin' that shit."

Jarvis gnawed at the corner of his lip before admitting, "Well, uh, it's been handled... already."

I raised an eyebrow. "Is that so? Care to explain to me who gave the motherfuckin' orders on that one?"

"Uh, your Ol' Lady... sir. She called in Knight—"

I let out a low whistle. "The British Butcher? Shit, between the two of 'em, I'd say they have it completely covered."

Knight was a Nomad known for dismembering club enemies while they were still alive, and the only other man who seemed to get off on torture as much as I did.

He'd earned every bit of his nickname but had a soft spot for Celia and would have done anything she asked.

"What else? Did you get a copy of her medical records? Tell me she ain't knocked up."

Jarvis's jaw tightened, and I wondered if I would have noticed had I not known about him and Kate.

"She's not pregnant, but she does have pneumonia, which could've been caused by any number of things—none of them related to the Sons. Although, the more I think about it, the more I'm startin' to think that Kate wasn't their intended target." He opened his laptop. "Look at these—"

"Fuck, Jarvis. You think I wanna see those again?"

"Just hear me out here. I want you to look at these images again and tell me who it looks like to you. You knew it was Kate because I traced the images back to the hotel in Vegas, but what if I hadn't?"

I tried to ignore the fact that I was looking at my little girl and reluctantly lowered my eyes to the screen. "Yep. Still looks like Kate. Thanks for—"

He pressed a button and an image I'd never seen before filled the screen. It was grainier than the others, as if it had been taken with a different camera. "This is the original. I simply ran them through my software to sharpen them like the others you've seen, but tell me, who does this look like?"

"It looks like Kate's mama."

Jarvis nodded. "Exactly. I think these images were meant to make you think your Ol' Lady was with someone else."

The only thing that kept me sitting in my chair was the fact that my wife was with Knight.

"Why do they want her?"

He minimized the image while shaking his head. "I don't know why, but we're getting a lot closer to finding out who's behind this."

There was a loud knock at the door that had both of us reaching for our guns. I pointed toward the bedroom. "Stay with her."

When I saw who it was, I shoved my weapon back in the holster and threw open the door. He took several steps back at the sight of me, and I stretched my fingers, aching to lay hands on him.

"Is, uh, Kate here?"

"She's sick and needs her rest right now," I stated flatly.

Proving that love turned people into idiots, he tried stepping around me to get into the apartment. "Look, I'm her husband. Just let me check on her—I'm a doctor."

Giving up any pretense of being a nice guy, I planted my palm in the center of his chest and led him out onto her front porch with a growl. "Nate, can I call you Nate? Look, I don't wanna be that guy, but that's my baby girl in there. You feel me?"

His throat bobbed up and down in a swallow, and he nodded.

I took another step forward, enjoying the way he looked ready to jump out of his skin. "Now, I believe fair is fair, so I'm gonna give you a warnin'. Stay the fuck away from her. If she wants you, she'll come find you. Disregard that, and you'll find out just how bad Kate's 'biker daddy' is. Alright?"

Goblin had filled me in on the things he'd said to my little girl the last time they were together; the things he'd accused her of doing all because his ex-wife had been a psychotic bitch. If he wanted to pin shit on someone, I'd gladly step up and volunteer.

His face went ashen. I grinned and threw an arm over his shoulder, leading him down toward the parking lot. "Jesus Christ, Nate. You're shakin'. I didn't hold a gun to your head... yet."

"R-right. I'm just parked—" He pointed at multiple cars. "Over there. I—just tell her I hope she feels better."

"I won't," I said with a chuckle. "Ain't your goddamn secretary. Now, you might wanna get a move on before I change my mind."

The tires on his black BMW screeched across the parking lot, and I walked back upstairs, shaking my head. The old me would have killed him and told Kate he died.

I'd gotten soft.

Hell, maybe I was turning into Wolverine in my old age, giving out warnings and shit.

Jarvis met me at the front door. "Was that him?" I nodded, and he grinned. "Wish I could've seen the look on that asshole's face. Are we sendin' him to the Reaper?"

"Nah, Jarvis. Poor fucker's in love."

He slammed his laptop shut, the muscles in his neck straining as he nodded. "Well, Sullivan called while you were downstairs. He said it's best if we go without colors for the time being. And, uh, he's runnin' a trace on that IP address. Between the two of us, we should have something shortly. If you've got this, I'll just take off."

"Yeah," I agreed. "I've got this under control. You just head back to the clubhouse." Feeling like an asshole for pushing his buttons, I added, "Really appreciate all that you've done for her, Jarvis."

"Thanks, Pres."

I locked the front door before going back to the armchair. It was pointless. I was up again within seconds, unable to sit still.

"Nate?" The handle on the bedroom door rattled, and Kate appeared, using the wall to support herself. Her dark hair was drenched in sweat, and her usually bright green eyes were glazed from fever.

She might've been the spitting image of her mama, but as she stumbled toward me, all I could see was my little girl.

Daddy, can you come to my tea pawty?

I crossed the room to her. "Katydid, let's get you back to bed."

She shook her head and stabbed a finger toward the front door. "No... it's Nate."

"Sweetheart, you're not well. You need to be restin'."

"Jolly Giant," she croaked. "I'm fine. See?" She managed two steps before falling into the back of the couch and then collapsing onto the carpet in a flood of tears. Her hands dug at the fibers like she was building a sandcastle.

Daddy, I builded a towah all by myself. Don't bweak it!

I lifted her in my arms, but she didn't struggle, just watched me with a curious expression on her face. I'd forgotten how her cat-like eyes seemed to bore right through my skull as if reading my thoughts.

"Grey?" she whispered, and I pressed a kiss to the top of her head, suddenly fighting back the tears. When Dakota told Celia she wanted a relationship with me, I'd been ecstatic. But with Kate, things were different.

She'd known that fairy tales were bullshit since the age of six; had been forced to learn that her heroes weren't invincible.

Daddy, hold me on yew awm like Spidewman...

"I've got you, Katydid. You're not makin' any sense. Let's get you back in bed."

I gently laid her back in bed before bringing the blankets up to her shoulders and pushing them under her body like a burrito. It was just like before, only she was twenty-six, not six.

Fat tears rolled down her cheeks as she looked up at me. "Nate... where did Nate go?"

"Nobody's been here but me."

She shook her head sternly, and I half-expected her hand to pop out from under the covers, going straight to her hip. "I saw him. Nate. He was here, and he wanted to take care of me."

I wanted to take care of her.

It was no one else's job but mine.

I sat down and, ignoring the fact that she was as warm as an oven, pulled her body up against my chest. "I think you're hallucinatin', darlin'."

When she was four, she'd had the flu, and I'd stayed awake all night, holding her in my arms, just like I was now. Her shoulders shook as she released an anguished sob and I tightened my grip, wishing like hell I could take her pain away. Any good feelings I had about letting Nate live were gone, leaving my monster aching for a kill.

"Which one heard voices? Was that Sylvia Plath or Virginia Woolf?"

Jesus, she was her mother's daughter.

I chuckled. "Well, I think it was Virginia Woolf. In your case, though, I'd blame it on pneumonia and not any mental break on your end."

"So Nate hasn't been here at all?"

I chewed on the inside of my cheek, debating on whether to tell her the truth. I badly needed a cigarette, but would wait until I was away from Kate. I wasn't doing anything that would make her worse.

My lower back ached from the position, and I toed off my boots before pulling her closer and settling back against the pillows. "There was someone who dropped by earlier—dressed like a cowboy? You were sleepin', and I didn't want to wake you."

"That was Garrett, Nate's brother. Nate must've not told him I'm insane yet."

It was official.

I was sending Nate to the Reaper.

My jaw tightened. "You know, when you were a little girl, you would refuse to go to bed until you'd had a bedtime story. Your mama would offer to read it, and you'd throw a fit—it had to be me. You loved for me to read comics to you—"

Daddy, wead this one!

"I think you're mixing me up with Dakota."

I shook my head, recalling the exact face she used to make to get what she wanted. She'd always had me completely wrapped around her finger. "No, it was you. Dakota wasn't even around then. You were picky about them too. You always requested the same comics. They had to be Spiderman, or they were no good. I once asked you why, and do you know what you told me?"

"Not a clue," she rasped before coughing into her hand.

I rubbed her back until it passed before continuing. "You told me you liked him because he wasn't perfect. He lost his uncle and the love of his life, but you said somethin' that day that's always stuck with me: 'he's been through so much, but he just keeps tryin' to do the right thing—even when it would be easier to give up.' You've always had a soft spot for broken things, Katydid. I can't imagine that Nate is much different. You were drawn to Peter Parker's story because it's your story, too."

Fuck, I sounded like I was selling her on the idea of staying with the prick.

"No, I'm uptight. Rigid. Unyielding—nothing like your friendly neighborhood Spiderman. Just Not So Fun Kate. What a terrible superhero I'd make."

I growled, "No matter what life has thrown at you, you've taken it all in stride, knowing that with great power comes great responsibility. You were Dakota's keeper when your mama left, but you don't need to do that anymore. You've shouldered that burden for too long—if I would've known things were that bad, I would've stepped in a long time ago."

She fell silent before asking, "What are you going to do? Shower me in money? Break anyone who crosses me? Because I've got quite the list, starting with my grandparents. And then Nate... obviously."

Kate could've named anyone, and I would've put them down for her. Her grandparents had yet to be held accountable for their actions, but their day of reckoning was coming.

Regardless of my take on the matter, I chuckled at the thought of her raising a hand to anyone. "I don't think you're cut out for this lifestyle, kiddo. Hell, there are days I don't think I'm cut out for it. Sleep, Katydid. I'm going to get you some more medicine."

Another coughing fit took over, and her body jerked violently against my chest. When it passed, she whispered, "You know, I'd argue with you, but I feel like dying. I can't handle one more thing. Grey, I am so tired. Tired of feeling guilty... tired of constantly being pulled in fifteen different directions. If I'm honest, I'm tired of living this life."

I squeezed my eyes shut and nodded, feeling as if a knife had lodged itself in my chest. There was no free will... never had been. No matter how much I fought it now, her course had been set before she was out of elementary school.

Just like her mama, she'd given up her own dreams to chase

someone else's. For Celia, it had been mine. For Kate, it was her sister's.

We might have come from different places, but I knew what it meant to feel trapped. We were backed into a corner, scrambling to find a way out. I tightened my hold on her body, wishing like hell that I was a man who deserved to be her father.

Daddy, you awe squeezing me.

The broken pieces of my heart fell from my eyes and onto her face, causing her to blink up at me in confusion for a few seconds before her eyes drifted shut.

"Daddy's here now." I kissed her damp hair as I rocked her in my arms. "Ain't got much of a plan yet, but I'm gonna get us out of this, Katydid. You just rest and let me take over for a while."

While she slept fitfully in my arms, I stepped inside the confessional and laid my soul bare. I found I didn't need a priest or a formal prayer as I prayed my Act of Contrition; the pain fell easily from my lips with every word.

There was no absolution for souls like mine, but in desperation, knowing there was a slim chance anyone upstairs would hear me, I recited the words I hadn't spoken since I was ten. "Hail Mary full of Grace, the Lord is with thee. Blessed are thou among women and blessed is the fruit of thy womb Jesus. Holy Mary Mother of God, pray for us sinners now and at the hour of our death."

Time was running out.

I couldn't do it on my own anymore.

CHAPTER THIRTY-NINE

Grey: December 2016 (Age: 52)

"Grey?"

I jerked awake, blinking, until the room came into focus. I'd fallen asleep in my office again.

I pressed my fingers against my stiff neck and tried shifting it from side to side before grumbling, "What is it, Jarvis?"

He held up his laptop, and I gestured for him to come in. There was an excitement in his eyes that I hadn't seen in years, and I leaned across the desk, suddenly wide awake. "You found them."

"I did—well, Sullivan and I did. Their proxy was shit."

Sensing I wasn't following, he clarified, "A proxy server is kinda like *Inked on Broadway*. It looks like a tattoo shop, but really, it's a front for the club. The proxy masks their location and could ping anywhere in the world, making it impossible to track. Normally, we use high anonymity proxies to keep everything under the radar."

I scratched at my forehead with a nod, trying to keep up. "So, how'd you do it then?"

"They used a transparent proxy," he said with a grin, before once again realizing I didn't know what the hell he was getting at. "It means that they told the website that they were a proxy, but it passed along their actual IP address, anyway. It'd be like putting a sign out in front of Inked that said, 'Tattoos, but also money laundering.' Took some digging, but we got their location narrowed down to a single block."

I jumped up. "I want eyes on that block. We can ride—"

"Pres," Jarvis said calmly. "We already got Nomads in place, per your orders."

"How? I didn't even know."

He tapped the screen and enlarged a surveillance image. When I saw their colors, I slammed my fist against the desk. "Goddammit. It was the motherfuckin' Serpents sendin' pictures of my daughter?"

"That's not all." Another image filled the screen, and I moved until my nose was almost touching it. I knew damn well I needed glasses, but was too stubborn to do anything about it. He enhanced the resolution until every patch on the kutte became crystal clear. "We got Cobra."

"They still down around the Houston area?"

His grin widened. "Nope. They wanted to be where the action was. I pinged 'em about an hour north of Amarillo. Gives us plenty of time to get there, take care of shit, and get you back in time for Dakota's wedding tomorrow..." He checked his watch. "Or I guess tonight, as it's after midnight now."

I glanced up at the light knock on my open office door, surprised by the two men standing in the doorway. "The fuck are you two doin' down here?"

Angel stepped inside while Wolverine remained where he was. "They're my girls... now and forever."

Wolverine nodded somberly. "We're ridin'. Been a few years since I laid eyes on 'em, but they're just as much family as my jackass sons. Someone crosses 'em, they've crossed me."

Sliding open my desk drawer, I retrieved a cigar and lit the end, fighting the urge to run and bury my face in a mountain of blow. I knew I needed a clear head, but I also needed the feeling of invincibility I'd only ever found with drugs.

This was the last of the men who'd hurt my wife. I'd given Celia the other two. This one was all mine. Ending him wouldn't stop the war with the Sons, but it would end the one I'd battled for sixteen years.

"Jamie," Wolverine said as he moved in front of me, planting his fists against the wooden desk. "We'll finish it like we started it. Together."

His words calmed the cravings better than the cigar, and I pushed my shoulders back with a firm nod. "Let's do it, old man. Let's send those motherfuckin' snakes to the Reaper for the last time."

I spent most of the ride up past Amarillo trying to account for any obstacles the Serpents could use against us and strategizing ways we'd be able to beat them.

Jarvis slipped out in front and led us within blocks of their hideout. "Nomads moved out an hour ago and formed a perimeter. Nobody's come in or out."

I checked and re-checked my gun as we moved. The building was silent as we approached, and I glanced over at Comedian. "This seem strange to you?"

He nodded. "Not a fuckin' prospect in sight."

"Could be a trap," Bear added, warily watching the grimy windows for signs of life.

My muscles tightened in readiness, even with all the variables in play. The monster in me craved a good fight, but I didn't like ambushes; didn't like not knowing what I was walking into.

"Nomads are sure they're here?" I asked Jarvis.

He checked his phone and nodded. "We've got a sniper nearby that is confirming no one has exited the building."

"But did anyone even fuckin' go in?" Wolverine snapped. "Place looks like a goddamn ghost town."

We moved around the building, but Wolverine was right, it was as if we were in the wrong place. "Check again, Jarvis," I demanded.

"Grey, they're here. If you wanna wait 'em out..."

"No. We're endin' it tonight." I raised my hand up. "Move in."

My skin began to crawl, and I tightened my hold on my gun when I realized a door near the back was sitting wide open.

None of this felt right.

Comedian moved toward it in a crouch before lowering his gun with a shake of his head. "Fuck!"

I quickly realized why. Serpents littered the ground, their bodies contorted in ways that shouldn't have been physically possible. The scent of death hung heavy in the air, but there wasn't a drop of blood anywhere.

"It's like motherfuckin' Jonestown around here," Crossbones noted as he picked up an empty shot glass.

Glass crunched under a boot, and we immediately turned, weapons raised.

"That's right." A man stepped into view, holding a blade to a Serpent's throat. "You wanna drive out a nest of snakes, go after the fuckin' rats first. A little strychnine and all your problems are solved."

We'd killed many people over the years, but had given most of them a fair chance at fighting back. Poisoning was a coward's way of putting a man down; something best left to bored housewives looking to move on to their next husband.

Wolverine didn't flinch. "You're wearin' the kutte of a prospect. You turned on your own brothers?"

He shrugged and moved close enough for me to see the patches on his hostage's kutte.

Cobra.

I didn't give a fuck if he put a million Serpents down, but that one was mine.

"Give him up and we'll let you go," I said, feigning disinterest. "Don't give a fuck what you did to them, but that one crossed my club."

"See, I don't think you will." He shifted forward, and Cobra winced before making eye contact again; pleading for me to save him.

He was facing the Reaper but begging for Hades.

I yawned, knowing full well I was going to put a bullet in both of them the first opportunity I had. "You just did me a favor. Way I see it, you no longer have a club. Hand over your Pres and join me. We share the same enemy."

The man grinned up at us. "Partner, that sounds like a great plan. There's just one problem—"

Cobra opened his mouth and tried to speak, but the words came out garbled as the blood spilled over onto his lips.

They'd cut out his tongue.

"The Sons don't negotiate." He ran the blade across Cobra's throat and shoved his body toward us before turning his back on us, casually walking away.

I took the headshot and dropped him mid-step before looking around in confusion. "The fuck just happened?"

Comedian stepped over bodies and turned the man over, firing another round through his forehead before relieving him of his kutte. "Prospect," he roared.

Alex reluctantly walked over. "Yes, Comedian?"

"You asked me the other day why we strip search new recruits. Ain't 'cause we wanna fuck ya, it's 'cause we wanna make sure you don't fuck us. What's this look like to you?"

He knelt beside him. "It looks like the Sons' colors... sir."

Comedian cocked his head to the side and looked back at me. "Why the fuck wouldn't they have checked for that?"

Nothing made a goddamn bit of sense anymore.

I toed Cobra's body with my boot and studied his face, feeling as if there was something I was missing. There was a double-headed snake coiled around a ruby on his middle finger, but no sign of the ring he'd branded my wife with.

With a low growl, I ripped the kutte off and tucked it under my arm. It'd be the only trophy I got.

I should've felt some sense of victory, but the uneasy feeling I'd had since we arrived only intensified the longer I looked around. The Sons had played us, but why?

Why had they gone after the Serpents?

They'd been known club enemies of ours for as long as I could remember. If anything, the Sons should've partnered with them to take us down.

Bear's cell phone began vibrating, and he stepped outside.

"Torch, light it up," I sighed, before following him out.

"You got it, Pres."

Ending Cobra should've ended the threats against my family, but the Sons had been one step ahead, and for the first time in my life, I realized just how bad things truly were.

There was no way out.

Putting a gun in my mouth wouldn't save them. Killing every man who ever laid a hand on her wouldn't end this.

I'd dealt with one breakdown after another before sobering up; had always been one step away from destroying my own life.

It never mattered.

The game changed once I got clean, but so did my responsibilities. The kid who couldn't see anyone past himself was gone, replaced by a man who knew what was at stake and who was counting on him.

Bear ended the call and ran a hand over his face. "That was Goblin. Carnage was shot—"

"Celia—"

"Is fine," he hurriedly added. "Goblin's got her, but he's sayin' Carnage was ridin' with colors... explain that."

I couldn't.

I finally understood what she'd had been trying to communicate to me after Dakota was arrested. She'd survived being beaten and raped, and never once admitted that she was afraid. Sure, she'd get jumpy over unexpected sounds, but anyone would've. I'd been convinced that there was nothing in the universe that could shake her.

Until that night.

She'd known then what we were up against and looked to me to be her stability... her defender. I'd survived Donald Quinn and gone up against clubs like the Sons without breaking a sweat, but the thought of doing anything that might hurt or put Celia's life at risk scared the fuck out of me.

I wanted to get them somewhere safe, but safe was a fairy tale; a bedtime story meant to help kids fall asleep. Places like that didn't exist in the real world.

They never had.

CHAPTER FORTY

Grey: December 2016 (Age: 52)

"We inserted a chest drain and his BP stabilized. He's sedated for now, but I'm going to watch him closely for the next hour." Nate addressed Mikey, doing everything he could to not make eye contact with me.

It was as if he knew I'd ignored the sign posted on the front doors that demanded I not enter the facility with a concealed handgun.

Although she'd had divorce papers drawn up, my daughter was still inexplicably married to the good doctor.

I sank back in the small hospital chair with a sigh. I couldn't shake the shit with the Serpents. It had eaten at me most of the drive down. There was something I was missing, but in my exhausted state, I couldn't figure out what it was.

"We've gone without colors and brought other chapters in, but the Sons have recruited everybody and their fuckin' mother for the sole purpose of outnumberin' us."

Mikey fidgeted with his wedding band before looking up at me. "No colors ever. Drop the kuttes. From there, we'll stake out what they're claiming is their territory and light 'em up."

I'd been fighting since I was sixteen. I wondered if I'd known what it was going to cost me then if I still would've sent Donald to the

Reaper. Maybe if I hadn't, I would've finished high school... gone to college.

I could've made something of myself; been a man who was worthy of Celia Cross.

The scenarios in my head had changed over the years, but she was my one constant. In a thousand lifetimes, I'd still choose her.

"Fuck, Mikey," I admitted. "I don't know how much longer we'll be able to hold on to that lower rocker."

I didn't want to fight anymore.

I wanted to be a husband; a father. The one thing I'd fought against my entire life I now craved.

I wanted to be a nobody.

His hands trembled, and he shoved them under his thighs with a small nod. "You know, there's a conversation we need to have."

I'd known the day was coming but had hoped it would take place under better circumstances, when I wasn't being pulled in fifty different directions.

He deserved better.

Mikey took my silence as hesitance and added, "Old man, I've listened to you my entire life. It's your turn to listen to me for once. We both know that you're my father and if Lauren figured it out based on our mannerisms alone, we're fucked."

I looked down at my boots. I should've known his wife was the one who'd made the connection. The girl was better than the FBI.

"It won't be long before others notice—my mother made it very clear if Comedian found out, all hell would break loose. Are you prepared to deal with that on top of everything else? Because I don't know that I am."

When I lifted my head, he was watching me intently, his chest rising and falling from exertion. If I'd just kidnapped him as a kid and moved us all out of the country, we could've been living on a beach somewhere, without a fucking care in the world.

"I was a fuckin' kid, Mikey. If I had it to do over again, I would've claimed you as mine from the beginning. I did my best to keep you safe from him, but I know I fuckin' failed you. I should have just put him in the ground when I had the opportunity."

As Mikey's eyes filled, I wished like hell I would've taken the shot the first time we went up against the Serpents.

I'm sorry, buddy. Daddy's so sorry.

"I know things look beyond fucked right now, but I'm going to do everything in my power to keep my family out of this—"

He clenched his jaw and nodded along, fighting to stay in control of his emotions. "Exactly what I was thinking. We could get the girls to a safe house, just until this blows over—"

"Mike—" I tried.

"I don't know that they'd listen right away, with Dakota getting married and all, but I think if they knew—"

"Mike—" I pushed out of the chair and dropped to my knees in front of him. "Listen to me—I said I was gonna do everything for my family. My entire family—includin' my firstborn." When he lowered his head, I reached up and gripped his shoulder. "Look at me, son."

He brushed away the tears with the back of his hand before meeting my gaze, and I squeezed tighter at the sight of his big blue eyes.

My eyes.

"I don't give a flying fuck what your birth certificate says. You're a Quinn, through and through. Known it since I first laid eyes on you. I have a plan, but what is it you always say?"

"A plan ain't shit if everybody knows about it," he finished with a sniff.

"I want you to run this club beside me."

I wanted no such thing, but needed to know he'd be open to living on the wrong side of the law if it came down to it. Something terrible was coming. It was no longer a question of if, but when.

He immediately shook his head. "I'm a fucking cop, Grey. In what realm does that pan out?"

It didn't.

In a perfect world, I never would've had to ask.

"Ain't no alternate universe where you could do both. It's one or the other—you've had to straddle that line for long enough."

I can't do this on my own, buddy.

Mikey sat back and scratched at his jaw. "I—I can't just make a decision like that on the spot. I've got Lauren to think about. In your line of work, you don't exactly make a lot of friends."

I grinned. "Same could be said about your job as well. Just think about it and let me know. Why don't you run on home and get some rest—I'll wait here for updates."

He stood up with a stretch. "Grey?"

"Yeah?"

"Tonight, with the wedding—wear a vest, okay?"

I froze. "You know something I don't?"

Not today.

I wasn't ready.

His shoulder lifted in a shrug. "Got it in good faith from Jeremy, uh, Jarvis, that the mole is going to show up tonight. In a room full of cops, he'll blend in perfectly. Just watch your back."

A rat in my clubhouse. Moles hiding behind badges.

I had to keep my family close.

"You're still going, right?" I asked, squeezing his shoulder again, needing the connection between us now that there were no secrets.

"Yeah," he said with a smirk. "And I'll be wearing a fucking vest, too. I want to make sure we coordinate, dammit."

Once he left, I wandered the halls of the hospital, unable to sit still. The stained-glass windows caught the first rays of sunrise, scattering colored light across the small chapel and drawing me in.

I sank down onto an empty pew and stared up at a large wooden crucifix near the front. Jesus's arms were stretched above his body; his chin resting against his chest as if he was simply sleeping.

The perfect sacrifice.

Hadn't that been what the church had beaten into my head as a kid?

When I was young, I recited the words and prayed the prayers, but it hadn't meant jack shit to me then. As a grown-ass man, I still didn't get it.

A father didn't sacrifice his son.

Sure, I'd heard the anecdotes—an operator forced to raise a moveable bridge, all while knowing it would crush his only son who'd been playing where he shouldn't have been but would save the lives of everyone on the boat below.

Fuck the people on the boat.

Fuck the Donald Quinns of the world who'd put their own needs above their children's.

I wasn't willing to lose one more person I loved. I'd climb up on that cross and sacrifice myself before I put them in harm's way.

"Oh, hello," the chaplain said as he entered. "I hope you haven't been waiting long."

"Father," I nodded, still looking up at the cross. It was supposed to represent sacrifice and redemption, but all I saw was a man who'd been abandoned in his hour of need by someone he relied on. A man whose prayers had fallen on deaf ears.

He shuffled into the pew next to me. "Are you here to receive Holy Communion? I'm afraid you're a little early, but—"

"I'm here for last rites, Father." I turned to him. "Is that something you can do?"

"Absolutely. Now, normally, the nurses will page us, and we'll come up to the room. I'm so sorry you had to leave your loved one's side and come down here. If you wouldn't mind sharing a little about them—"

I blinked back tears and looked away. "Ain't for someone else, Father. It's for me. Figure we better start with the confession... it's been forty-two years since my last one."

Sooner or later, your clock stopped, and that was it.

I'd cheated Death once, but any luck I had ran out a long time ago. The best I could hope for now was that I'd go to my grave with a clear conscience and some legacy to leave behind for my family.

Growing up, Ma had always told me that death would come like a thief in the night. This time, I was going to be ready for him.

CHAPTER FORTY-ONE

Kate: December 2016 (Age: 26)

Out of all the things I expected on my sister's wedding day, being locked out of the dressing room was not one of them. Her best friend, Ava, came out and apologetically informed me I would need to get ready elsewhere.

Running into my grandparents as they tried to sneak in a back door at the event center hadn't been high on my list of possibilities, either.

"Mary Katherine, there you are," Nan crowed. "Where have you been? I've been calling you for months now."

Her hair still had a faint purple tint to it and I suppressed a smile, knowing who was responsible. It was the coldness reflected in her eyes, though, that told me everything I needed to know.

She stole our money and didn't feel a shred of remorse.

"Nan. Pops," I said, my tone indifferent. "I didn't think you got an invitation."

Pops took in the decorated tables. "We didn't. Will you just tell us what's going on? Your Nan and I have done just about everything, trying to get in touch with you girls. When I saw the announcement in the paper, I told her we had to at least try. So, I'm here to say we're sorry for whatever we've done to upset the both of you."

I blinked rapidly, fighting against the lump in my throat. It had been there for so long; I was beginning to think it was a tumor. "Pops, I think you know why Dakota and I are so upset. Mama told us everything."

My grandmother's eyes bulged. "Your mother? What lies did she feed you this time? She's always tried to turn you away from us!"

Little Ricky rounded the corner, only to retreat immediately upon seeing the commotion.

Some help he was.

My fingernails dug into my palms, and I took a deep breath. "My mother sent money from the moment we moved in with you. Money to cover clothing, college, and cars. We never saw a cent, though. Oh, and my father is alive. Which part is a lie?"

Pops shook his head adamantly. "We never received money from your mother and had to dip into our retirement savings to keep you two as comfortable as possible. As for your father, he isn't exactly an upstanding citizen and your mother felt it best for you to believe he was dead. If we're guilty of anything, it's honoring her wishes."

I narrowed my eyes at Nan, giving her the sweeping once-over she'd often used on me and Dakota growing up. "Really?" I asked with a bitter laugh, jerking my thumb toward my grandmother. "Care to explain how she's afforded all her little surgeries and that expensive Cadillac?"

His face darkened, and a vein bulged in his forehead. "Mary Katherine, what your grandmother does is none of your damn concern! That money was an inheritance from a relative of hers that passed a few years back! Young lady, I ought to—"

"Ought to *what?*" a voice growled from behind me, raising the hairs on the back of my neck. "Choose your words carefully, old man. That's my baby girl you're speaking to."

Grey stepped in between us, and Nan's face drained of color. Even Pops stumbled back in fear.

"Which relative was it, Norma? Last I checked, not a single one of 'em had a pot to piss in."

"J-J-Jamie, we don't want any trouble," Pops stammered. "Mary Katherine was mistaken."

Jamie?

I really thought his name was Grey and had long assumed his parents were hippies who had a thing for the names of colors.

My father stood in a wide-legged stance, effectively blocking me from getting around him to defend myself.

"Dick," he said, keeping his voice low. "Kate ain't mistaken and I never for a minute thought you knew jack shit about what went on under your roof. But I'm out a fuck ton of money—money that was meant for my girls. Norma knows all about it, though, and she's gonna come clean, ain't she?"

Nan nodded shakily, lowering her head as she admitted, "I—I did it. I took the money."

Pops gasped. "Jesus, Norma! How much did you take? We can fix this. Please, let me make this right."

"The time for fixin' it is long gone—"

"I still have some of it left!" Nan interjected. "There was a lot—I put it in savings. I thought if I let it earn some interest, it'd be like it never happened. Please..."

My stomach churned, watching my grandparents beg for their lives. "Don't."

He jerked his head back and looked down at me in surprise. "Katy, what they put you and Dakota through?"

"Is over now. Let it go." I took a deep breath. "Daddy... please."

I tried not to think about how long it had been since I last said his name—tried not to think of the years we'd lost because of his lifestyle.

He froze at the term, nostrils flaring as he stared down at me. I saw the war raging in his eyes—the battle between ruthless biker and the man who had been my safe place for the first six years of my life.

"They're about to start," Little Ricky announced, popping his head around the corner.

I squeezed my father's arm, praying he made a decision he could live with.

Little Ricky escorted me back to the event center, practically bouncing with excitement. "You ready for this, Hail Mary?"

I forced a smile. "Sure. Let's just hope it lasts."

He stopped in his tracks. "Why would you say that? Escúchame— what Caparina and Big Guy have is the real thing. He'd do anything for her and vice versa. For all your education, you don't know a lot about love. It makes me sad for you."

"And what would you know about love?" I snapped. "Please enlighten me."

His eyes went dark with pain, and I regretted asking. "I was in love before. What's with the face? Are you surprised?"

I nodded dumbly.

"You think you're an expert on love, because you got burned, but you're not. When it's the real deal, nothing can stand in the way of it. Now, let's go. I ain't about to get my ass chewed out by Caparina, because you're late."

I tightened my grip on his bicep. "I'm sorry."

He squeezed me back. "Apology accepted. You and Nate will figure things out—just need to stop gettin' in the way of it first. Love can't be neat and tidy—"

"Well, it wasn't love," I quickly interjected. "It was just—"

He held a finger to my lips. "Shhh... you're not the love expert, remember? So, you know nada. Okay, good talk."

When the music started, I couldn't help but smile. It wasn't traditional, therefore perfect for my sister.

Zane stood like a statue with his hands clasped in front of his body, watching the back of the room with an expectant smile. Maybe Little Ricky was right—maybe they were perfect for each other and I couldn't see it because of my own broken heart.

After the ceremony, I'd apologize to both of them.

The doors opened and my smile faded when I realized it wasn't my sister coming down the aisle, but Little Ricky. People began murmuring when he reached Zane's side.

Zane leaned down to hear him before stiffening in response. Then he turned to me and growled, "What the fuck did you do, Kate?"

A collective gasp worked through the room, and my cheeks heated.

"Nothing!" I turned to Ava. "Was she fine when you left?"

The bridesmaid frowned. "She just said she needed a few minutes alone. What's going on?"

"She's gone," Zane said, almost too quietly to hear.

"Did she mention anything to you that would help us figure out where she is?" Little Ricky directed the question at me.

"No." I sank down onto a nearby step, recalling the things I'd said to her during the rehearsal the night before. Why had I taken it upon myself to warn her not to go through with the marriage just because she was pregnant?

Maybe she hadn't run—maybe she was still in the building.

"Wait, is Jeremy here? He could track her phone, right?"

Zane pulled me up and propelled me toward the exit, telling the confused guests, "Hey, we're having a slight technical difficulty. Excuse us for a moment."

"We're gonna find her and everything will be good. It will be—"

"What. Did. You. Say. To. Her?" he growled. "She wasn't right after your little chat last night."

I swallowed nervously. "Um... I just wanted to ensure she was getting married for the right reasons and not because she's pregnant—"

Zane's fist collided with the brick wall above me. I yelped and tried to squirm out of reach.

"Found her," Jeremy announced, holding up his laptop. I wondered if he took it everywhere and couldn't recall ever seeing him without it. "Her phone's pinging near the gym."

"I'll do it," I declared when they began bickering over who should go.

Zane snorted. "Sure, so you can convince her to leave town and change her name? You ruined what was supposed to be the best day of our lives."

I placed a hand on his arm, pleading, "Let me fix this, please!"

"Fine. Thirty minutes and then I'm coming after her on my own."

"I won't let you down, I promise," I said with a nod.

I hoped.

CHAPTER FORTY-TWO

Kate: December 2016 (Age: 26)

On the way to the gym, I tried coming up with a list of reasons Dakota needed to marry Zane. Most led back to the fact that he looked like Thor. One was because I didn't want him to kill me.

Dakota stood near a leg press machine in full wedding attire. When she saw me, her lips curved up into a wide grin. "Took you long enough to get here."

I tried to ignore the sinking feeling in my gut at seeing her so happy. There was a good chance she wasn't going to be coming back with me. "Why aren't you at the event center?" I asked tentatively. "You know, getting married?"

"I've got plenty of time to kill," she said with a careless shrug. "Thought I'd round up all the guests who hadn't RSVP-ed yet. You know how rude that is."

The gym was deserted. Not only was it a Friday night, but New Year's Eve. Most people were probably out partying.

I opened my mouth and then immediately closed it, not sure if it was even worth asking.

The satin on her dress swished as she walked over. "Remember when I told you Nate was your Bucky?"

I nodded, more than a little thrown off by the change in topic. "Yeah, and you said I was Black Widow. But then Grey said I was Spiderman, which just confused everything. You might have to reiterate your point."

"Spiderman?" she blurted, nose crinkling in disgust. "You aren't even a good climber! No, you're definitely Black Widow. So, Bucky and Natasha trained as assassins, brainwashed and used as weapons for years."

She paused to acknowledge my raised hand. "Uh, I've never been used to kill people, so..."

"Maybe not," she agreed with a grin. "But you're pretty dang uptight. I think it's because you're afraid—afraid to fall in love and lose control. I get it, I do. But what is it you always say? Fear is just a blanket—"

"Don't you dare psychoanalyze me, Dakota Mae," I snapped, ignoring the tears pooling in my eyes. "It was never going to work out between me and Nate. We're just too different."

"Why won't you let yourself be happy?" she sobbed. "What's wrong with someone wanting to take care of you?"

"Because when you love someone, they leave," I blurted, the words like poison on my tongue. I wasn't thinking of Nate, but of my parents. It seemed everyone I loved left me eventually. And even when they reappeared years later, it didn't make it hurt any less.

"I'm not Black Widow. And Nate's not Bucky. We're two messed up individuals who will never make it work. He left the first time because he trusted his ex-wife's word over mine. And maybe it makes me a coward, but I know I won't survive losing him a second time."

Dakota took my hands in hers. "You've both been used by people, Kate. Nate's ex-wife was a psycho crazy person, and he still tried to stay loyal to the vows he made—even when she used him and left his heart broken. You—you've had to take care of everybody since we were kids and I'm sorry for that. I'm sorry for the ways I used you—"

"Don't," I warned, the tears now flowing freely down my face. "Don't apologize—not to me."

"You wanna know the reason I love comics so much? It's because of all the broken heroes—the ones who redeem themselves in the end. Bucky and Natasha are at the top of the list because, despite all the bad they lived through, they continued to fight for the good."

I blinked to clear my vision and cleared my throat. "That—That's a lot to process—"

"He still loves you," she interjected. "Despite everything you two have gone through, he loves you. That's why he is and will always be, your Bucky."

I glanced around, as if the gym might magically alleviate my confusion. "How could you possibly know that?"

Dakota stepped back with a triumphant smile. "Who do you think I've been talking to this whole time?"

"But you left your own wedding... no one knew where you were. You came here? For him?"

"I left a note," she insisted, eyes suddenly widening in horror. "Biscuits and gravy, I didn't leave a note! Zane must think I—"

"Pulled a runaway bride," I helpfully finished for her. She gathered up her skirt and hurried toward the exit. "Wait—where's Nate?"

"Locker room," she muttered distractedly. "Said he needed to shower."

After urging her to get to the event center, I hurried to the locker room, my heart beating double time. I didn't know where to begin and wished I'd written something down. Dakota's speech had been eloquent and moving. I had nothing.

A man with gray hair stepped out of the sauna and I bypassed him, searching for the showers.

He tightened his grip on the towel slung around his waist. "Miss, you're in the—"

"Men's locker room. I know. I'm trying to find my husband."

Nate was right where Dakota promised he'd be. He shut off the water and stepped out of the shower to grab a towel,

Speech time. I was gonna say something great—*just as soon as I finished shamelessly drinking in the sight of him naked.*

"You know this is the men's locker room, yeah?" he asked when he caught my stare.

I shrugged and blurted, "Turns out, I don't even need alcohol to make poor decisions anymore."

He wrapped the towel around his waist with a raised brow. "Did you come all the way down here to tell me that?"

I sighed and tried again. "Is it true?"

"Is what true, Katy?" Instead of moving closer, he turned away.

A strand of hair fell from my updo, and I nervously tucked it behind my ear. "You still love me?"

He gave me his profile, his jaw tight with tension. "Does it matter at this point?"

"Answer the damn question," I demanded, refusing to give in to the sob in my throat.

"Yes!" he snapped. "You fucking happy now? You run so deep in my veins there's not a chance in hell I could ever get rid of you!"

I closed the gap between us, wrapping my arms around his warm body. "Then don't. Don't get rid of me. Stay."

He pulled back with a frown. "I got the divorce papers, babe. What's changed in the last two weeks? What—I'm supposed to just believe you want to stay now? You seemed pretty cozy with Jeremy last I checked."

I resisted the urge to walk out and held my head high as I told him, "Jeremy's nothing more than a friend—well, minus the one time before I met you. Look, maybe nothing's changed and we're still too damaged to make it work. Maybe this whole idea—"

"Let's do it right, then."

"What—what do you mean?" I asked, my head swimming in confusion.

His mouth split into a wide grin. "Let's get married, Katy girl. A real wedding—one we'll hopefully remember this time around. What do you say?"

I'd say I needed this man. *Badly*.

I kicked off my heels and launched myself into his arms. His hands came up to grip my ass, holding me steady as I wrapped my legs around his waist.

"I say yes," I breathed against his lips. "And also, what is the gym's policy on sex?"

He laughed and his mouth slid over with mine before he whispered, "Anything for you, babe."

Keeping his arms locked around me, he backed me against the wall. I shivered against the cold tiles on my back and the feel of his fingers brushing against my core. He tugged my panties to the side with a barely repressed growl.

"Tonight, when you're back in our bed, I'll go slow. I'm going to take my fucking time worshiping every inch of this body." His lips moved down the column of my throat. "But right now, I need to feel you around me."

"Please," I begged.

I'd missed everything about him. His voice, his smell, the way he touched me, just like—

I bit down on his shoulder with a moan, the edges of my vision already blurring. His hand moved between us, stimulating me—encouraging my body to open up for him.

"I'm close..." I whispered, feeling my inner muscles flutter around his length.

Taking it as a challenge, he rolled his hips forward, forcing me to take more—to take all of him. I gasped when his thumb and forefinger squeezed my clit before coming apart with a loud cry.

Nate's mouth sought mine, silencing my cries while he continued to push my body to the brink of another orgasm. I sucked his lip into my mouth to keep from screaming and he groaned, his thrusts becoming shallow.

The room faded away, and I saw stars. Well, and the old man from the sauna. But I was beyond caring at this point. Nate held himself deep, releasing a low growl as he chased his own release.

"I—I love you, babe," he panted, crushing me against the wall with his body.

I dropped my head onto his shoulder with a contented sigh. "I love you too, Nate. I don't want to navigate this life with anyone but you."

The older man cleared his throat. "And I'm happy for the two of you, but I'd really like a shower before the new year. Do you mind?"

"Guy, do you mind?" Nate snapped. "We're trying to have a moment here."

He threatened to call gym security before stalking toward the exit, grumbling about public fornication.

I dissolved into giggles. "We may have to find a new gym."

Nate glanced over at the clock on the wall. "Let's go, Katy girl. We missed the wedding, but if we hurry, we might still make the reception."

CHAPTER FORTY-THREE

Dakota: December 2016 (Age: 22)

I burst through the side door of the event center, shoes tucked beneath my arm. Several employees jumped back in fright, but I didn't slow down. I was late enough, as it was.

"Do not be alarmed," I said with a breathless wave and a British accent. "'Tis only me."

"Holy shit, you came back!" Little Ricky intercepted me as I rounded a corner, spinning me in a small circle. Then he set me back on my feet with a stern expression. "Why the hell did you run away?"

"I had some unfinished business," I panted, still out of breath from running. "And I forgot to leave a note explaining where I was. Where's Zane—is he still here?"

"Right here, Dakota." I turned to face him, my mouth immediately going dry. Even without a cape, he was the sexiest superhero around with his slate gray three-piece suit and golden waves of hair cascading down over his shoulders.

And he was all mine—just as soon as I cleared up some confusion.

"I meant to leave a note—"

He jerked his chin in a brisk nod. "You had second thoughts. Maybe we rushed this."

I ran a hand over his chest, stopping to pat his rock hard abdominal muscles. "Look at me, Big Guy. Do I look like a woman who's having second thoughts?"

He cupped my cheek in his hand, studying my eyes, as if trying to read my thoughts. "Babe, you look incredible. But you left and I—"

"I know," I blurted, resting my chin on his chest. "This is the happiest day of my life and call me crazy—I wanted to share it with my sister. So I may have gone out to get the happily ever after she deserves —superhero style."

Zane rolled his eyes with a chuckle, eyes sparkling with amusement. "Jesus, babe. You're absolutely insane, but I love you." His hands moved down to cup my rounded belly. "You're feeling okay, though? Baby's good?"

"Big Guy," I began with a grin, feeling as if my heart might burst. "If you haven't broken me, I doubt running around will, either. When you're carrying a superhero's baby, you're pretty much invincible."

"Babe, you're killing me over here," he said in a low voice, nostrils flaring. "Get your ass down that aisle so I can make an honest woman out of you."

I narrowed my eyes. "Language."

He smirked. "Sorry. Get that fine ass of yours down the aisle."

"Shouldn't we wait for Kate?" I argued as he helped me slip my masquerade mask over my eyes.

"Oh no, I'm not waiting a minute more. See, I need to be inside of you in the next half-hour—we can't stall this wedding any longer."

I breathlessly agreed. "I mean, Kate's done this before, so surely she knows how it goes. Right?"

CHAPTER FORTY-FOUR

Mike: December 2016 (Age: 34)

"I know I said I'd be there by now, but I just left the office. I still have to change."

The entire day had been one kick in the nuts after the other. The sheer amount of paperwork for Carnage's shooting alone had me chained to my desk for hours.

Grey sighed, "Shit. Just get here when you can—maybe you'll see something that I'm missing."

I agreed and hung up. When I left the hospital, I called David and told him to get Elizabeth and Kaden out of town. I didn't think they'd ever go after him, but I wasn't taking any chances. My gut feeling was too strong to ignore. He said they would be on their way to Beaumont to see his mom by lunchtime. No questions asked.

The sun was gone by the time I pulled into the driveway and I wanted nothing more than to crack open a beer and fall asleep in front of the television with Lauren in my arms.

If I knew her, though, she was going to be fully dressed, tapping her foot impatiently for us to leave. She'd been invited last-minute and had been looking forward to wearing that dress for over a week now.

God help the man who stood in her way.

I walked inside to see all the lights on, but no wife. I frowned and checked the kitchen, on the off-chance that she'd decided to start baking again. The birthday cake she'd made me had been to die for. Come to think of it, the sex right as I walked in the front door had been pretty fucking amazing as well.

As if on cue, my cock stood at attention, ready to serve. Maybe she was still getting ready. I began switching off the downstairs lights as I moved toward the stairs.

If that was the case, then I could probably talk her into a quickie before we headed out. I took the stairs two at a time, but the landing was dark, as were the bedroom and bathroom.

Fear settled in my chest, until I saw the outline of her body in our bed. I waited for my eyes to adjust. "Red? Are you okay?"

She pulled a washcloth from her face and moaned. "I think I've got a migraine—either that or my skull is collapsing in on itself. I've never actually had a migraine before, so the jury's still out."

I kicked off my shoes and climbed in next to her. "Does the light bother you?"

She nodded. "Yep."

"Sounds like it could be a migraine. Let's try something." I jogged downstairs to grab an ice pack from the freezer, only stubbing my toe once in the dark on the way back up. I turned on the taps full blast, filling the tub with hot water, before getting her out of bed.

Lauren had been doing so much better over the last couple of months. I couldn't remember the last time I'd come home to find her in bed or on the couch—it might have been on her birthday. So, we still hadn't had a formal discussion on children, but I think she'd caught onto the fact I was happy with just her.

Fuck everything else.

I wrapped an arm around her shoulders and led her into the dark bathroom. "Just take your pants off—"

Lauren laughed weakly. "Mr. Sullivan, are you trying to take advantage of me?"

I swatted her on the ass playfully. "Mrs. Sullivan, I think you know by now that you can't take advantage of the willing."

I held her steady as she slipped her sweats off, realizing she hadn't even gotten her dress on before the headache hit. I checked the water and turned the faucet off before guiding her feet into it. "Okay, sit just like this on the edge of the tub and look down at the water."

She lowered her head, and I placed the ice pack on the back of her neck.

"Oh, that feels really weird. I'm hot and cold at the same time."

I knelt down on the tile and massaged her lower back. "The heat pulls the blood down to your feet and the cold constricts the blood vessels around your head."

She looked over at me, her expression almost dreamy now. "You learn all that from the History Channel?"

"No, darlin'. I learned that from personal experience."

"You should go—if you leave now, you might make the reception."

I shook my head. "I'm not fucking leaving you here when you're sick."

We slipped back into a peaceful silence and I knew we weren't going to make the wedding. But it wasn't a bad way to spend New Year's Eve.

When the water grew cold, I helped her out and handed her a towel. It was hard to tell in the dark, but she looked like she was feeling a little better. I'd just bent down to retrieve her sweats when a flash of light hit the bathroom window, as if someone had just pulled into the drive.

The bathroom plunged back into darkness as the lights cut off and I stood frozen for a second.

"Mike?" she whispered. It was like she was afraid whoever was outside would hear.

I handed her the pants and pulled her away from the window. "Red, I want you to go into the closet and stay there until I say it's safe. Okay?"

I'd expected an argument, but she heard the tension in my voice and nodded. The low rumble of a motorcycle suddenly cut out, and I knew they were trying to mask the fact that they were getting closer to the house.

It was someone from the club.

The only problem with that logic was the fact that most of the guys were at the wedding. And I wasn't supposed to be home.

I still had my carry gun on me, but grabbed my Grey Special from the safe. Part AR15, part M16—and fully automatic. I hadn't used it off the range. Lauren watched me with wide eyes as I began dropping loaded magazines into the small bag near my feet.

"Stay right here. Do not come out—no matter what the fuck you hear. Do you understand me?"

She nodded shakily, and I pulled her into my chest.

"I love you."

"I love you too—Mike, please be safe."

Her words echoed in my ears on my way out of the closet and I only hoped I could do as she asked.

Please be wrong.

Please don't be what I fucking think this is.

CHAPTER FORTY-FIVE

Grey: December 2016 (Age: 52)

I glanced toward the reception tables with a scowl while twirling my daughter in my arms across the dance floor. "Care to explain to your old man why Nate's here?"

Dakota winced. "That was my toe again, Daddy. And, he's here because he's her Bucky."

"No shit?" I looked back at him again, arm slung over the back of Kate's chair, whispering in her ear. I clenched my jaw. "Him? Kota-Bear, thought we were on the same page about Dr. Douchebag."

She gripped my hand tighter. "Did Mama never teach you how to dance? God of thunder, you're killing my poor feet!"

Several couples turned their heads, and I adjusted the cheap plastic masquerade mask, feeling like Batman's delinquent brother. "I'm doin' the best I fuckin' can right now, darlin'. Didn't exactly host a lot of square dances at the club."

Her nose crinkled up in amusement. "What's a square dance?"

"Jesus Christ. So, you're sure Nate's her Bucky? Maybe she's more of a Spiderman—"

Dakota snorted and stepped up onto the toes of my motorcycle boots. "Here. We'll just do this. As for the Spiderman thing? Absolutly not. Kate was and will always be Black Widow. Maybe you need to reread the comics—oh! Did you know that Mama's best friend is Little Ricky's mom?"

I nodded, trying to keep up with her rapid subject changes while also watching the people around us for any sign of the mole. "I, uh, I did know that. Did you see Angel and Wolverine were here?"

"What?" she screeched in excitement, leaving me almost deaf in my right ear. "Why didn't you tell me sooner?"

"Thought you saw them, darlin'."

I found Angel watching the room from a corner and waved him over. Dakota no longer cared that we hadn't finished our dance as she hopped off my feet and threw herself into Angel's arms.

"I can't believe it's you! Nan, my grandmother, she told us you died."

"Did she now?" he asked, narrowing his eyes at me from over the top of her head.

They'd shown up before the ceremony, begging to be let in. When Kate confronted them, Norma had denied taking the money, throwing Celia under the bus like she had hundreds of times before. It was only when I stepped in that she came clean, but I'd let them walk out alive because my daughter had asked me to show mercy.

Something Angel strongly disagreed with.

"Dakota, I'm gonna find your mama, okay?"

She grinned. "Sorry we didn't get to finish our dance. Guess I'll just have to dance with Angel here until I can find my husband—did you see him? He looks just like Thor!"

"Oh, I saw him, sweetheart." Angel chuckled. "He's kinda hard to miss."

Celia stood against the bar, holding a still full glass of champagne in her hand. "Anything?"

I shook my head and pulled her into my arms. "Dance with me."

The corner of her mouth tilted up. "You know, I seem to recall that not being something you're the best at—"

I hated every second of shuffling my feet around, but the dance floor was the perfect vantage point without being obvious. I patted her ass with the palm of my hand and cocked my head as the next song started. "Let's go, princess. Don't leave me hangin'."

She listened to it for several beats. "Jamie, I haven't heard this in years."

"Know you're more of a George Michael fan, baby, but this'll have to do."

Even with knowing what was headed my way, I took her hand and led her out onto the dance floor like we were two people without a care in the world.

"Why don't they play 'Silver Springs' more?" Celia asked.

I shrugged. "I don't know. Maybe Fleetwood's afraid Lindsey and Stevie would end up killing each other mid-song?"

"I bet you're right," she said with a laugh before resting her chin against my chest. The smile faded, and she jerked back in surprise. "Are you wearing a vest? Oh my god, Jamie. Are they coming here?"

"Celia, just dance with me." I tightened my hand on her waist, silently pleading with her to not make a scene. Mikey and Lauren were late, and I was running out of ideas as to who the mole was.

"Jamie," she whispered, her eyes filling with tears. "Tell me a story... something with a happy ending, please."

Stevie's voice rose to a howl, and I lifted my eyes, scanning the room again for anything I might have missed. Almost every one of my men was doing the same. My prospect, Alex, hung back by the bar, deep in conversation, but I didn't miss the way his eyes moved over every person who walked up to order a drink.

"When I was a kid, I used to love sittin' out on my front porch, listenin' to the radio. I'd wait until the weatherman came on before hopping on my bicycle and ridin' to the outskirts of town to watch the summer storms roll in. Thought I'd grow up to be a storm chaser or some shit."

She watched me with wide eyes, and I brushed away a tear that had caught on her lower lashes before continuing. "Desert land makes it easy to see for miles. Where we're at now, though, ain't the desert, and this time I ain't sittin' back to watch it come to us."

"What are you saying?" she asked quietly.

I took a deep breath. "I'm sayin' what I should've said on Kate's first birthday. We can't fight these guys, Celia... not anymore. So, fuck the plan. Let's kidnap the kids and run. You, me, Mikey, Lauren... the girls. Wolverine has a cabin in New Mexico we could hide out in... club can go underground until we figure out what to do."

Celia's lips pursed. "And the girls' husbands?"

"Fuck," I growled. "One's a cop, and the other's a doctor—"

"They're family, and they're coming with us," she finished with finality.

Goblin stood up and stretched his arms overhead before nodding to me.

"I gotta go, princess. Grab what you need. We'll leave in an hour."

She caught the sleeve of my suit and tugged me back, placing her hand firmly in the center of my chest. "I don't want you to leave—"

I took her left hand and brought it up to my mouth, kissing just above her diamond ring. "Ain't leavin' you, darlin'. Never again. I just need to take care of a few things before we get on the road."

Her thumb moved over my wedding band, and she swallowed. "Come back to me, Jamie."

I dropped my head to hers, tangling my fists in her perfect curls, before roughly taking her mouth with mine. My tongue slipped between her lips, and her fingers moved over my biceps, squeezing me to the point of pain. Reluctantly, I pulled back. "Love you, princess."

She pressed the heel of her hands to her eyes and nodded. "I love you."

I lowered my head and whispered, "Who's in control?"

"We are," she breathed with a resolute nod.

CHAPTER FORTY-SIX

Mike: December 2016 (Age: 34)

I'd assumed that if the Sons ever grew a pair and attacked, they'd go after Grey or another biker.

Never here, though.

Not with my entire fucking world hidden in a closet, fifteen feet away from me.

Why hadn't I told her to run?

I tossed the bag down on the landing overlooking the downstairs before finding a semi-protected spot to crouch. I was near a wall I could get behind if needed. It was a good vantage point to see who the fuck was about to waltz into my house.

I wasn't sure whether to hurl or shit myself as the sound of boots hit the front porch. *A fucking coward with a gun—hadn't that been how I'd always seen myself?*

I popped the mag in, but it was impossible to determine how many of them were outside. Unfortunately, I didn't have to wait long.

The front door imploded, sending shards of wood and glass flying everywhere as they forced their way in. I lost count after five—more focused on trying to keep all of them in my sights.

I had the element of surprise on my side until I depressed the charging handle and pulled it back. It moved forward with a loud click and suddenly every fucking eye was on me.

I didn't even think about the ramifications of firing a full auto inside my fucking house. I just emptied the mag as they finished coming through the door before dropping it and grabbing the next one.

Spray and pray.

The bikers hadn't stood still like good little boys and began firing back at me. Bits of drywall and bannister joined bullets as they whipped past my head and I rolled back behind the wall.

Jesus Christ.

My house had become a fucking war zone. It was apparent I hadn't grabbed enough ammo.

Keep Lauren safe.

It was the only thing I could focus on at the moment. I rolled onto my stomach, praying they wouldn't get another shot off before I could.

I'd only ever used this gun standing up, and I was fucking struggling to get my grip right in my current position. The gas block grew hot, forcing me to adjust my grip because I didn't have gloves on. It just gave the bikers plenty of time to return fire and move closer.

How long had this been going on?

I ducked back behind the bullet riddled wall, reaching for the bag, as the air whistled with bullets. I'd hit maybe one or two. Not enough to end this soon. Our wedding picture shattered and fell to the floor with a crash, and a quick check around the corner confirmed they were getting closer.

I reached into the bag.

Fuck.

One mag left.

If they got up here, we were dead. I dropped the empty and looked down at my only salvation. I had to make it count.

I let them move up the stairs, their bullets ricocheting off every goddamn thing around me.

Wait for it.

Wait for it.

I'd been in some tight spots, *but this*? It'd be a fucking miracle if I made it out alive. It wouldn't even matter as long as she was okay.

Now.

I went to slide the mag in, but it wouldn't click—it was like it didn't fit suddenly. Drywall broke off above my head and I ducked, before yanking the charging handle back and trying again. This time it slipped in and I rolled onto my stomach before emptying it on the stairs.

It hadn't been enough.

CHAPTER FORTY-SEVEN

Grey: December 2016 (Age: 52)

I found Goblin pacing the sidewalk just outside the event center, rolling up his sleeves with flared nostrils.

"Did we get somethin'?"

He loosened his collar before shaking his head. "Jarvis texted, said he hacked our mole's computer and was going through his messages. *El cabrón* never came tonight. Someone tipped him off we were gonna be lookin' for him."

"Fuck," I growled, catching Goblin as he stumbled forward. "You drunk, kid?"

He held his thumb and forefinger a few inches apart with a nod. "*Sí*, because I'm so happy for *Caparina*."

I made sure he stayed on his feet before taking off toward the parking lot. He bounced along behind me, making small talk about the wedding. I grinned at the appropriate times and responded as if nothing was wrong, but my head was spinning.

The mole had known not to show up because someone in my clubhouse had gotten to him first. I glanced back at Goblin as he patted at the air in front of him like it was a dog. He was out, for obvious reasons.

No, the guy who'd rolled over was someone with a motive.

I'd taken the club back from Bear after Celia's attack, but never once gotten the impression he held it against me. Plus, he'd been a patch longer than I had. If anyone knew what our colors meant, it was him. He might have had the motive, but wouldn't have destroyed the club from within to take it back.

If love was a motive, then Jarvis should've been a suspect, but turning on the club wouldn't guarantee him Kate. Not only that, he'd been giving me solid intel and stood to lose his entire career if the club went down.

It had to be someone who would benefit if Silent Phoenix fell.

I quickly ruled out Angel and Wolverine. The two had been riding since God was a boy and had made more than enough money for several lifetimes. One by one, I went down the roster, ruling out members.

When I got to Mikey, I paused. He'd been forced into club life by a man who'd lied about being his father. His motive for taking down the club was stronger than anybody else's. And if my club disappeared, so did the crimes of his youth.

It wasn't him, though.

I didn't know how I knew it. But I did.

Convinced I'd gone through every member, I stumbled when it hit me.

The one man with the motive and means. I knew who my rat was. It had been right in front of my face all along. The biker who should've been a brother but had always been an enemy.

Comedian.

I'd been going about it the wrong way—trying to figure out who would have the most to gain financially.

It was never about money, though.

It was about revenge.

I'd just opened my mouth to tell Goblin when something shifted. The air around us felt as if it was suddenly charged with electricity. I glanced up, expecting to see lightning, but there wasn't a cloud in the sky. Still, the hair on my arms stood on end, warning me I was in danger.

A black suburban turned into the parking lot, engine revving and tires slapping against the pavement as it barreled toward us. Time seemed to slow down, drowning out anything other than the steady thumping from my chest and the sounds of my heavy breathing.

Goblin's mouth fell open, and his hand dropped to his hip as the tinted glass on the vehicle rolled down with a hum. A rifle moved through the open window, a ring on the shooter's hand glinting from the streetlight overhead as he shifted into position.

Only one of us was wearing a vest.

I didn't hesitate, knocking Goblin off his feet as a deafening crack of thunder pierced the surrounding silence, echoing around us until I was convinced they surrounded us on all sides. My back ignited, the flames bursting through the front of my chest like a fireball, dropping me to my knees against the asphalt.

The scent of gunpowder and burning flesh filled my nostrils as I collapsed onto Goblin with a sharp exhale, knowing the next explosion would be the one that sent me to the Reaper.

Only, it never came.

Tires screeched against the pavement, and smoke from the rubber coated my lungs, choking me with the knowledge that I was a dead man. The vehicle roared out of the parking lot and sped off; the sounds growing fainter until the air fell silent again. I'd prepared for everything but a slow death. I should have known a monster like me would be forced to suffer before being sent to hell.

Goblin moved me onto my back, and I looked up at the stars with a grin, consumed by a memory that hadn't taken place in this lifetime.

Maybe that was what the Reaper did.

Showed you how things could have been had you made different choices. It was like something out of a Dickens novel, only I wouldn't wake on Christmas morning to right my wrongs.

"You see those, Mikey? They're called constellations."

"Daddy," he said with a grin, displaying a mouth full of missing teeth. "Those are stars."

I squeezed his little body and pulled him onto my lap. "The stars create a picture when you put them together. See that one?" I traced the sky with my fingertip, his blue eyes tracking my every movement. "That's Perseus. If you look hard enough, you can see the head of Medusa in one hand, and a jeweled sword in the other."

His eyebrows drew together. "I see it, Daddy!"

"That's my boy. He was a warrior who went up against the monsters and married the princess."

Mikey stuck his tongue out. "Ew, I don't want to have to marry a princess. Kissing a girl would be worse than fighting monsters!"

I tickled along his ribs until he was squirming. "Is that so? You gonna tell your mama that when she tucks you in tonight?"

He pulled his chin onto his chest and hunched his shoulders with a giggle. "Daddy, Mama doesn't count as a girl. She's just a mom!"

"Is that so? And what about your sisters?"

He scrunched his nose. "Katy and Dakota? No way! I'll fight the monsters and keep them safe, but I'm not kissing them. They have to find a prince for that."

"Boys, time to wash up for dinner," Celia called through the open kitchen window.

"What if I wanna kiss your mama?"

He hopped off my lap with a shrug. "I guess, but don't do it in front of me. That's gross."

"Mikey, someday you'll realize that killin' the monsters and fallin' in love with a princess ain't a bad gig. Maybe that's all Perseus wanted... maybe that's all any of us could want."

"Sure." He grinned. "When I'm a hundred."

The vision faded, leaving me in darkness. If the Reaper wanted to torment me, he'd failed. I'd made a million mistakes, but even while dying, I knew the things I hadn't accomplished didn't matter.

They never had, because I'd had the love of a woman I didn't deserve and three kids who had turned out better than I ever could have imagined.

Even if we'd never been under the same roof.

Wolverine had given me the name Grey, but Jean hadn't just become more powerful as the Phoenix. She'd been corrupted; turned into something else. Something that made her a danger to the ones around her.

The power I'd held within the club was second to none. I'd thought nothing else would ever come close. Until Celia. My actions had almost destroyed her, but maybe me giving my life now would set things right.

Jean Grey was most known for her suicidal sacrifice and not how she'd failed the ones who loved her. Instead of living as a god, she'd chosen to die as a human.

CHAPTER FORTY-EIGHT

Mike: December 2016 (Age: 34)

I t was now between me and my piece.

I reached for my Glock just as gunfire erupted over my shoulder. One of them had snuck past me and was about to blow my head off.

I glanced back, surprised to see Lauren instead, a look of complete concentration on her face. She began picking the men off as they came up the stairs. Not a drop of sweat on her.

Who the fuck was this woman?

I'd known about her little hobby at the gun range, but I never imagined she was this good. Every time she depressed the trigger, it was a kill shot.

When a bullet embedded in the wall next to her head, I snapped out of my stupor long enough to lose my shit. I emptied my Glock like a fucking madman.

She stood over me like a fucking goddess, never once taking her eyes off her targets.

My girl, coming through in the clutch.

Within seconds, they were no longer returning fire, and she paused. The house was deathly silent, my ears ringing like a motherfucker.

"Jesus Christ, darlin'," I hissed. "Told you to stay in the fucking closet!"

"I've got your six, Tex!" she matter-of-factly yelled. "How many did you get? I think I hit more!"

I sat there, openmouthed. "Where in the fuck did you learn how to shoot like that?"

Her hands began to tremble, and she lowered her gun. "Um, from Jimmy." Then she stumbled back into the wall before dropping to her knees with a sob.

"I've got you, baby. I've got you." I wrapped her up in my arms, feeling along her body. "Are you hit? Where does it hurt?"

Jesus.

She'd been shot and was so calm because she was going into shock from blood loss. The problem was, I couldn't find any blood.

Lauren shook her head and began crying harder. "I'm—I'm pregnant."

My hands stilled. "Are you fucking kidding me right now?" I all but roared the words in her face.

She sniffled and nodded.

I lowered my voice, trying to stay cool, while gripping her tightly. "You're carrying my baby and just put yourself in the middle of a fucking gunfight?"

Oh my god. The realization that I could have lost not only her, but our child as well hit me hard.

"Ssss..."

"What the fuck does that mean?"

She gave me a small smile before burying her face in my chest with a muffled sob. "Babies. I'm carrying your babies."

This time, I began shaking. "There's more than one in there?"

Lauren nodded. "I didn't want to say anything for a few more weeks, but I found out a couple of days ago that we're having twins. I'm going to have to have a long talk with Abuelita about her fertility rituals." She laughed softly to herself before dissolving into tears again as I rocked her in my arms.

I didn't know what Gloria had to do with us having twins, but maybe once the shitload of adrenaline left my system, it would make more sense.

I was going to have to call this one in officially. There was no way around it—not with as many bodies on the stairs as we had.

My cell phone rang. Once I saw Grey's name pop up, I immediately answered. "Yeah, not gonna make the reception. Just had a fucking Wild West shootout with the Sons inside my fucking house!"

"Mike, we got a problem," Little Ricky began, and my heart immediately sank. His voice was different. Gone was the goofy jokester, replaced by something else. Something I'd never heard before. "Grey's been shot, and it doesn't look good."

CHAPTER FORTY-NINE

Celia: December 2016 (Age: 44)

The Fleetwood Mac song ended just as the glass doors of the event center closed behind Jamie and Rick. Another song immediately began, but I stayed where I was, standing on the edge of the large dance floor, panic tightening the noose around my neck.

After ensuring that Dakota was with Zane, I searched for Kate. She sat at a table with Wolverine and Lucy, absently picking at a piece of wedding cake with her fork while laughing at something one of them had said. The hospital had paged Nate over an hour ago, and with it being New Year's Eve, the chances of him making it back before the reception ended were slim.

If we were really going to run, we'd probably have to pick him up at the hospital on our way out of town. Knowing Jamie, though, he was going to insist we leave the doctor behind.

"Grey took off in a hurry. Did they find something?" Molly asked as she sidled up next to me. Concern filled her eyes, but she continued swaying her hips to the beat of the music as if to hide the fact that anything was amiss.

"I don't know," I mumbled, straining to see where they were going. "Rick got up, and he just left. Something bad is coming. I feel it in my gut."

In the entire time I'd known him, Jamie had never once backed down from a fight, but the cocky biker who'd ruled as if his club were untouchable was gone. In his place was a man who'd been shaken up enough to put on body armor.

It seemed since Carnage was shot that he wasn't willing to take any chances.

And if he was willing to run, it meant he no longer felt he could keep us safe.

"They're going to find the rat that rolled over on the club," she said confidently. "Bear said Jarvis was keeping them up to date. I guess he hacked the mole's computer. Prick's a cop. He could even be somewhere in this room, and we wouldn't know it."

A chill ran the length of my spine, and I surveyed the room before asking, "How'd you find out?"

Molly's mouth moved into a flat line as she raised her eyebrows.

"Seriously?" I hissed with a grimace. "Please tell me you're joking. Tell me you didn't hook up with Bear at my daughter's wedding."

"Of course not," she blurted. "What do you think I am, a heathen?"

Dakota waved to me from across the dance floor, a wide grin stretched across her face. I'd just raised my hand to return it when Molly leaned in to whisper, "We waited 'til the reception... like normal people. Did you know there are couches in the bathroom? Not only that, but the door has a lock on it. It's like they're practically encouraging people to fuck."

"Jesus Christ, Molly—"

"Hello, ladies," a voice purred from behind us. We turned in unison to see the same cop who'd spent most of the reception hitting on any woman who'd come within ten feet of the open bar. Judging by the way he was swaying, he'd saved his best pickup lines for the alcohol. His beady eyes moved over us, lingering on the bodice of our dresses as if hypnotized.

He winked at me. "I can see where your daughter gets her good looks."

Molly looked down at him in disgust. "She has two daughters, which tells me you must be a friend of the groom's. So, does that mean you're a cop as well?"

I knew for a fact that she didn't care one thing about what the lecherous hobbit in front of us did for a living. She was hunting for a mole.

He smirked and extended a hand. "Detective, actually. Kyle Barton."

The desperation seemed to roll off of him in waves.

Instead of taking his hand, she stared down at it as if it was diseased. Given the way he'd behaved most of the night, it very well might have been.

"Detective, huh? Not a very good one, though, to have missed the fact that the bride has a sister—"

"Oh, I was talking about the bride's sister. Dakota and I—we don't really get along."

"And why is that?" I asked, searching for a motive that would connect him to my family. Something that would've given him a reason to want to hurt us.

He chuckled. "Well, it's a funny story, really. Zane and I were working undercover at the gym, and I got assigned to be her trainer. She wasn't happy with the way I did things, but I'm pretty much responsible for all of this. Introduced the two of them and the rest, as they say, is history."

As if sensing there was a problem, Dakota's eyes met mine from across the dance floor, and she pantomimed sticking her finger down her throat after pointing to Kyle.

"It sounds like the two of you have a unique bond," I deadpanned. "It's a shame you're not closer."

"Well," he said, puffing out his chest. "I think she wanted there to be more between us, but I just didn't feel the same, and had to let her down gently. It's obvious—"

At the sound of a loud pop, I jerked my head back toward the front of the building. Torch and Bear nodded to me before getting up, their hands already moving toward the holsters on their hips.

Molly gripped my arm so tightly that her manicured nails embedded in the skin. "Celia, do you think—"

"That someone's starting their New Year's fireworks early?" Kyle asked with a chuckle. "Yeah, I do. Doesn't matter that the city has ordinances in place to prevent this very thing—"

Kyle began rattling off statistics, but I'd stopped listening. I stalked toward the doors, dragging Molly behind me, feeling as though I'd just gotten off a trampoline. My heart was lodged somewhere in my throat, and the ground felt foreign beneath my feet. Jamie's newest prospect, Alex, met me halfway.

"Torch and Bear told me to keep an eye on you. They're checkin' it out, so we can—"

"No. I will not sit here and act like everything's fine. I'm going with them. Watch the girls."

"Celia," Molly begged, tightening her hold on me. "Just—we don't know. It could've been some idiot setting off fireworks."

It wasn't.

I'd been around bikers long enough to know the sound of a gunshot when I heard one.

"It could be Pres caught the mole," Alex added confidently. "We'll just wait here and let him take care of it, okay?"

"You've got a lot to learn, kid," I said flatly before pushing the door open. The hair on my arms instantly stood up, not at the sudden drop in temperature, but at the sight of Bear. He paced the parking lot; one hand tangled up in his dark brown hair while the other held a cell phone in a death grip against his ear.

"Jesus, fuck," he groaned when he saw me. "Crossbones, get her the fuck away from this!"

I kicked my heels off and jogged toward him, scanning in between vehicles for Jamie. "Where is he?"

"Don't take him to Eli—fuck! Listen to me!" He roared into the phone. "Jarvis, fuckin' listen! We're beyond that right now. Get him to the goddamn hospital—"

"C'mon, Celia," Crossbones held his meaty hand out for me, but I shook my head.

"No. Tell me where he is. Tell me what happened." My voice was quiet. Calm. As if a part of me already knew the answer.

I looked down at a large, dark oil stain near Bear's boots. It shimmered under the lights above the parking lot as if it was still fresh. A car leaking oil like that wouldn't have gone very far, but the trail cut off just feet from where he stood.

Crossbones' fingers had just closed around my bicep when I realized I wasn't looking at oil.

I was looking at blood.

Jamie's blood.

"Fuck, they're losing him! Torch, you and Angel get the girls." He looked up. "Molly, thank Christ! Grab Wolverine and get her to the hospital. Crossbones, you follow. I want protection in place for every member of his family! Are we clear?"

White-hot heat flooded my veins, along with a sort of manic energy that left me feeling jittery.

It wasn't possible.

He'd been wearing a vest.

Bear yelled something else into the phone, but all I could hear was the ringing in my ears, like the screeching feedback from a microphone, drowning out everything else around me. I blinked, and Molly was by my side, leading me to her car.

"The girls?" I asked, the swirling emotions wrapping around my vocal cords, choking me.

"They're safe with Torch and Angel. Zane's with them too, okay?"

She clenched her jaw, wiping away the stray tears on her cheeks as she navigated away from the crowd of bikers in the parking lot, punching the accelerator once we reached the streets. I noticed as she expertly weaved in and out of the holiday traffic that she was keeping a close eye on the rearview mirror.

"Are we being followed?" I forced out through clenched teeth.

Molly checked again before shaking her head. "Crossbones is right behind us—he's gonna be okay, Celia."

I nodded while hearing Bear's devastating proclamation on repeat in my head. The car slowed, and I looked up at the bright red emergency sign looming over my head like an omen.

Maybe it had always been there; a warning that Jamie and I were forever doomed to tragedy. We'd been staring down the barrel of a gun for years yet had convinced ourselves that it was unloaded. The sirens had been nothing more than background noise, easily ignored as we'd fought our way back to each other and rebuilt a life together from ashes.

I heard them now, though.

The sliding doors opened silently, blasting our bodies with air before filling our nostrils with the stench of antiseptic. Every chair was filled with people in various states of distress. A disheveled man in a tracksuit pushed an empty shopping cart in a slow circle around the room, mumbling about the cartel being after him. While one woman vomited down the front of her sequined dress and onto the linoleum in front of her, the man next to her, clearly still under the effects of his party drug of choice, batted the air around his head with an impaired grin, oblivious to the state of his shoes.

I hugged my shoulders, letting my chin rest against my chest as Molly guided me toward the front desk. My mouth moved, but I couldn't recall a single thing I said before they led us to a private family room.

Instead of sinking down onto the loveseat beside me, Molly slipped into her more familiar role as caregiver and sprang into action, requesting warm blankets and a pair of socks. I frowned until I glanced down and realized my feet were still bare, my shoes lying abandoned in a parking lot fifteen miles away. My toes were almost blue from the cold, but I felt nothing.

Crossbones waited until the nurse left before taking up his post near the door, one hand resting on the handle of his gun.

"They're sure he's here?" I finally asked.

Molly nodded. "He's in surgery now. It could be awhile, though. I'm gonna find you some coffee, okay? Crossbones, you need anything?"

He shook his head, never once taking his eyes off of the small rectangular window in the middle of the door as she stepped out.

Someone paged a doctor over the intercom, but otherwise, the room stayed quiet. Molly returned a few minutes later with a cup of coffee and two nurses carrying supplies.

"Alright, let's just get this on you." She handed me the coffee and wrapped a blanket around my shoulders before directing me to lift my feet. I obeyed and let her slip plum-colored socks onto my feet as if I were a child. They were covered in white rubber flowers, and I didn't know whether they were a fashion statement or only there to keep me from falling.

If it was the latter, it was too late.

I'd been falling since I heard the gunshot.

Once Molly had me bundled from head to toe, she sat down and urged me to drink my coffee. I took a small sip and instantly recoiled at the overly sweet taste. At her stern expression, I took another drink, wondering if she'd added every sugar packet in the hospital to the cup.

Crossbones opened the door when he saw Wolverine leading Kate and Dakota down the hall. Zane and Angel brought up the rear like a team of bodyguards.

"Mama?" Dakota asked, the train on her wedding gown swishing softly as she approached me. "Have they said anything?"

"Here, Kota-Bear. Sit," Molly interjected, jumping out of her seat. "Do you want some coffee? I think we all need coffee."

I made eye contact with Dakota and discreetly shook my head.

"No, thank you," she blurted. "Kate, do you want coffee?"

Kate's head jerked up, and she gave Molly a strained smile. "No, I'm good. Thank you."

Wolverine pulled me into a rough hug. "He's gonna be fine, doll. Ain't a goddamn thing that can take him down."

I nodded and mashed my lips together, knowing if I said anything, I'd likely fall apart. Kate's legs bounced up and down, and she stood up, only to drop back into the chair with a heavy sigh.

"Did you call Nate?" Zane leaned over to ask her, keeping Dakota tucked under his arm. She stared right through me with her bloodshot eyes, seemingly lost in her own thoughts.

I had to stay strong for both of them.

"Yeah. He didn't answer. I'm sure he's in—" Kate's voice broke off in a sob, and she held a shaking hand up over her face, gasping for air.

I got up and moved into the empty seat next to hers, pulling her under the blanket with me. "I've got you, Katydid. Deep breaths, baby. In and out."

Somehow, I kept my voice calm while reciting words I hadn't used since she was a child, grieving the loss of her father.

The irony wasn't lost on me now.

"Mikey," I said suddenly, looking at Angel. "Someone needs to call him. He should be here."

In case he doesn't pull through.

Wolverine shook his head. "Sons showed up at his house, Celia. Place looks like a goddamned bomb went off inside."

The breath hitched in my chest, and I brought my hand up, running my knuckles roughly over my sternum before wheezing, "Is he? Oh my god, and Lauren?"

"They're both alive... thank Christ, but it don't sit right with me. Why tonight? Why'd they choose to go after the badge we got in our pocket same time as Grey?"

The meaning behind his question hung heavy in the air.

How had the Sons known what Jamie had fought to keep hidden?

The same way they'd known where to find him. Someone he trusted had betrayed him.

But who?

"Maybe they planned on cleaning house... anyone associated with the club was fair game? I don't know." Zane ran a hand over his face, clearly fighting a yawn. He'd probably imagined his wedding night going differently. I almost felt bad for him until I remembered that one of his cop buddies had been working with the Sons, too. My husband might as well have had a flashing neon sign above his head.

Minutes blended into hours with no updates. Wolverine paced while Molly pushed her sugar-laden coffee on every single person in the room. Kate would doze against my shoulder, only to jerk awake seconds later, frantically checking her phone for messages that weren't there.

Finally, just as the first rays of sunlight streamed in through the cracks in the blinds, someone entered, and the world as I'd known it for twenty-seven years ceased to exist. The ringing in my ears intensified to where I wanted to clap my hands against the side of my head, drowning out the words of the chaplain.

I'd been in a perpetual freefall for what seemed like forever, but saw the ground rapidly rising up to meet me with five simple words.

"Your husband didn't make it."

CHAPTER FIFTY

Mike: January 2017 (Age: 34)

"Did you see anything out of the ordinary?" Zane asked, as the crowd began dissipating, everyone in a rush to get out of the cold.

I looked around the cemetery and shook my head. Lauren was over talking to Kate and Dakota near Grey's casket. I wasn't going over there—not yet.

Eight Sons had ambushed me in my own fucking home and I hadn't even been able to warn Grey because they'd gone after him ten minutes prior. Lauren had taken out six of them on her own—with ten bullets left in the mag. Every single one of her shots had been deadly accurate. Apparently, Jimmy had taught her to always carry cocked and loaded.

I hadn't known whether to be proud or scared shitless. Thankfully, the department had been willing to overlook my highly illegal weapon of choice and just congratulated me on keeping my family safe.

"How did they know I was going to be home? I was supposed to be at your fucking wedding."

He crossed his gargantuan arms over his chest. "I've been trying to piece that together myself. Even if we factor in the rat in the club and the fact that there are multiple moles inside the station, nobody knew you were planning on being home. And if their goal was to eliminate you, wouldn't they have brought more men? They know that you're a cop."

Little Ricky walked over to us, his eyes rimmed in red. "I got some ideas about that, but you're not going to like it so much."

I sighed. Other than finding out that my wife was pregnant, I couldn't recall the last time I'd gotten good news. And even that had come with its own set of problems. I now had to keep three people safe.

He waited until he knew we were listening. "It didn't click until this morning. Who knew that *mi sirenita* would attend the wedding? Besides Grey and me? But I don't count, for obvious reasons."

I ignored the spark of anger that flared at his term of endearment and really listened. "Are you saying—"

Zane interrupted. "That you were never the target."

My blood ran cold. It was why they'd only sent eight men in—how I'd escaped without a single scratch. I leaned over, struggling to get air into my lungs.

Jesus Christ.

They'd gone in that night to kill my wife. I looked over at her—comforting Kate—our babies still hidden from the world under her black dress and gray wool coat.

Nate came up behind me. "Mike, are you okay? Look at me."

I brought my fist up to my mouth and pointed at Lauren, unable to speak through the absolute rage I was feeling. Nate looked at Little Ricky and Zane for interpretation.

"He just found out the Sons of Death were trying to put down his wife, not him," Little Ricky offered helpfully as Nate's face blanched.

I wiped the rain from my forehead and stood up, ready to massacre their entire fucking club. I pushed the fury down and made my way over to her. As much as I wanted to get her somewhere safe, I didn't know that such a place existed anymore.

Lauren gave me a soft smile as I walked up, before wrapping an arm around my back, stroking me gently. She still looked a little green around the gills. A side effect of pregnancy hormones, times two. "You okay?"

I looked over at the casket. "I'm going to say my goodbyes and then I need to get you out of here."

She nodded and led me over to my father. I stared down at the metal casket, suddenly without words. I couldn't imagine how Lauren had handled losing her mom on her own. This was a fucking nightmare I wanted to wake up from.

I slammed a fist down on top of the metal, sending the spray of flowers off the top. Lauren let out a cry of surprise and I turned back to reassure her I was fine, only to see her pointing a shaking finger behind me.

I spun back around and immediately saw what she'd seen. A business card rested on top of the metal—a smiley face with a gun pressed to its head.

I felt as if a bomb had just been dropped on me the longer I stared at it. Lauren's hands came up to her mouth as she trembled and shook her head. "It meant nothing. I didn't think it meant anything," she whispered.

Torch came running up and had an arm around her within seconds. "Lauren, is it the babies? Are you okay?"

She shook her head again and pointed at the card. His face went white, and he looked at me. "You know about this?"

"No," I forced out. "And given where it was hidden, we weren't supposed to."

He whistled, and the men began gathering.

Not the man responsible, though. He'd already left.

That would've been too fucking simple for me to be able to put him down right in the middle of a goddamned graveyard.

He'd rolled over on his own club. I never thought I'd live to see the day that someone defied Grey. Lauren fell against my side and I snapped out of it, holding her upright. "Do you know what it is?"

Her chin quivered as she nodded. "It was in my mother's purse, but I thought it meant nothing!"

Kate and Dakota came over and pulled her into a hug as Zane met my eyes over the tops of their heads. "You know who it is."

It was a statement.

I'd seen that goddamned image my entire life—it had practically been burned into my brain. The motherfucker thought he needed a calling card, a way to let the world know that he was responsible for the destruction. I never thought the world was under any illusion that he wasn't. It made perfect sense. The Sons had been targeting who they considered weak—prospects and women. They'd even attempted to take out Carnage while he was riding, with no way to defend himself.

It was his M.O.

Comedian.

The man I'd called father had just claimed responsibility for killing my actual one. The Sons had been one step ahead of us the entire time because the fucking VP was giving up intel.

It all clicked. Monica claimed she'd overheard something she shouldn't have—she'd known he betrayed the club. Torch had just put it together too, judging by the clenched fists at his sides.

"Just make it look like a suicide."

Fucking hell—he'd even used the same advice when trying to convince me to kill Katya. Monica dying of an overdose was never supposed to arouse suspicion. Comedian never imagined Lauren would look into it. He'd probably been the biker in the parking lot, watching her, seeing if she was going to give up his secrets.

"Where's Celia?" I demanded, searching the cemetery.

Zane answered. "Your mother took her home—is she in danger?"

I didn't know.

That had always been the problem. I'd never known how deep the corruption ran.

I let go of Lauren and sank down onto my knees. I'd told him about her plans—when she was going to go down to the station to reopen her mother's case. I'd given him everything he needed. Carnage was fighting for his life in the hospital because of him. Men he'd known for decades and he'd easily handed them over to our rivals.

"Comedian rolled over on the club," I began, forcing myself back up. I had to be strong. For them. "He betrayed his Pres and his brothers. The Sons of Death knew our every fucking move—lives were lost because of his actions."

Sun Tzu had been right. *If you know the enemy and know yourself, you need not fear the result of a hundred battles. If you know yourself but not the enemy, for every victory gained, you will also suffer a defeat. If you know neither the enemy nor yourself, you will succumb in every battle.*

Grey had kept the club running without knowing his enemy, but it came at a steep cost. I'd studied the Comedian my entire life; learning his every move to avoid facing his wrath. If the club was going to take him on, they'd need my help. Without Grey to lead, it fell to me. I knew not only him, but his every weakness.

I took a deep breath and walked back up to the casket. It was time to say goodbye and vow to put Comedian down. I owed that much to Grey.

I lifted the lid and paused in confusion. Where I'd expected to see my father, there were sandbags instead.

"Mike? Where's Grey?" Zane asked, peering down into it alongside me.

"Not fucking here," I growled. Had that been part of Comedian's plan, too? Stealing his body?

Lauren reached down into the casket and pulled out a single flower, turning it over in her hands. "A daisy," she marveled.

Everyone turned as she began laughing wildly, tears streaming down her cheeks. "Red? You gonna be alright over there?"

She nodded and then shook her head before falling apart again. "Gerbera daisy. I told him they were my favorite flower..."

"If shit goes south again, I won't hesitate to remove myself from the equation to keep the club intact."

No. No. No.

"He's still alive."

Little Ricky punched the air in victory. "I knew it! I knew he wasn't leaving us without saying goodbye. Let's find him and take mother-fuckin' Comedian out!"

I wasn't throwing my fists up in excitement. I had the sensation that I'd just tripped and was falling. It didn't matter what I did; I'd never be able to catch myself. Grey had faked his death because, in his mind, it ended the war. In actuality, though, it was just beginning.

Fuck you, Grey.

I turned back around to face the bikers and my family. Dakota and

Nate were holding Kate upright, while everyone else looked up at me with matching expressions of shock and confusion.

"What are we gonna do, boss?" Torch asked.

"Don't call me that shit," I ordered. "I can help, but I can't—" I lost my train of thought and fell silent. I'd watched Grey lead SPMC my entire life, but I didn't know that I could fill even one of his shoes. I didn't even own a fucking motorcycle. That should've been the biggest indicator that they had the wrong guy.

I wanted a life with Lauren—sitting on our front porch swing, watching the babies run around the yard. I fucking deserved that—I'd given him everything. Anytime he'd snapped his fingers, I'd come running. Now, he got to play dead while I once again stepped in to fix his mistakes.

Life was dangerous enough as a detective. How in the actual fuck was I supposed to lead an outlaw club?

Lauren put her hand over mine and squeezed. "You're the boss now, Tex. We've tried it on the other side and gotten nowhere. You're the only one that can end this."

I had no idea where Grey was, but if he'd been here, he would have laughed his ass off at the thought of me running his club. Maybe that had been his plan all along—to retire on some goddamn beach and leave me to clean up his mess.

Little Ricky looked over at the girls. "*Caparina*. Hail Mary. The last thing Grey said to me was to tell you both everything. Meet your brother, Michael Sullivan—uh, Quinn."

I wasn't sure I would have dropped that on them after just finding out their father was still alive, but Little Ricky seemed to think now was a good time for all the skeletons to come out of the closet.

I thought Kate was going to pass out from hyperventilating, while Dakota just gave me a chin tip, like the little badass she was. "Thank the god of thunder! I was stressed, thinking I was going to have to go after these guys alone and my shooting skills still leave a lot to be desired. Plus, what are the odds I could even find maternity ninja wear?"

Zane interjected, "Excuse me? You're not fucking going anywhere —you're pregnant."

Kate wheezed out, "We're going after them?"

I nodded and faced the club, even though everything in me screamed to grab my wife and haul ass out of the country. This was my club now. Grey's good little soldier was once again going to step up to the motherfucking plate. "Michael Sullivan, Sr., otherwise known as Comedian, is club enemy number one and should be shot on sight. I'm calling in the other chapters. As of today, SPMC is at war with the Sons of Death—and this time, they aren't going to know what fucking hit them."

A prospect let out a whoop from the back before yelling, "I'm in!"

Jeremy nodded. "You'll need my help—I'm in."

Little Ricky grinned. "In it to win it, boss."

Torch agreed. "You know I'm behind you."

One by one, every biker present pledged their loyalty to me, solidifying my position as leader. A position I never fucking wanted.

Zane watched with a bemused expression before announcing, "Count me in. Get me a patch and a bike and I'll ride wherever the fuck you want me to."

"I'm in." Lauren's voice was quieter, but her loyalty packed a much bigger punch.

I shook my head. "Darlin', you're staying out of this one. I will not risk losing you or the babies."

She held her ring finger up against mine. "You see these? We made vows, Mike. You go, I follow. That's the way this works."

I leaned down and kissed her lips fiercely as Dakota remarked, "See, she's knocked up and she gets to participate. I'm in. I'll obviously be Captain America, but you may all call me Cap for short. What do you say, Big Guy?"

Zane sighed and pulled her to his side protectively. "Fine, but no guns. I just got my shoulder back to normal."

I laughed, despite the absolute insanity of it all. This morning when I woke up, I'd been a cop and grieving son. Now, I was in charge of the club and declaring war on the man who'd raised me.

Dakota nodded approvingly. "Good—now I do want to discuss all of our names—"

I held up a hand. "Not right now. Please."

"Oh, okay. I'm in," Kate forced out, still very much being held up by her husband. She sounded surprisingly optimistic, given the circumstances.

Nate kissed the top of her head before shaking his head. "No way. We're not getting into this. I've got the hospital and things... things were finally calming down. We can't get into the middle of a biker war. That's crazy. People don't do that."

Some people did.

People who'd seen the sociopath that Comedian was firsthand. The people who'd lost loved ones by his actions. Sometimes, when faced with the injustice of the world, people had to stand up and fight back.

Some people never got a chance to enjoy the calm.

Grey had known that the only way to take the focus off the club was by making them think that they'd won. He was a fucking pussy to tuck tail and run—even Comedian was better than that. He'd abandoned his club in their time of need—saving his own ass while leaving his family's out on the line.

This time, we were going to move silently, taking the time to build our numbers before falling from the sky like a bolt of lightning.

I could've chosen to stick my head in the sand, hoping the threat would disappear, but they'd made a grave mistake. They'd come after my girl. They'd blatantly attacked my family, and that was an unforgiveable offense in my book.

I wasn't just coming for Comedian and the Sons of Death—Grey was going to be held accountable as well.

Little Ricky might've called me a Quinn, but from what I'd seen, a Quinn ran at the first signs of trouble. No, I was a motherfucking Sullivan, through and through. And I was going to bring hell down on anyone that crossed my family.

After all, I was my father's son.

CHAPTER FIFTY-ONE

Celia: January 2017 (Age: 44)

The rain that had been coming down in sheets for most of the morning turned to icy sleet, pelting my skin with fury. Still, I remained on the small stone bench, utterly immune to the cold. The pale pink blossoms were long gone from the Redbud tree Jamie had planted for our baby; leaving behind flat brown seed pods and frozen branches.

I looked up at it, feeling empty.

Hollow.

Just like that tree, I'd been left bare, stripped of my protector.

My dream of the two of us on a beach had been just that. A dream.

I squeezed my eyes shut, still seeing his blood against the asphalt... hearing the sounds I'd made when the doctor finally appeared in the waiting room.

"You need anything?"

I pulled myself from my thoughts and looked over my shoulder. "Louisa? When did you get here?"

"Oh, Celia." Her lips trembled, and she pressed her fingers to them before joining me on the bench. "I've been here since... since the day he... passed. You know, it's a lot warmer inside the house—"

"No," I stated firmly. Lucy had already gone into nursing mode, pushing me to eat and sleep as if that alone could piece me back together.

There was a traitor masquerading as a biker inside my house. And I refused to break bread with a man who'd given up Jamie's location; a man who'd sentenced him to death at his own daughter's wedding.

"It was a lovely service," Lou tried again.

Was it?

I'd been forced to say goodbye to my blond biker in the same cemetery I'd fallen in love with him in. As I'd looked around at the other mourners, I was seventeen again, sitting underneath a large oak tree, discussing mythology.

The tree was long gone, lost to an errant bolt of lightning. It didn't matter. If I squinted my eyes and stared long enough, I could still see us... two naïve souls, blissfully unaware of the problems life was busy stacking up against them.

If I would've known that dance was going to be our last one, I would've paid more attention. I would've moved my feet a little slower and traced the lines that time had left along Jamie's face with my fingertips.

By now, they'd probably lowered him into the frost-covered ground. I shuddered at the thought of him being surrounded by dark and wondered if I could've given the funeral director something warmer for him to wear. It had only seemed fitting to send him off in the leather vest he loved so much, but maybe it wasn't enough.

I knew it wasn't rational.

Jamie was gone; oblivious to the fact that he now resided in a steel box. He didn't care if it was pitch-black. A fear of the dark was something that only plagued me. I couldn't sleep, convinced that the Sons would come for me the minute my eyes closed.

That was how they worked, wasn't it?

Going after Mikey and Lauren in their own home... coming for Jamie at Dakota's wedding. They struck close to home when it was least expected. It was how they'd been so successful.

And someone within the club had given up both Jamie and his son.

There was always the possibility it wasn't a man. For as much as I knew, it could have been the woman sitting beside me. Slim had always had a bad heart, but maybe Lou blamed the club for his early death. It could've been the woman who'd driven me home from the cemetery. A woman who had gone out of her way to make my life a living hell.

Betsy.

"Celia?"

I clenched my jaw with a jerky nod and pushed my thoughts aside before admitting, "Yeah, it was nice, but he would've hated all the flowers."

She laughed. "I said the same thing at John's funeral. Our men weren't really the type to be showered in roses, were they?"

Ignoring the pain in the back of my throat, I agreed. "They could be soft... but never in public."

The breath hitched in my chest, but the tears wouldn't come. It was just one more thing my husband had taken with him when he left.

"I didn't ask, but did you spend any time with him? After he passed, I mean. They let me sit with John for about an hour. I just ran my fingers through that gorgeous long hair of his and kissed his face." Lou paused and wiped the tears from her cheeks, thawing some of the ice around my heart.

"I knew he was gone. I'd known it when he went down in our bedroom, but just touching him again gave me a sense of peace. It let me know he was okay. He wasn't hurting."

There was no way she could've been the traitor. She'd loved Jamie almost as much as I had.

My nostrils flared, and I rubbed at my wrists before coldly replying, "No. The doctors wouldn't let me back in the room. They said there was a lot of blood—I don't know if it was a health code violation or what the exact reason was. By the time I met with the funeral director, I'd decided I didn't want to see him like that. I didn't want to remember him that way."

She didn't need to know that even the funeral director had denied me access to my husband's body.

Jamie was bigger than life, and no matter how many people told me he was gone, I just couldn't wrap my mind around the fact that something as small as a bullet had taken my husband from me. He was the god of death... he should've been unstoppable.

Mrs. Quinn, we've done the best we can for him, but it'll be a closed casket funeral. Trust me, it's better this way.

Louisa turned away from me, shoulders curled over her chest. I didn't understand why people hid their grief from me, as if I was somehow unaware of my loss.

It wasn't as if I was still expecting him to come down the driveway on his bike, covered in sleet and laughing about a mix-up at the hospital.

That would have been crazy.

"Are the girls coming back here?"

I nodded, studying the bare branches on the tree again, wondering if they'd always looked like this in the winter and I'd just missed it. "They are. They were still at the cemetery when Angel and I left."

She rubbed her hands over the soaked sleeves of her coat to warm herself. "We really need to get you inside, Celia. You'll catch your death out here."

"Good."

Her eyebrows drew together. "You don't mean that. Your girls need you, just like David needed me. Sure, it'd be easier to admit defeat, but when have the two of us ever done things the easy way?"

Maybe David had figured out that his father was involved in more than just construction. It seemed if I looked hard enough, almost everyone had a motive.

"They came for him, Lou. It's only a matter of time before they show up for me. Hawk warned me—said death was coming. I didn't listen then, but I'm listening now."

She glanced back toward the house, ensuring we were alone, before leaning in. "Why would they want you, Celia?"

I shrugged. "I wish I knew. Jamie looked into it, but as far as I know, nothing ever panned out."

"Is this about what happened to you—the night you were attacked?"

As her eyes scanned my face, searching for answers I didn't have, I wondered if she knew more than she was letting on. Despite all their bluster about nothing leaving the clubhouse, it was apparent that, when push came to shove, the bikers were incapable of keeping secrets from their Ol' Ladies.

I pinched the bridge of my nose before getting to my feet. Mud squished out from under my ballet flats as the soles sank into the soft earth, and I sighed. "I don't know anymore, Lou. I don't see how any of it connects, and unless someone can explain it to me, I'm lost!"

My voice rose over the storm, and I threw my hands up, practically begging for a bolt of lightning to put me out of my misery.

It wasn't supposed to end... not like this.

"Celia!" Molly hurried across the yard toward us. "Let's get you inside. Lucy's got a plate of food with your name on it. Then, we'll let you rest—"

"Stop!" I roared. "I'm not a goddamn child! I don't want a plate of food or to take a nap! I want to know who killed my husband. Jesus Christ! Is that too much to ask? I swear to all the saints, the next person who tries to give me a goddamn sandwich or casserole is going to the Reaper!"

Her eyes widened as she put some distance between us. "Fair enough. Are you planning on staying out here until you turn into a snowman, or what?"

"Maybe I am," I petulantly replied. "Maybe I'm going to stay right here until I figure out who the traitor is."

Louisa's mouth twisted up as she fought a grin. "You know she'll do it too, don't you? She's as stubborn as a damn mule."

Molly nodded. "Oh, I don't doubt it. Just thought you'd want a last meal before freezing to death."

CHAPTER FIFTY-TWO

Celia: January 2017 (Age: 44)

"I can't eat," I admitted. "And if one more person tells me how sorry they are, I'm going to snap. I don't want sympathy! What I want is for someone else to be as angry as I am!"

"You think we're not angry?" Molly asked. "Bear has been working around the clock to find the rat. The club won't rest until they know who's responsible."

Swirling flakes of ice struck my face, and I swatted at them before snapping, "Nice of them to step up now that my husband is dead. Would've been nicer had they done it—oh, I don't know, maybe before he was shot to death?"

"Celia, please."

A truck pulled into the driveway, and I brushed past her, my shoes sinking further into the mud with each step.

Dakota's foot slipped off the running board as she climbed down from the passenger seat of Zane's truck, and she fell to her knees in a puddle with a groan.

"Dakota, wait!" he yelled as she scrambled to get to her feet. "You can't just—"

"What's going on? Dakota, are you alright?"

The baby.

I should have been thrilled at the prospect of becoming a grand-mother, but we were at war with men who didn't fight fair.

Men who preyed on innocents.

Her pregnancy would only make her a bigger target in their eyes.

I'd lost my baby at the hands of monsters, but I would hand over my own life before letting her suffer the same fate.

"Mama," she panted. "You need to sit down..."

Another truck pulled down the driveway, the wheels churning up a wall of mud on either side.

"Mike's my brother," she hurriedly finished, before clapping a hand over her mouth with a choked sob. When Zane shook his head, she added, "I'm sorry. I had to tell her at least that part!"

The truck screeched to a halt just inches from the bumper of Zane's vehicle, and Mikey got out. "Jesus, Dakota! I told you to wait!"

Lou hurried toward us. "Is everything okay? Did something happen?"

Dakota nodded. "Mike is my dad's son. We just found—" She froze and looked toward the porch to where Comedian sat on the porch swing with a clenched jaw.

The atmosphere shifted, and I leaned into Lou's side when Mikey drew his gun, calling across the yard, "Thought you'd be running, old man. Isn't that what a traitor does?"

I reached for Dakota, but she moved toward the porch with her chin high in the air, planting her feet like a superhero from her one of her comics. "We got this, Mama. We'll protect you."

Lou pursed her lips, eyes darting from one person to the next. "Celia," she whispered. "What—"

"The fuck's goin' on?" Bear demanded, coming around the side of the house.

With a sigh, Zane drew his gun and held it on him. "Stay where you are. This is club business."

I pulled in and slowly released a deep breath, wondering what had happened after I left the cemetery that warranted a stand-off in my front yard.

Since when did the comic club members carry guns?

"Mikey?" I tried.

"Not now, Celia. Gotta deal with my old man first, and then we'll talk."

Comedian ran a hand over his face and stood up with a nod. "'Bout time we had this talk. There's no need for the gun... I ain't stupid, Junior. Knew when you were born that the timing didn't add up—"

"You knew I was Grey's kid. It's why you went after him," Mike snarled. "Admit it! For once in your worthless existence, tell the goddamn truth!"

"No." My legs buckled beneath me at the revelation, sending me down into the muck.

Someone yanked me up at the last second, pulling me back against their broad chest. "I got you, girl," Angel said firmly. "Kota-Bear, get your ass back here."

Dakota turned around, mouth already opening to object. When she saw who it was, her posture sagged, and she stomped back over to stand at his side. "I could've handled it," she hissed.

"Ain't a doubt in my mind you could have, but you ain't got a gun. You remember what I taught you when you girls were kids?"

"Don't go running into things with your dick out," she recited proudly before her eyes widened. "Oh! I get it now!"

Comedian loosened the collar on his dress shirt before bringing his arms down to rest against the railing. "Just because I knew I wasn't your daddy don't mean I knew Grey was. And, as I recall, Sons came after you that night too. How's that work out, detective?"

"Did you do it?" I croaked, freeing myself from Angel's grip. "You?"

Somehow, I remained upright as I stumbled toward him, but inside I was reeling. Comedian had ridden with Jamie for even longer than I'd known him.

Fury ignited in my bloodstream as I climbed the steps, bringing my body temperature back up.

"Celia," Mikey called. "Get away from him!"

"No," I seethed. "Not until he looks me in the eye and tells me what he did to my husband."

Comedian lifted his head and met my gaze, nostrils flaring. "I've done a lot of fucked-up things in my life, but I swear to you, I didn't lay a hand on your old man, Celia."

The porch felt as if it were tilting beneath my feet, like a boat on rough water. I latched onto the railing with clammy hands, blinking to clear my vision. "Then who did?" My words came out on a whimper, but my eyes remained dry.

"I don't know, darlin'."

Mike's boots connected against the porch steps with reverberating thuds. "Gave you an opportunity to come clean—"

Comedian dropped to his knees. "You wanna put me down, son? Do it. If you think it'll make you feel better, pull the goddamn trigger! Just know I would never sic a bunch of deranged bikers on you and Lauren. You think I ain't hurtin' here? Grey was my best friend—"

"Your fucking calling card was on the casket. Explain that," Mikey ground out through clenched teeth, pressing the barrel against Comedian's forehead.

"What are you saying, Mikey?" I stared up at him, acutely aware he was no longer a little boy, convinced I was giving birth to an alien. The lines on his face were more pronounced, his accusations more damning.

The sinking feeling in the pit of my stomach threatened to capsize what little of me still remained.

It had been right in front of my face the entire time, but I'd refused to see it, never imagining that the man who'd been so gentle with me after the attack could destroy my family.

He kept his eyes on Comedian. "Tell her. Tell her what you did."

Comedian jerked his chin up and looked at me. "I didn't kill him—"

Bear shoved past Zane and put himself in front of me. "You got two seconds to tell me what the fuck is goin' on, kid," he snarled at Mikey. "From where I'm standin', it looks like you're holdin' a gun on one of my brothers. Tell me I'm wrong."

Mikey ran his tongue over his teeth with a grin. "From where you're standing? Bear, sweetie, might be time for you to invest in a pair of glasses. Maybe if you'd had some, you would've seen that this piece of shit rolled over on the club. Now that I'm in charge, I'll be taking care of it for you. Okay, pumpkin?"

Bear's body went taut, but he remained where he was, clearly holding himself back. Whether it was out of respect for Jamie or me was anyone's guess.

"In charge? How the fuck do you figure that... sweetie?"

Mikey cracked his neck and rolled his shoulders. "I was named Pres about..." he looked down at his watch. "An hour ago. So, from where I'm standing, I call the motherfuckin' shots."

Still on his knees in front of us, Comedian lowered his head, shoulders shaking with laughter. "Jesus Christ, I needed a laugh. Kid's got better jokes than me."

He wiped at his streaming eyes and got to his feet, ignoring the gun trained on his head. "You ever consider that I might've been set up when you saw my card, or was the idea of sendin' me to the Reaper just too good to pass up?"

"You aren't important enough to be set up, old man. Oh, and one more thing. If anyone here has a problem with me taking over, speak the fuck up now," Mikey demanded.

"I do. I'm the VP—" Bear began, only to be cut off.

"No... Comedian's the VP," Mikey said slowly.

Comedian chuckled again. "Nah, son. I'm the SGT at Arms. Bear's the VP—well, actin' Pres now."

"That's right," Bear said in a low voice. "So, I actually call the motherfuckin' shots. Any changes within the club have to be approved by the officers. Seeing how almost every ranking officer was here, whatever the fuck was decided in the graveyard, don't mean shit—"

"Was this why you came here?" I asked, and the laughter around the yard stopped immediately. "You didn't come to pay your respects, but to take over the club?"

Mikey holstered his weapon, shaking his head. "No, Celia. Just listen to me. I've got a plan to go after these guys—"

"You ever ridden in a club?" Bear asked. When he didn't get a response, he sneered, "That's what I thought. You badges are all the same... assumin' you're above everyone else, or that you know more. Why don't you leave the big boy stuff to the grown-ups, okay?"

Mikey licked the flakes of ice from his lower lip with a smirk. "Big boys? Is that what you call yourselves? Jesus Christ, no wonder you couldn't defeat the Sons. You gonna hop on your Power Wheels motorcycle and take out the bad guys?"

He held up his thumbs and drove his forefingers into Bear's chest with a snarky, "Pew, pew! Pew, pew!"

Bear grinned and grasped Mikey's shirt in his fist before dragging him into the yard. "Seems no one ever taught you respect, kid. I'm gonna remedy that right the fuck now."

"You got him, Bear," Rick called out. "Just take his legs out from under him!"

I flinched when Comedian touched my shoulder, extending my hands out in front of my body as I backed away. "Don't touch me—"

"Celia—"

"Don't—he trusted you." I looked to where Bear and Mike were circling each other like boxers in a ring. Dakota's mouth hung open in shock as she watched grown men fight over Jamie's club like starving dogs being thrown a steak.

Take a good look around you, baby girl. This is the last of your father's legacy going up in flames.

"He trusted you!" I screamed hoarsely. "All of you! You two want to have a pissing contest, do it somewhere else. Not here. Not today."

Bear lowered his fists and took a step back. "You're right—"

Taking advantage of his momentary distraction, Mikey glanced a blow off the side of Bear's jaw just as he turned to face me. "That feel respectful, motherfucker?"

Shock gave way to anger as I stormed down the steps and planted my palms in the center of Mike's chest, sending him stumbling back. "How dare you! After everything he did—just go."

"Wait."

I shook my head and wrapped my arms around my body before walking away. The damage was done. My only comfort was that Jamie wasn't around to see the club imploding and the people he loved at each other's throats. My jaw tightened. He wasn't around because one of them had wanted him gone.

"Celia, wait a fucking second," Mikey snapped. "This concerns you too—"

"Does it?" I roared. "Because to me, it looks like the men my husband trusted more than anyone couldn't wait for him to die so they could take over!"

The screen door slammed shut, and Wolverine stalked out onto the porch, surveying the scene with cold eyes. "Anyone wanna tell me what the fuck is goin' on?"

"Yeah." Dakota stepped forward. "Um, so Mike is my brother, and he's going to take over the club, which is great because I have some ideas on nicknames—"

Zane shook his head and gestured for her to get on with it.

"Oh, right. So, Mike declared, in his first order of business as Pres, that..." She lowered her voice dramatically. "Comedian is club enemy number one and should be shot on sight."

Wolverine's eyes narrowed. "Okay... anyone else care to explain it to me?"

Angel stepped forward. "Kid says Comedian had somethin' to do with Grey's death."

He popped a toothpick into his mouth before glaring at Mikey. "Better explain yourself, kid. And do it quick, before I lose my shit."

"Comedian's calling card was hidden under the flowers on the casket. With the way the Sons had been targeting people, it just made sense. They didn't bust into my house that night to kill me; they came for my girl."

"Why the fuck would I come after you or your family?" Comedian snapped.

"Celia..." Wolverine looked at me, his scowl deepening. "What do you say?"

I shook my head. "I don't know—it just doesn't make any sense. Wasn't Comedian with the club the night he was—the night that it—"

I couldn't say it.

It felt wrong.

Bear pulled me into his side, his chest vibrating against my cheek as he spoke. "She's got a point. Comedian was with us the entire night. Fuck, he even helped us get him to the hospital. There's only one of us here that looks guilty as fuck, and it sure as hell ain't Comedian."

"What are you saying?" Mikey growled. "You think I'm the traitor?"

"That's exactly what I'm sayin', detective." Bear led me back to the porch. "Who better to dismantle a club from the inside out than a motherfuckin' cop? What are they givin' you for takin' us down? A bigger badge? Gonna give your dick a couple of extra tugs? What'd you trade his life for?"

"Fuck you, Bear!" Mikey spat. "You wanna look at every possible suspect? Great. Let's start with Grey. He told me he'd do it—night Carnage was shot. He said he had a plan... what if this was it?"

Wolverine rubbed at his temple with a sigh. "How exactly is gettin' killed a plan?"

Mike looked up at the heavy clouds, nervously tapping his index fingers against his thumbs. "You're tellin' me that Comedian had nothing to do with what happened... maybe we need to consider the possibility that Grey worked a deal with the feds—"

"That's impossible! Wolverine, you were with me at the hospital when the doctor came in and told us he didn't make it. There was no deal."

There'd only been one plan, hurriedly discussed on the dance floor at our daughter's reception.

Fuck the plan. Let's kidnap the kids and run.

"Bear?" Wolverine asked, gnawing on the toothpick.

"No fuckin' way. Who would voluntarily take a bullet to the chest as part of a plan? There're too many variables. Given that he's no longer with us, I'd say if there was a plan, it fuckin' failed."

Mikey crossed his arms over his chest with a laugh. "I can't believe I didn't see this before. I told him to wear a vest that night."

"He did!" Rick and I exclaimed at the same time.

"The bullet..." I tapped my fingers lightly against my chest, shifting my jaw back and forth. "The bullet went through. He lost too much blood..." my voice tapered off.

"Maybe you're the mole," Bear growled at Mike. "How else would they have known to use armor-piercing bullets? We've already established that you had the most motive out of any of us. Now you wanna rule it all."

Wolverine moved the toothpick up and down with his tongue, regarding the two of them thoughtfully. "That's a damn good question,

Bear. They hadn't used ammo like that before... why'd they suddenly change their MO the night Grey went down?"

"What if it wasn't the Sons?" Zane asked.

Wolverine cocked an eyebrow before turning back to Bear. "Instead of sittin' around, measurin' dicks, I'd start there. I, for one, don't believe for a second that Grey had plans of rollin' over, but if I were in charge, I'd look into everything. Then again, I'm just an old man. What the fuck do I know?"

Losing Jamie had damn near killed me. To even entertain the idea that he would've turned on his own club was unfathomable.

"I just put him in the ground, and you're already ready to dig his body up—to crucify him all over again?" I dropped onto the bottom step, wishing like hell I could shed my rage as tears. The heels of my shoes dug into the mud, and I wanted to coat myself in it until the soft earth swallowed me whole.

I'd done my time above ground.

It was time to go home.

Mikey's blue eyes met mine, and the chasm in my chest widened. There was so much of Jamie in him it left me aching. He chewed on his lower lip and looked over at Dakota, who nodded as if giving her approval. "Casket was empty, Celia—"

Blood roared in my ears and slivers of black clouded my vision as I took in the admission; turning it over and over in my head, struggling to make sense of it. Voices rose all around me in disbelief.

Panic.

"Oh, Jesus. Celia!" a deep voice shouted. It was distorted, like a slow-motion scene in a movie. The frozen earth that I'd longed for only moments ago now came up to greet my face as my heart pounded a furious rhythm in my chest, warning me I was in danger.

Convincing me to run.

He'd promised me.

I tried lifting my head, but oblivion won, sending everything into darkness.

If he was still here, I should've felt him.

I would've known.

CHAPTER FIFTY-THREE

Grey: January 2017 (Age: 52)

I struggled to open my eyes, squinting against the blinding white surrounding me. Despite my surroundings, I knew I was in hell.

My throat felt as if I'd been gargling with broken glass and even the smallest movements sent searing pain through my chest. I managed to lift my head a few inches, only to see thick foam restraints on my wrists.

"Well, there he is." A smiling face appeared. "Thought you were gonna be out forever, Sleeping Beauty."

"Who—" I coughed and the burning feeling in my chest spread to my limbs. "Who are you?"

He ran a hand over his face with another grin, and I saw the diamond thirteen on his middle finger, confirming his identity.

"I can't believe she hasn't mentioned me to you. We have such a good thing going on."

"Cobra," I rasped. "You're supposed to be dead."

"So are you," he said with a shake of his head, rolling one of his diamond cufflinks between his fingers. "But Saint wants you alive, so here we are."

I pulled against the restraints. "I'm gonna tear you apart—"

"Are you, though? You barely survived the bullet I sent into your chest. Trust me, I wanted to aim for your head. We could've continued our little game, but you got too smart, didn't you?"

"Where's Comedian?" I snarled.

Cobra's face went blank. "Who the fuck is Comedian?"

"Don't fuck with me. I know he's the one givin' the Sons their intel." I winced as another jolt of pain shot through my body, sweat running from my hairline and down my neck.

He rocked back onto his heels. "You really don't know shit about what goes on in your clubhouse, do you? Saint was right. You're too old and tired. Lucky for you, I'm not. Maybe I'll let you watch when I take your girl this time—"

"You ain't gonna lay one goddamn hand on her!" I forced myself up, yanking at the restraints until something popped in my chest, sending me back down with a groan.

"Grey, you're tearing your stitches. I'd hate to sedate you. You'll miss all the fun. Now that your girls are old enough, I might even let my brothers take a turn with them. That oldest one looks like her mama, doesn't she? I wonder if her cunt is just as tight."

Nausea rose up, and I realized why Manny's taunts had never gotten under my skin before. Deep down, I'd always known I was still the one calling the shots; knew they'd never get near my girls again.

Now, I was helpless.

My eyes filled, and I tried blinking the tears away, but not before Cobra saw.

"Are you crying? The big bad Grey is fuckin' crying? You've gone soft in your old age, Pres. What is it that's got you down? Is it knowing I'm going to fuck your girls raw and there's not a damn thing you can do about it?"

I clenched my teeth and strained against the restraints until my vision blurred.

Cobra leaned over me, pinning my forearms in his grip with a manic grin. "Your youngest... she's knocked up, right? Maybe you can listen to her screams for mercy while I gut her like a fish."

"Kill me!" I roared. "You've wanted me for sixteen years! Fuckin' do it!"

The mad look in his eyes faded, and he released me, suddenly thoughtful. "It's not about you anymore. It's about Celia... maybe it's always been about her. There's a certain... what's the word? Feistiness when it comes to her. What is it about possessing a woman that makes you feel like a man? To know that only you have the power to crush her spirit using your body..."

"You'll never break her," I forced out through clenched teeth.

Something like lust flashed in his eyes. "I never understood how you left her. I would've kept her handcuffed to my bed, reminding her of what she is. An object to be brutally broken or something to be handled with care, depending on the mood of the owner. Maybe I won't fuck her... maybe I'll take my time playing, letting you hear every moan I draw from her pretty lips—"

"Celia!" My voice was hoarse, but I kept screaming her name until Cobra injected something into the IV in my arm.

His face faded out of focus, but I heard his laugh as he whispered, "Don't you worry about her. She's in excellent hands."

To be continued...

––––––

Where is Grey?

Keep reading for a sneak peek of The Savior, the dramatic conclusion to the SPMC series. Are you ready to unmask the traitor? Order today by tapping **HERE**!

––––––

Confused about the recommended reading order? Look no further!

Savior (Book 5 in the Silent Phoenix MC Series)

* Operation Fit-ish (Book 1 in the Operation Duet)
* Operation Annulment (Book 2 in the Operation Duet)

*Optional, but will enhance your reading experience.

————

Worried that you'll miss my next release? Click here to receive an email notification the minute it goes live!

Want to be the first to know when my books go on sale?
Follow me on BookBub!

For new release alerts, follow me on Amazon!

PREVIEW OF THE SAVIOR

Grey: February 2017 (Age: 53)

Forgive me Father for I have sinned...

I've shed enough blood to flood the streets with red... broken every rule in my climb to the top.

It seemed my reach knew no bounds...

Until I almost lost her...

And I was forced to realize that I'd become the very thing I hated; the monster I feared the most.

I fought my way back from the brink only to have everything I loved ripped away from me again. Sooner or later, death comes for us all. The best I can hope for at this point is that I go to my grave with a clear conscience.

I vowed to be their protector.

Just another promise I couldn't keep.

Maybe in the end, we get what we deserve.

All I know is that love is sacrifice, and I'm a man with nothing left to lose...

The Savior is available now! Order by tapping HERE or read on for a sneak peek at what's coming next...

THE SAVIOR

Grey: February 2017 (Age: 53)

My head shot up as the door swung open and I surged forward. The metal that encircled my wrists bit into the skin, warning me to back off. Instead, I pushed my body to its limit, tendon and muscle straining in a futile attempt to break free from my restraints.

"Happy... whatever the fuck today is." Cobra pulled his phone from his pocket and tapped the screen with his index finger. "Let's see, tomorrow is Valentine's Day, so why don't we just celebrate early? Isn't that what you used to do with your prisoners? Spout off all the inane holidays as if they needed to be reminded of how long they'd been with you?"

None of my captives had ever lived long enough to need to know the date, except one.

Manny.

I wracked my brain, struggling to recall how many of my men would've known that detail. To my knowledge, there were only two—Crossbones and Bear.

The chains rattled as I jerked my arms forward, suddenly convinced I was the goddamn Hulk thanks to the adrenaline that had just been dumped into my bloodstream.

Had it been one of them?

I didn't want to believe it.

"Trying to escape again? What's that—the third time this week?" Cobra sank into a chair in the corner, crossing one leg over the other with a wry grin. "Thought you would've realized by now that you aren't walking out of here."

It seemed I had nothing but time.

And I'd spent every second trying to find a way out. The chains around my wrists were bolted to a stone floor. I'd used something similar in my kill rooms, knowing that unless my prisoner knew how to tunnel through rock with his hands, there was no way out. It hadn't stopped me from trying to break my own body down, piece by piece, to get back to my family, though.

Something that had fascinated Cobra to no end.

"Tell me, did Manny think he was going to be saved?"

I shook my head and sank down against the wall, completely spent. "He knew he was a dead man the second we showed up. My club's gonna come lookin' for you, and when they do, you'll know exactly how that feels."

My fingers twitched from the tremors that had wracked my body for days. I didn't know whether it was from the wound in my chest or the stress put on my joints from being shackled to a wall. Fuck, for all I knew, it was nothing more than nicotine withdrawals.

Cobra pulled a cigar from the inside of his jacket and lit up with a smirk. "Is that so? You really think your men are out combing the streets to find you?"

I nodded, wanting nothing more than to puff on the cigar in his hand until my head cleared. "They won't rest until—"

"Until what, Grey? Do you see them going on television to plead for your safe return? Passing out flyers? What exactly is it that your men are doing?"

I didn't know.

Everything had gone dark after I was shot, punctuated by only the briefest bursts of color. I saw Rick above me, pleading with me to stay alive. At one point, there'd been a blinding whiteness directly overhead, like the headlights on a Mack truck, and then everything was a blur. Maybe that was when I'd gotten separated from my men. All I knew for sure was that I'd woken up here, in nothing but my jeans with stitches too perfect to have come from any club doctor running the length of my chest.

As long as the club was still searching for the Sons, I had a fighting chance.

"That's what I thought. Nothing." He exhaled a stream of smoke toward me and glanced at his watch. "I think it's time for a little bedtime story. You've been looking more... worn down. What do you say?"

I shook my head. It was just another ploy to fuck with my mind.

"No?" he asked. "Alright then, how about this? Your family had a lovely funeral in the middle of a goddamned ice storm; so, tell me again how hard they're looking for you. You should've seen Celia; not one single tear. Why do you think that is?"

My heart plummeted to the concrete. I knew exactly why; in fact, I was probably the only person alive who was aware of how she shut down when shit got too heavy. Only this time, I wouldn't be there to shoulder the weight and bring her back.

She thought I was gone.

They all did.

I'd always known I'd never survive without her. Now, it was apparent, neither would she.

"Why the fuck am I still kickin' then?" I growled. "Saint got what he wanted, didn't he? Took a fuckin' bullet to the chest—why not end it already?"

"See, now it's interesting to me you're willing to give up so easily. Manny? Sure, I expected that cocksucker to go to his grave sniveling like a toddler. But, you?"

He clicked his tongue against his teeth with a shake of his head before bringing the cigar back up to his lips. "I had a lot more riding on you fighting until the end. Manny, he thought he knew better than everyone because he spent more time on the streets. He was too impatient to see the big picture. I cut my losses when he wanted to go after your daughters—"

"Don't sit there and act like you weren't talkin' of doin' the same

goddamn thing to them. Ain't that what you said when I got here?" I
was baiting him into doing something stupid in the hopes he'd give up
more information. The more he talked, the more I'd learn.

If my family thought I was six feet under, then I was going to have
to work twice as hard to escape; even if the wound in my chest was
nowhere near healed.

Cobra freed another cigar from his jacket and held it out. "You
want this? Then shut the fuck up. I have no interest in going after children, but news flash, your girls aren't so little anymore. Now, before
you lose your head, just know that as long as you're cooperating, they'll
stay safe."

"Like you kept my wife safe?" I growled, my wrist popping against
the chain. "So, you caught a fuckin' break and got me. Just gonna leave
me chained up to the goddamn wall until I die of old age? Oh, that's
right. You don't call the fuckin' shots. That's what Hawk told us
anyway—said you answer to Saint. What I don't get is what's in it for
you?"

There had to be a plan in place. Saint had worked too hard moving
us around like pieces on a chessboard for it to have all been for
nothing.

I just couldn't come up with anything that made sense.

He grinned. "You still want to believe that what happened to you
was a random attack, something completely unplanned. Sure, you got a
little suspicious when we wiped out the Serpents—which, you're
welcome for that—"

"That's where shit goes off the rails for me," I drawled, fighting
against a sudden wave of dizziness. I needed water but refused to beg
my captor for a goddamn thing.

"Which part? That your enemy took out another rival club, or that
you saw my kutte and immediately assumed you'd found me? Speaking
of, I'm going to want that back."

With a heavy sigh, he snagged a small black bag off the table beside
him. "Look. Let's start over, yeah? What do we have here? Camels?
Nice choice."

I watched through narrowed eyes, fighting to figure him out as he walked over and tossed the pack next to my foot. For the longest time, my enemy had been a faceless entity.

Not anymore.

If I wanted to make it out alive, I needed to learn everything I could from Cobra.

When I made no move to grab it, he rolled his eyes and bent to tap one from the pack. "And... nothing. C'mon, Grey. I'm feeling generous tonight; you might take advantage of it while it lasts."

He offered the cigarette to me, and this time, I took it. My shoulders screamed their protests as I brought it up to my mouth and leaned toward the lighter in his hand. The urge to numb myself by filling my lungs with smoke outweighed any of the risks associated with him holding an open flame near my face.

Once it was lit, he calmly stood and walked back over to the chair, leaving me more confused than ever. If he was trying to convince me he was a nice guy, he was barking up the wrong tree.

I'd seen what he'd done to my girl.

Fuck, I'd seen what he'd done with a rifle and decent aim.

"Why the fuck are you doin' this? Tryin' to earn brownie points with your boss?"

"Told you," he replied, crossing one leg over the other again like he was on the cover of a fucking fashion magazine. "I was feeling generous. Plus, the story I'm about to tell required something stronger. From what I understand, you don't drink. That's something we have in common. So, we find other ways to kill ourselves."

I took a long, desperate drag before leaning back against the wall to let my shoulders rest, hating that he made sense when nothing else did. "Fair enough."

"Haven't ridden with the Serpents in years. That's something you would've known had you actually bothered to look into the club, or, I don't know, call a meeting with them. They wanted to hold on to the old-school way of thinking and weren't big on me going after your family to get to you. It didn't matter. With the money we took from Celia, I had enough to start over with more... like-minded individuals. Remind me, what is it we call brothers who turn their backs on us?"

"Enemies," I answered, blowing a stream of smoke in his direction. We weren't friends by any stretch of the imagination. The closest I could come to describing us was death row inmate and jailer, but damn, if it wasn't nice to have some company.

Even if I was considering all the ways in which I wanted to send him to the Reaper.

"Exactly. I didn't have the stomach for a long, drawn-out death, even if it was exactly what they all deserved. Their new Pres, Viper, was a different story, though. He'd been the one to rat me out, claiming that my actions had started a war. When the fuck did that happen? When did bikers get soft? Back then, we loved nothing more than a good fight..." his voice trailed off, and he puffed on his cigar in silence, reminiscing about the early days.

He wasn't wrong.

When I'd patched in, it seemed there was always another club to go up against; someone else that needed to be reminded of who we were and what we could do.

Death had been my first love, replaced only by Celia.

Maybe it was as simple as that. We'd all gotten older and realized that there was more to life than getting bloody.

"You're thinking about her again," he said with an unreadable expression. "I can tell. Your face changes. Is that why we all became pussies in the end, Grey? Because finding a nice warm cunt to sink our dicks into was suddenly more important than keeping a stranglehold over our territory? You know, you might've just solved the entire goddamn mystery. We let our dicks do the thinking."

The vein in my forehead throbbed steadily as I bit out, "And what would you know about that?"

He laughed softly. "The club whores are all the same after a while; more concerned with their next fix. They don't care what you do to them as long as you fill their veins with something nice afterward. No, it's better when the woman has a certain look in her eyes, like maybe you're the only man who's ever gotten her. She hands over her trust, knowing you'll keep her safe. You could fuck countless women, but you'll never have that kind of loyalty."

In a fucked-up way, I understood.

"I'd never experienced anything quite like it until Celia," he mused. "It didn't matter what I did to her body, she still believed I was going to hold true to my word and keep her girls safe. I told her I was going to let her live, so she trusted me completely. Fuck, I'm getting off-track. You didn't come here to hear about my love life—"

"I'm gonna force-feed you your own cock and watch you choke on it, you piece of shit motherfucker!" I roared, rattling the chains on my arms as I reached for him, losing my cigarette to the concrete floor.

Cobra raised his eyebrows. "Is that so? And how exactly do you plan on doing that from where you are? As I was saying, before I got completely sidetracked, taking out the Serpents was my own personal brand of karma for all the ways I'd been fucked over. Knowing Viper had already ratted me out once, I decided to not take the chance of him spoiling the surprise early and cut out his tongue. Did it work? Were you surprised?"

"Surprised? Not really. When the fake prospect announced that the Sons didn't negotiate, it kinda gave away the punchline. What I don't get, though, is how he thought he was gonna waltz out of that building. Don't make a damn bit of sense."

I couldn't let him get into my head.

He bit down on the cigar and clenched his hands into fists before relaxing with a deep breath. "Kid knew it was a suicide mission from the start. That's why we're on top, and every other club is in the ground. We're willing to give our lives for our cause. Can you say the same?"

"Wait a minute, so this Saint guy is actually convincin' people to die for him? What kind of fucked-up, Koresh-soundin' bullshit is that?"

My men had always been willing to die defending our colors, as were most of the other clubs, but never once had I asked them to sacrifice themselves for me personally. I thought back to the months and years after Celia had been attacked and realized that maybe I had. For all I knew, that was what had landed me in this prison.

Wolverine had pushed us into a battle over Molly, but I'd started an all-out war over Celia.

Cobra gave me a hard smile and drummed his fingers on the thigh of his slacks as if he was bored. "We're all Saint."

He held the lighter under the tip of the cigar until it was glowing red before popping it back into his mouth. "Now, here's where it gets fun. I know for a fact that you spent that entire wedding searching for a dirty cop. You want so badly to believe it was a coincidence that we showed up when we did, because it's easier than knowing one of your own tipped us off. Tell me, Grey. Who was it?"

Days and nights blended into one, making it seem as though Dakota's wedding had taken place years ago. I thought back, struggling to see what I'd missed. Almost every biker in my clubhouse had been in attendance to ensure that nothing happened to my family.

It was like searching for a needle in a haystack.

As far as I knew, it was just another trick. Another way to get me to let my guard down.

"You're wrong." I shifted forward, trying to ease the worsening ache in my neck and shoulders, fighting not to imagine Bear and Crossbones betraying me. "My men are loyal—"

"Are they?" Cobra asked with a low chuckle. "Look around you! If they were loyal, you wouldn't be with me. Why would I tell you this now? We both know you're not getting out of here. Now, think. Who wanted you gone?"

"Besides you and your imaginary friend, Saint? No one."

My list of regrets had only grown longer the more time I spent in here. If I hadn't been strung out, I could've ended the Sons before they even began.

Fuck.

Maybe if the club hadn't been my number one priority, I could've saved my wife from ever crossing paths with Cobra.

Keeping the cigar in his mouth, he slipped the jacket from his shoulders and laid it across the chair before slowly coming toward me.

As sick as it was, I was looking forward to it. The monster that was hard-wired to need violence was still in there, rattling the bars of his cage.

Cobra's face tightened in irritation as he looked down at me. "Saint wants you alive, but he didn't say jack shit about roughing you up a little. I try to do something nice, but it seems there's still only one way men like you know how to communicate."

I jerked my head back in shock when he grabbed a rope from the ceiling, looping it around my neck. A sudden coldness descended over me. I knew torture, but this wasn't it.

"What's wrong, Grey? Is this not how you do things? Last chance, tell me who betrayed you? If you guess right, I'll let you rest." He tapped an index finger against my skull. "C'mon... think!"

The implication of his words hung heavy in the air. If I told him what he wanted to know, he wouldn't string me up. For all I knew, he'd take the name for their next target, and I wasn't willing to put anyone else's life at risk just to save my own ass. I'd take whatever he wanted to do to me if it meant that my family stayed safe.

"Told you," I growled. "You and your buddy, Saint, are the only two who had anything to gain by takin' my club."

"Fair enough." He calmly walked over to where the rope wrapped around a hook on the wall. A quick glance upward confirmed my suspicions. He had a multiple pulley system almost identical to mine. If he wanted to hoist me up to hang to death, he'd have no trouble. "Last chance..."

I spit a mouthful of saliva onto his fancy leather shoes in response, and he yanked the rope, jerking my body until just my bare feet rested against the concrete. I took slow, deep breaths, bracing myself for what was to come, only to remember Cobra didn't do predictable.

He took a step back, wrapping the slack around his hand with a grin. Somehow, the cigar remained clenched in between his teeth, and he shifted it to the side of his mouth before speaking. "Do you know how hard my job was that night? I had to factor in the fact that you'd decided on a vest last-minute, on top of ensuring that your wound wasn't fatal, but something that would require more than a club doctor to fix. I go to all that trouble and can't even get a goddamn thank you?"

I looked up from the floor. "How'd you know I was wearin' a vest?"

"It's funny; I toss a rope around your neck, and you suddenly want to chat. You know the answer. The one cop you never investigated— tell me, how does it feel, knowing that your own son turned on you?"

Even though I was one good pull away from being hanged, I

exhaled a laugh. The evidence against Mikey looked solid on the surface, but it wouldn't hold up. He and I might've had our differences over the years, but I knew without a doubt that there was one person he'd never turn on. One person he'd move heaven and earth to keep safe.

Lauren.

Even if he'd considered taking me down, there wasn't the slightest chance in hell that he would've partnered with the same club responsible for killing his wife's mother. They'd gone out of their way to make it look like an overdose, never expecting anyone to look into it.

Unfortunately for them, they hadn't accounted for Lauren.

Cobra's admission only proved that he didn't know as much as he wanted me to believe he did. Not only that, but he'd also inadvertently given up their mole.

At Dakota's wedding, a cop had stumbled into me on his way out of the men's room. At the time, I assumed he'd just spent too much time at the open bar and let him lean on me as I led him over to a table. Looking back on it now, it was obvious he'd been planted to check me for body armor.

It had never been one of my guys.

One dirty cop had been more than enough to give the Sons everything they needed to take me out that night.

"Detective Sullivan came to blows with another club member after your funeral; claimed the club was his to run. If that isn't a motive, then I don't know what is."

No, it wasn't a motive.

It was a sign that my son had heard me when we were sitting in the waiting room at the hospital. He was willing to become a renegade to protect our family, and I was going to have to play along to keep him safe.

"Maybe you're right," I rasped. "Told his mama to take care of it when she told me she was knocked up, but the bitch didn't listen. Kid's been nothin' but trouble since he came into this world. We covered up his shit, and he pays the club back by tryin' to kill me."

Cobra tipped his head to the side, watching me intently. "You aren't going to argue?"

I shrugged. "Why should I? You're right. I never saw it before; never imagined that he was capable of doin' it. Kid was so strung out on drugs and alcohol; I'm surprised he managed to pull it off at all."

"You know Saint's all bent out of shape over Sullivan ruining the surprise early," he slipped.

At my blank stare, he elaborated. "In the cemetery. He stayed back to open the fucking casket; realized that you weren't in it—"

"And? What's that got to do with anything?" I fought to keep my voice steady. Mikey knew I was alive and was willing to run the club to find me. Instead of feeling relieved, I was more worried than ever.

The Sons were going to be watching their every move.

Was that what Saint wanted—me, chained up, watching the people I loved getting picked off one by one?

He tightened his grip on the rope. "Saint wanted them to believe you were dead until the last possible second. Now, we're being forced to speed things up. Can't make a fucking omelet without cracking a few eggs though, am I right?"

I'd been shot New Year's Eve. It was now almost Valentine's Day. More than enough time had passed for Mikey to assemble an army. Pain shot through my chest, the rope around my neck the only thing keeping me upright.

Too fucking bad his old man was out of commission.

"So, like I said before... they're gonna come lookin' for you," I forced out through clenched teeth.

Cobra grinned. "Yes... and no. Your son wanted to take over the club to hunt you down, but Bear refused. Declared himself Pres unanimously and, even knowing you were still alive, ordered the club to stand down. Don't you see? Without you, your enemies get what they've always wanted... power."

Wrong.

I fought the grin playing on my lips, knowing he was seconds away from stringing me up. Bear wasn't my enemy, and he'd never wanted power. All he'd ever wanted was for the kid he'd raised as his own to acknowledge him. Family had always been the most important thing to Bear, and like Mikey, he never would've allied himself with the same men who'd tried to kill his Ol' Lady and son.

Initially, Saint had wanted them to believe I was dead. Thanks to Mikey, he was now going to try to convince me that the people I'd loved had betrayed me. I still didn't know how the puzzle was going to come together, but was at least aware of where a few of the pieces fit.

Cobra had yet to give up my rat, and I wondered if it was because he didn't know.

If Silent Phoenix had suddenly decided to stand down, it was because they knew they were being played.

And a plan wasn't worth shit if the enemy knew about it.

"Why does Saint want me alive, then?"

He walked around me in a slow circle, eyeing my body like a slab of beef. Having spent decades dealing in torture, I knew what he was going for even before he did. With an amused grin, he plucked the cigar from his lips and stabbed it out against the festering wound on my chest. Instead of jerking away, I leaned into the pain, letting the burn work its way down under my damaged skin, keeping me focused.

"You're the key, Grey. Without you, there's no war, and you go down like a fucking hero. It brings me back to my original point—nobody wants to fight anymore. Even Saint leaves the dirty work to everyone else. It's up to men like us to convince them to change their minds. They just need a cause." He pulled on the rope until my toes skimmed the ground, and regretfully stated, "It's gonna hurt."

I clenched my jaw and nodded. "Alright, let it hurt."

The pulleys creaked and groaned as he jerked the rope, the chains around my wrists stretching until they were taut. I'd been so preoccupied with what had been around my throat that I'd momentarily forgotten the arms shackled to the floor. He wasn't going to hang me; he was going to tear me in two.

My shoulders screamed in agony, momentarily distracting me from the rope compressing my jugular.

It didn't last.

Desperate for air, I began kicking my legs wildly, struggling to find something to hold my weight—anything that would relieve the pressure around my neck. My jeans grew warm with piss, but I was too far gone to care. A healing wound on my chest tore with the jerky movements, sending fresh streams of blood down my body. Involuntarily, I jerked my legs again, knowing I was only making things worse.

Cobra's mouth widened into another grin as he gave one last vicious tug, and my right shoulder popped. The excruciating pain sent everything into darkness just as I opened my mouth to scream.

The Savior is available now. Order here.

ACKNOWLEDGMENTS

A writer is only as good as the people behind her. I'm lucky enough to have an entire city.

Rebecca Pau- Thank you for designing a cover that matched Renegade's so perfectly, you'd think you'd designed them both. *Ha!* Seriously though, thank you for keeping me sane and making the cover process painless.

Bloggers- Your responses to Renegade blew me away and brought tears to my eyes. Thank you for believing in me and my characters. Your support means more to me than I will ever be able to articulate.

Readers- Your endless messages of support pushed me to give you (and Mike!) a fitting conclusion. I try to make each book better than the last and feedback from the readers helps me greatly. Thank you for taking a chance on my stories.

J. Law- Thank you for being my person. You are the Lauren to my Beth and the Reese's to my Pieces. Your willingness to discuss the inane facts of my stories and work them into something that makes sense keeps me sane. Bitches for life!

Wendi- You're the best PA ever. Seriously, your willingness to drop everything and help me out has made my life so much easier. Thank you for keeping me organized and prepared during this crazy journey and for becoming my friend in the process.

Ashley- Thank you for all of your information on Indie publishing this year and for being the one who broke the news that Renegade was going to be two books. I appreciate all the motivation you send my way and am lucky to call you my friend.

Family & Friends- Thank you for supporting my crazy little dream and for your willingness to promote my smut to your friends. I love you guys to the moon and back.

Zach- There are never enough words for me to communicate how much you mean to me. It doesn't matter how busy you are, you always have time to hear my troublesome plot points and help me gain a better understanding of the male psyche. Never leave me, because I'll find you!

ABOUT THE AUTHOR

Shannon is a born and raised Texan. She grew up inventing clever stories, usually to get herself out of trouble. Her mother was not amused. In junior high, she began writing fractured fairy tales from the villain's point of view and that was the moment she knew that she was going to use her powers for evil instead of good.

After an unplanned surgery in 2014 and a long pity party, she decided to pen a novel about the worst thing that could happen to a person in order to cheer herself up. She's twisted like that. Thus, *From This Day Forward* was born and the rest, as they say, is history.

She resides in the Texas desert with a posse of men (nothing like she'd imagined in fantasies) and plethora of fur babies.

Find her online at: http://shannonshaemyers.com
Or in her reader group: https://www.facebook.com/
groups/630229377127363/

ALSO BY SHANNON MYERS

From This Day Forward Duet

(David & Elizabeth's Story)

From This Day Forward

Forsaking All Others

Standalone Novels

(Travis & Katya's Story)

You Save Me

Operation Series

(Dakota & Zane's Story)

Operation Fit-ish

(Kate and Nate's Story)

Operation Annulment

Silent Phoenix MC Series

(Grey & Celia's Story)

The Deserter (Book One)

The Protector (Book Two)

The Renegade (Book Three)

The Traitor (Book Four)

The Savior (Book Five)

The Mercenary (Book Six) *Coming 2022*

Fairest Series

(Charm & Neve's Story)

Through The Woods

Made in the USA
Middletown, DE
18 September 2024

60610039R00186